Sons of Glory

SONS OF GLORY

CRAIG & JANET
PARSHALL

HARVEST HOUSE PUBLISHERS

EUGENE, OREGON

All Scripture quotations have been taken from the 1611 edition of the King James Version of the Bible. The spelling has been modernized for inclusion in this book. An electronic transcription of the translation was used, courtesy of Jeff Garrison of StudyLight.org. Their online Bible resource site, which can be found at www.studylight.org, "is packed with the most Bibles and study resources found on the Net—everything needed to help you in your study of God's Word."

Cover by Left Coast Design, Portland, Oregon

Cover photo © David H. Wells / Corbis

This is a work of fiction. Names, characters, places, and incidents are products of the author's imagination or are used fictitiously. Any resemblance to actual persons, living or dead, or to events or locales, is entirely coincidental.

SONS OF GLORY
Book 3 of the Thistle and the Cross series
Copyright © 2008 by Craig and Janet Parshall
Published by Harvest House Publishers
Eugene, Oregon 97402
www.harvesthousepublishers.com

Library of Congress Cataloging-in-Publication Data

Parshall, Craig, 1950-
    Sons of glory / Craig and Janet Parshall.
    p. cm.—(The thistle and the cross ; bk. 3)
    ISBN-13: 978-0-7369-1326-3 (pbk.)
    ISBN-10: 0-7369-1326-2 (pbk.)
    1. United States—History—Colonial period, ca. 1600-1775—Fiction. 2. Boston (Mass.)—Fiction.
3. Adams, John, 1735-1826—Fiction. 4. Lawyers—Fiction. I. Parshall, Janet, 1950- II. Title.
PS3616.A77S65 2008
813.'6—dc22

                                                                        2007017278

Printed in the United States of America

08 09 10 11 12 13 14 15 / RDM-NI / 10 9 8 7 6 5 4 3 2 1

Chapter 1

Boston, Massachusetts
February 22, 1770

The crowd that had gathered on the frozen mud street outside of His Majesty's Royal Customs House was growing larger and more unruly. They had braved the frigid New England weather to congregate on the corner and listen to a Colonist protestor who was standing on a small wooden crate as he addressed them. The men pulled their wool coats and capes up around their necks, and a scant number of ladies, who stood farther off, tugged their bonnets down tight against the cold breeze. In the crowd, a twelve-year-old boy name Christopher Seider, tall for his age and with cheeks that were flame red from the cold, had elbowed his way to the front to get a good view.

The street crowd would not be deterred by the falling temperatures. They were there to hear the local orator and often yelled out in agreement as he spoke.

The speaker was getting more animated as he raised his voice and gestured toward the Customs House.

"You know…every one of you," he called out, pointing to a few of the men in the front, "why we decided on a trade embargo with England."

"Taxes!" one man replied.

"King George's troops have taken over my house," another man added, "without so much as a *by your leave*...or a *pardon me sir!*"

At that several more men began to shout out several complaints against the oppressive policies of King George of England. Several of them shouted out that the Crown of England had consistently denied them fundamental rights of religious freedom, arbitrarily jailing dissenting preachers and forcing other ministers to be licensed by the Royal authorities or else be imprisoned as well.

"All of those abuses," the speaker continued, "yes, and many, many more. Depriving us of the rights of Englishman...taking away our rights to a jury trial by our peers. Now replaced by His Majesty's Admiralty Courts, stacked with judges bought and paid for by the Crown of England, whose only aim is to convict and punish our fellow colonists!"

The crowd yelled back in agreement.

"So we all agreed," the speaker continued, "tradesmen and craftsmen, and shopkeepers...merchants all...to refuse to receive or sell any English goods until these infractions of our civil liberties are corrected."

More hearty voices were raised. The noise of the crowd was now attracting the attention of people in the row houses down the street. They were opening their second story windows and peering out into the cold air to get a look.

"But an embargo against old King George is only as good as the strength of our unified commitment...all of us...no exceptions...must continue this refusal to trade with England."

"What about Rudolph Skillings, the cotton broker?" one man yelled out. "I know for a fact, as sure as my eyes, that he's gone and broke the embargo…took several shipments of linens from England to sell in his clothing shop, he has!"

"Let's round him up!" another yelled out.

"Hot tar and feathers for the likes of him!" a voice rang out.

But the orator was now waving his arms to gain control of the crowd.

"There will be no tar and feathers tonight," the speaker shouted out. "But rest assured that I will be having a stern talk with Mr. Skillings…and not about the fabric for my fine lady's dress, either!"

A round of laughter rippled through the onlookers.

On the other side of the street a man with a walking stick, and dressed in a long, rich coat and beaver's fur hat was standing still, momentarily, and shaking his head in disgust. Ebenezer Richardson, an outspoken loyalist to the Crown of England, began muttering to himself loudly, and then began to walk briskly, jamming his walking cane down onto the frosty ground with each step. He crossed the street closer to the crowd as he passed by.

When the orator took a pause in his address, Richardson, a mere thirty feet away, took the opportunity to make his point.

"Traitor!" he yelled loudly, directing his scorn to the speaker standing on the crate. "A liar and a traitor!" Then he motioned to the crowd as he continued, lifting his cane to make the point. "Don't listen to this man…he's a traitor to King and to country…"

"And what country would that be?" the speaker retorted. "Would that be England? The land of Magna Carta? Home of the legal canons of the great jurist Blackstone?"

"Ye know well that ye're a traitor to England!" Richardson replied.

"Then if England be my country," the orator shot back, "then why, pray tell, am I denied the rights of an Englishman? Why do the rights of Magna Carta and the legal principles of Blackstone stop cold at the shores of England? Why does King George keep them for himself, and keep them hostage from visiting the shores of these good colonies?"

"I will see you hanged by the same laws that you cry out for, sir!" Richardson yelled back. "Hanged in the street like a dog!"

"You ought to talk!" one of the men, a well-dressed Boston merchant, shouted back. Then, pointing to Ebenezer Richardson, he addressed the crowd, his voice screeching with anger: "This same man," he yelled, "who would hang one of our patriots, is, himself, a vermin spy…yes I know this to be truth! He is a paid informer for the Crown's Royal Customs office…sneaking over to their office, right here on this street, and then secretly telling them which of us merchants ought to be closed down!"

Now the crowd was quickly turning into an angry mob. But Richardson had retreated to the other side of the street, and was willing to match their mood.

"I will have you all dancing from His Majesty's rope!" Richardson yelled back, his face twisted in a violent rage. "I know your names, I do. And will have every one of you strung up, and your houses sold, and your children starved! And will be glad of it!"

That is when the mob began surging toward him. But Richardson had reached his brownstone house, and quickly entered it, and then hurriedly bolted the door.

The group of men, with young Christopher Seider in their midst, were gathered outside Richardson's house yelling up to the second story where they could see a window was open.

One of them threw a bottle against the bricks, and a shower of broken glass rained down. Someone launched a rock upward, hard and fast, and it passed into the open window. Standing inside the room, Richardson's wife was struck with the rock, as it caught part of her bonnet, and she screamed out in fright.

"Now they shall have war from me!" her husband yelled out as he was entering her room, and saw his frightened spouse. Richardson ran down to the fireplace, grabbed his musket from over the mantel, loaded it and ran up the stairs and over to the open window.

Richardson looked out of the window, down toward the crowd. The men gathered down below on the street were chanting something which Richardson could not quite make out. But it did not matter. The die was cast.

"I'll not wait for His Majesty to hang you!" he shouted down to the mob. "I'll dispense with you street scoundrels myself!"

Richardson poked the barrel of his musket out of the window, pointed it downward, and pulled the trigger.

There was a sickening explosion of gunpowder.

Suddenly the mob jumped backwards in a wave, leaving a single body laying facedown in the snow. Bright red blood was now ebbing from the body.

Christopher Seider lay dead on the frozen ground.

The crowd stood in stunned silence, as one of the men leaned over the body and checked for a pulse. After a full minute, the silence was broken.

"He's dead," the man whispered.

"He's killed the Seider boy!" another man screamed out.

Around the corner a muster of red-coated English soldiers were approaching at a fast clip to restore order. From the other direction, a mother was running toward the scene. She was calling out the name of her son.

"Christopher!" she cried out. "Is he with you men?" she cried out again.

But when she was close enough to see the grave looks on their faces, and then, as they parted, close enough to spot the body of a boy laying on the ground, she screamed out in a pitiful moan.

The mother staggered toward the body of her son, and her knees buckled and she began to collapse. A burly dockworker grabbed her, and began to move her away from the scene, and to safety.

But by then the English soldiers were at the crowd, and with the butt-end of their muskets, were bashing the heads and torsos of the men.

The mob scattered. Several of the soldiers gave chase. Richardson, up in his house, quickly pulled his musket back, and slammed his window shut.

Soon, the only thing left on the street was the stone-still body of Christopher Seider, lying dead on the streets of Boston.

Chapter 2

The Evening of March 5, 1770
Boston

That winter the frigid temperatures were a constancy in Massachusetts, and particularly in the city of Boston, where the winds whipped off Boston Harbor and blew through the narrow streets. Before the latest snowfall, many of the roads in the bustling downtown area that were inlaid with red brick had been clear and mostly dry. In the other areas of town without the brick-ways, though, the mud was frozen solid, and the puddles were frozen over, posing a threat to ladies in hoop skirts who might have to cross the roads unescorted, and who worried that they might slip and fall to the ground with great indignity.

But then the snow began to fall, cascading down from the sky in sheets. And so, on this evening, Boston was still blanketed in a layer of wintry white.

The sun had set several hours before, and Bostonians were now scurrying to their homes and for the warmth of burning fires and hot bread, roast beef, and bread pudding with raisins.

But there was an air of unsettled anxiety among the inhabitants.

11

On a few corners of the city, here and there, English soldiers were posted in squads of half a dozen, leaning on their muskets, eyeing the passersby.

The killing of the twelve-year-old boy during an anti-Tory protest, less than two weeks past, hung over Boston like a suffocating pall. A grand jury had been convened to investigate the shooting. Locals were clamoring for the indictment of English-sympathizer Ebenezer Richardson for murder. But in a stunning, infuriating move, the English Governor disbanded the grand jury to protect Richardson. A smoldering fury was building against the various tyrannies imposed on the colonists by a Monarchy that sat an ocean away, seemingly oblivious to the violations of such fundamental legal rights.

And to make matters worse, the English overseers appointed by King George to run the colonies, and their military troops, appeared to be even less caring for basic justice than was the King himself.

The number of English soldiers stationed in Boston was in a constant ebb and flow. On that evening, there were two large garrisons still in the city: the Fourteenth and the Twenty-Ninth.

That night, a young lawyer named Nathan Mackenzie was scurrying down the streets of Boston, keeping pace with John Adams, another Boston lawyer. Though Adams was only two years Nathan's senior, Nathan paid him the traditional respect due to a legal mentor by a younger associate.

"Mr. Adams," Nathan asked, "I greatly appreciate your permitting me to escort you tonight to the meeting of the Sodalitas club...and particularly for the honor of sharing a treatise with the other lawyers."

Adams answered quickly.

"I invited you because I do see some promise in you, sir," Adams said. "Now, what text do you bring with you tonight?"

"*Lex Rex*," Nathan said, "the treatise by Mr. Samuel Rutherford."

"Rutherford," Adams mused as the two men walked together, high-stepping through the snow, trying in vain to avoid soaking their knee-high stockings. "Ah yes...the Scottish reformer. Wrote about the limitations of monarchy...and the rights of man to be free under God. Yes, fine choice!"

"Thank you, sir," Nathan replied, feeling good to have his mentor's approval.

Adams was slightly shorter than Nathan, and with a less athletic build; and a studious look about him, sometimes appearing even introverted. Nothing like his firebrand cousin, Samuel Adams.

But Nathan had learned, while he apprenticed under Adams, that such appearances could be deceiving. Adams was admittedly shy in some matters—in the social niceties of party banter, particularly with the members of Boston high society, and with the wealthy gentry. He would often look ill at ease making polite, but empty chatter. Other times, when comparisons to other, more successful lawyers arose in discussion at the local tavern house, Adams would look perfectly distraught. Nathan had concluded that his mentor probably suffered—for reasons that were entirely unknown to Nathan—from intense feelings of professional inferiority.

On the other hand, when Adams found himself in conversations that drifted—as they almost always would—to matters of justice, social policy, or politics, then that was an entirely different matter.

In those circumstances, and Nathan had witnessed it several times, there would be a dramatic transformation: John Adams would be uncommonly passionate, sometimes even fiery in expressing his convictions.

As the two lawyers walked, suddenly down the street from them under a lamp light they could see a small squad of English redcoats on patrol.

Adams slowed down for an instant, eyeing them, and then picked up his pace.

"*Lobsterbacks*," he muttered to Nathan. "King George has no idea how their presence has only thrown oil on the bonfires here in Boston."

"My wife tells me," Nathan said, "that one of the soldiers recently accosted a lady in broad daylight—knocking her to the ground, and stealing her cape and bonnet."

"Well, here is the problem," Adams said, his voice rising in agitation, "the Crown pays its soldiers neither amply nor on time…so they roam the streets looking for mischief…feeling entitled to strip us of our belongings…to quarter themselves in our homes, demanding food and drink…I've heard more than one story that one of the redcoats tried to extort a local merchant into hiring him for night duty so he could supplement his military wages. When the merchant refused, they came to blows."

"I know that same merchant," Nathan interjected. "It was Mr. Sam Gray, was it not?"

"The very one," Adams replied. "I fear that the shooting of poor Mrs. Seider's boy is simply a harbinger of things to come. I crave the liberties to which we are entitled," he continued. "Yet I fear with all my heart the terrible cost at which they might be purchased."

Adams and Nathan had reached the front door of the home of one of the barristers. Adams grabbed the brass door knocker and gave it the characteristic three clangs, followed by a single knock.

After a few moments, a well-dressed lawyer in a finely powdered wig swung the door open.

"Mr. Adams!" he said with a smile, then turning to Nathan he added, "and your protégé, Mister…Mister…"

"Mackenzie," Nathan replied. "I am privileged to be invited to your…discussion group."

The lawyer beckoned the two men inside, then poked his head out of the doorway, looking down the snowy street first one way, and then the other, to scout out the presence of any snoops or spies. Having been satisfied that there were neither, he closed and bolted the door to his home.

As the small group of lawyers warmed themselves in front of the fire, and were served up with hot cider and sweet breads, they were oblivious to the confrontation that was unfolding only two blocks away.

Down off of King Street, the squad of English soldiers had been trapped in a narrow alley by a mob of angry protestors who had blocked their way. The officer in charge ordered the soldiers to charge with bayonets fixed, so as to clear the way. The mob scattered but circled around to follow the redcoats to their barracks, shouting at them as they went.

At the same time, two other groups of yelling colonists were confronting English troops nearby, and throwing ice-balls and rocks at them.

It was all rapidly beginning to boil over.

Nathan Mackenzie was politely introduced to the other lawyers by John Adams; and as Nathan began his short reading from the book he had brought with him, called *Lex Rex*—the text written by Samuel Rutherford to show that the laws of God were paramount to the laws of any single monarch—a screaming mob had encircled a group of armed British soldiers.

"*Filthy Lobsterbacks!*" the protestors were crying.

The troops nervously fingered the triggers of their muskets as they retreated into a tight line.

Captain Preston, the officer in charge, was holding back his orders for a defensive assault. But he knew that several of his soldiers were men who had gained a reputation for brutalizing the civilian colonists, and he did not know how long they could be restrained.

One of them, Private Killroy, a particularly brutal English foot-soldier, was staring into the eyes of Sam Gray, a local merchant, who was in the front line of protestors.

Killroy recognized Gray immediately.

Sam Gray was standing next to a tall African freed man named Crispus Attucks, who was armed with a long club and was poking it, menacingly, in the direction of the redcoats in front of him. Samuel Maverick and James Caldwell were also in the front line of colonial protestors, well-known to Bostonians and to the English troops as well. Just behind them was a young apprentice to a wheelwright, named David Parker, and next to him the leather crafter from Queens Street, Patrick Carr.

"That's the ugly toad," Killroy growled to Hugh Montgomery, a fellow soldier standing shoulder-to-shoulder with him, and nodding in the direction of Sam Gray, "who's the fellow wouldn't give me work at his shop. And called me a few choice names to boot..."

Killroy was gripping his musket tightly and pointing it directly at Gray. His finger was laid against the trigger, tensed and ready.

And there was a devilish grin on the English soldier's face as he did.

Chapter 3

"It was so kind of you, Mrs. Adams, to invite me for tea."

"Oh for pity's sake, I get so busy with the babies here in the house, sometimes it's good just to hear the sound of another woman's voice. And please, call me Abigail. As I shall not call you Mrs. Mackenzie, but rather, Deborah. And, it's a special delight to be able to share our…well…*expectations* together…"

With that, Abigail Adams tapped her pregnant belly with a forefinger. Deborah Mackenzie laughed and cupped her own pregnant form with both hands.

Instinctively, Abigail craned her neck to look over at a trundle bed and a crib, where her two small ones, a five-year-old and a three-year-old, were sleeping in the corner of the front room. After satisfying herself that they were both still slumbering peacefully, she settled back into the rocking chair.

"It's good to finally meet you," Deborah said. "My husband has told me such wonderful things about your husband, John."

"Just one more item we have in common," Abigail said with a smile. "Both of us married to lawyers."

Then, with a sly smile she added, "or should I say…*sentenced* to marriage with a lawyer!"

They both had to muffle their laughs at that.

"Oh, they can be so insufferably arrogant," Abigail said with a half smile, shaking her head a little.

"Well," Deborah said, looking down into her lap and chuckling, "I often tell my Nathan…just because you can go to court and argue the *points of law*, doesn't give you license *to be pointed with me!*"

"Oh that's grand!" Abigail said, throwing her hands up in the air.

Both of the women fell silent, though, when one of the Adams infants squeaked, and whimpered for a second. Abigail, with some effort, rose from the rocking chair and quietly tiptoed over and peeked into the crib. Then she smiled and padded back to the rocking chair, where she slowly settled in after a bit of labored breathing.

"Yes," Abigail said, picking up the conversation again. "My John can be quite haughty at times. I gauge that he doesn't even realize it…but he acts the part nevertheless. Once, when he was courting me, he actually chastened me by telling me that I shouldn't sit cross-legged, as was my habit to do. He said that ladies should refrain from that kind of posture."

"What did you say to that?" Deborah asked, wide-eyed.

"I told him," Abigail said with a grin, "that a gentleman had no business paying such close attention to the legs of a lady!"

With that, they both had to muffle their laughter in their hands.

When they had both gained their composure, Abigail was going to offer her guest some more tea.

But then she heard something outside. It came from a point down the street.

Then she heard it again, and yet again just a split second later. It sounded like gunfire.

"Did you hear that?" Abigail asked in a hushed voice.

Deborah Mackenzie nodded immediately.

"Musket fire," Abigail whispered.

Both women stood up.

But before they could reach the door, they heard the alarm being sounded by the tolling of the tower bells at Trinity Church.

By the time the two women had quickly waddled to the door and swung it open, they saw several men running, with knees pumping, at a quick pace through the deep snow, down Draper's Alley toward King Street.

Off in the distance there was sound of screaming voices and yelling back and forth.

In the home of the barrister, John Adams and Nathan Mackenzie and the other lawyers heard it all too—the musket fire, the tolling bells, the cries from the mob, and the counter commands from the English captain of the guard.

John Adams and Nathan sprinted to the door, stopped only momentarily, and then saw the streaming of men running toward King's street.

"Another shooting," Adams said through gritted teeth.

"Our wives," Nathan said with a shocked voice.

"Yes, Nathan," Adams said with some panic in his voice. "We must get to them...make sure they are safe."

The two lawyers excused themselves rapidly from the meeting, and then ran through the streets, leaping over snowbanks and making their way through the snow covered streets until they had reached John Adams' brown-bricked row house.

When they finally reached the house, and sprinted up the stairs and burst into the front room, and were at last assured that the women were secure and unharmed, they both embraced their wives and held them tight.

By then, the two Adams infants had awoken and were crying in their beds.

Down at King Street, the Redcoats, after they had discharged their weapons into the crowd, had rapidly retreated into the safety of the Royal Customs House by the orders of Captain Preston, and then bolted the door behind them.

The icy night air was filled with the screams of mourning family members who were now arriving on the scene in the snowy street, and were beholding the carnage that had resulted from the fire-power of the English squad.

Large pools of bright red blood lay everywhere on the white, frosty ground, clearly visible in the yellow illumination of the light from the half-moon above.

Crispus Attucks was lying on his side clutching his chest, with a startled look, his mouth half open, and was dead. He had been killed instantly. Next to him, face down, was Sam Gray, only barely alive, but not for long. He had been shot in the head. Samuel Maverick was bleeding from the belly profusely, and James Caldwell was giving a throaty rattle as he slowly expired, having been shot at point-blank range, as had the others.

The young apprentice David Parker was screaming and writhing in pain on the ground, grasping at his thigh where he had taken a musket ball.

And the leather worker Patrick Carr was laying close by, also crying for help in a voice filled with miserable pain. He had sustained a shot through his hip.

As the wives and sisters and brothers of the slain and wounded clutched their fallen loved ones, suddenly a British troop appeared around a corner and rushed them, with their bayonets fixed.

"Off the streets, you vermin!" an officer shouted to them without pity. "Up and off the street! Or we'll shoot you like the trash you're crying for!"

Nathan and Deborah Mackenzie stayed late at the home of John Adams and his wife, Abigail. They waited until the sounds of riot and death had subsided before Nathan and Deborah slipped out of the house and scurried back to their own home.

By the time Nathan and Deborah fell into bed for a fitful sleep that night, the mournful, frightening sounds from the street had subsided.

Then, late in the evening, when the streets were cleared, the British soldiers made their way among the victims. The dead were dragged to a saddlery shop that had been converted into a make-shift morgue. The wounded were taken to the home of a physician on King Street. The doctor was wakened and told to save them—if he could.

Meanwhile, the snow began to fall again, in quiet sheets of white, down on the city of Boston.

Eventually, the ponds of blood in the snow would be covered. But it would take all night for the snowfall to finally accomplish that.

Chapter 4

In the First Church of Boston, the Rev. Edward Mackenzie, Nathan's older brother, was standing hickory-board straight in the high, vaulted pulpit. He was taller than Nathan, but thinner, with a face that was possessed of a kind of plain serenity, a determined confidence. He had a strong voice, and a winning delivery. He was a good orator, and his preaching always kept his listeners awake.

That Sunday, because it had followed the killings at King Street of a few days earlier, every seat in every pew was taken. The entire congregation, grief stricken, frightened, enraged, had flocked to the worship service looking for something. For solace. Guidance. Spiritual assurance in a time of violent confusion.

Their faces showed the eager anticipation of the faithful looking for a bulwark for their faith after recent bloody events had sent their spirits reeling.

Edward Mackenzie, in his clerical robe and starched white frock, gripped the polished wooden handrails of the pulpit with both hands as if it were the wheel of a ship; as if he was struggling to keep the wheel true to course even as the howling winds and surging tide threatened to spin the wheel out of his grip.

"All government is instituted by God," Edward said boldly. Then he paused.

"And of that fact," he continued, "there can be no greater certainty. For Scripture tells us plain, brothers and sisters. Plain and clear. Dare we declare to be unclear what God has made clear?"

His right hand unfastened itself from the rail and then rose in the air, with a pointed finger.

"And if government comes to us from the hand of God...then how shall we treat it? Shall we strike, with our hand, that which has been given us from the very hand of Almighty God? Shall we? Blasphemy! Better that we cut off our hand than to allow it to resist the ordinances of God!"

The members of the congregation were shifting in their seats.

Edward Mackenzie saw their faces. His parishioners had known well the men who had been killed and maimed by the muskets of the British troops. The week before the shootings they were hailing them by their names, and exchanging small talk with them in the marketplace. And now those same men were dead. *Surely there must be,* they were thinking to themselves, *a cry for justice from the minister...a demand for retribution against the English murderers.*

"So, if government is from God, and we dare not resist it...then it shall be called sin...sin repulsive to God and in flagrant violation to his Holy Word...to raise our hands against our English overseers. For they are given us by God for our protection."

A few men in the pews were scowling and shaking their heads.

"I know, yes, brethren, I know what you are thinking. *What shall become of the murderers who have slain our fellow citizens?* Here is my answer: This same government bestowed upon us by God for our protection shall be the same instrument to wield swift and certain judgment against the wrongdoers who slew our friends. Let government run its course, and then, and only then, shall a true and righteous justice prevail."

Nathan Mackenzie and his wife Deborah were seated toward the back of the sanctuary. Nathan had been listening intently to his brother's sermon. But Nathan's face betrayed his inner turmoil. He bore the expression of a man questioning what he was hearing. And more than that, he was struggling against the words of Edward, his older brother for whom he had always harbored the greatest respect.

After the service, Edward stood in the vestibule by the open front door as he always did, and shook the hands of his departing parishioners as they filed past. A few men milled around the minister to engage him politely on the text of his sermon. But Edward held fast to the conclusions he had articulated in his message. Resistance against England, even when England was behaving with malice, he reminded them, would be a sin.

"Shall we simply forget, then, about *those murderous lobsterbacks* that fired on our friends?" one of the parishioners asked.

"Most certainly not," the pastor assured them. "Those soldiers responsible for the shootings will be brought to punishment. Just wait and see."

Later that day, Nathan and Deborah attended a lunch at the large parsonage belonging to Edward and his wife Edith. Edward enjoyed a handsome salary from the church; meals at his three-story, brown brick house were always sumptuous affairs: sweetmeats, baked pears with cinnamon, boiled potatoes, and fairly fresh vegetables from the market that imported them from the southern colonies.

The meal was prepared by a full-time cook and two serving girls. Edith wandered in and out of the large kitchen a little aimlessly, looking like someone who had the task of overseeing the culinary details, but who couldn't focus on the task. As Nathan and Edward were talking in the parlor, Deborah found Edith in the kitchen, just as the servants scurried, with arms loaded with serving dishes, out of the kitchen and toward the dining room. Deborah walked up to Edith when they were alone and then took her hand in hers.

"Dear Edith," she said. "It's so good to see you."

Edith managed a smile, but didn't respond.

"Please know how very sorry Nathan and I are," Deborah continued, "about your loss...your..."

"I *shall not* speak of it," Edith said, with no energy, no emotion to her voice, but with a listless, faraway quality.

Deborah was surprised by that, but her sweet demeanor was unflagging.

"Then, I also, shall refrain," she replied, and smiled, trying to warm her husband's sister-in-law.

"It is..." Edith said, "done...and gone."

Then Edith gazed over at Deborah's pregnant figure, and fixed her eyes on the rounded shape beneath the dress. And, as if she were dipping a quill in an inkwell, and then dotting a period down at the end of a long and tedious sentence, Edith said just one more word.

"Done."

It was a curious note to end their conversation, and Deborah did not understand it. But she was determined to be cheery around Edith.

"Please," Deborah said, when she saw the serving girls quickly entering the kitchen again and begin taking up the large silver plates full of food, "let me help. Edith, you sit down on a comfortable chair."

Deborah waddled over to help the servants. As she did, Edith turned and left the kitchen.

The oldest servant girl whispered to Deborah.

"Please Mum," she said in a low voice to Deborah, taking a dish from her hands, "we girls can handle the meal. You shouldn't be exerting. Not in *your state*." And when she said those last words, she glanced over at the door to the kitchen to make sure that Edith, the matron of the house, had left.

With a little protest, Deborah was urged to leave the carrying to the serving staff. She and Nathan lived modestly, and had no household staff themselves, except for a woman who came in occasionally to clean and prepare a few meals. Deborah did much of the work in the home, and was not used to being pampered. Having come from a family of seven, Deborah was raised to believe that pregnancy was not a disabling condition, at least until the last month.

When dinner was served, and the four were seated, Nathan and his brother, Edward, continued the conversation that had occupied them in the parlor.

In between bites, Edward expounded on the point he had been making to his younger brother. "So, brother, it is simply the radicals," Edward said, waving a two-pronged fork, "the fire starters, and the roustabouts...the *agitators* who dare to call for armed resistance against the Crown of England. Not decent folk."

Nathan was chewing slowly, and thinking hard on Edward's point. Then he offered a rebuttal.

"Yet, that certainly cannot be the standard by which we resolve this question," Nathan said.

"Why ever not?" Edward retorted. "Look at the fruit from the tree, and thereby judge the tree, that is what I say."

After Edward said that, he looked to the two women at the table for approval of his wisdom. Deborah smiled politely, but Edith, his wife, gave him only a blank look.

"Edward," Nathan said, "what I mean is this—how you define a *radical* and an *agitator* may be prudent enough—but how will your neighbor define them? And will the answer to the question be found in *his judgment* or *yours?*"

"It is not a matter of opinion or judgment, brother," Edward replied with a bit of condescension. "But of fact. Just look at the proponents of revolt..."

"Like whom?"

"Well," Edward said, "just take the cousin of that legal associate of yours—the cousin of Mr. John Adams...that brewer and merchant, Samuel Adams. There's an agitator...and a man devoid of spiritual judgment no doubt."

"I know Samuel Adams only slightly, I admit...but he is known as a devout man, a God-fearing man," Nathan responded.

"And what church does he attend?" Edward shot back.

"That, I cannot answer."

"There!" Edward said loudly. "My point exactly. If he is devout, his godliness should be shown to be such in the streets, and in the markets, for all to see."

"And yet," Nathan said quietly with a smile, "did not our Lord and Savior protest of those who made sure their 'righteousness' was seen in the streets, even though it did not appear in their hearts?"

"So, you would play the lawyer with me now?" Edward said.

"No," Nathan said. "Only the humble follower of Christ and his holy religion. Trying to sort it all out."

Then, after a few more mouthfuls of food, Nathan spoke.

"And even further, brother," he continued. "What do you make of our most honorable ancestor...the Reverend Ransom Mackenzie?

He fought the tyranny of Queen mother Marie de Guise in Scotland two hundred years ago, to establish the Reformation there, alongside the likes of Mr. John Knox, and other notables of the faith. What do you make of him? Was he a mere *agitator*...a *radical?*"

Edward was about to pounce on that point, but Deborah threw a glance at her husband, and then cleared her throat loudly.

"I am afraid," Nathan said, "that my wife is much tired. And our conversation is probably tiresome."

"Not at all," Deborah replied brightly. "And I would have opinions myself on the subject at hand..."

With that, Nathan and Edward both stopped, and gazed with some surprise at her.

"But," she continued, "my concern is with Edith, your good wife, Edward. She is, I am afraid, much tired. I am sure that the demands on the wife of a reverend are great."

"Yes, yes, you are right, of course," Edward said, looking over at Edith. "You are quiet tonight, dear heart. Are you all right?"

Edith nodded, and managed a thin smile, but did not speak.

Shortly after that, Nathan excused himself and his wife. They said their goodbyes and were escorted out to their covered carriage where Deborah was wrapped in a thick woolen blanket for the short ride home.

"She seems so melancholy," Deborah said to her husband as he jiggled the reigns and hurried the single horse pulling the carriage through the snow. "Poor Edith."

"First, a daughter born dead, and then a baby son with the same fate," Nathan said.

Deborah snuggled closer to him and pulled the blanket tighter as she saw a squad of redcoats leaning up against a building, warming themselves at a small fire.

She wanted to say so many things, but they were jumbled up in her mind, and her heart was full of yearning. The world in Boston seemed to have become suddenly so violent, and disruptive, and unpredictable. She felt safe, for the time being, next to her husband. But there was fear in the air. What she cared about most of all was the safety of her soon-to-be expanding little family.

Shall our little baby, Deborah wondered silently to herself, *know the tranquility of peace...or the ravages of war?*

Chapter 5

While Boston, to the north, was still snow covered and frigid, down in the southern colony of Virginia, they were enjoying mild weather. The light snow on the ground had melted in a sudden thaw, and there was the smell of an early spring in the air that Saturday.

A large crowd of men were crossing the small wooden bridge over the Rappahannock River in the direction that led away from the shops, warehouses, and docks and over to the far side of the river. The conversation was lively, and they were laughing and talking loudly about the day's sporting event.

"I'll bet a guinea on the laddie from Culpeper!" one of the men chimed out.

"And I'll take that bet, and up it to a guinea and a pence...but not on him, but rather on the Mackenzie fellow," Jared Hollings, another local merchant, shouted out in the group.

"Who's he?" a third man asked.

"Robby Mackenzie. He's the red-haired lad that works the livery for the Sunrise Tavern."

"And why is it, exactly, that you think he'll best the Culpeper chap?"

"That," Hollings, the merchant, said with a smile, "is my secret to keep…and yours to find out!"

Several of the other men chided the merchant, but he maintained a smug smile and would elaborate no further.

When they reached the other side of the bridge they turned south, down the steep incline of a small rocky path in the woods until they intersected with a larger dirt road that was smooth and straight and ran parallel to the river.

One of the men took out his pocket watch.

"Seventeen minutes, gentlemen," he announced.

A few of the men stretched out on the ground, to wait there until the competition began. One man found a clean stump to sit upon.

Someone produced a flute and struck up a tune on it.

After the musician played a quick tune set for dancing, someone asked for another song.

"Do you know 'Come, Fair Rosina, Come Away'?" he called out.

The flute player nodded and commenced a slow, lyrical number.

"And does anyone know the singing of it?" he asked.

A tall, lanky fellow who led the music in one of the city's church choirs stood up, brushed off his knickers, and his vest and coat, and placed his hands formally in a folded position in front of him as he commenced to sing the romantic ballad:

> *Come, fair Rosina, come away,*
> *Long since stern Winter's storms have ceas'd;*
> *See! Nature, in her best array,*
> *Invites us to her rural feast:*

The season shall her treasure spread,
Her mellow fruits and harvests brown,
Her flowers their richest odours shed,
And ev'ry breeze pour fragrance down...

"Better throw your guinea and pence in the good singer's hat, Mr. Hollings," the man with the watch said, as he checked the time once again. "For in exactly one minute, the footrace begins...and you will most certainly lose that sum in the pursuit of the vice of betting. 'Twould be better, instead, that you donate it to the musicians here. At least it would be to a worthy cause."

There was a hearty round of laughter among the men, but Hollings held fast.

"You'll be the ones quite somber soon enough," Hollings shot back. "And I will be the one laughing."

The men who had been reclining all stood up. They stood on either side of the dirt road where a red ribbon had now been stretched between two familiar oak trees. The road had often been used for horse racing. But today, the galloping would be done by men.

One mile down the road, four young men, despite the merely mild weather that still had a coolness about it, had stripped off shirts and opted for bare chests and suspenders, and readied themselves at a straight line drawn across the road in the dirt.

Tom Partridge, the reigning footrace champ of Culpeper, a town about twenty miles to the west of Fredericksburg, was a blond young man with a lean, tight body. He moved his legs and arms about with a restrained confidence as he warmed up.

Next to him were two good racers, both from the countryside to the south of Fredericksburg, in the Virginia colony.

And at the other end, farthest from Partridge, was Robby Mackenzie. He was a relatively unknown athlete. Robby had fiery red hair and a short, muscular body. Though his legs were shorter than Partridge's longer shanks, they were powerfully built.

Robby leaned forward next to the other racers, steadying himself at the line.

"Mr. Partridge," he cried out to his competitor down the line.

"What is it?" Tom Partridge yelled back, but looking straight ahead, his body tensed for the sound of the starting gun.

"I heard you are a dandy runner."

"You've heard right," came back the reply.

"Then—out of due respect for you—I will have a bowl of water and a towel for yer face ready at the end of the race."

"Quite accommodating," Partridge shouted back. "But to what do I owe the honor?"

"It is because of my regrets," Robby called back.

"For what?"

"For kicking dust in yer face from now until the ribbon—which I shall be breaking ahead of you."

Tom Partridge had to smile at that, but didn't move, nor flinch. His eyes were fixed on the road ahead.

All four of the young men were poised and still, and were waiting for the gun.

To the rear, a man with a watch and a pistol glanced at the time, then raised his pistol toward the sky, and pulled the trigger.

The pistol barrel exploded loudly with smoke and a short blast of fire.

The four men burst forward, their legs churning.

Partridge quickly took the lead, taking long, graceful strides like a gazelle. Behind the leader by only a few feet was one of the country boys, and then right behind him was his fellow runner from Culpeper, and then Robby, who followed closely behind, but in the rear.

As the men ran down the dirt road there was only the sound of their pounding feet and heavy, labored breathing.

This was a mile race, and Robby knew he would have to pace himself for the finish; he had a powerful kick and wanted to use it in the last eighth of a mile. But just the same, he couldn't afford to lag too far behind. Partridge, and the country boy who was right behind him, were both long-legged fellows, and were capable of big strides.

Robby was studying the other country boy just ahead of him by two feet. Here was his first victim.

The man in front of him had a wild, untamed gait, and was pumping his arms wildly. Robby kept his eye on him, and after about a third of a mile Robby made his move.

Robby lunged forward, throttling his pace up, and shot past the other young man whose expression showed a look of complete surprise as he was being passed.

Now there were only two runners ahead of him. But they were about thirty feet ahead. There was a red kerchief tied to a tree branch at the edge of the dirt road that marked the half-mile point. And when Robby saw it he suddenly was seized with panic.

He had raced quarter-mile and half-mile races before. But this was his first miler. And his breathing was already uneven and almost convulsive as he gasped. His lungs seemed to be lit with fire, and his legs were beginning to feel as if they had been filled with poured iron.

But as Robby closed the gap toward the other two racers he noticed something about the country boy: He was starting to dip his shoulders, and drop his arms to his sides, and then he had to pick them back up. And his feet were taking missteps. He was getting sloppy.

I can take him, Robby thought to himself.

After another hundred feet of pounding on the hard dirt road, and fighting for breath control, Robby began to push himself faster.

Now he was only fifteen feet behind his next closest competitor. His legs were telling him that they wouldn't last. But Robby would have none of it.

No you don't! Robby shouted out to his own exhausted body, pushing it on.

He shouted so loud, the country boy in front of him turned his head around to see what the commotion was about.

That is when Robby kicked it in again.

Only five feet separated them…then three…and then two.

Now Robby could taste the victory that he felt was just barely within his reach. And that fueled his fatigued muscles.

Robby pumped his arms like the rotor of a cotton gin. In perfect, mechanical locomotion. Unceasing. As if powered by an energy source outside of himself.

He strode past the other country boy, who tried to speed up so as to avoid being overtaken, but as he did, he nearly stumbled with exhaustion, and when he next looked up, Robby was already ahead of him.

Then Robby increased his speed, ignoring the pain that was exploding in his thighs and calves. Partridge was too good a runner to look back at Robby's approach, and miss a few steps. But he did turn his head ever so slightly to the right and listened.

Tom Partridge could hear the footsteps of Robby thundering up from the rear.

Partridge had a strategy of his own. He would not give a sudden burst of speed...instead he simply increased his speed ever so slightly, taking long, galloping strides.

He would simply wear Robby out.

Now there was a mere two hundred feet left. Both men could see the red ribbon stretched across the road ahead. There were groups of cheering men on both sides of the road, jumping up and down and waving their hats.

Robby knew it was do or die.

His mouth was open and slack jawed with pain, and his body had been pushed into a state of nothingness, beyond exhaustion.

But he pushed. He rammed his arms up and down as if to force his legs to follow suit.

He was closing in on Partridge.

Partridge turned slightly to the right again. He was hearing the thundering steps of his challenger.

And they were coming faster than he had gauged.

Partridge panicked, and jettisoned his strategy altogether. He pushed himself to the fastest pace he could muster.

But somewhere down in his long legs, they were not cooperating. There was no more speed.

Robby was just a foot behind. Partridge had a look of an animal being hunted by a more deadly predator—eyes wide and his face contorted in painful, physical effort.

Then Partridge turned his face around, just enough to miss a step.

And just enough to see Robby's grimacing face pull up next to his.

They were perfectly even. Shoulder to shoulder.

Fifty yards to go.

Then thirty.

Still nose to nose.

Ten yards.

Then Robby made a funny little grunt.

And his torso lunged ahead of his feet…as if by some force of will that defied the gravitational pull that was trying to slow down his legs, he burst ahead.

When Robby hit the red tape he was a full foot ahead of Tom Partridge.

The men at the tape were jumping up and down in furious disbelief.

All except Jared Hollings, of course.

He was dancing and yelling up into the air with a holler of delight.

Robby staggered to a stop and held his arms out like a dying man looking for someone to hold him up.

He finally made his way over to a tree and collapsed against it, unable to stay standing.

After several minutes, when he and Partridge had both managed to catch their breath and begin breathing in and out like humans, Partridge, on wobbly legs, made his way over to Robby.

"How…how long…you trained?" he asked, breathlessly.

Robby didn't answer, but just stared back, still panting.

"I trained…for a month. How long…did you train?" Partridge said holding his side and barely able to breathe.

When Robby was finally able to put words to get, and muster the strength to talk, his answer was simple.

"Train?…Well…I didn't."

When the bitter losers had paid Hollings his winnings, he finally approached Robby.

"Here are your winnings," he said, holding out several coins.

But Robby shook it off.

"Nope. Can't take yer money," he said. "I'm a Christian man. Don't wager…but I would take one thing…"

"What's that?" Hollings asked.

"A job with you, Mr. Hollings. Know ye're an important merchant. Very influential."

After a moment's consideration, Hollings bent down close to Robby and whispered a question.

"Where do you stand on the English question?"

"Well," Robby said with a smile, "I don't believe we're in England, now, are we? So, where I stand, is…well…*where I stand*…is with the colonies, sir, and Virginia in particular. I hope that doesn't displease you."

Hollings straightened up with a wide grin.

"No, Robby. That doesn't displease me in the least!"

Chapter 6

"Nathan, dear, did you have a pleasant day?"

"As pleasant as can be, Deborah, considering that I am a fledgling lawyer with few clients, in a city that is more interested in discussing the recent riots than retaining lawyers."

Nathan Mackenzie had made his way home through the snow after a long day in the offices he shared with Mr. John Adams. He was later than he had expected. Deborah's dinner for him, set properly on the table, was already cold.

"Your practice will grow," Deborah said, trying to be reassuring.

"I wonder," Nathan said, setting down his leather satchel. Then he walked over to the fireplace in the kitchen, and warmed his hands before the fire. The logs were starting to burn low.

"Why do you doubt it?"

"Because," Nathan said, shaking his head in half-bemusement, "of Mr. Adams, who has agreed to take me on, he as my senior, and I as his legal apprentice."

"What about Mr. Adams?"

"Just that he seems more interested in talking about his farm in Braintree, which he left to set up office here in Boston, and worrying aloud about the state of his cows, and the revenues he expects from next year's harvest."

"He is a gentleman, and a farmer, as well as a lawyer," Deborah said. "What is wrong with that?"

"It's just that if I am going to tie my fortunes with another lawyer, I want to know that he is dedicated to the pursuit of the law, and not milk cows or nanny goats!"

"And you talk of me being fickle," Deborah countered with a laugh.

"Why so?" Nathan asked, and plopped himself down on the spindle-back chair in front of his plate of now cold beef and potatoes.

"You told me yourself," she said, "that you considered Mr. Adams a brilliant lawyer and a highly able mentor."

"Perhaps," Nathan replied, putting a small piece of potato in his mouth and chewing it thoughtfully. "But he is sometimes odd, and full of quirks, and very unpredictable."

"You see, that's what I mean," Deborah said. "It is men that are fickle, not just women as you often accuse me."

"Fickle?" Nathan said, and then swallowed his food. "You, my dear, can be as *fickle as a pickle*."

"There you go again, using that little turn of a phrase. And for the life of me I cannot make sense of it."

"It makes perfect sense," Nathan replied, now enjoying the roast beef even though it was no longer warm. Deborah had a way with beef, and had concocted her own special gravy for it that tasted slightly of blackberries and coffee.

"You see," Nathan said, chewing again, "*fickle as a pickle* means that wives can be very much like pickles—"

"I beg your pardon!" Deborah responded in mock anger, struggling not to laugh.

"Yes, quite so. Here is the similarity between wives and pickles. When you eat a pickle that is served to you at the house of another…you aren't quite sure what you will get. It is always a bit of a surprise. Pickles can be very sweet. Or—well—very tart!"

Deborah waddled over to her husband and stood next to him with her hands on her hips. Her back was tiring, as usual, from the growing weight of the little one within her.

"Are you lecturing *me* on the process of preserving pickles, then? It is not enough that you aspire to be a master of the law of the royal burgh of Boston, but you also pretend now to be a culinary expert as well?"

Nathan considered the point for a few moments while he finished the rest of the roast beef, and sopped it up with gravy.

"No…not an expert…"

"Well, then," Deborah continued, sensing now that she could best him in the debate and setting herself down in the chair next to him at the table, "because you are *not an expert,* you cannot liken me to any pickle—for you lack the necessary understanding of the process by which they are preserved!"

"May counsel ask the witness a question?" Nathan requested with mock formality.

"Granted."

"Are not pickles brined with two different kinds of liquids?" Then Nathan added quickly, "And be careful how you answer. You are under oath, and must be truthful. And remember that I myself have watched you many a time preserve pickles in this very kitchen."

Deborah paused and smiled at her sly husband.

"Alright, then. The answer is *yes*…two kinds of brine."

"One with vinegar…"

"Yes," Deborah answered cautiously.

"And the other with sugar."

"Yes..."

"Well then, that answers it!" Nathan said, rising from the table, and stepping behind his wife's chair, and surrounding her with his arms from behind.

"But what is the answer?"

"It is merely this," Nathan said, reaching down to kiss her neck. "You are clearly constituted with the choicest sugar, and the sweetest brine."

"A lawyer's trick of language," Deborah said, smiling as he kissed her. "Nothing else."

"Indeed," Nathan said, kissing her again. "My lawyer's turn of a phrase is but a poor token, a failed offering made to the beauty of your demeanor and the sweetness of your character."

"Delightful words," Deborah said, "but may I ask that your offering to the sweetness of my character take a slightly different form—like bringing in some more firewood?" Then Deborah nodded toward the kitchen hearth, where the fire was almost out.

Nathan sighed, but agreed, and trudged out to the shed, gathered an armful of slow-burning hickory logs, and then brought them back into the house. He loaded them into the fireplace and prodded them with an iron poker until the fire started blazing again.

Deborah finished clearing off the table and cleaning the dishes in the wooden rinse bucket.

"Tell me, dear," Nathan said. "Share something of your day today."

"I visited with your brother's wife, Edith. Or tried to, that is."

"What do you mean?"

"Well, she is in such a state of melancholy that she scarcely conversed at all."

"I wonder what ails that woman."

"I have heard of it, Nathan. It is sometimes common with women after childbirth."

"But she didn't give birth. Not actually. Both of her confinements resulted in stillborn infants."

"But can't you see," Deborah said, with an urgency to her voice. "All the more reason for her present state of despair."

Nathan was thinking over his wife's observation.

"And, with all due respect," Deborah continued, "to your brother, Reverend Edward Mackenzie, I do not believe he really sees the depth of her inner darkness."

"My brother is a good husband, Deborah."

"I know that. It's just that sometimes men…well…look—but still don't see certain things about women."

"Perhaps the woman simply has poor humours of the blood," Nathan remarked, but not convincingly. Yet his face took on the stubborn resolve that his wife knew very well.

Deborah could see that she was not about to change her husband's mind on the matter, at least at that time. So she decided to change the subject.

"And your work today, Nathan dear? What else can you tell me?"

Nathan was kicking off his boots. Then he walked over to the hearth and placed them before the fire to dry out for morning.

He thought for a moment, and then spoke up.

"Heard the news of the day," he said. "A grand jury was convened to look into the shooting near King Street. They issued an indictment today. Mr. Adams heard it from someone who was at the courthouse. They've indicted that British captain and several of his soldiers—for murder—for killing Samuel Gray, and that

Maverick boy, and Mr. Attucks the mulatto, and the others, in the riot."

"Thank God," Deborah said. "Perhaps, as your brother said in his sermon, now justice can be done."

"I wonder," Nathan said.

"Why would you ever say that?"

"Oh, nothing. Just that I've heard so many contrasting stories about what happened."

"It seems quite clear to me. The British soldiers shot several unarmed citizens. Put them in their graves. Cold-blooded murder."

Then Deborah studied her husband. Nathan had a pensive look on his face.

"Whatever could you be thinking?" she asked. "Of all the people who detest the injustices brought on this city by the Crown of England, you, my dear husband, are the prince."

"Prince, yes. But not king. The king of outrage, I think, is Mr. John Adams. He is much quieter about it than his outspoken cousin, Samuel. Sam Adams is a good man, and driven to the goal of increased freedom for the colonies. But I sense an even deeper current that runs within Mr. Adams, in a way."

Nathan was speaking from firsthand experience. He had sat in on some local meetings of Samuel Adams' Sons of Liberty; and he had even heard his mentor, John Adams, give a speech or two to the group.

"Well," Deborah said, concluding her thoughts, yet refraining from commenting on her husband's obvious inconsistencies in his attitude toward his mentor, Mr. Adams, "when that Captain and his troops are all duly and severely punished for the deaths of those poor men, perhaps this city can finally return to peace and tranquility."

Nathan was silent. Deborah looked again into his eyes, but could not understand her husband's wordless expression—a look like the face of a sailor on a ship who is on the high and windy crow's nest.

And who has seen the storm, rising ahead and inescapable, like a great, dark vortex.

Chapter 7

Following the announcement of the criminal indictment against Captain Preston and his soldiers for murder, the city of Boston could talk of little else. The merchant stores, the taverns and inns, the stables, and craftsmen's shops were all abuzz about the extraction of revenge against the "lobsterbacks" who had long tormented them.

The quick issuance of felony indictments should not have been a surprise. The royal legate of Massachusetts appointed by King George himself, Lt. Governor Thomas Hutchinson, had no choice but to appease the furious population following the shooting of unarmed civilians. On the night of the shooting, he received word that the grounds of his mansion in Boston might be mobbed. He raced down to North Square, where the incident had occurred, and met with English officials in the town hall. Then he appeared personally in the balcony of the building, and there Hutchinson pleaded with the shouting mob down below to disperse.

They would only do so after Hutchinson shouted out to them that "justice will be swift and severe against those responsible for firing on innocent citizens—now let the law have its course!"

The criminal charges were issued from the grand jury which

had been convened by Queen's Bench prosecutor Samuel Quincy, who laid out a bloody and shocking case of premeditated murder. Quincy was under orders from Hutchinson to make sure he got indictments, and he did.

Hutchinson was pleased that the English captain and his squad would now be prosecuted. If they were convicted, as Hutchinson fully expected them to be, the local rabble-rousers would be satisfied—they would have been plied with a "pound of flesh." With that revenge settled, Hutchinson hoped to restore order once again to Boston. His plan would then be to write to London for more troops—not less—to fully control the unruly Massachusetts colony, even though he had agreed with the locals to rid the city of Boston of all British troops. He knew that King George's aim was to subdue the whole of the colonies up and down the eastern seaboard. But it would have to start with Boston.

And as for Captain Preston himself, there was some evidence, Lt. Governor Hutchinson had been told, that the English officer might actually be innocent of any wrongdoing—that Preston never gave the order for the soldiers to fire their weapons.

But Thomas Hutchinson was willing to allow the wrongful conviction of one English officer and a handful of unimportant British regulars to save his own political station, and perhaps his own life.

After all, five years before, when colonists became outraged at the passage of the Stamp Act, another ploy of the Crown of England to further suffocate the colonies with more taxes, a Boston mob swarmed to Hutchinson's house, destroying much of it.

Lt. Governor Hutchinson would rather sacrifice Preston and his men than risk more destruction and plunder of his own property.

But the English governor was not the only one hoping for a quick conviction of Captain Preston.

Four days after the infamous shooting in North Square, three men appeared in a silversmith's shop on a side street of Boston.

The shop belonged to Mr. Paul Revere, a successful engraver and silversmith. Revere crafted a variety of pitchers, mugs, and plates. His copper ones were not well regarded. But his silverwork, on the other hand, was renowned. And he had a good drawing hand, good enough to receive regular commissions for woodcuts of important persons when their likeness needed to appear on the front cover of the *Boston Gazette*.

So, on March 9, a trio entered his shop and discreetly closed tight the shutters.

"Why the secrecy?" Revere asked, stepping into the front room to greet the men, wiping his hands off on his leather apron as he did.

"This is a special commission we have for you," said Benjamin Edes, the publisher of the *Boston Gazette*.

"Yes, quite special," added Mr. Gill, his partner.

That is when Revere looked over toward the third man and recognized him.

Now Revere was starting to understand the need for secrecy.

The third man was Samuel Adams, the fiery leader of the Sons of Liberty and considered widely to be the most ardent and radical opponent to English rule. He was short and stocky. He wore no wig nor fancy cloak, but dressed plainly, even poorly. But his eyes were steely and fixed.

"We have need," Samuel Adams said, "to fashion a woodcut for the front cover of the *Gazette*."

"What manner of woodcut?" Revere asked.

Edes took his leather letter case, opened it, and produced a drawing.

Revere took the drawing over to his drafting table, laid it down, and studied it. "This is the shooting—the British shooting of the citizens that you have in this drawing," Revere remarked.

"We prefer to call it a *massacre*," Samuel Adams said sternly.

"I have been working on some rough drawings myself," Revere said, "based on some witness accounts. But, this one you have here is different..."

"How so?" Mr. Gill asked.

"Well," Revere began, "from what I know, Captain Preston was not in the *rear* of the squad as you have in this drawing. But in fact *was* in the *front of* the soldiers. And secondly, this drawing has his arm raised as if giving the signal for the soldiers to fire their muskets—"

"Exactly," Mr. Edes said, interrupting him. "This is the version that has come to us. We consider it the authentic account. Now, Mr. Revere," he said, stepping over to Revere and putting his hand on his shoulder, "we propose to advertise your engraving of this massacre in the next *Gazette*. Offering it for sale in reprinted pictures."

"For the sum of eightpence per picture," Mr. Gill chimed in.

Mr. Revere considered it for a few moments. Then he nodded.

"Well enough," the engraver said, and reached out to shake Mr. Edes' hand in agreement.

By the time the two newspaper printers and Samuel Adams left the Revere silversmith shop, two things seemed very clear to them all.

By the following week, the entire town of Boston would be viewing the picture of the "Boston Massacre" and would be agreeing on the guilt of Captain Preston and all of his men.

And secondly, they firmly believed there wasn't a single lawyer in all of Boston, regardless of the truth that lay behind the entire bloody incident, who would be willing to defend the English officer nor any of his soldiers.

Chapter 8

James Forester, an Irish merchant, was sitting at the rough-hewn pine-board table across from a Boston lawyer named Josiah Quincy. Forester's eyes were welling up with tears, and there was deep emotion in his voice as he spoke.

"I tell ye, Mr. Quincy, I have known Captain Thomas Preston many a year, and he is one of the most decent and honorable men I've yet to meet."

Quincy was listening carefully, but he was shifting in his high-backed wooden office chair uncomfortably. He would have wished to have been anywhere but there at that moment. Josiah was a young, frail lawyer, with a bad eye and a timid nature. Unlike his older brother, Samuel Quincy, Josiah was shy and ill-at-ease on his feet in a courtroom. Samuel, on the other hand, was an accomplished royal prosecutor for the Crown, and had been given the assignment of prosecuting Captain Preston and his soldiers.

At twenty-six, Josiah was just a year older than Nathan Mackenzie, and was trying to forge a lucrative law practice. But, like most of the Boston lawyers during the boycott against England, he had found that tough sledding. Hard financial times had made the law wells run drier than usual. Merchants were reluctant to pay attorneys when their own trades had suffered.

In light of that, Josiah should have been overjoyed to have a prosperous merchant like James Forester solicit his services.

But the case he was bringing was a nightmare for Josiah.

"So tell me sir," Forester continued, "is there any way you can help poor Captain Preston?"

"Well, you…you…know," Josiah said with a bit of a stammer, "that my brother Samuel is, well…"

"The royal prosecutor? Yes, man, of course I know that. I'm sure that Captain Preston would have no objection to your going after your own brother in court. Happens often. Sometimes legal fights between brothers draw the best blood."

Josiah went silent. Forester could see the torment on his face. Then he asked a question.

"You said you've tried other lawyers in Boston," Josiah said, "and they've turned you down."

"Turned me down flat. I told them what the good captain told me—about his innocence. And how almost all of his men are wrongly accused."

"How about the Tory lawyers in town, the pro-English fellows?"

"They are the first ones I consulted. Refused me, they did. Down to the last man."

"Why was that?"

"Because they all feared they would be ruined. It's bad enough to be a Tory in this town they say, but to then side with an English captain charged with the murder of citizens, they say they would be tarred and feathered for that."

Josiah was quiet again. Forester was growing impatient and

began shaking his head, and muttering to himself, and then finally he could wait no longer.

"Mr. Quincy, are ye not a lawyer? Is not the defense of a man who stands to be hanged by the neck for a crime he dinna commit something that is within your province? Are ye not called to help bring justice, now man?"

There was another awkward pause, and then Josiah spoke up.

"I am not as skilled in…in the arts of courtroom debate as some lawyers," Josiah said slowly. "I could not take on the case myself…could not do it myself…"

"Whatever else you need, Mr. Quincy, I will attend to it."

"What I mean to say," Josiah continued, "is that I would need to have you secure a leading trial counsel, and perhaps others as well, to take the forefront of the defense, with my participation merely as an assisting attorney."

Now he had Forester's attention.

"Yes, go on," Forester said.

"I know a lawyer here in Boston. You may know him too."

"Aye, I know many lawyers."

"He is no Tory," Josiah said, and then he caught himself chuckling a little at the mere thought. "No, indeed he is not. Just the opposite. He is very much a patriot to the colonies and to the rights of our citizenry."

"Who do you speak of?" Forester asked.

"Mr. John Adams," Josiah said.

"Yes, I know him full well. Cousin to that Sam Adams fellow who is always rousing up the public against England on this point or that."

"The very man," Josiah said. "I consider Mr. Adams a very able lawyer. Quite brilliant on occasion."

"You said that he might need additional legal help?"

"Yes. But Mr. Adams is often assisted by a young associate about my age—a fellow he takes with him to the Sodalitas legal club. A man with a Scot's last name...MacHenry? No, not that...MacItrick? I can't rightly recall his name, but perhaps if you could convince John Adams to take up the defense of Captain Preston, then perhaps Mr. Adams would engage his Scots associate to join in as well. And with me, that would be three."

"Well then," Forester said with a new sense of enthusiasm. "There is hope."

"If you can get Mr. Adams on the case, then I will pledge my assistance," Josiah said.

Forester stood up and reached over the table and shook Josiah's hand vigorously.

"Thank you very much, Mr. Quincy," Forester said.

"It appears that my task is now clear," Forester called out as he headed out the door. Then he turned and added, "I must secure the services of Mr. John Adams, Esq."

As James Forester was heading at a fast clip down the street toward the offices of John Adams, the wagons of the *Boston Gazette* were rumbling down the cobblestone streets. Newsboys were standing ready to unload the bundled newspapers.

When the wagon stopped, the boys pulled the newspaper bundles down and cut the cords. One of the boys stopped to look at the front page. And when he did his eyes widened and his mouth went slack.

"Cooee!" he cried out as he lifted up the front page of the *Gazette*.

The top half contained the woodcut drawing by Revere depicting the shooting by the British troops, with the title "Bloody Massacre perpetrated in King Street, Boston, on March 5, 1770 by a party of the 29th Regiment."

Beneath it was the poetic and highly inflammatory verse that described one very slanted version of the violent episode. A grand jury had already issued a first, formal criminal indictment. But now, in the court of scandal journalism, the *Gazette* had issued a second:

> *Unhappy Boston! See thy Sons deplore,*
> *Thy hallowed walks besmeared with guilt & gore.*
> *While Faithless Preston and his savage Bands,*
> *With murderous rancour stretch their bloody hands,*
> *Like barbarians grinning over their prey.*
> *Approve the carnage and enjoy the day.*

Chapter 9

By the time James Forester had located John Adams' law office and then had banged on the outer door, Adams and his young associate Nathan Mackenzie had both fetched copies of the *Boston Gazette* and were each poring over the front page.

Nathan had the accompanying office off to the side, which was much smaller, but he was allowed access to the law library, which separated Nathan's office from that of John Adams. The library also doubled as a conference room, as it was housed with a long maple wood table suitable for seating a number of clients and visitors. It was an old dining-room table that Adams had brought from his farm at Braintree, but it passed as a conference table well enough.

Adams was in his larger office, reading the front page intensely in the swivel wooden chair at his desk, and there was a perplexed scowl on his face. As he read further, the perplexed expression disappeared and melted into quiet rage.

With the banging on the door, Nathan had put his copy of the newspaper down and then hurried to the front door. Since the most recent riot, they had taken to locking the front door unless they were expecting clients.

Nathan swung the brass cover away from the peephole and saw Mr. Forester standing outside.

"Yes, may I help you?" Nathan asked, having cracked the door a bit to speak to their visitor.

"Mr. James Forester, a local merchant of some reputation here in Boston," he replied.

"And the manner of your business?" Nathan asked politely.

"To see Mr. John Adams on a matter of great urgency."

Nathan closed the door and walked over to Adams, who was gesturing to the newspaper as if he were engaged in a debate with a sheet of parchment.

"Excuse me," Nathan began, "but there is a Mr. Forester—"

"Have you read this article on the 'massacre,' as they are now calling it?" Adams said, interrupting him as if he had not heard Nathan's comment.

"The front page story? Why yes I have…"

"This is an outrage," Adams continued.

"Yes…but…Mr. Adams, there is a Mr. Forester here to see you."

"Who?"

"Mr. Forester."

"I don't know any Mr. Forester."

"He says it is a very pressing matter and he needs to speak with you immediately."

"Is it a legal matter?"

"I rather think it is," Nathan said, hoping to increase their clientele by at least one new prospect.

"Good. Could use some new clients. I have just received word from my farm manager at Braintree that another of my cows just died. They are having a hard time of it, what with the animal pox that seems to be afflicting all of my livestock."

"Should I show him in?" Nathan asked.

"Yes, do that," Adams said, and then returned to his newspaper, shaking his head in disbelief at what he was reading.

When Forester entered, he took off his tri-cornered hat, bowed slightly, and introduced himself.

"Have you read this claptrap?" Adams asked, shaking the newspaper in front of his visitor.

"I have," Forester replied somewhat confused.

"The *Gazette* has taken this whole business a step too far now," Adams said, "poisoning the well. That is exactly what they are doing."

Forester was trying to figure the lawyer out. He had come under the impression that Adams was a Whig, and opposed England's rule over Boston, and was a patriot to the citizen cause. But now, Adams' comments condemning the anti-English *Boston Gazette* were confusing the Irish merchant.

"You are John Adams," Forester asked. "The lawyer?"

"I am a lawyer today," Adams remarked. "And will likely be even more so tomorrow, if my farm continues to wane, and my livestock persist in failing me…I'll have no choice…"

After a few moments, while Forester continued to size up the lawyer across the desk from him, Adams laid down the newspaper and leaned forward on his folded hands.

"You didn't tell me what brings you here," Adams began.

"*That,*" Forester said, nodding to the newspaper on Adams' desk.

"This? The *Gazette*?" Adams asked. "You want to sue the newspaper?"

"No," Forester said quietly and soberly. "I want to find justice for a man wrongly accused."

After a few seconds of deliberation, Adams understood and then slowly nodded.

"I see," the lawyer said in a voice that was subdued, and reflected an understanding that was growing by the second. After a few more moments, he said, "You used the phrase *wrongly accused*."

"Yes, and I used it advisedly, and on purpose, sir," Forester replied.

"Upon what basis do you assert, sir, that *this certain man* to whom you refer has been wrongly accused?"

"Upon the fact that I know him as a friend, and have spoken to him face-to-face about the entire incident for which he is charged with capital murder."

"*Capital murder*, you say?" the lawyer asked.

"Yes sir. And I am sure that you know who I am referring to."

Adams suddenly thrust up his hand to halt the man's conversation in its tracks.

"I have not undertaken to consult with any man on this subject," Adams said. "Including you. I have not been retained as any man's lawyer having anything to do with the incident that I gather that you are describing. So, before you go any further and divulge private and confidential confessions, I must consider my stake in this case very carefully."

With that Adams stood up and straightened his long coat and the white frock that covered his neck and upper chest.

But he was simply buying time. And he was weighing his own resolve. Whether to wade into this morass of deadly quicksand. Or to remain safely at a distance. Away from danger.

"I should like to consult my associate," Adams said, and strolled to the door of his office. "If you will excuse me for a moment..."

Nathan had been standing just outside eyesight around the

corner of the opening to Adams' office, listening to the conversation that was quite audible, as Adams had not shut the door.

When Adams came around the corner, Nathan was startled and stepped back with surprise.

"So you've been listening," Adams said. "Good. That will save me the breath of repeating what has transpired. I would wager that this merchant is seeking legal counsel for Captain Preston. What say you to that?"

"It seems clear that is his purpose," Nathan replied.

"And?" Adams said, persisting.

"And…it would also appear that any lawyer taking up the case—"

"Would be inviting the demise of his professional career? Is that what you were going to say?"

"Yes. And perhaps even more than that. Perhaps even endangering his home and family as well."

"Quite so," Adams said, in a voice that was barely audible. The two men stood, looking at each other in the vestibule of the office for a minute or two.

Finally Adams spoke up.

"I was in the street that night as you were. The night of the shooting. I saw men wielding clubs. And swearing violence. Now what," he said with a voice that was tensed like a mistuned piano string, "what would you say if in fact this Captain Preston *never gave the order to fire?* But some of his men were instigated into firing on the mob out of self-defense. Would Captain Preston then not be wholly innocent of any murderous intent?"

"It would appear so," Nathan said reluctantly.

"And yet, would his innocence ever be proven in court, sir, in this town of Boston, with the flames of instigation being flamed by the likes of the *Gazette* and by my own cousin Sam—*without the benefit of legal counsel at his side?*"

Nathan did not want to answer. Because he knew the answer, and he knew the disastrous consequences if he admitted it to be so.

"Will you answer me or not?" Adams asked his young associate, growing impatient.

"The captain will hang, most certainly, if matters run their course without a vigorous legal defense."

"Hang."

"Yes, Mr. Adams."

"For a crime he did not commit."

"Possibly so…"

"*Probably* so, would you not agree?" Adams said, pressing the matter.

"Probably so, yes," Nathan had to admit.

John Adams exhaled loudly. He tensed his face slightly and then turned to his associate.

"I believe we should discuss with Mr. Forester, you and I, exactly what he knows about the alleged innocence of Captain Preston. That would be the logical step, would it not?"

"It would," Nathan said in a low voice, filled with resignation and defeat, and feeling all over his senses that numbness that one feels when impending catastrophe comes fully into sight—too quickly, and too certainly for any chance at escape.

Chapter 10

At the very moment that his brother and John Adams had been meeting with James Forester, Rev. Edward Mackenzie was attending a conclave of his own.

But Edward found it difficult to concentrate on the proceedings.

Once a month prominent members of the clergy in the town of Boston would meet and discuss matters of common concern. Edward, at first, considered it a great honor to have been invited. The ideas of ministers from a variety of different denominations meeting together was a decidedly revolutionary idea. But it had been born out of necessity.

Since the current disturbances in Boston between the citizens and the British regulars, and going back even farther to the decision by Boston merchants to boycott English goods in protest over exorbitant taxes, the local clergy felt they needed a council of their own to help to keep peace and propriety in the town.

They had not been successful.

The topic of conversation in that particular meeting was, according to the agenda, "The Current State of Civil Unrest in Boston, and the Presence of British Troops as a Debilitating Influence on the Morals of the People."

Edward took exception to that agenda item—believing that it was an essentially political question, and ministers of the Gospel were to stay clear of such matters. But in preparation for the meeting he decided to suffer through the discussion for the sake of propriety and to avoid unnecessary discord.

But earlier that morning, as he was preparing to leave their house for the clergy meeting, and as Edward was adjusting his powdered wig and then carefully placing down on it his best, black silk lined tri-cornered hat, he saw something out of the corner of his eye.

His wife, Edith, was standing in the inner doorway of the parlor, staring at him, with a puzzling look on her face.

"Whatever is it?" Edward asked, looking at her closer.

He noticed that she was holding both hands out, as if carrying something. But her hands were empty.

Edward approached her, but she did not move. He took her hands and closed them with his, and then said, "Edith, what is it?"

"It is nothing," Edith said.

"Your visage tells me otherwise," Edward said.

"Nothing bears nothing," she said. "Nothing hopes for nothing."

He thought it a queer saying and was going to question her on it, but chose not to. He knew that Edith had been exceedingly melancholy since the loss of their last baby. *She simply needs time for the healing of her soul,* Edward had decided.

Edward bent forward and kissed her on the forehead.

"I am off to my meeting, my love," he said.

"Have a good day, dear husband," she said in a small, distant voice.

"May I…is there something I may do for you, Edith?" he asked.

"Nothing. Nothing at all," was her reply. She managed a smile and reached out to stroke his face.

Then Edward smiled back and turned to leave.

The meeting was droning on, but Edward had been distracted with thoughts of Edith, and her strange posture, appearing in the doorway as if she were a disembodied apparition, holding out her hands for some unseen possession.

But something caught Edward's attention and drew him back into the discussion. Someone had brought up the matter of Captain Preston's criminal indictment. Several of the ministers ventured opinions about whether his certain conviction would bring peace to the town.

Finally, Edward spoke up.

"I dare say, his conviction and swift punishment should not be justified on the grounds of bringing peace and tranquility to Boston, even though that would be an enviable result."

"Then what, pray tell, is the point of his being brought to justice?" one of the ministers asked.

"Just that…the achieving of *justice*," Edward answered. "God is a God of perfect justice. A swift rebuke to Captain Preston's immoral and outrageous incitement to violence will show forth God's sense of justice. That is the only end we need to justify the trial of that malicious British officer."

"And what if this Captain Preston gains a clever lawyer and escapes judgment?" another minister asked. "Then is God mocked by such a perverse verdict?"

"I have faith," Edward said, "in God's sovereign will. That He will not allow it to be so, gentlemen. Whatever the lawyers may do to try to win his acquittal, with whatever corrupt contrivances they may muster…still…God's justice will prevail."

Near the end of that day's meeting, one of the clergymen suggested a novel idea for the next meeting.

"I have heard," the minister said, "that over in Philadelphia, there is debate regarding the illegitimacy of the institution of slavery. Some have suggested an organized opposition to the keeping and bartering of slaves."

Then the minister added, "Perhaps we could discuss that issue in our next meeting."

There was an uncomfortable silence in the room.

Finally Reverend Jonathan Mayhew, a Boston minister who was, in Edward's judgment, a man of genuine brilliance and spiritual temperance, though of some theological unorthodoxy, spoke up.

"Slavery is, I believe, a moral issue. And because all moral issues derive from spiritual verities, and from scriptural principals, perhaps we could address that issue in a future meeting."

"It is, I fear," another of the clergymen said, "an unanswerable proposition. The Bible seems to condone the practice. Slavery is simply an assumed part of human institutions and practices—"

"So is sin," Edward Mackenzie found himself saying out loud. "Do you suppose we should condone that too?"

The speaker was taken aback by Edward's directness. After clearing his throat, the other minister rebutted.

"Sin is clearly condemned by Scripture. Therein lies the difference."

"I beg to differ," Edward replied. "Galatians 3:28 says, *There is neither Jew, nor Greek, there is neither bond nor free, there is neither male or female: for ye are all one in Christ Jesus.* Now, if there is no distinction 'in Christ' between slave and free, then why is one in chains and the other not?"

"Reverend Mackenzie, what exactly are you proposing by your extraordinary remarks?" the other minister asked.

After a moment of reflection, Edward answered simply, "I propose nothing, sir. I only make an observation."

As the meeting disbanded, Reverend Mayhew approached Edward, and shook his hand as the two left the church hall together.

"Be very careful, Reverend Mackenzie," Mayhew said with a smile.

"Of what, good sir?" Edward asked.

"Of the consequences of your controversial ideas."

"I truly did not set out, in our meeting, to be *controversial*, but only *biblical*," Edward replied.

"Interesting," Mayhew said over his shoulder as he went his way, "how those two things so often find themselves to be next-of-kin."

Chapter 11

It was the end of day, and John Adams was trudging home with a heavy burden on his mind. He knew that Abigail and his two young children would be there, waiting for him. He had something to tell Abigail, and it would be very hard. But in their relationship candor was always prized as part of the cement that bonded them so closely together.

He would be forthright and plain with her.

It was all because he and Nathan had returned back into Adams' office after their short, but terse, discussion in the office vestibule. Once they had returned to the interior of the office and sat back down with James Forester, they began to pepper him with aggressive questions, challenging his assertion that the British captain of the regiment was not guilty of murder: *How long have you known Captain Preston? Has he lent you any money or done any favors that you would vouch for his innocence? Have you opposed the boycott against English goods—or have you sided with the English on that question? What did Captain Preston tell you personally about his involvement in the "massacre" at King Street?*

Forester looked them in the eye and calmly answered every question. Forester explained that as an Irishman, he had his own bundle of complaints against the Crown. That said, he was also a "loyal supporter of the king, though not of all of his policies." He personally thought the boycott was a bad idea, but he participated as best he could in any event. He had known the captain from his very first appearance in Boston. He knew him to be a conscientious man, who had privately confided in Forester that he was concerned about some of his soldiers and it was a struggle to keep them within the bounds of the law and of decency. Forester had personally observed Captain Preston, on more than one occasion, chastise some of his men for harassing the citizens of Boston.

And on the last and all-important question, Forester was equally open.

"The good captain told me, after his arrest," Forester explained, "that he had been *in the fore* of the squad of soldiers, not behind them as popularly imagined. And that he had *never* given them the order to fire on the mob."

On that particular point, regarding *where* Preston was standing at the time of the shooting, Nathan pressed Adams on it when they were later alone in the office.

"What difference would that make?" Nathan asked. "Whether he was behind the troops as some have suggested, or was at their forefront, as Preston insists?"

"Why it is paramount, absolutely *paramount*," Adams replied, spreading his arms out like a stage performer. "Can't you see?"

Nathan thought it over for a moment.

Then the lamp was lit in his mind.

"Of course," Nathan said. "If Captain Preston was indeed in the forefront of the armed soldiers and had ordered them to fire, he would have exposed himself to certain harm."

"Precisely!" Adams shouted out. "Which makes it unlikely he ever gave the command at all. Besides, the proper place for a regiment commander is *behind* the line of fire, so he may appropriately direct their shot."

But Nathan was still concerned at one point.

"But Preston was uninjured, and was never shot himself. Doesn't that tend to indicate," Nathan wondered aloud, "that he was *not* in the front?"

"There is one possible explanation," Adams said. "But I do not want it coming from me. Instead, I suggest it come directly from Captain Preston himself. Nathan, I believe we must interview Captain Preston in the jail and do it so posthaste."

Adams and Nathan hurried over to the jail and quickly gained access to the British captain. Preston had been told by Forester that he was hoping to retain Mr. Adams and his associate, and the prisoner was half-expecting, and more than hoping, to see John Adams personally.

"I was indeed in the front of the squad," Preston said in a hushed voice, bending forward in the jail cell across from Adams and Nathan.

Captain Preston was still dressed in his tan pants and white stockings, but had removed and carefully hung on a hook his red English officer's coat trimmed with gold. His white frock shirt was slightly dingy from his having slept in it in the dirty cell. His wig was carefully placed on a small stand next to his bed, and his reddish hair was untidy. A few long strands were hanging down on either side of his face, uncombed. Preston's face was weary, and there were dark circles under his eyes.

"To the very point," Adams said, launching into the gist of the matter after a quick introduction of himself and Nathan. "If you were in the fore of the squad as you allege, then why were you not hit with shot from their muskets?"

"Because," Preston answered with a certain amount of fatigue in his voice, "I was indeed in the front, but off to the side, trying to quell the mob's further threats. I was fearful of a clash—"

Adams interrupted him, not letting him finish.

"So, then, you *knew* that there might be violence."

"Of course. There already was," the British officer answered. "Rocks and large chunks of ice were thrown at us. Clubs were wielded. Mr. Attucks, the tall mulatto fellow, he was swinging a club. I was hit—"

"Where?" Adams asked.

"In the forearm."

"Show me," Adams said sharply.

Preston paused for a second and considered the two attorneys sitting across from him in the dank, foul-smelling jail cell.

Then, the captain slowly began to roll up his sleeve.

As he did, he winced slightly.

When his sleeve was fully rolled up, he displayed it to Adams and Nathan.

The forearm was black, green, and red from bruises, with a long purplish ridge through the middle of the arm where something hard had struck it.

"You may roll down your sleeve," Adams said, after he was satisfied that Nathan also had a good look.

After a number of additional questions, Adams turned the conference over to Nathan.

"You told us, Captain," Nathan said, "that you were trying to quell the mounting threat of violence."

"Clearly, yes."

"You told us of the rocks and other missiles that were being thrown by the colonists."

"Correct."

"Yet," Nathan said, "was your apprehension of violence perchance also based on *something else?*"

Preston eyed him closely, trying to discern his meaning.

"What do you mean, sir?" he asked.

"Only this, that the colonists played their part, perhaps. Yet…was there some concern on your part regarding the violent tendencies of some of your soldiers?"

Preston leaned back in his chair, and a flash of indignation crossed his face.

"Answer Mr. Mackenzie's question, Captain!" Adams said in a loud voice, so loud that he startled the officer slightly.

After regaining his composure, Captain Preston looked out into space for a moment, then looked directly at Nathan when he answered.

"There was a concern on my part…of a sort…"

"What kind of a concern?"

"For unruliness—"

"By your soldiers?"

"Yes."

"How many?"

"Two…in particular…that I could think of."

"Which two?" Adams interjected now, being swept into Nathan's line of questions.

Preston, now being pelted with rapid-fire questions from both attorneys, took a deep breath, but before he could answer, Adams was on him again.

"Names, sir. Give us the names…"

"Killroy was one," Preston said.

"And the other?" Adams asked.

"Montgomery, also, I would think."

Adams now settled back in his chair and looked over at Nathan, nodding for him to finish with any more of his questions.

"Did those two," Nathan asked, "Killroy and Montgomery—the two that you knew may have violent propensities—did they *fire upon the crowd?*"

Captain Preston clasped his hands together before he replied. He knew his answer would not help his defense.

"They did."

Nathan was now absorbed in contemplation of what that might mean for their defense. If the captain knew that Killroy and Montgomery were unruly soldiers, would he thereby be held responsible for their shooting into the mob? Or was the attack by rocks and clubs sufficient to have given rise to the doctrine of self-defense?

But while he was considering that, Adams was looking over the haggard British captain.

For the most important question of all still had to be asked.

"Sir," Adams asked him. "Did you ever give, by word or deed— *ever* give any order for your soldiers to fire their weapons?"

Preston straightened up, stiff and formal, before he answered. As if he were under parade review by a superior officer.

"I did not, sir," he replied.

Those words, *I did not, sir,* were still floating around in John Adams' mind as he entered his Boston house, and kissed Abigail and then kissed his two small children, and tossed his hat down and slowly peeled off his long coat and his inner coat, and stripped down to his vest and sleeves.

He and Abigail compared notes of their day. But she was astute and saw right off that he had something on his mind.

So Adams recounted, in very general terms, his encounter with Mr. Forester, the Irish merchant, in his law office; and then his interview with Captain Preston in the jail.

Abigail's countenance fell as she was holding one of their children in her arms.

She waited for the inevitable blow.

"I have agreed to represent Captain Preston," Adams said softly.

Tears were now welling up in Abigail's eyes.

"And…one other thing," he said reluctantly.

What else can he tell me that could possibly be worse? Abigail wondered to herself as she tried to fight back her emotions.

"I promised Captain Preston, at his urging," Adams continued, "that we would also defend all of his soldiers as well. He did not want to abandon his men…"

Finally, Abigail could hold it back no longer. A flood of tears came pouring out.

"Dear Abigail, I am sorry that this will be such a trying ordeal…" he said. And then, without thinking of its effect on his wife, he added, "I have already been paid ten guineas for the case."

And then in a show of complete candor he added, to his weeping wife, "Perhaps that will help offset the eventual toll my law practice will surely suffer…when all of Boston knows I am the lawyer for a British officer accused of murdering Boston civilians."

Now Abigail's weeping was mixed with a flash of anger. "Mr. Adams," she began sternly, "you should hope and pray to the Almighty that a loss of your law practice is *all they will do to you*…to us…to our home, and our children."

Chapter 12

When Nathan arrived home in the evening, he was struggling with whether to announce he would be assisting John Adams in the defense of the most notorious and politically divisive criminal case in Boston history.

Deborah could see that her husband had things on his mind that night. But Nathan did not tell her that he had visited Captain Preston in jail with Mr. Adams earlier that day, or that they had agreed to represent the British officer and his men.

But when Nathan showed up at the office the following day and Adams began telling his associate of his interaction the night before with Abigail, his wife, Nathan volunteered that he still had not informed his own wife of his entrance into the tumultuous case.

When Adams learned that, he scolded Nathan severely.

"When God joins you to a wife," Adams said, "He gives you both a friend and a lover. Domestic tranquility requires candor, Nathan. You must tell her."

"But did not you tell me just moments ago of your wife's tears and weeping?" Nathan said. "Do I want to impart that kind of suffering on my wife?"

"But I did not finish my story," Adams said. "Yes, she burst into a flood tide of tears and lamented the fact I had committed myself to Captain Preston's case. But that is not the end of the matter. She and I talked until the wee hours of the night."

"And what was the resolution?"

"My dearest Abigail finally said she understood that I was acting in the fashion that I thought was right," Adams said. "She knew full well the danger to our family from the riotous reactions of the mob once it all became known that I was Preston's legal counsel. Yet, despite all of that, she also said that she was willing to share in any of the travail that may come. And that she was placing her trust in the Providence of God to have the whole matter end well."

Nathan nodded when he heard that. He was ashamed.

"I'll tell Deborah tonight," Nathan answered.

Yet privately he wondered how he was going to confide in his wife that he was imperiling their safety. And not only that, but he was almost assuredly guaranteeing that his ability to find future legal clients would be decimated. That last point would undoubtedly strike Deborah badly, because Nathan had been the one who repeatedly complained to her about the fledgling nature of his law practice. Yet now Nathan was the same person who was single-handedly destroying his own professional future by teaming up with Mr. Adams in the criminal case.

But Nathan did not have much time to ponder how he would face his wife with all of that bitter news. Adams, minutes later, dashed into Nathan's small office.

"Well, my boy," he said almost out of breath. "What are you doing here? Come into the law library at once. You and I have a great deal of work to do on this 'massacre' case."

After grabbing a quill pen, several long sheets of cheap printer's paper, and a small silver inkwell, Nathan hurried into the conference room. Adams was already there, jotting down a list of items they needed to cover.

"The arraignment's coming up shortly," he said as Nathan sat down. "Of course there shall be a plea of not guilty for our client. But the point is, Captain Preston's defense requires some particular finesse if it is going to be successful."

"And what of the fact," Nathan asked, "that we are committed to also represent numerous of his soldiers as well?"

"That does pose several problems. The first is the manpower we need to muster a defense."

"There are only two of us..." Nathan began. "But there are numerous prosecution barristers, I have heard, who are going to be assisting the Crown in trying to prove their murder charges against our clients."

"Yes," Adams said. "And Samuel Quincy is the special prosecutor appointed to head up the prosecution effort. And Robert Treat Paine has been named as his chief legal assistant."

Nathan studied Adams' face. There was a look of distress on his senior partner's face. Adams had often spoken of Robert Treat Paine before. Paine was an aggressive, fire-breathing trial lawyer with an impressive practice throughout Massachusetts.

And every time that Adams talked about attorney Paine, he had the same expression on his face—dismal and slightly tortured. There was clearly a history between the two men, but what it was, and why it so afflicted John Adams, was a mystery to Nathan.

"Only two defense lawyers...you and I," Nathan reiterated with a defeated tone. But Adams, who had regained his composure, wouldn't let him finish.

"Not true," Adams retorted. "Josiah Quincy has agreed to join us."

"A reticent kind of advocate, I am afraid," Nathan grumbled.

"Well, man, we have to accept what we have," Adams said with an edge to his voice. "And I've already made some inquiries…I believe we can also get Samson Salter Blowers."

"Quincy's partner?"

"The same."

Nathan had run into Samson Blowers in court on one occasion. All he could recall about Blowers was that he was a particularly dour and gloomy man, who spoke in a low, moaning cadence when he addressed the judge.

As he thought about the power and influence of the prosecution team, and then as he considered the unimpressive group that was being assembled for the defense, Nathan's heart sank.

He saw the very likely scenario of not only losing most of his law practice, and having his home assailed by anti-English vandals, but also suffering the ignominy of losing the case and seeing his client convicted and then hanged for a crime he didn't commit.

He wondered how things could get worse.

But by the end of the day, they did.

Adams breezed into Nathan's office and announced he had lined up one additional member of the legal defense team.

"Who is it?" Nathan asked.

"Robert Auchmuty," Adams answered. "An accomplished attorney."

That gave Nathan a momentary lift of optimism—until he asked his next question.

"What is his background?" Nathan inquired.

"He is a vice-admiralty judge," Adams said, "appointed by King George. An obvious Tory in his politics."

There it was—the final, detestable blow: Nathan would be

publicly linked with an English sympathizer who had close ties to the English Crown, in a case that was likely to incite all of Boston into a conflagration of massive, violent proportions.

And Nathan, a neophyte lawyer with a struggling practice and no reputation to speak of, would be right in the center of it.

Chapter 13

In the short time Robby Mackenzie had been working for Jared Hollings down in Virginia, he had showed himself to be every bit the eager, industrious worker Hollings had pegged him for. Hollings had, at least to Robby's mind, a vast empire of business interests and investments spread all over the colony of Virginia, and stretching up to Maryland, and down to North Carolina as well. And there was plenty of work for Robby to do. And he did it with zeal.

Every day his duties seemed to change. One day he might supervise the loading of wagons full of Hollings's cotton bales onto longboats that shipped out of the small port in Fredericksburg, and then would float down the Rappahannock River. He worked with teams of slaves from Hollings's country plantation that loaded the bales; he had already made an acquaintance with most of them. By and large they seemed friendly, but they also were very quiet around him, and the slaves eyed him with a mixture of suspicion and curiosity. Robby had a Bostonian's accent and was, in neither his manners nor his speech, a Virginian. Perhaps that was what made him a mild curiosity to the Africans on Hollings's plantation.

The slaves seemed to be fed regularly and Robby had not seen them physically mistreated. But he detected a genuine sense of fear that seemed to lurk deep in their eyes. Robby shared the antislavery sentiments of his brothers, Nathan and Edward, but he wasn't known as an advocate of liberty like Nathan, nor was he a religious idealist like his older brother, Edward. Robby was a good-natured young man with a practical way about him, and a sense of humor that made him tend to laugh off a situation as a first response. It was only when he was pushed—and pushed hard—that he would use his considerable physical strength. And then only as a last resort.

So, as Robby worked side by side with the Africans, he made friends with them quickly, but he nevertheless kept himself from thinking too deeply about their state of poverty, or their lack of liberty, or their status as one man's property. He knew that Jared Hollings had taken a liking to him, and he would do nothing to hinder that, even if it meant turning a blind eye to the condition of fellow human beings.

Mr. Hollings owned a share, with his brother, in an ironworks mill in Baltimore and promised that one day Robby would accompany him there. In Virginia, Hollings also owned a tobacco plantation outside of Richmond.

Robby soon learned that Hollings was an astute business man, who seemingly could turn a profit in anything he attempted—whether it was the running of various mercantile shops in Fredericksburg, or playing cards till late into the evening with local shop owners, whom he relieved of their coins and paper money. But that was not Hollings's passion. His true obsession lay in politics. He had been elected a member of the House of Burgesses in Williamsburg. The house was currently out of session. But it was never out of mind with Hollings, who endlessly talked about laws, either passed or proposed, dealing with taxes, and surcharges, and levies, or more often than not dealing with the abrogation of the same—and land regulations, and court procedures, and elections, and the need to stimulate commerce by what he called "sensible legal provisions," rather than the "legal monstrosities enacted by a distant monarchy."

Hollings had three daughters by his second wife, Ruth. Hollings's first wife had died of influenza. The oldest Hollings daughter was Rachael, who was Robby's age. Rachael was a blonde-haired maiden with a pretty smile, pale blue eyes, and a laugh that, to Robby, had a rare musical quality to it. He had exchanged but a few words with Rachael, mostly at the few dinners in the mansion house when Mr. Hollings invited him to join the family.

That is, until the day when he was in the plantation office, tallying figures in the written feed register for his employer.

"So, you are good with numbers, Mr. Mackenzie?"

Robby looked up from the tall desk where he had been standing, hunched over the angled top, with a quill pen in one hand, and the register book in the other.

Seeing Rachael's smiling face, tucked neatly within her yellow bonnet, Robby had to break into a wide, uninhibited grin.

"Fair enough with numbers, Miss. Fair enough," he answered.

"Poppa says that it is rare that a man who has such physical talents should also be endowed with mental faculties as well."

Robby blushed, and looked down, trying to hide his smile which was now threatening to eclipse his entire face.

"Well that is certainly the kindest compliment I have ever received," he started to say. "And from the prettiest source, I might add—"

But Rachael interrupted him.

"Why Mr. Mackenzie," she retorted, in a convincing voice that made it sound as if she were genuinely surprised at his comment.

Robby's smile dissipated, and for a moment he struggled in a pool of embarrassment and confusion.

"Oh, I…that was my mistake…I shouldn't have…" Robby stammered.

Then he caught Rachael's smile, which she could contain no longer. It erupted into a pretty laugh.

"So, you make sport of me?" Robby countered with a laugh.

"I certainly do, Mr. Mackenzie. For footracing is not the only sport, you know."

"Indeed not," he said, feeling better about things by then. "Your wit is faster, I would wager, than my feet are in a race."

There was a pause, as Rachael stepped a little closer to the desk where he was standing.

"You use the phrase *I would wager*—that is interesting."

"Just a manner of speaking."

"Perhaps," she said. "But I remember Poppa saying that he won a great deal of money on your race, but that you would have none of it. For you said you could not wager, as that would be a sin."

"What your father said was true."

"So," Rachael said with a twinkle in her eye, "do you say then that my dear father is a sinner, inasmuch as he wagered on your race?"

Now Robby was caught. For a moment he wished he had his brother Nathan's keen logic or Edward's ability to exhort. Somehow he knew he had to escape the implication that he was condemning Jared Hollings—his employer and benefactor, and just as importantly, the father of Rachael, with whom he had been secretly enthralled from the first day he saw her.

Then Robby's posture relaxed and he smiled confidently.

"No, miss, I would never say that."

"But why not?" she shot back, taunting him. "My father was wagering, was he not?"

"Not really."

"Oh? How could that be?" Rachael said with surprise.

"Because," Robby explained confidently, "a wager is something that one man bets with another when the outcome is so uncertain as to be a speculative game of chance—"

"Quite so," Rachael said. "But then—"

Robby cut her off and moved just an inch closer to her as he spoke.

"But then," he concluded, "your father could not have been betting on an outcome that was uncertain—for I was most certainly destined, my dear miss, to have won that race."

Rachael laughed a little at his clever reply, but then her laughter stopped. She was gazing into the dark brown eyes of Robby Mackenzie, who was now standing so close that she almost believed she could hear his pounding heart.

And then she heard her father calling her outside.

She bowed quickly and scurried to the door of the office. But before she turned to leave from his sight, she cocked her head slightly toward him as she stood in the doorway, smiled, and then disappeared.

Chapter 14

The evening after he had been scolded by John Adams, Nathan decided to share everything with his wife about the Boston Massacre case. Including his retainer as co-counsel to Adams. He would be forthright about the risks. He had no other choice.

Nathan envisioned the argument that he would inevitably have with his wife. Deborah was loving and obedient in public. But in private, though no less loving, she nevertheless could be direct, even blunt with her husband's mistakes. This decision of taking on the criminal defense of English soldiers in Boston, of all places, was the most outrageous risk of all.

And to make matters worse, Deborah was expecting. To Nathan, in light of his wife's vulnerability, it seemed that his professional decision could not have come at a worse time.

When the two of them were preparing for bed, Deborah donned her nightcap and long frilly bedcoat. Nathan decided to delicately raise the issue.

"Darling," he began.

Deborah did not answer, but she climbed into the four-poster bed and crawled in beneath the goose feather comforter. Then, sitting up, she puffed her two pillows and placed them behind her back, so she could lean back against the headboard.

She turned to Nathan and gave him a little thin-lipped smile, but said nothing.

"Darling," he began again. "I was wondering…"

"Wondering about what?"

"About my career."

"Oh?"

"Yes."

"What about your career?"

"Well, my law practice…"

"Yes, well, I thought that was what you might be getting at," Deborah interjected with a controlled smile that barely lingered on her lips but did not spread to any greater part of her face. "After all, you are not a sailor, or a merchant, or a tinker, or anything else for that matter. You are, for better or worse, a lawyer. Are you not?"

Nathan recognized the tone from his wife. She was making a point.

"Yes, of course I am a lawyer. Though I do not know why you insist on pointing out, as you do, that it is for better or worse. You make it sound like our wedding vows."

"Indeed," she continued. "Much the same as our wedding vows. You vowed to me, and I to you. Though there was someone else in the church that day of our wedding—a mistress."

"A mistress, you say?" he retorted.

"Yes. That grasping, selfish, demanding woman—the lady of the law, holding a law book in her arm, draped in those robes…those horrible robes. And what I did not know then, but I know now," and with that Deborah had to fight back tears, "what I know now is that she took a vow from us both. That *she* would be the cruel mistress of our home—that *she* would rule our lives—and that *she* would place us, body and limb, in such great peril—"

"Peril?" Nathan asked, but inwardly wondering whether Deborah had already known about the soldiers' case.

"Yes, peril. And do not act the innocent with me, husband. You know exactly what I am referring to."

"The case."

"Indeed."

"But how—"

"I learned it from Abigail Adams. Nathan. How could you? Waiting a day and a night before telling your own wife."

"I regret that, Deborah," he said a little meekly. "I just wanted to spare you—"

"Then you should have refused the case—that is how you could have spared me."

"It did occur to me to turn it down."

"Then why didn't you?'

"Something compelled me."

"Money? Was it a matter of the fee, good sir?"

"No, not that. He has only paid a modest retainer. And I would guess that all our efforts will ultimately far exceed a captain's wages, or even what his friend Mr. Forester might be able to raise for the defense."

"Then what?"

"Just this—that I felt compelled, even against all my natural instincts of survival. Compelled, much as I believe Mr. Adams was also compelled, to do the right thing. To see justice done."

"There she is again," Deborah said coldly. "Lady justice. Demanding our obedience. Our sacrifice. And to what end? That our home be burned to the ground? That I be accosted on the streets by a mob because I am married to a lawyer for an English captain with blood on his hands…"

"There is no blood on his hands," Nathan said, raising his voice. "And that is exactly why we must take this case. Would God have me just watch silently, as an innocent man is hanged for what he did not do? I would be judged by the Lord—and well I should be—if I ever allowed that to happen without a protestation or a fight."

After a long pause Deborah gave him a long stare and an icy look. Then she spoke.

"So be it," she said. "May it be on your head. You are master here, and I am your wife. If disaster befalls us by this case you have chosen, then you, Nathan, shall bear that fault. And not I. May that be on your head."

And with that, Deborah clumsily reached over to get closer to the candle that burned on her nightstand.

Then she blew it out, and the room was plunged into darkness.

Chapter 15

Nathan Mackenzie and John Adams were walking to their office. The air was still cold; it was, after all, Boston. But the promise of spring was all around. The snow had melted, and there was the scent of hay and grass and manure from the fields in the countryside that wafted into the city from time to time.

It was morning, and the two lawyers were consumed in conversation as they walked together to the law office. So engaged were they that they did not see a half-dozen roustabouts lounging on the street corner two blocks down as they approached. Most of them were sailors and dockhands who worked the ropewalk down in the harbor.

"I seem to be forever obsessed," Adams was saying to his co-counsel, "by the fact that we find ourselves in the most hostile judicial atmosphere imaginable for this case."

Nathan was studying his mentor's face and didn't notice the small gang of toughs waiting for them.

"Agreed," Nathan said, nodding. "Of all the cities in all the colonies, Boston is surely the one that contains the bitterest enmity against the English Crown, and her soldiers."

"You can hardly blame the city of Boston," Adams said, a little defensively, suddenly taking the tack of protecting the reputation of the very city that he had been lambasting just seconds before.

Nathan knew what was going on in Adams' mind. It was not logical inconsistency, nor was it hypocrisy. It was just that John Adams had a particular talent for parsing down a matter to its thinnest slices, like a hard apple being carved down in paper-thin segments with a sharp paring knife. It was just that some of the slices fell to the left—and some to the right.

"Boston," Adams continued, "has suffered beatings by the red-coated militia of His Majesty; it has seen homes taken over in illegal quarterings; silks, silver, and china dishes stolen by the soldiers; women harassed and assaulted. And, of course, citizens slaughtered in two separate shootings by English troops."

"But how do you respond to the argument," Nathan countered, "and I have heard it myself—that England has a right to post her armies here because she is the dominant power—and the colonies are the subservient."

"Yes, yes," Adams snapped back. "I've heard that prattle myself. But here's the fact, Nathan…England did not invade and conquer the colonies. Just the opposite…King James gave charters for the founding of the Americas with a written guarantee of not only our protection by virtue of English law, but the freedom of land owner-ship and representative rule in our own legislatures."

"Which we have," Nathan said, arguing the point, not be-cause he believed it, but because he enjoyed hearing how Adams would demolish it. "We have the House of Burgesses in each colony—"

"You mean those legislative house dogs—never allowed to go out and hunt, but only allowed to sit at His Majesty's feet—and then to suffer collars and leashes whenever it pleases England's king, or

England's arrogant parliament? Where are our promised rights as Englishmen, man? Where are they?"

By this time, Nathan and Adams, who had been engaged in lively discussion, finally looked up ahead, and some three feet away, the small gang was waiting. Two had clubs.

"If it isn't Mr. John Adams, lawyer to the bloody murderers of our Boston families. Turn about, Mr. Adams," he sneered. "Let's see if your back is as red as the English lobsterbacks who shot some of our friends in cold blood."

"I dare say," Adams snapped back, "you haven't the good sense to tell red from yellow. Now—do you wish me to tell you straight which color bedecks your back, sir?"

But the gang was in no mood to debate. The men began swinging at Adams, who quickly crouched to miss the swing of a club aimed at his head. But he could not avoid the other club, which landed squarely on his back, knocking him flat to the ground.

Nathan lunged at the closest man and landed a punch on his jaw, sending him reeling back. But the other man turned to Nathan and swung, but as he did, he tripped over Adams' prostrate body and tumbled down.

That is when a squad of English soldiers came running to the scene, shouting. The gang of tarjackets leaped to their feet and scurried off, yelling profanities at the two lawyers and the soldiers who came to their aid.

Adams caught his breath and struggled to his feet, brushing off his clothes. Nathan stood up, and noticed that he had torn his waistcoat, and also ripped his best pair of knee-high, white silk stockings.

The captain of the squad called out to Adams and Nathan, but Adams waved them off.

"We need no help from you," he called out. "But thank you for your courtesy."

"Did you get a good look at them?" the captain called out.

"No—couldn't recognize them if I was paid a gold sovereign to do so," Adams called out. Then walking quickly toward their office, he reached out and patted Nathan's arm.

"You landed a powerful blow," he said with a strange kind of admiration. "I am afraid I took the worst of it."

"Not really," Nathan said with a smile, glancing down at his ripped jacket. "The big jack-tar with the club would have cracked my skull for sure, had it not been for your body lying in the way."

Adams was still bending over as he walked, trying to regain his breath, but he couldn't help but laugh. It came out sounding more like a gasp.

"Looks like," he said trying to laugh it off, "I am more good to you on my face in the road than on my feet!"

Both of them laughed as they unlocked the front door and entered the office.

Nathan was glad they had escaped real harm. But only narrowly. And he could only shake his head at the irony of his life at that point—having been assaulted by colonists for whom he and his law partner secretly harbored loyalty against the tyrannies of the English Crown, yet saved from true brutality only by the intervention of British troops for whom they both held little but contempt. And the entire incident occurring because the two lawyers had been bold enough to represent an innocent English Captain, whose men had shot several of their fellow Bostonians to death.

Could the world be any more turned upside down for me? he wondered silently to himself.

It could, and it would, as he was soon going to learn.

Chapter 16

John Adams had, from all appearances, forgotten the violent episode in the street, and was soon foraging through the papers on his desk to locate some of his notes.

"Here it is," Adams shouted out when he located the papers he had been searching for. "My list of the jurors from the last jury trial held here in Boston."

He thrust the paper in front of Nathan, as if assuming that Nathan would be able to immediately comprehend its meaning.

But Nathan, after looking at the list, just shook his head, not understanding Adams' point. Adams simply smiled back at him, as if to say, *Look again, counselor, look closer.*

So Nathan looked at it again. And then the light broke.

The paper contained the jury list from a recent case, with the typical name and occupation, and place of residence. The document was the standard one supplied to barristers from the magistrate court. Studying it, Nathan was now able to appreciate John Adams' point.

In every instance, each juror was listed as a resident of "The City of Boston."

"I see what you mean," Nathan said, waving the paper in front of him. "The court has been consistently drawing its jurors from within the city of Boston."

"Exactly!" Adams exclaimed. "Understandable, of course. They're closer at hand. It takes less effort to hail them in for jury duty. And in most cases it wouldn't make any difference in the eventual outcome of the case."

"But not in ours," Nathan remarked, joining in. "The 'massacre' occurred right here in the city. Almost every Bostonian knows someone personally who was either injured or killed in the melee. And the publicity in the papers would have been read by every citizen of the city."

"So," Adams replied, "there is our challenge—to try to secure jurors from *outside* the city of Boston, so that our clients can at least receive some semblance of a fair trial."

"And how do we do that?" Nathan asked.

Adams shrugged, then answered, "Let me think on that one."

"We have an arraignment coming up soon," Nathan added, "where we will have to enter not-guilty pleas for our clients. I am sure that the court will want to set a court date."

"Yes," Adams replied with a somber look, "and a quick trial date will be disastrous. That dramatic etching by Mr. Revere in the *Gazette* depicting the whole bloody incident is burned into the brains of folks throughout the colony of Massachusetts. Let us give the sands of time some ability to erase that manipulative and inaccurate depiction—so that the better nature of men's reason and conscience will guide them to a verdict, rather than the pages of the *Gazette*."

Nathan agreed. As usual, John Adams had placed his finger on the nerve center of the matter. The two of them agreed that the defense had no other alternative but to request an adjournment of the trial to the latest date...perhaps all the way to the fall.

Those procedural matters were occupying Nathan's mind as he wandered into his office. But when he looked up he was startled to see his brother Edward standing with his back to Nathan and gazing out the window onto the busy street, where carts, horses, and pedestrians were traversing Boston's central thoroughfare. He was leaning on his walking stick, but turned around when Nathan entered the room.

"Edward," Nathan said slightly startled. "I am surprised to see you...pleasantly surprised, of course. Is everything alright? Your good wife? And yourself?"

"Yes, yes, well enough," Edward said briskly. Then he paused for a moment. He was tempted to mention something about Edith. But he chose not to. Instead, he dived into the subject that brought him to his brother's law office.

"But there is something amiss, brother," Edward said.

"Amiss? What?"

"You, Nathan. You are amiss. And apparently..." and with that Edward lowered his voice and glanced through the open door of Nathan's office to the outer area which led to John Adams' office, "so, as well, is your association with this lawyer, Mister Adams..."

Nathan was able to guess his older brother's meaning.

"I gather you object to my entering the case on behalf of Captain Preston and the English soldiers..."

"I object? No sir, the entire city of Boston objects. The Boston Clergy Council, of which I am a member, they object. And today as we met," Edward continued, and as he spoke there was visible embarrassment on his face, "that council ridiculed me for my prior assurances that God would ensure the hasty punishment of those murderers...only to discover, to my everlasting humiliation, that *my own brother* is working to acquit those very same British brutes."

"Edward," Nathan said, trying to calm his brother, "you know I would do nothing to intentionally embarrass you."

"Then why, brother, did you allow my reputation to be stained by your reckless choice of legal clients—and law partners!"

"I mean no disrespect, Edward," Nathan replied sternly. "But I would suggest that as a learned minister of the Gospel of Jesus Christ, you base your opinions of the current affairs of the day on the *Word of God*—rather than the opinions of the Boston Clergy Council."

"So, you mean to preach to me, sir?"

"Perhaps I do," Nathan added. "Amos, chapter 5—*Take thou away from me the noise of thy songs: for I will not hear the melody of thy viols. But let judgment run down as waters...*"

"And would you," Edward quickly countered, "have me quote the scripture that admonishes fools in the pursuit of their follies? Or the younger men who despise the wisdom of their elders?"

"I mean no disrespect to you, Edward. I mean no disruption to this good city of Boston..."

But as Nathan spoke, Edward noticed his brother's torn coat and ripped stockings. And as he looked at Nathan closer, he noticed a small bruise on his cheek.

"It appears," Edward said, "that it is too late for that. The disruption, brother, has apparently already begun. Starting with you."

And with that, he stretched out his walking stick and flipped the end of Nathan's torn waistcoat.

"You have already alienated your own brother," Edward said as he prepared to leave. "I wonder, now, whether your wife and future child will be safe in this city."

When his brother had left, Nathan tried to settle down for more work. But his soul was so terribly troubled that he gave up the effort.

Instead, he packed up some papers, thrust them into his leather satchel, and quietly fled the law office without saying another word to Adams, who was busy at work at his desk.

The sun was setting, and there was a cold breeze blowing, belying the coming promise of spring. Nathan looked around to see if he was being watched, and then scurried home to Deborah.

Chapter 17

When Robby Mackenzie was told he would be traveling to Williamsburg, Virginia, he was dumbfounded. Jared Hollings, his employer, had made reference in passing to possibly taking him there when the next session of the House of Burgesses commenced. But Robby thought initially that Jared's comment was just friendly, idle banter.

Robby was beginning to learn something important about his benefactor. That though Hollings was a confident and winning man, with a quick smile and a way of putting others at ease, he did not talk in idleness. Words spoken had meaning. Few words were ever wasted. And when something was said in passing by Hollings, Robby was discovering he must make careful note of it. He never considered himself as book-smart as his older brothers Nathan or Edward. But Robby knew he possessed something else—a knowledge of the ways of the world, and a good deal about people.

His "worldly" travels began when Robby was only fourteen years old. He took work on a fishing boat harbored in Boston. He then graduated to a merchant ship that took him up and down the eastern seaboard. He eventually made his way to Charleston, then up the Carolinas, and finally settled for a while in Fredericksburg, Virginia, where he had met Mr. Hollings.

And so it was his knowledge of the world and of the men who conducted its businesses and industry that gave Robby the knack of knowing what his superior wanted from him and then working hard to accomplish it. Hollings had recognized that particular ability.

"You shall accompany me to Williamsburg," Hollings announced to Robby. "We leave in the morning."

The next day, Robby rose before sunrise and packed his blanket and bundle, and then went down to the barn to prepare the horses and the coach in which Hollings, together with his chief overseer, Miles Habner, would ride.

But a third passenger would be riding in that coach.

Robby was approaching the main house and was on the back porch, ready to knock, when he heard the voice of Ruth Hollings, Jared's wife, mildly scolding her husband.

"Dear Jared," Ruth was saying. "I cannot take Rachael with me while I tend to my sister's smallpox. Rachael is of a tender disposition and hasn't been exposed before. Do you wish to jeopardize the health of your own daughter, husband?"

"Of course not!" Jared thundered back. Then there was a silence, followed by another comment by Hollings.

"It's just that the House of Burgesses is no place for a young lady," Jared said. "And for that matter, neither is Williamsburg. It has become populated by questionable establishments. I cannot, for the life of me, understand why the royal governor, Mr. Fauquier, has permitted the capital city of this colony to become so abused and so ruined."

"I am sure you will keep her safe," Ruth replied. "Jared, there really is nothing more that can be done."

Jared groaned and muttered something indistinguishable. Robby knocked, and Jared came to the door, and before Robby could explain that he had prepared the coach, his employer interrupted him and barked out an order.

"Go fetch my daughter, Rachael, and tell her she must pack, and do so posthaste. We leave in the hour, whether she is ready or not."

Trying to hide his enthusiasm at the turn of events, Robby ran down to the gardens, where Rachael was walking and shading herself with a small parasol.

"Excuse me, miss," Robby said with a smile. "But your father says you are to pack your necessities immediately."

"Whatever for?"

"Because you will be accompanying him on his trip to Williamsburg."

"I shall do no such thing!" she blurted out. "Why ever must I go to that boring old city where, from what I hear, all the men do nothing all day long but argue over politics, and land, and money."

"I gather it is because your mother cannot take you with her, and I assume your father will not leave you here alone."

"But I won't be alone. I have the slaves. Mama Bess will be here to care for me. Besides, it's time I think that I be given the responsibility over the household in my parents' absence."

"Well, in that case," Robby said with a disappointed voice, "I should have enjoyed your company..."

"Why, are you going too?"

"Your father requested it specifically."

Rachael paused, and glanced over at Robby and then pretended not to be looking at him.

"Oh well," she said, trying to be casual, "I suppose that such a trip will do me some kind of good. Travel is educational, and is a refining experience, I have heard."

"I can vouch for that," Robby interjected quickly. "Travel has given me a true education of sorts. It has, if you will excuse the expression, made me who I am today."

"And what kind of man might that be?"

Robby laughed at his own foolish statement, and then replied, "Well, miss, that still remains to be seen."

"Then, Mister Mackenzie, I shall be watching," Rachael said with a smile.

Rachael made her way up to the bedroom in the main house to pack. More than an hour later, Robby was lugging the trunk full of her clothes and personal items out to the coach, which would be driven by Jared, and Miles, his plantation overseer.

The ride down to Williamsburg took all day and into the early evening. Robby drove a two-hitch team and a cart behind the coach, with a slave man named Solomon as his only passenger.

They arrived at a three-story rooming house on the outskirts of town, and Robby and Solomon unpacked the coach and carried the luggage into the house and up the stairs. Rachael was on the third floor, as was her father's room. Robby and Miles shared a room on the second floor. And Solomon was told to sleep outside in the smokehouse.

"Good sleep, Mista Robby," Solomon said as he turned away. Robby felt awkward and embarrassed at that moment, though he could not exactly explain why.

The following day, Rachael was left at the house with the matron, while Jared Hollings, Miles, and Robby made their way on horseback to the House of Burgesses. It was situated on the same grounds as the governor's palatial mansion with its tall, stately spire and large arched opening that ran between two adjoining buildings.

But once Robby entered through the heavy doors to the hall, it was as if he had been thrust into complete pandemonium. Men were jammed in a space that did not appear large enough to accommodate them. And they all seemed to be talking at once, and loudly. The hall was a small room, crammed with chairs and tables, with a high, vaulted ceiling and a balcony overlooking it. There was a speaker's desk at the front, slightly raised above the floor level.

Most of the men carried sheaths of papers and waved them about as they talked. There seemed to be little order, dignity, or procedure.

Most of the men knew and greeted Jared Hollings. Miles followed along behind and smiled courteously and shook a few hands as they bumped in between men, avoiding elbows and arms.

Jared pointed out a few of the better-known delegates to Robby as they walked through the crush. But he had a hard time remembering them.

"Patrick!" Jared said at one point to a red-haired man with a sharp, angular face and a slightly hooked nose. Then the two men shook hands and Jared turned to Robby.

"Robby Mackenzie, this is delegate Patrick Henry. A lawyer now, I hear, recently admitted to the bar, is it?"

"Indeed, just last year," Henry replied with a smile, and then reached out to shake Robby's hand.

Jared was hailed by another man, and they launched off to meet him. As Jared was talking in a corner, Robby was surveying the men in the room.

Two rather tall gentlemen were standing at one end of the hall. One lanky man, dressed smartly in a red-coated uniform with brass buttons, was standing amidst a small group, listening to their comments. The other man, a few feet away, was leaning against a pillar and, despite the conversational din in the room, seemed to be absorbed in a book.

"Who is that?" Robby asked Miles, pointing to the stately man in military uniform in the small group.

"Planter and surveyor," Miles replied. "Owns a huge tract of land up past the Rappahannock River. Thousands of acres. Our Mr. Hollings has been aching to buy up some of it, but can't get him to sell."

"Why's he wearing a uniform?"

Miles laughed.

"Oh, he does that for the beginning of every session. He's the formal type. Fought in the French and Indian Wars. Made a name for himself—that Mr. Washington is one of our veterans. Been in the House of Burgesses about ten or eleven years by now."

"And the book reader over there?" Robby said, pointing him out.

"Oh that," Miles said with a snarl. "Just another lawyer who just started up a practice but also likes playing politics on the side. That one's Jefferson. Tom, I think his moniker is. They've got more lawyers here than is healthy, in my opinion. Which is why," he said shaking his head, "they sure talk up a storm here but don't get much work accomplished."

Chapter 18

Deborah Mackenzie had been, by all appearances, getting over her initial dread of the calamity that might befall her husband and his family as a result of taking on the "Boston Massacre" case. But then Nathan entered their home, earlier than usual, the same day of the assault that he and John Adams had suffered on the street.

Looking at his ripped coat and the tear to his best silk knee stockings, and the bruise on his cheek, Deborah knew instantly what had happened to her husband. She burst into a new flurry of tears. But then, just as quickly as the flood tide started, it stopped. Deborah wiped her eyes and changed the subject.

"Our little one has been kicking all day today!" she exclaimed.

Nathan rushed over to her and put his hand on her. He waited there for a kick.

After a few moments, Nathan felt a little flutter, like a butterfly beating its wings.

"Oh, that feels like a girl for sure!" Nathan exclaimed.

But he kept his hand on her belly for a while longer. Then he felt a kick so strong his hand visibly moved.

"So, sir, are you confident it is a girl now?" she said laughing.

Nathan's face was close to hers, and he bent over and kissed her tenderly on the cheek, then again, and then fully on the lips.

"I can start working out of the house from now on rather than the office, to be closer to you, in case…in case there is any disturbance against our home. I still have my pistol and musket here. I can prime them and have them ready to go."

But Deborah put her hand over his mouth and smiled.

"God has spoken to my heart," she said. "That all will be well. That this will all end in good somehow…though, for the life of me, I do not know how."

"It is a bit of a puzzle, isn't it?" Nathan said. "If we win the case, and those soldiers are acquitted, all of Boston will despise us. And if we lose, then the British Crown will cry out that we were merely pawns in a conspiracy to railroad those soldiers into a hanging, and perhaps arrest us when it is all over—"

"So, what shall we do?"

After a moment of reflection, Nathan replied.

"Pray that God will use us for His greater purposes. And try with all my might to see that the truth is put on trial, rather than the raw emotions of this confused city. That's all we can do. And when we have done all, then we must leave the rest up to the Lord of Hosts."

While Nathan was confiding quietly with his wife in their home, at a nearby tavern in Boston Sam Adams and the group of revolutionaries named the Sons of Liberty were meeting.

Their meeting was considerably louder.

"I say we do something about this outrage!" one of them was saying.

"Sam, I never thought I would find myself speaking against your kith and kin," another said, "but this is the last straw. Your cousin or not, this John Adams has got to be stopped."

"I am not above taking direct and forceful action against him. And against that young upstart assistant of his, this Nathan Mackenzie. Never trust a Scotsman, I say. Both of them, John Adams and Mackenzie, are traitors. They ought to be hung by the neck, naked as jaybirds, in the main street."

Samuel Adams, who had been uncharacteristically silent during the discussion, now stood up in the sight of the small group that gathered around the worn oak table. He took his pewter tankard and slammed it down on the table so forcefully that all of the men present were surprised he hadn't dented in its bottom.

"I will not have my cousin called a traitor—now or ever!" he shouted out.

Then after a moment of collecting himself, he continued.

"But lest any man doubt me, know you this, men—that I will do whatever is required—*whatever is required*—to get the deadly grip of King George and his madhouse parliament off the necks of the colonies."

"Talk plainly," one of the men said, lowering his voice. "You, Samuel, are known for that. What is it that we are to do?"

"First," Samuel Adams said, "I need each of you to talk to every resident of Boston within two or three blocks of the town square where the shooting took place. Take down their sworn depositions, on oath. Get them to swear to the brutality of the English soldiers. We will present all of those to the special prosecutor, lest he and his deputy attorneys plan to simply let the case fall apart so the soldiers all go free."

The group all nodded in agreement.

"And what about your cousin John and his co-counsel, Mackenzie?" another man asked. "How do we handle them?"

"Let me remind every one of you here," Samuel continued, "what is at stake here. The drums are beating. Beating for a confrontation. There is bound to be more bloodshed. More murders. But we have to keep our eyes fixed on the prize ever before us. As the Scriptures tell us, to forget what lies behind, but fixing our eyes on what lies ahead—to reach forward to the prize of the calling of God."

"Now you sound like one of the Methodist preachers!" one man shouted out.

"Do I?" Samuel Adams said, with a smile. "But what is the calling for us, men, that calling of God? Is it not for freedom—to burst the chains of tyranny? To secure liberty?"

"We all know that—" one man began to say.

"Oh, I know we know it somewhere down here," and with that Samuel pointed to his gut. "But how about here," and with that he took his index finger and jabbed himself in the chest, "or here?" and Samuel tapped the side of his head.

"We have to have the idea set, not in tar or pitch, but in stone," Samuel continued, "why we deserve liberty—why it is right and true and just. That we were given a charter at Jamestown, from no less than King James I of England, dismantling the feudal land rights of ancient England and granting private land ownership to all. That was our beginning, gentlemen. But where are we now? We are taxed as English slaves but not given the rights of English citizens. Troops are quartered in our homes as if we were a vanquished foe who had lost a war, rather than a partner in the empire of our parent."

Then Samuel lowered his voice and concluded.

"And in our sister colony to the south, in Virginia, Baptist preachers are jailed for nonconformity to the Church of England. Now, gentlemen, in light of all of this, let us remember this is a crusade that must be based on sound reason, and not brute strength."

Then, adding one final comment, Adams remarked, "Besides, men, if it finally comes down *only* to a matter of brute strength, then we all know who will win this struggle. And it won't be Boston, nor Massachusetts, nor any of our American colonies. It will be a king who is resolved to bring us to our knees and force us to beg for scraps at the table of his arrogant empire."

The men all nodded, but one of them was far from satisfied.

"A fine speech, as usual," he said with a scowl. "But you didn't answer our question…"

"Oh?" Samuel Adams asked. "And what might that be?"

"What is to be done with John Adams and Mackenzie?"

Samuel Adams smiled, then leaned forward to quietly emphasize his point.

"When the Boston Massacre trial is over and done, I have my own plans for those two men."

The group was silent, waiting for the revelation. But it did not come.

"Plans," Samuel Adams said, "that for the time being I am keeping safe and sound—right up here."

With that, he added a tap to his forehead.

Then he dismissed the meeting.

Chapter 19

"Oyez, oyez, all those having business before this court, the Honorable Benjamin Lynne, Justice of the Superior Court of Judicature, Court of Assize, held this day in Boston, within and for the County of Suffolk, in the tenth year of the reign of His Majesty, George the Third, by the Grace of God, King of Britain, France, and Ireland, being also the Defender of the Faith..."

The court clerk then took a quick breath and, as the packed courtroom was standing silently at its feet, he finished his pronouncement.

"...Now, if any man has business before this court, may he approach the bench forthwith, giving honor and diligence to the sitting justice herein."

The clerk sat down promptly. At the high bench at the far end of the courtroom, Justice Lynne, with ornate curled wig and scarlet robes edged with white ermine at the cuffs, leaned forward only slightly. Then with one raised hand, with only two fingers, he motioned the counsel to approach the bench.

John Adams and Nathan Mackenzie stepped forward. From the other side of the courtroom, through a previously locked door, Captain Preston, in handcuffs but spared the indignity of leg irons, still decked out in his wrinkled red English officer's coat, was escorted to his position next to Adams.

"You are the prisoner, Captain Preston, the accused in this cause—that is correct, sir?" the justice asked.

"I am he, that is correct," Preston replied.

"And you are here with legal counsel," the justice continued, "that being Mr. John Adams of Boston, and his associate, one Nathan Mackenzie, correct?"

When the name of John Adams was spoken, a loud murmur rippled through the crowded courtroom.

"Yes, Mr. Adams and Mr. Mackenzie are my lawyers," Preston said.

The low din of gossip in the courtroom persisted, and Justice Lynne reached over and grabbed his heavy, round wooden paperweight and slammed it down on the bench with a loud bang.

"There will be silence," Justice Lynne said in his controlled cadence, "lest I call upon the bailiffs to clear you all from this room."

The noise stopped.

"And the King's Special Prosecutors...?" Justice Lynne continued.

"Present, Your Honor," Samuel Quincy said and quickly approached the bench. He was a well-dressed attorney with a fine wig, a waistcoat with black silk lapels, and a starched white frock.

"And I present my co-counsel for the Crown," Quincy continued, "Mr. Robert Treat Paine."

Paine stepped forward, dressed in equally fine waistcoat and expensive wig; yet he carried himself with an arrogance that gave the appearance it would be he—not Samuel Quincy—who would be leading the prosecution in the case.

Paine was a handsome, broad-shouldered fellow, a highly successful barrister throughout Boston. His appearance and stature was in visible contrast to the squat figure of his opponent, John Adams.

Adams shot a quick, uneasy look over at Paine and then focused again on Justice Lynne.

"As a matter of rule, Mr. Quincy," the justice remarked, now addressing the chief prosecutor but glancing down occasionally at the papers before him on the bench, "it appears that your brother, Josiah, is listed in this case as one of the several of the defendants' attorneys."

"That is correct," Quincy replied with a smile.

"And do you vouch that, in this cause, there is nothing untoward in the fact that you and your brother are in full opposition in this cause, each representing clients at odds—you for the Crown, and he for the accused?"

"Nothing untoward," Quincy replied with an even broader smile, "unless by that Your Honor means to recognize the fact that I shall be giving my good brother a legal education in this case that he shall long remember."

Justice Lynne barked a laugh, and the courtroom full of spectators joined in.

When the chuckles died down, John Adams spoke up.

"If it may please Your Honor," he said to the justice, "Josiah Quincy is but a lesser assistant defense counsel in this case—a welcomed help, but he shall take no prominence."

Then Adams continued with a wry smile, turned slightly toward the two prosecution attorneys and added, "So if Mr. Quincy has any legal education to impart, then he should send it to me instead of his brother. Though I fear he will find me a rather unwilling student of his brand of legal pedagogy."

"Noted, Mr. Adams," Justice Lynne said, cutting him off. "Now, may we stop wasting the court's time and proceed? Captain Preston…"

The English officer straightened to attention.

"How do you plead to the indictment specifications of murder?"

"Not guilty," Preston answered with a face that contained no show of emotion or hesitation.

"Very well, plea entered," the justice said. "Now then, the trial of this matter. It shall be in this session, in a few weeks hence—"

"Your honor," John Adams interjected, "there is a matter for you to consider on the scheduling—"

"Oh, Mr. Adams, I hope," the justice said with a little groan, "that you will not burden this court with more of your metaphors or figures of speech."

"Quite the contrary," Adams replied, "I intend to burden this court with a letter from Lt. Governor Hutchinson."

Adams scurried to the bench with a paper and carefully handed it to the justice, quickly bowed, and then returned to his place between Captain Preston and Nathan.

After reading the letter, Justice Lynne looked up and addressed the array of attorneys.

"It does appear that His Majesty's Governor for Massachusetts has instructed that this trial be put over to the fall of this year."

Pausing only for an instant, he continued.

"Therefore, the trial shall be at the first jury session following the summer recess."

Hammering his paperweight on the bench again, Justice Lynne called for the next case.

"How did you ever manage that?" Nathan whispered to Adams

as the two lawyers left the court room together. "The letter from the Governor I mean…"

"I simply explained to him," Adams said, "that if this case is tried now, with tempers in Boston still at full pitch, there will be more riots. And more shootings. I told him to his face in a meeting recently that I would hold him responsible and would carry that message to King George personally if need be."

Nathan would have replied, but Robert Treat Paine rudely stepped between him and Adams.

"Mr. Adams," he said with a sneer. "Always a pleasure—of sorts—to see you. Have you, sir, any more good writs for the courts here in Boston?"

Then Paine chortled loudly and turned and left, walking into the dense crowd departing the court building.

When Adams and Mackenzie were a good half block away from the courthouse, Nathan opened his mouth. But he was not quite sure how to address the strange interaction between his senior partner and Paine. Adams, as they were walking, appeared to be in a foul mood, thinking intently on something.

Finally, Adams broached the subject himself.

"Do you have any idea why Paine said such things to me?" Adams snapped. "Well, do you?"

But he did not give Nathan a chance to answer. He then addressed his own question.

"Because," Adams went on briskly, increasing the speed of his steps as he spoke, "when I first commenced my law practice in Boston, I had a case…and Paine was on the other side. I filed a writ for my client. But Paine was able to convince the justice presiding that my writ was composed defectively. The case was dismissed.

The man has never ceased ridiculing me about it…to other lawyers…to local merchants…"

Then Adams stopped in his tracks and wheeled around.

"The man even called me a *numbskull!*" Adams snorted. "I oppose dueling—always have. Yet I think I would be willing to make an exception for Mr. Robert Treat Paine."

The rest of the walk of the two lawyers to the office was in silence.

Nathan was now deep in thought about Adams' comment.

And he wondered how his lead counsel's personal animosity against the prosecutor's co-counsel might color his objectivity.

"*Numbskull*," Nathan thought to himself. "Good heavens."

Chapter 20

In the weeks following the arraignment hearing before Justice Lynne, in addition to the other press of legal business they had in other matters, Nathan and John Adams began venturing out into the streets of Boston that intersected the King Street square where the shooting had taken place, looking for witnesses.

But what they discovered was most disconcerting. Samuel Adams' Sons of Liberty had already beaten them to the punch. A half dozen of them had talked to most of the residents and merchants in the area, and in many cases, taken written, sworn statements.

"I already told Sam Adams' men what I know," one elderly widower remarked. His row house was on King Street, not a hundred feet from the scene of the riot.

"And what did you tell his men?" John Adams asked.

"What did you say your name was?" the elderly man asked, looking at John Adams with suspicion.

"*John* Adams," he replied. "Samuel is my cousin."

"Oh-ho," the man said in the doorway, nodding his head and then adding a frown to his face. "So ye're the one who's the lawyer for the murderous lobsterbacks..."

Adams' face flushed a bit, but he was careful to control his temper as he tried to answer the man.

"I am one of the lawyers for the accused soldiers, including the unfortunate Captain Preston, who most assuredly did *not* provoke the shooting that occurred—"

"Oh I don't know anything about that," the man said, abruptly cutting Adams off. "All I know is that the British troops were cold-blooded killers, they were, and I'll swear by my beloved and departed wife's grave on that, I will."

"Did you give a statement saying as such to Sam Adams' men?" Nathan asked.

"Sure did. Would do it again."

"Did you actually see the shooting?" Adams asked.

"Didn't need to," the old man replied. "Walked out and saw what came after…the blood and the dying…it was an awful sight. Won't ever forget it…"

"But how did you know who started this altercation?" Nathan asked. "Perhaps the Bostonians provoked the troops into firing their weapons. There was a riot going on."

"Riot!" the man blurted out. "By my father's whiskers, I say there was no such thing going on. No riot! No, sir."

"But how can you say that, having not seen the actual incident?"

"Why, Mr. Adams," the elderly man said boastfully, "I ain't no lawyer like you, but I can figure out a thing or two—I am surprised being such a bright attorney you can't figure it out either."

Nathan and Adams looked at each other. Then Adams spoke up.

"Where were you standing during the incident?" he asked.

"Now ye're catching on," the aged man in the doorway said. "I was standing right on the other side of my door. Inside my house. And I didn't hear no riot—no screaming—nothing. Until I heard the shots from the guns of those murderous English marauders who were posing as soldiers."

"You heard no riot occurring? No threats? No commotion?" Nathan asked in disbelief.

"No, sir. Nothing—until the firing of the muskets. Bang, bang, bang—and more shots. It sent a cold chill right up and down my spine."

"Would you be willing to sign a statement for us?" Mr. Adams asked.

"Certainly not!" the man said and then reached for the door. "And one more thing," the man added before he closed the front door. "I hope they hang every one of your clients!"

Then the door swung shut with a bang.

As Adams and Nathan walked away, Nathan was crestfallen. The one hope he had held out for his involvement in the disastrous case was that somehow they could vindicate their representation of such despised soldiers by showing their innocence.

But now, the full brunt of one very clear and very disturbing realization was dawning on Nathan: There might simply be no way that he and John Adams and the other defense lawyers could prove that their clients were innocent.

And if they were all found guilty, that would be the worst of all outcomes. Surely, if that happened, Nathan's legal practice would be ended. And he and Deborah and their child would be driven out of the city as English loyalists and collaborators with the Crown; perhaps even labeled as accessories after the fact, men who assisted the murderers in their effort to escape responsibility.

Yet, as he glanced over at John Adams, his colleague had a satisfied expression on his face.

"Nathan," Adams said calmly. "You need to do something right off when we get back to the office."

"What is that?"

"Make a written record, while the conversation we just had is still fresh in your memory, of everything that old gentlemen had to say. Leave nothing out. Will you do that?"

"Of course," Nathan replied. What he would have liked to have said is something along the order of *Certainly, Mr. Adams, I will write down what the man had to say...so we can read it regularly... just to remind ourselves how impossible this defense will be, and how ridiculously mistaken we were to have taken this case.*

But he didn't. Nathan had to believe that John Adams saw something in this case that Nathan was missing. Some faint ray of light off in the distance.

In the air everywhere, the bells from the church steeple overhead were now chiming that it was noon. As Nathan and John Adams were crossing the street passersby glanced at them, some walking by, and a few on horseback; each, when their eyes would lock with Nathan's, would quickly look away.

Nathan felt the heat of their distasteful looks like the burning end of a torch singeing the hair off his head.

Lord, Nathan prayed silently, *help me figure this all out. Show me where You are in all of this.*

Chapter 21

In London, England, spring was well on its way. It was late in the hours of the night, and the tall windows of the diplomat's suite of rooms were wide open. The heavy draperies were billowing slightly in the mild breeze. Benjamin Franklin had long believed in the medicinal powers of fresh air, and enjoyed basking in it while he sat at his ornate desk to write.

Franklin adjusted the small brass knob on the oil lamp to heighten the flame. He took off his spectacles and rubbed his eyes. Then he put down his quill pen and listened for a moment to the ebbing tide of humanity that was still passing by on the street down below. Outside there were the sounds of carriages and horse hooves on the brick streets, and a few random wisps of voices, all men, drifting up in the night air as they paused under the flickering street lamps to converse. London was a city that rarely slept.

Which was, for Franklin, a good thing, as he was a man who needed less sleep than many, and preferred to write, or even better, to fraternize with his contacts and friends until the wee hours of the morning. Sometimes enjoying the pleasantries of the theater or the opera. Or dining at the finer taverns on Fleet Street. Always talking, passing wry jokes to the enjoyment of the local politicians and merchants, waxing wisely on the state of affairs of the world as he saw it.

But behind his keen humor and good-natured exterior, Benjamin Franklin was of a mind that was deadly serious on a deadly serious subject: the future survival of the American colonies, and their right to be as free as possible from the stranglehold of English overreaching.

Franklin's presence in London had been, for several years, of a purely diplomatic nature. He now was the paid representative agent for several American colonies in negotiating trade and other issues with the English Parliament and with the Crown itself. The list of his clients had grown to four: Georgia, New Jersey, Pennsylvania, and Massachusetts.

He enjoyed receiving multiple stipends, of course. As much as any of his other talents, Franklin's business sense was highly refined. In addition to his diplomatic duties, Ben Franklin was still serving as Deputy Postmaster General of the colonial postal service.

Now, as he bent over the heavily carved walnut desk and studied the stack of correspondence and news dispatches he had received on one particular subject, Franklin's face took on a somber cast. He took a hand and flipped his long cascade of hair away from his face, sending it over his shoulder.

What a bloody mess this is, he muttered to himself.

He had visualized that such a turn of events was bound to happen. He reached over and picked up a letter from Reverend Samuel Cooper that he had received the week before, recounting the terrible events of March 5, 1770, in the streets of Boston. Franklin had read the local English version in the newspapers. Now, Reverend Cooper's letter would be added to the growing pile of accounts

Franklin had accumulated on the "Boston Massacre" as it was now universally known.

Franklin carefully set his spectacles back on his face and lifted the piece of parchment paper he had been writing on closer to his eyes so he could read it over. It was his reply to the correspondence from Reverend Cooper. He knew that once read by Cooper, it would be quickly disseminated among the American patriots: the Samuel Adams group in Boston, perhaps too, John his cousin, and John Dickenson up in Pennsylvania; and maybe even distributed down to Virginia among the hot-blooded members of the House of Burgesses in Williamsburg; then down to North Carolina among the farmers who had been fed up with British tyranny over their livelihood; and then over to Georgia, where the plantation owners and merchants and entrepreneurs were waiting nervously to learn the news about England's attitude toward taxes, and the attitude of Parliament toward the only moderately successful American boycott of English goods as a protest against the backbreaking and, as argued by Franklin and others, unconstitutional taxes imposed by Britain.

When he thought about that, Franklin couldn't help but think back to his last meeting with the Crown's appointed secretary to the American colonies, Lord Hillsborough.

It was a state dinner in the House of Lords, and Franklin had been seated next to Hillsborough. The dinner, as usual, was sumptuous. The long table was covered with pheasant and duck, and an assortment of filleted trout and grouper; and there were soups, and stews, and sweetbreads and candied carrots and cheesed potatoes. The feast was not helping Franklin avoid the pitfalls of gout.

During the dinner Franklin had made a few humorous comments about life in the colonies.

One English lord asked him about the typical, day-to-day trials and tribulations of living in the "frontier" of the colonies.

"Oh, thievery is a common problem in the colonies, as it is here in London," Franklin noted.

"Really?" the lord intoned, not realizing that Franklin was poised for one of his famous quips.

"Certainly," Franklin replied. "I recall one poor tavern owner complaining to me about the constant theft of the cheap beer he would house in his tavern's cellar. Which, from my perspective, was a crime that could be easily averted."

The English lord was now fascinated.

"You must tell me," he said, waving a fork weighted with a large chuck of duck at the end, "exactly how you advised that unfortunate merchant."

"Well," Franklin said with a glint in his eye, "to me the entire problem seemed to have a very elementary and very obvious solution..."

"And that would be?" the lord inquired.

"I simply told the tavern owner," Franklin quipped, "that if he wished to end the theft of his cheap beer, all he needed to do would be to place cases of his most expensive wine right next to the beer."

After a moment of silent reflection, the lord burst into raucous laughter, and the two listening members of the House of Lords seated next to him, who had been listening in, also joined him.

On the other side of Franklin, Lord Hillsborough, who also had been listening to the joke, was not laughing. He smiled politely, but only barely. He decided to dump a pound of sobriety on the breezy table conversation.

"Mr. Franklin," he inquired, "do you think that this ridiculous and illegal boycott by the colonies against English goods will ever accomplish anything?"

"Perhaps only this," Franklin said, munching on the lemon-basted trout, "that our illegal boycott may best be measured by the lessening of England's illegal taxes on our colonies!"

The lords to his right chuckled loudly at that.

"Ah, yes," one of the chuckling lords noted, "however, as you well know, Mr. Franklin, the Crown has still imposed onerous taxes on English tea to the colonies."

"Yes, and the port city of Boston has seemed to have lost its nerve," Hillsborough said, "and abandoned the boycott in order to secretly secure stores of tea to sell to the colonists."

"Yes, I am aware of that," Franklin replied. "English tea is a fine product, worthy of the English empire. Though the Americans are gaining a newfound reputation for craftsmanship in areas that will soon surpass England—"

"Like what?" Hillsborough remarked, his face showing an expression of insult.

"Gunsmithing, Lord Hillsborough," Franklin said, his face suddenly losing his impish character. "Gunsmithing…"

The three lords to his right were struck serious for only a moment, but when Franklin broke into a smile, the three of them burst into loud laughter once again, thinking it to be a joke.

But Franklin's smile soon faded, and next to him on his left, Lord Hillsborough was not amused, but cleared his throat loudly.

Benjamin Franklin had seen the gunsmithing advertisements himself. The colonies were beginning to arm themselves. And their fear that England would force an eventual military confrontation was fueled by the arrogant attitude of those who, like Lord Hillsborough, felt that the colonists were to be treated as of only a slightly higher rank than the island slaves that populated the British Caribbean.

Changing the subject, Franklin inquired about the status of his letters of introduction that he sent to Hillsborough, requesting a meeting with him on behalf of his four colony clients.

"I think those letters of authority," Hillsborough said, with his broadest smile of the evening, "are being scrutinized, Mr. Franklin. For…how should I put this…for *irregularities*."

It was a lie, of course, and both of the men knew it. There were no irregularities with Franklin's letters of authority that permitted him to represent the four colonies in dealings with the English Crown. But Hillsborough was toying with him. The new English secretary to the colonies was refusing to deal with Franklin, hoping to undermine his effectiveness and betting that the four colonies would soon abandon Franklin as their agent in favor of someone decidedly more amiable to the interests of the King of England.

But Hillsborough was wrong. And tragically so. Like the king and the majority of parliament, Hillsborough had failed to appreciate the determination of the leadership of the Americans: Franklin and Dickenson from Pennsylvania, and the Adams' of Boston, Patrick Henry and Jefferson in Virginia, even up to the north in New Hampshire with Nathan Hale and his "Green Mountain" militia, these men had all agreed on one basic fact—that the king had imposed taxes on the colonies unconstitutionally, having failed to secure consent of the parliament. Further, the king had imposed on the colonies a large number of British troops in time of peace—in direct conflict to the most basic rights of Englishmen.

As Franklin looked over at Lord Hillsborough, who was sipping wine from his crystal goblet with a look of smugness and arrogance, he decided to peel away the niceties and diplomacy, and get down to the base truth of the matter.

"Lord Hillsborough," Franklin said bluntly, "I think that it is of little importance whether you recognize my letters of appointment from my four colonies or not. It is clear to me that no agent on behalf of the colonies can be of any use at the present time in trying to deal with you, or the Crown of England. Such a task is futile. You won't have to worry about my bothering you anymore on this subject."

Hillsborough's eyes widened. A number of the other lords had been listening, and a pall of embarrassed silence swept over the long banquet table.

As Franklin sat in his rooms that evening, studying the letter he was penning to Reverend Cooper, he recognized something: There in his handwriting there was a sense of foreboding, resignation, yet steely determination.

I am saddened by the incident of slaughter you have described in the streets of Boston. Yet, I must confess, I am not surprised. The installation of an English standing army in the colonial streets, in a time of peace, and without the permission of the lawfully constituted assemblies in those colonies violates the Charter from King James for the founding of the colonies; and it violates the British idea of constitutional rule. It is an outrage and an act of tyranny, but just one more tyranny among many. Where this will lead, I must confess, seems darkly predictable. There will be a final and fatal break I fear. Whether it will entail the ultimate enslavement of America—or the slow ruination of England by the loss of her vital and prosperous colonies remains to be seen.

But this I know—the history of many great empires shows that they can eventually collapse from such arrogant indifference as I have seen of late.

Chapter 22

"Three stitches down and to the right…"

"Oh, yes, of course."

"That is the box stitch, like this one…"

Deborah Mackenzie took her stitching off her lap and showed Abigail Adams. Abigail laughed at the mistake she had made in her own pattern and, nodding in understanding, she took her needle and plucked out the threads that had been misplaced.

"Deborah, you are a marvel with cross-stitching!" Abigail said.

"It's merely a craft my mother taught me. She was the skilled one."

"Isn't she a marvel?" Abigail asked again, this time directing her comments to Edith Mackenzie, who was working on her own project, a small quilt square about thirty inches by thirty inches.

Edith looked up absently, half-smiled, and then lowered her head and resumed her needlework.

In the next room, there were sounds of crying babies as Abigail's housekeeper was minding her two small children.

"It's a fine thing that Mr. Adams saw fit to hire a housemaid for you," Deborah said.

"We had to," Abigail said. "I've been taking over more and more of the oversight of the farm in Braintree for John. Keeping the ledger of accounts. Last week I traveled there to see how our livestock and animals were doing. I couldn't take the children with me."

"You traveled by yourself?" Deborah asked, amazed.

"I had no choice. I certainly could not have asked you, dear. You are a ripe pear—nearly ready to explode!" With that Abigail reached over and tapped Deborah's pregnant belly lightly.

"Just a few weeks at most," Deborah said. "It has been so long."

Then thinking of something, Deborah said, "*You*, Abigail, you are the accomplished one."

"Why do you say that?"

"You're a businesswoman of considerable means. You keep your husband's books for his law office—manage the family farm. And you are so up-to-date with the political goings-on."

"I simply do what needs to be done. My mother was a minister's wife. There is no end to that life. Meetings, hosting suppers, visitors at all hours. Helping with the children. Providing music for worship. My mother did it all."

"Does…does your husband, John…does he tolerate well your views on matters of politics and such?"

Abigail smiled.

"Tolerate *well*? No, certainly not *well*. Tolerate, but not well. But I take some comfort in the fact that Mr. Adams does not tolerate *any* opposing viewpoints very well!"

Abigail and Deborah giggled. Edith smiled quietly.

"Why do you ask?" Abigail said.

"It's just that my Nathan…he listens intently enough to me. Takes on an earnest look on his face. That caring look. But sometimes it strikes me that it is more the look that a father has for a child than the expression of a husband for his wife's well-thought opinions."

Deborah was going to go one step further. She was going to use the illustration of her husband's decision, against her better judgment, to join John Adams in the defense of the English soldiers. But she decided against it. She knew Abigail had felt the same way initially. But then later supported her husband's decision. Deborah had harbored some intense feelings of anger against Abigail. Somehow thinking that it was her friend's fault—that if Abigail had continued to oppose her husband's thinking, perhaps things would have been different. Perhaps then the men could have been talked out of their stubborn insistence to have taken on the Massacre case.

But after a while, Deborah realized that such blaming was foolish. Abigail was loyal to her husband, and how could that be blamed? And in some ways, her steady, implacable faith seemed to exceed Deborah's. So, eventually, Deborah let go of it and rekindled her friendship with Abigail.

"Our husbands are accomplished men," Abigail said. "They deserve to be respected for that. But they are men, after all—it is as if, sometimes, they are on a far-off continent, sending faraway messages to us. Remote. Often simply misunderstanding our very basic nature and heart's desire."

"The way you describe it," Deborah said, "makes our husbands sound like old King George—and we women are the colonies!"

"Well said!" Abigail said brightly. "Indeed, you are very quick-witted. That is exactly what it is like. So, if they understand the need to secure liberty as a blessing from God, then why for heaven's sake would they fail so consistently to understand our need as wives to garner some respect ourselves—indeed, even some measure of independence?"

"You speak *treason!*" Deborah whispered and laughed.

"No, hear me out," Abigail said. "Not opposition to the rule of husbands. Scripture plainly commands that there be but one master of each house. But there is to be partnership as well. That is all I am saying."

"Did I tell you? I am reading in my Bible," Deborah said, "the book of Numbers in the Old Testament. The wandering of Israel...in the desert."

"It's so odd you should mention that," Abigail said. "I have thought back to that story so often lately. The breaking of the bonds of slavery from Egypt..."

"Only to find themselves in the wilderness..."

"Totally dependent on God for guidance..."

"And then landing in the Promised Land. Canaan. The creation of a new nation."

There was a quiet understanding between the two women that their conversation, on such an apt comparison between the Israel of old and the plight of the American colonies, must end there. They did not dare to say anything further on the matter.

Instead, Deborah glanced over at Edith and decided to try to bring her into the conversation.

"Edith, what is that you are stitching? A little quilt?"

"It's a baby's quilt," she said, and then held it up. "For my baby..."

"Oh, Edith, that's wonderful news—that must mean that you're—"

But Abigail intervened quickly, reaching out and putting her hand on Deborah's hand to stop her from continuing. Instead, Abigail finished the sentence.

"That must mean, then, that you and the reverend are hoping for a child, isn't that so?"

"Indeed," Edith said. "Yes we are. Trying to make a family. Yes. And Hannah of old was barren, and God touched her. And Elizabeth thought she was barren, the mother of John the Baptist, but God touched her too. And in the same way, I know God shall touch me—the birds whisper it, the clouds of the sky seem to speak it to me…"

"God's will is unknowable," Deborah said, trying to manage a smile as she spoke. "But we shall pray to that end, however," Deborah continued. "That God, in his divine intention, will provide a child for you."

"It must be. It simply must be," Edith said. "Otherwise I cannot go on."

"Let's pray now," Abigail said, and invited Deborah to pray for Edith. The two women bowed their heads and prayed.

When the praying was over, they looked up to Edith; she had not closed her eyes, but had been gazing into vacant space.

Then she collected herself, and resumed her quilting.

Chapter 23

John Adams and Nathan had, after several days, finally finished canvassing the Boston downtown area for witnesses. When Nathan sat down at the law library table with his senior partner to review the various statements they had culled from those who lived near the market square area of King Street, however, there was simply no clear picture of what happened on that dreadful day in March.

"The facts from these various witnesses," Nathan said, "seem to go out in all directions…with no clear pattern."

Adams listened to Nathan's comment, and then grew silent and thoughtful. After considering it for a few moments, he spoke up.

"On my farm in Braintree," Adams said, "we have some sheep. And we have a goodly sized barn, where, up in the loft, and in the hay, we also have some mice."

Nathan looked at Adams quizzically, wondering what in the world the lawyer was talking about. But he had learned that with some patience, usually the connection would come. And this time, as before, it did.

"But there is a true and substantial difference, don't you see, between sheep and mice when they are loosed?"

Nathan still didn't get the point.

"You see," Adams continued, "when I open the sheep gate, the sheep come pouring out, but in a group, and clinging together mostly. But when I go into the barn, and swing my pitch fork this way and that, into the hay where the mice are hiding…well, they scurry out… but all pell-mell, and in different directions. This way or that…"

Now Nathan was getting the point.

"So, you believe the witnesses here, in Boston," Nathan said, "the folks who heard or saw something about the massacre, they are like the mice scampering out of the barn."

"It appears so, yes. Which means they are not sheep, Nathan. Not at all. And that is something to be glad about…it appears that, despite my cousin Samuel's attempts to sheepfold the townsfolk in Boston into the same story…that Captain Preston gave an unjustified and criminal order for the soldiers to fire on peaceful civilians, and the soldiers knowingly complied with an illegal order, that these witnesses are apparently refusing to act like sheep. And that is good for the defense of this case. Better facts running willy-nilly, than a carefully controlled story that puts the necks of our Captain and his men in the noose of a rope."

"True enough," Nathan replied. He could see Adams' logic in wanting a variety of stories rather than a fixed picture of guilt coming out of all of the witnesses' mouths. But he still saw a lingering problem.

"Yet, we still have a deep trench we need to safely cross."

"What is that?"

"Differing facts may help…but in the end, it seems to me that we cannot simply confuse the jury. We have to show, somehow, that Captain Preston did not give the order. And that *most* of the men could not have knowingly fired into a peaceful crowd, and that there is some explanation for why they did fire their muskets."

"You said that *most* of the men must be found innocent," Adams retorted with an edge to his voice. "Why not all of them? We represent the Captain and all of his soldiers, do we not?"

"Perhaps," Nathan said. "But I have been thinking on this. We have a dilemma, Mr. Adams. There must be some explanation as to how and why the shooting started in the first place. Now if we can but discover the cause of this terrible incident...and if, in our investigation, it happens to be this soldier, or that, who started the musket assault, and the other may have joined in thinking they were under attack...would that not lend itself to my exact description? Where most would be innocent, with only a few truly guilty?"

"I am a lawyer!" Adams said indignantly. "Which means I must defend *all* of my clients."

"Precisely," Nathan countered. "But we have several other attorneys who you say have pledged to help in this defense."

"Yes, and I have given both you and the court their names."

"What if we were to conclude," Nathan continued, "after much prayerful and effectual consideration, that a certain soldier was the responsible one...and then we assigned our co-counsel to fully and aggressively represent such a soldier, while you and I represented the rest...all the while collaborating together for the common defense...would that not better serve the interests of our innocent clients, while nevertheless also providing, at the same time, a vigorous defense for the ones most likely *guilty?*"

Leaning back from the table, Adams stood up, stripped off his waistcoat, showing his blousy shirt sleeves and vest, and then stretched.

When he was done, he sat down. He looked over at Nathan.

"There may be some merit in your plan," Adams remarked, sounding slightly exasperated. "We'll consider it—"

But before Adams could finish his sentence, Nathan went onto a related subject.

"But there is, if you will permit me, Mr. Adams, yet another procedural point that must be considered."

"Well?" Adams blurted out, growing a little impatient with Nathan's diversions from the central focus of the case, and taking them down narrow, procedural alleys.

"It has to do with Captain Preston."

"What about him?"

"His innocence."

"Yes, of which we both, I believe, are convinced..."

"But how to protect his innocence..."

"Well isn't that the point?" Adams said, with a tinge of incredulity in his voice.

"Yes," Nathan said, plowing ahead, "but how exactly can we accomplish that, if some of the soldiers say, as we know a few of them do in fact say...that they *thought they heard* the order come from Captain Preston?"

Adams pursed his lips together, making his round face lined and grimaced.

"And what is your solution to that conundrum?" Adams asked wearily.

"A procedural motion...a motion to sever and separate the trial of Captain Preston from that of the rest of the soldiers. That way, we may focus the jury's attention, in the first trial, on Preston's innocence...while in the second case, we can put light on the confusion among the soldiers and the riotous threats of the crowd."

"And you believe such a motion would hold merit—and might be granted?"

"I have witnessed the same motion a year ago in a case involving a tavern brawl…though I cannot recall which justice it was who granted the motion."

"Who was the successful attorney who was granted such a motion for severance?"

"I am sorry to say," Nathan said, "that it was your nemesis… Robert Treat Paine. Now that he would be on the other side of such a motion from us, no doubt he would be even more prepared to anticipate our arguments, and even more able to undermine them in court."

"But you said that such a motion might have merit."

"In theory, yes," Nathan replied. "But in actual practice…"

"Actual practice be hanged!" Adams blurted out. "You sir, shall draft the motion. And you, Nathan, shall be the one to argue it in court."

Nathan was about to argue the propriety of that, but Adams' determination was apparent in his face. He was not to be dissuaded.

"If you insist," Nathan said, suddenly realizing that his arguing the motion would catapult him right into the epicenter of the legal nor'easter.

Adams answered simply and bluntly.

"Oh yes, sir. I insist."

Chapter 24

Deborah, now that she was nearing her expected date of delivery, was barely able to get about. Yet she wanted to serve Nathan breakfast—it was a kind of badge of honor for her—but he would have none of that. He fried eggs for both of them, along with some slices of ham, and a few cooked tomatoes. But even as he served up the food for his wife and tried to make small talk, Nathan gave the appearance of a man greatly burdened.

"You look distressed, dear heart," she said.

"I must confess," he said with a sigh, "I am apprehensive."

"About how the court proceeding will turn out today?"

"That, yes. But also the fact that it is I who will be arguing the motion. And against Robert Treat Paine, no less. He has even managed to make John Adams, a fine lawyer, look like a bumbling apprentice. Imagine what he shall do with me…"

"So, you are afraid of him?" Deborah said, knowing exactly how to goad her husband.

"No, of course not!" Nathan said defensively. But then he softened. "And yet, I know his skill…and his willingness to use any tactic to win. And then there is my concern about the Bostonians who may be there in the courtroom."

"The families…of the dead and wounded?"

"Yes. That more than anything. Will they ever be able to understand why Mr. Adams and I have undertaken this defense?"

"I am not sure I can fully understand it," Deborah said softly, "so, I think you cannot expect much consideration from those who lost their loved ones and friends to musket fire from your clients…"

"You're quite right. Whatever rightness lies in our decision to take up this case cannot depend on any supposed support from the good people of Boston. We are alone in this cause…so, that is that."

Nathan changed the subject and asked, again, how Deborah was feeling. And asked, as he had before, whether the midwife was on the alert and was ready to attend to the delivery when the contractions began.

"Not to fear, husband," Deborah answered. "Olivia, the midwife, is at the ready. She comes by daily to check on me. I feel quite pampered actually."

Then Deborah thought of something else.

"Oh, did you see the letter from your brother Robby? I put it on your desk…"

"Yes, I did. I read it with great excitement. It has been a while since I've heard from Robby. Believe it or not, he has been taken on as some kind of assistant to a Virginia merchant…and of all things, Robby has accompanied him to the Virginia Assembly. Imagine it! Robby in politics, for heaven's sake!"

"That doesn't surprise me much," Deborah remarked. "He is an outgoing lad. Talkative and friendly. Isn't that what politics is made of?"

"I would certainly hope that it requires more than that…"

"But isn't it important for a person of politics to have passion for what he believes?"

"Passion? Some measure of it I suppose. But a good head and a right understanding of government would help…besides, he should be looking for a wife and starting a family. He has, I fear, been too prone to wander about without direction or purpose."

"Well, I think, once he settles down, that he will make a fine husband."

"I wonder…"

"Oh, you always play the older brother, Nathan, really. I think Robby has a good heart. And he loves God. He has a very charitable spirit about him. He is your brother. You should speak more kindly of him."

Nathan thought on that, and then something came to mind.

"You never told me about your day with Mrs. Adams, and Edith."

"Oh, Abigail is a delight. It was a wonderful day. Poor Edith was quiet as a clam most of the time. She and your brother Edward are trying to have a child. She seems very much taken up with that idea. At least it seems to have lifted her spirits a little."

"You know," Nathan said, "Edward has not spoken to me since he confronted me so abruptly in my office that day. I never meant to hurt him by taking up this case. Yet he acts as if I became embroiled in this massacre case just to spite him. Which is absurd. I don't know why he is taking this so personally."

"Nathan," Deborah said, trying to be diplomatic, "everyone in this city is taking this personally. Your case is nearly all that I hear about when I venture down to the market…which reminds me. We need some salt beef and potatoes. And milk. And some thread so I can finish the baby clothes I have been working on. If you could leave some money for me…"

Nathan's face took on a grim expression.

"What's the matter?" she asked.

"It's just that…over the last few weeks…there has seemed to be a decline in business at our office. I am sure things will pick up."

Deborah did not look surprised. She had been expecting it—the financial toll that would be extracted when Boston decided to punish Adams and Mackenzie for their controversial choice of clients.

Before heading to court, Nathan left Deborah a few coins. It was all he could afford.

When he arrived at the courthouse, Adams was already there. He had learned who the presiding judge would be.

"It's Justice Cushing today for the motion," he told Nathan.

"I don't know him."

"He is a humorless fellow," Adams said. "Dark and gloomy and overprecise…like a clerk in a bank."

"I wouldn't think he is going to favor our motion."

"Likely not," Adams said plainly.

When Cushing appeared at the bench, he took a moment to carefully adjust his robes before he took his chair. He wore a small, tightly curled wig, and he had perfectly trimmed sideburns that came down the sides of his cheeks. His face was thin, and had dark shading in the pale and hollow cheek areas. His eyes contained little spark in them.

The case was called by the clerk. Nathan introduced himself. As expected, Robert Treat Paine, the prosecution second, was entering an appearance for the Crown to oppose the motion.

Nathan's presentation of the motion was cautious, logical, and painstaking. Before another justice, his presentation may have just been considered tiresome and uninteresting. But before the bland, meticulous Justice John Cushing, it was, perhaps, the perfect argument at least in style, though inadvertently so. But as for the substance, Justice Cushing saw the problem with Nathan's argument immediately.

"Counsel," he said in a monotone, "sweeping away all of your concerns about justice and equality among the various defendants, and particularly what you say is the need for special fairness for Captain Preston requiring that his trial come first, and that it be separated from the other defendants—I have one concern that you have utterly failed to address."

"What is that, Your Honor?"

"The court's good time and pleasure in running an expeditious court docket. You are calling for two separate trials. Captain Preston's first...and then the remaining soldiers in a second trial. Double the expense and bother for the court, it seems to me. Two juries. Twice the amount of time. Have you no concern for the court's time and calendar?"

"Actually," Nathan said politely, but firmly, "I have considered that exact point, Your Honor. And my conclusion is this—that in one single trial, the issues would become so complicated, and the procedural matters so numerous in trying to keep straight the issue of Captain Preston's superior authority as an officer as opposed to the lower rank of the other soldiers, that such a trial might well run *longer* that the combined time of two separate trials."

"Well, now," Justice Cushing remarked, "what you say on that account is just a matter of pure speculation, is it not? About the differing lengths of time if there were one combined trial?"

"No more speculation than Your Honor's comment about the potential length of two separate trials. With all due respect, Your Honor, if one is a mere hypothesis, then so is the other..."

Justice Cushing let out a low grumbling noise of dissatisfaction from his throat as Nathan took his seat at the counsel table next to Adams.

Robert Treat Paine strode up quickly before the bench to make his counterargument. He raised several objections. That Captain Preston would seem to be receiving undue favoritism by having his case tried separately. That great confusion would be created by having two trials dealing with the same incident.

But he saved his most devastating argument for last.

"And finally," Paine said, swinging his arms about him dramatically. "The reputation and integrity of this very court—indeed of the Crown itself, is being called into question by Mr. Mackenzie. He urges two separate trials—yet the subject of those trials? Both trials would deal with the same bloody massacre which happened in one single, tragic incident. Now what if the juries in the two cases were to yield verdicts which are inconsistent? What if, in the first trial, the jury were to find that Captain Preston gave the order to shoot…but in the second trial of the soldiers, a different jury were to find just the opposite? In the minds of the public, this court—which is a function of His Royal Majesty—would then appear to be double-minded, and contradictory."

Then Paine wheeled around, and pacing over toward Mackenzie and Adams at the defense table, he pointed to them and landed the lowest blow of all.

"But then, Your Honor," Paine added with a sneer, "perhaps that is exactly what these two colonial radicals have in mind all along…to show this English court, and the English Crown, to be double-minded and contradictory. To hold Your Honor and this Court up to public ridicule. To fuel the hatred that sadly exists in some corners of Boston toward the British Empire."

Then Paine sat down with a self-righteous scowl.

Nathan stood up at the table.

"I have only one observation," he said. "If arguing a legitimate point of law is interpreted as treason against the Crown, then what is Mr. Robert Treat Paine…but a man who has committed the same treason himself?"

"I shall not tolerate such insults!" Paine said, rising to his feet.

"For Mr. Paine and the prosecution," Nathan said, ignoring Paine's standing objection, "have deigned to suggest that a British officer and a gentleman should be placed in the same category as ordinary foot soldiers. In England, that would be deemed to be clear treason."

"Outrageous!" Paine shouted out.

"And the prosecution," Nathan continued, "is seeking to hang an entire English squad for defending themselves against a violent mob. Would that not be called treason if we were in London today, rather than Boston?"

Justice Cushing's face had the look of a fragile boy who had just been bullied. He waved Paine back to his seat with one hand while holding the fingers of his other hand to his forehead.

When calm was restored, Nathan concluded. "I fear," he said, "for the future peace and tranquility of Boston, if we do not exercise the utmost caution to insure the highest form of justice for Captain Preston, a respected officer of the Crown's army. If we fail to do that, English soldiers will refuse to do their duty, for fear of being treated unfairly in the courts. When that happens, riots will be untamed. Disorder will prevail. Chaos will be the legacy, Your Honor, of a wrong decision here today."

That was the linchpin for Justice Cushing; not the niceties of the law or the passions of the prosecution. But the frightening specter of civil strife sweeping across Boston, and perhaps even into the inner sanctum of Justice Cushings's own chambers.

"Motion for severance granted," Cushing said quickly. Then he stood up, dismissed the courtroom, and disappeared into the shadows of his inner chamber.

Chapter 25

The surprise of winning the motion before Justice Cushing had stunned Nathan. For a moment he was slightly numb. John Adams reached over the table and shook his hand vigorously.

"Well done," he said.

Then Nathan started tasting the sweet rush of victory over the arrogant Robert Treat Paine. He had done it. Nathan had successfully argued a small, but highly significant procedural point. Strategically, the minor success would, at a minimum, begin to place the defense on a level field of battle with the Crown's prosecution. He wanted nothing more, now, than to rush home to Deborah and share the good news with her.

But Nathan's sense of satisfaction would be short-lived.

As he rose from the defense table and gathered his papers in his brown leather satchel, he gazed over the crowded courtroom. He had been so absorbed with his legal presentation that he had paid no attention to the spectators.

In the front row of the courtroom, there were several members of the victims of the shooting. Two women were weeping into their handkerchiefs. The men sitting with them, brothers and sons and friends of the dead, were grave-faced and angry.

One man, a tough-looking fellow in a sailor's blue wool coat and striped pants, stood up and pointed his finger at Nathan.

"Traitor!" he called out. "Ye're nothing but the King's toady... Crispus Attucks was a friend of mine. Now he is a dead friend. His blood is on yer head."

The sailor would have gone on, but Robert Treat Paine appeared in front of Nathan and Adams. He bent forward and addressed Nathan.

"I will not bother to congratulate you, Mr. Mackenzie. Though, unlike your mentor, Mr. Adams, at least you can carry an argument without dropping it. But this was merely a small skirmish. It means nothing. Captain Preston and the others will be hung. The stupid Boston mobs will have their blood revenge...I will happily grant that to them. And then, when this case is done, the Crown will, no doubt, begin a more quiet—but much more effective investigation into the causes of turmoil here in Boston."

"You're daft, Paine," Adams growled.

"Am I?" Paine replied with a smile. "We shall see. I know your game, Mr. Adams. You and your cousin Samuel. And those so-called Sons of Liberty. Liberty indeed! I should say you are all sons of *perdition*...sons of civil turmoil and disorder. Haters of England and all she stands for. I am proud to be a Tory," he said with a whisper. "But for you, there will be a reckoning. Your game will soon end, mark me well. And the ending will not be good for either of you, nor your associates."

Then, half-turning to the crowd in the courtroom, all of whom were now standing and staring at Nathan and Adams with disgust on their faces, Paine gave one last, parting shot to the two lawyers.

"Behold your constituency, gentlemen...the fine citizens of

Boston whom you seek to represent in your radical strategies, your game of civil strife against the Crown...even *they* now hate you."

Robert Treat Paine chuckled at that and then exited through the crowd.

Adams and Nathan had to elbow their way through the spectators, a few who gave unnecessary shoves to them, and jostled the lawyers as they made their way through the courtroom.

When the two men were finally on the street, Nathan looked across the town square at Robert Treat Paine, who was striding down a side street.

"What did he mean by that?"

Adams did not respond.

"What did Attorney Paine mean," Nathan persisted, "when he referred, several times, to our supposed game?"

"I cannot hope to speak for that man," Adams snapped back.

"But you must have some idea what he was talking about. Why did he act as if he knew something about our plan—about our strategy in this case that I am not aware of?"

He continued to walk, but Adams, who rarely held his tongue when the opportunity to voice his opinions arose, was strangely quiet.

"Permit me, Mr. Adams," Nathan continued. "But I must insist on an answer, if you have one for me. I have risked my practice, my livelihood, the well-being of my marriage...I believe I deserve an answer to my question."

Adams stopped dead in his tracks, and turned to Nathan. There was an ignited spark, an indignity in his eyes.

"You forget yourself, sir!" Adams retorted. "And I will remind you to remember your place as my associate, and I as your superior.

And I would also remind you that I have suffered from this case as well. My legal reputation, which I have long worked to establish here, is permanently injured, I fear. My name is mentioned now only with disdain."

Nathan suddenly realized that in his zeal to learn whether he had been deliberately made an outsider to some of Adams' plans for the defense, he had crossed the line of propriety with a lawyer whom he had always held in such high honor.

"Please pardon me, Mr. Adams," Nathan said, with regret in his voice. "I meant no disrespect."

"None taken," Adams quickly responded, but his face was not agreeing with his words.

"It is just that, if I am to be of assistance to you, and to our clients," Nathan said, "I feel that I must know whatever designs you might have for this case."

That was as delicate as Nathan could put it. But John Adams now had his point. Nathan was not about to rest until he had been given some intelligence as to Robert Treat Paine's meaning.

"Let me just tell you two things," Adams said, lowering his voice. "First, I have considered Mr. Paine's comments. And I believe that I understand some of his intention. I can only tell you that my cousin Sam is a good and honest man. Know that, even though he is reputed to be a sower of civil disturbance. He is a patriot."

Yet, Adams had another thought, which he was reluctant, at first, to share with his junior partner. But he knew he had to say something. And when he finally said it, it would give vitality to Nathan's vague feelings that he had been sheltered from Adams' private thoughts about the case.

"And there is a second response I have," Adams said in a quiet voice as they reached the front step of their law building.

"That Robert Treat Paine's statements confirm my suspicions—that he and the Crown's men have their spies about...and we had better watch carefully in whom we place our trust."

Chapter 26

After several weeks in Williamsburg, Virginia, Robby was getting to know the town well. Nearly every day he would escort Jared Hollings and Miles, his overseer, to the House of Burgesses, carrying piles of papers for Hollings, and fetching him food during long meetings, and shuttling messages to others of the assemblymen during the loud, confusing sessions.

Whenever he would be given tasks that took him close to the rooming house where they were staying, he would run over to the house, hoping to see Rachael, who was spending her days with the matron of the house.

That day Robby had been told to retrieve a statute book that Jared had left inadvertently back in his room. When he sprinted up to the house at a full run, he found Rachael sitting on a front porch swing, with a bored look on her face.

She brightened up when she saw Robby coming up the front steps out of breath.

"Do you always run about like this?" she asked.

"I like to run fast," he said, still panting. "It gets me to where I am going...and I see no reason not to get there sooner rather than later!" Robby remarked with a grin.

"And where would you be going today, Mr. Mackenzie?" she asked. Robby had asked her several times to pay him the privilege of calling him by his first name, but she continued to call him by his surname. He wasn't sure whether it was her playful nature or something else that led her to continue with him so formally.

"I have been given the task," Robby said, "of fetching a book for your father. But it was doubly a pleasure for me to do that," he said, with an even wider grin, "because I had hoped to see you at the same time."

"How interesting!" Rachael said, enjoying the attention. "And you find pleasure in doing my father's bidding?"

"Of course."

"And what of me? I am sure my father would not approve of me sitting idly here at the rooming house, no one to talk to for hours on end. By myself..."

"Where is the matron of the house? She was to look after you..."

"She has tasks around the house to attend to. She asked if I wanted to join her in her work...but I could hardly want to do that, don't you see?"

Robby tried to understand the source of her complaint, but failing that, he simply smiled back and put his hands on his hips, and looked around the porch a little nervously.

"The point is," Rachael continued, "that you would be doing me a great service if you would escort me around town and show me some entertainment."

"I would love to do that!" Robby blurted out.

"Then, Mr. Mackenzie, what is stopping you?" she said with a bright smile.

"Well, your father is waiting for the book I am here to fetch..."

"Oh that!" Rachael said with a laugh. "My father pretends to play the scholar. But he relies on the others here in the House of Burgesses to tell him the law, and suggest how to vote. He is quite good at shaking hands, and being a good fellow to the politicians here...but I doubt if he will even read that silly old book!"

Robby was taken a little aback at Rachael's comments. Had he not been so enamored with Jared Hollings' pretty daughter, he would have interpreted her words to be troubling, and disrespectful.

"I am afraid that I must decline, for the moment," Robby said, trying his best to put a good face on it. "But I will do my best, I promise, to honor your request. It will be my great pleasure to do so. As soon as I can, I shall ask your father for permission..." Robby said, and as he spoke, he started toward the front door of the rooming house.

"Oh, that won't be necessary," she said, following him into the front room of the house.

The house was quiet. There were no signs of the matron about, nor any other guests, who apparently had all left for the day. Suddenly, Robby was aware of Rachael right behind him.

He turned, and she was very close to him. Rachael moved up to Robby, until she was leaning fully against his chest, and he could smell the lavender bath oils that she would use to scent herself.

"My father need not know," she whispered in his ear, and then she slowly placed her full lips against his cheek. It was a slow, deliberate kiss that stunned Robby.

Rachael was so close to Robby that the lace from her cuff had hooked on one of his large vest buttons.

"Rachael, I beg you to be careful," Robby said, taking a step backward. But as he did, he tore a bit of the lace off her cuff. Robby plucked the small bit of lace off his vest button.

"Careful of what?" she said a little indignantly. "I am asking you not to speak of this to my father…is that so hard to understand?"

"I owe him so much," Robby said, trying to mend things quickly. "But not least of all my loyalty…and respect for both you and him."

"You treat me like a little girl, Mr. Mackenzie. You really do…"

Then she turned and ran up the stairs to her room, crying. Robby looked at the small piece of lace in his hand, and placed it in his vest pocket.

As Robby looked up the stairs after her, there at the top, he saw the house matron, who stood there as a crying Rachael swept by her. The matron threw a stern look down to Robby. He quickly ran up the stairs, turned down the hall to Jared Hollings's room, and after finding the book, sprinted down the hall again.

The matron was still standing there with a glowering look on her face.

"Good day, mum," Robby said to her, trying to be cheery. But she did not break a smile.

Robby kept up a good pace all the way back to the House of Burgesses. He sprinted in the huge front doors.

But the minute he entered the front foyer, he knew something was amiss.

Men were rushing around and arguing, and pointing at the unusually large presence of a contingent of red-coated British soldiers stationed in each corner of the rotunda of the House of Burgesses. They had muskets at their sides, with bayonets fixed.

"Mr. Henry, can you tell me what is going on?" Robby asked, grabbing the attention of Mr. Patrick Henry, whom he had encountered several times since their first meeting the day Robby first arrived.

Henry was rushing to an emergency meeting, his coattails flying. He couldn't stop to converse, but yelled behind over his shoulder as he went.

"He's shut us down, Robby. Can you imagine the arrogance!?"

"Who has?" Robby shouted after him.

"The English governor himself...closed down the House of Burgesses!"

Robby made his way through the confused, arguing crowds, until he finally spotted Jared Hollings and Miles walking quickly toward him.

"Robby, get the carriage ready. Miles and I must attend an emergency meeting that is being assembled crosstown. It appears that we will be continuing the business of the House of Burgesses whether the governor wants us to or not. He may shut us out of the governor's buildings, but he can't stop us from meeting somewhere else."

"Shall I go with you also?"

"No," Hollings shouted. "You will have to walk back to the rooming house. Wait for us there."

Robby brought the horse-drawn carriage around to the front of the entrance to the assembly building, and Hollings and Miles jumped in, with Miles behind the reins.

"You mind my slave, Solomon, until I return."

After the carriage had disappeared down the road, joined by men in other coaches and on horseback, riding quickly to a rendezvous point for a meeting of the Virginia assemblymen, Robby started walking slowly across Williamsburg.

But a thought came to his mind as he walked.

Jared Hollings did not also ask me to look after his daughter.

It was a thought that hung over Robby's mind like a gathering thundercloud.

Chapter 27

As Robby strolled slowly through the city of Williamsburg, toward the rooming house, his mind was not on the political turmoil and chaos he had left behind at the government buildings adjacent to the Governor's mansion.

Rather, his mind was fixed on his last troubling encounter with Rachael.

Her forward advances had taken him by surprise. But equally distressing, was her insistence that he violate propriety and break trust with his employer; Rachael knew full well that if Robby was to personally escort her for the purpose of entertainment, or out of mutual attraction, that he would first have to ask permission from Jared Hollings, her father. Yet she was *insistent* that Robby not disclose their plans to her father, but to secretly and clandestinely travel together to the sites in the city.

Why was Rachael so adamant about Robby not disclosing any information about their being together, to her father?

Those thoughts led Robby to believe that he needed to avoid the rooming house as long as possible—at least to a point in time closer to when he knew that Jared Hollings and Miles might show up. Robby now feared being alone with Rachael, at least until he could straighten some things out in his own mind. But he kept wandering back, mentally, to the image of the house matron standing at the top of the stairs, glaring down at him, as a tearful Rachael ran into her room.

Looking back later, Robby should have prepared himself for what was about to befall him. With all of his worldly-wise experience in life, he should have expected the final, devastating blow, and steeled himself for it. But in the affairs of the heart, he was about to learn that the understanding can become clouded. And the cold, brutal facts can become easy to ignore.

So Robby spent several hours wandering the streets of Williamsburg. Past the shops crowded door-to-door. Along the dirt streets with occasional bricked market squares; along the boardwalk sidewalk designed to avoid the spring muds, which were now dried from the last cold rain. The boxwoods, which ran between the houses and shows and which lined the lanes, were now starting to give off their floral, piney scent. The streets were crowded with horses and carts.

For some reason, Robby was suddenly flooded with loneliness. He yearned to see family. To perhaps go north to visit his older brothers Nathan and Edward and their families. He had only written one letter, that to Nathan, weeks before, telling him of his life with the Hollings household and his initial impressions of Williamsburg. But now he wanted to see them all, and to converse with them, and joke with his brothers, and tell them of the recent turn of events in his life.

Those feelings, the yearnings for home and family, and safety, were perhaps the way in which Robby's heart was trying to warn him of the impending trap that was being set for him.

By the time the sun was starting to set, Robby thought that he had to return to the rooming house.

When he arrived, the front porch was empty. But he did notice that Jared Hollings's coach was there, and the horse had been apparently taken back to the barn for grooming. He wondered how long Jared and Miles had been back from their meeting.

Suddenly, Robby had a terrible, sinking feeling.

He remembered Jared's words to look after his slave, Solomon.

So immediately, Robby hurried behind the rooming house, to the smokehouse where Solomon had been staying.

He swung open the door.

It was a small room, with a bedroll spread out on the floor, and a large fireplace at the end of the room.

At the end of the room, Solomon was bent down, tending to the fire, cooking some food on an iron skillet.

He turned around slowly, and then spoke.

"Mista Robby," he said. "What you doing here? You are supposed to be at the roomin' house with Mista Hollings…"

"I am on my way," Robby said, "but I just wanted to check on you first."

"Better not be worryin' about me," Solomon said. "You got yer own worries aplenty…"

Robby gave him a perplexing look.

"You ain't been to the house yet, have you?" Solomon said.

Robby shook his head.

"I can't talk to you about that…you got to go to the house right away…I fear there's some trouble brewing against you…"

"What kind of trouble?"

"Can't say…not my place…"

"But you know something…"

"What I know is what I shouldn't know, 'cause I heard something up at the house just now that I wasn't supposed to hear…don't you make me spill it all out...don't do that to me, Mista Robby. I like you, and feel bad for you...but don't make the fury come down on me for tellin' you."

"You must tell me something..."

"Only this, and this is all I can say to you," Solomon said, his face clearly reflecting fear or retaliation, "it is about Miss Rachael...now that's all I can say about that..."

Robby turned to leave, thanking Solomon for his somewhat cryptic warning.

Solomon looked at him and had one final admonishment.

"I didn't tell you this, now," he said softly. "Mista Hollings is a fine man. I got few complaints, as far as that goes, compared to some slave owners. Now Mista Miles, he seems nice enough, but he will lay into anyone when he gets a mind to...jest that..."

Then the middle-aged slave looked at the dirt floor of the smokehouse, and then looked up and finished his sentence.

"Jest that...you see...when a slave runs away, they got to stick out, their black faces are out there alone, running along the countryside...in the *white folks'* countryside...but if you, to take a *for instance*...wanted to run away from somethin'...a lot harder to find you...a *lot harder*...and Mista Hollings...he is a man who thinks on a matter...and the longer he thinks, I figure the *angrier he gets*...you hearin' that, Mista Robby?"

Robby didn't understand all of it, but he soon would, and so he thanked Solomon, and then dashed up to the house.

He entered through the back door, which led to the kitchen. There was no one there.

But he could hear voices in the front room. He could hear Jared's voice. It was low, and angry. He thought he could hear a woman crying. It sounded a little like Rachael. But he couldn't be sure.

He walked down the narrow hallway that led to the front hallway, and he turned to the right, through the open doors of the front room.

Jared Hollings was seated at the far end of the room. Bending forward, he had his hands clasped together. On one side of him was Miles, who was standing, his hands behind his back. He had a stern look on his face. On the other side of Jared was Rachael, who had a handkerchief covering her face, and she was crying.

When Robby walked in, Jared looked up, and there was a look of rage on his face.

Robby said nothing. The first words would come from the mouth of his benefactor, and employer, Jared Hollings.

"I must first decide," he said, "whether to horsewhip you myself, or perhaps to have Miles here do the honor…or whether to have the local constable grab you by the scruff of the neck, and throw you into the Williamsburg jail."

"I don't understand what you are saying, Mr. Hollings," Robby began.

"You will keep your filthy mouth shut!" Miles shouted, "until Mr. Hollings here gives you permission to speak."

"What I cannot comprehend," Hollings continued, his face reflecting a pained sense of betrayal, "is how you could return my respect and my trust with this kind of outrage."

Robby had to struggle not to cry out that this whole conversation was making no sense to him. But it was now about to become excruciatingly clear.

"How could you accost my dear daughter, Rachael, in such a brutish manner? The poor girl is engaged to be married to a fine merchant in Fredericksburg in a few months, and now comes down to Williamsburg to suffer this kind of indignity."

"I accost her?" Robby cried out, not being able to contain himself. "Sir, I cannot say loud enough that I did no such thing!" And then Hollings's other comments—those about Rachael's engagement—started to sink in. Robby was dumbstruck.

Miles yelled out for Nathan to silence himself, and took a few steps toward him, holding his right fist out in front of him. That is when he noticed that Miles had a horsewhip in his left hand.

But Hollings stood up and brushed Miles aside and strode up to Robby's face.

"Are you calling my daughter a liar?" he said in a barking, guttural tone.

"I am calling no one a liar, sir," Robby said, now with his voice trembling with emotion and confusion, "unless they claim that I ever hurt your daughter or accosted her in any way…and any such person who says so is telling you a brazen lie."

Jared swung his arm toward Robby, and slapped him powerfully across the face.

"That is for my daughter's honor," he said.

"My daughter says that after accosting her, and ripping her sleeve as she struggled to escape, you kept the lace from her sleeve as a trophy…"

At first Robby was about to challenge Hollings again defiantly, but then, suddenly, his heart dropped.

"Show me your vest pocket!" Hollings called out to Robby.

Slowly, with a mixture of humiliation and anger, Robby produced the small piece of ripped lace from his vest pocket.

"Who is the liar now?" Hollings said with disdain.

Then Hollings turned to Miles and ordered him to secure Robby in a room locked from the outside, until morning, "when I shall then decide what form of ruination I shall bring down on your head."

Miles shoved Robby up the stairs and down the hall to a door to the attic. He shoved Robby through the doorway and walked him up the short stairway to the attic with low-lying rafters.

There, when they were alone and there was no one else about, Miles instructed Robby to stay put. Miles disappeared and then a few moments later he appeared with Robby's satchel with his belongings in it and tossed it down on the wooden floor of the attic.

"I shall be locking the outside door to the attic," he said nonchalantly. Then Miles threw a glance over at the small window at the end of the attic, and then looked back at Robby. "I cannot wish you Godspeed I am afraid, as that would be disloyal to my employer."

Then, before he left, Miles turned and added one final thought.

"I've known Miss Rachael from when she was a small little girl…and what was said about you…this is not the first time, with a man…but if you say that I have ever said such a thing, I will put a knife between your ribs!"

Miles walked down the steps and closed the door.

Robby could hear the key in the lock, as the door was locked from the outside.

Robby stood for a moment, trying to figure out what had happened.

He looked down at his satchel that Miles had brought to him. Then he walked, stooping down, to the end of the attic, where he reached out to the small window. He gave it a shove, and it opened up to the outside. Robby pushed his torso through, halfway. The window was just large enough to fit his body through.

He looked around to the left, and there was an iron railing around a small porch, just within reach. And then, down below that, about four or five feet, there was a small roof that connected to the roof that covered the porch. It would be only a moderate jump from that roof to the ground.

Robby pulled himself back into the attic. The day had disappeared, and it was dusk. He would wait until it was fully dark. And then he would make his escape.

He walked over to his satchel and carried it to the window, where the last, dim light was coming through. Robby lay down on the floor, under the window, laying his head on his satchel, and folding his hands over his chest.

Now he would wait until the late watches of the evening, when he would climb out the window.

He thought at first of running north to his kin in Boston. But he realized that Jared Hollings had connections all the way up through Virginia and into Maryland. His chances of making it, without detection, all the way to Massachusetts, which necessitated travel through those two colonies, seemed diminished.

On the other hand, just to the south of Williamsburg was the border with the Carolinas, the colonies where Hollings held no business interests, and an area through which Robby had traveled previously.

His escape would have to be into North Carolina.

That having been decided, Robby's mind drifted to the thought of Miles, and how he brought him to a room from which he could easily escape; even bringing him his bag.

And he thought about Solomon's warnings.

But mostly Robby considered Rachael, and her vicious, inexplicable betrayal.

Laying there in the attic, in the vanishing last light of the day, Robby's eyes welled up with tears. He said a prayer, and then lay and waited; listening to the sounds outside, of horses clopping along the street, and random voices, and then the chiming of the bells from a nearby church.

Robby wondered what was ahead of him, and whether he would make it safely away, as far away as he could flee, from the rooming house, and from the Hollings household.

Chapter 28

Spring came and went in Boston, and then faded into summer. Nathan was busy with the massacre case, but by midsummer most of the preparatory work for the trial was fairly complete. He had hoped that, by some miracle, his flagging law practice would be reinvigorated.

In all of the months since taking on the controversial case, Nathan had only received two new clients. One involved a nasty boundary dispute. The landowner who retained him was an ill-tempered farmer whose crops had failed the prior year, and who paid Nathan a pittance for an initial fee, but with a promise of paying more money when his summer corn came in. Nathan worked on the case feverishly, but despite his letters to the client, the additional fees never appeared.

The other client was a merchant from Pennsylvania who wanted to sue a Boston merchant. The client traveled all the way from Philadelphia, and met with Nathan. The client conference went well. The client promised to send a fee by way of a banknote drawn on his bank. Instead of getting the banknote, Nathan received a bulky envelope from the client. Inside, there was an article that had been torn from a Philadelphia newspaper about the Boston Massacre case, and mentioning Nathan and John Adams as the lawyers for the British soldiers. The client circled Nathan's name and jotted a note down that read simply: *Is this you?*

All the way over to Pennsylvania, Nathan said with exasperation. How could he ever successfully practice law again?

There was one saving grace in all of that; Nathan was able to spend more time with Deborah as she neared the date of her delivery.

They talked of names for the baby—if it was a girl, it would be Abigail, not only because of the Old Testament namesake in the Bible, but because of Deborah's fondness for her newfound friend, Abigail Adams.

They had a harder time trying to decide on a name for a boy. Deborah favored Stephen, her father's name. Nathan preferred Lawrence, the name of his own father.

There was only one way to resolve the impasse: they agreed to a third name.

If a boy, it would be William.

When Deborah began her contractions, it was slow progression. It was so slow that they went on for several days. Then one day Edith, anxious to find out how Deborah was doing, stopped by Deborah's house. Deborah was in a chair, moaning.

"It's coming...so quickly," she cried out, "oh, Edith...you will have to run...get the midwife...run quickly...and fetch Nathan!"

Edith scurried out and down the street to the midwife's house. Deborah's water had broken, and her contractions had sped up considerably. By the time the midwife was located, and was led to the house, the baby's head was already crowning.

"So, ye're a quick one!" the round, merry-looking midwife shouted out as she rolled up her sleeves.

"Can I help?" Edith asked expectantly.

"Fetch me everything I ask for...and be quick about it," the midwife ordered.

A few minutes later Nathan came rushing into the house, and into the bedroom.

"Out!" the midwife shouted at Nathan. "Husbands have no business in the business of a baby delivery..."

"But, my wife..." Nathan stammered. "She...is she...?"

"Yes, she's having a baby..." the midwife countered. "Now content yourself, good sir, in the front room until ye hear the cry of your young one..."

Nathan trudged out of the room.

In fifteen minutes, he heard the faint cry of a newborn.

Nathan rushed into the room.

The midwife was slicing the cord, and laying the baby on Deborah's stomach. The baby was a chalky white, and was shivering with each lung-filled wail.

"What's the name?" the midwife asked.

Nathan looked at Deborah.

Deborah looked back.

"Don't look at me," Deborah said weakly, trying to jest a little.

Nathan looked closer at the baby's form.

"William!" he cried out. "My son is named William!"

Later that day, when Edith joined her husband over supper, she described the delivery of Deborah's baby with excited delight.

Edward was listening cautiously, half expecting Edith to plunge into despair over her sister-in-law's blessed event while she seemed chronically unable to conceive. But there was none of that. In fact, Edith seemed to be in high spirits, and brightly optimistic.

"As I watched God's miracle," she gushed, "I was so amazed.

Deborah's baby was so alive, and beautiful, and crying his little lungs out!"

They both laughed, but Edward remained silent, letting his wife do the talking, and studying her closely.

"And then I thought back to our two little ones…each born so terribly still and lifeless…and my heart breaking into pieces as if it was made of fragile china, and had been smashed with a mallet…"

"Dear heart," Edward said, reaching over and grasping her hand. "There is always hope…of the kind that does not disappoint…"

Edith's face brightened as she nodded in agreement.

"That's so true…we are still trying, trying so that I can be with child…that hope is not quenched, is it Edward?"

Her husband was not thinking of that kind of "hope," but rather, of the theological kind. Of the fact that God's will was sovereign and inscrutable. That it might simply be His providential hand that, for whatever reason, was keeping them childless.

But Edward had learned some things about Edith over the preceding months. That her melancholy was not her problem only, but that it was his, as well. That he had been too long detached from the depth of her distress.

Now he would try his best to comfort his wife, and to be cognizant of the mysteries of her heart.

So, his answer was simple.

"No dear, that hope is not quenched."

She smiled and nodded, as if she were agreeing with herself in some secret way.

Then Edith abruptly changed the subject.

"I saw Nathan at the delivery. He was overjoyed."

"I am happy for my brother…"

"Oh, Edward," she said, suddenly taking on an earnest, pleading tone, "must things be at odds between you two? Can you approach him on this matter of disagreement...about the case he is handling...to mend things? I believe he does respect you so much. And you are his older brother."

His wife's comments came as a jolt to Edward. It had been several months since he stormed into Nathan's office and confronted him about his error in defending Captain Preston and the others. Lately he had felt the inward press of the Spirit to reconnect with Nathan.

Things have never been this way between us, Edward had found himself thinking. *How did Nathan and I have such a falling out?*

Edward had a keen knowledge of the Bible, and, even though he could be stiff-necked and rigid when it came to matters that he believed to be true, he knew full well the admonitions of the Gospel of Matthew, chapter eighteen. That when a "brother" sins against you, God's Word directs that the offended party must privately and directly meet with the offending brother. In the case of Nathan, Edward knew him not only to be a spiritual "brother" in the Christian sense, but he was also kin to Edward in the familial sense.

For Edward, there were no more excuses. He would have to reach out to his brother.

"You know, Edith dear," he said, "I have been thinking and praying on that exact matter. I do believe I will call on my brother... but this time, I will try my utmost to reconcile our differences."

"How wonderful!" Edith said.

And then she added, "Perhaps that will help make everything absolutely perfect...your decision, husband, may chase the shadows away even yet..."

Chapter 29

The trial of the Boston Massacre was only a week away. When he trudged into the office, Nathan was blurry eyed from their newborn son crying off and on for feedings through the night.

As always, John Adams seemed possessed of some unnatural energy. He darted out into the front room when he heard Nathan come through the front door, and beckoned to him.

"Nathan, good, it's you," he said exuberantly. "Come in! Come in...wanted to talk about the jury issue..."

"Jury issue?"

"Well, yes," Adams snapped back, wondering why Nathan didn't recall the point he had raised several months back. "You will recall my concern that we will pull an all-Boston jury at our trial. That would be disastrous."

"Agreed," Nathan said, still a little groggy from lack of sleep. "Do you have—"

"Any ideas? Of course, that's what we are being paid for isn't it? To come up with clever ideas, so that our clients have the better chance to secure justice."

Adams motioned for Nathan to sit down across from his desk.

When Nathan did, Adams did not sit down, but paced around the room.

"If every juror is from Boston, as is usually the case, they will have been predisposed against our clients. So we must extend the jury pool..."

"Yes, but how?"

"I have been thinking," Adams said, still roaming the room, "how the English sheriffs of the county are responsible for assembling potential jurors."

"Yes, that is right—"

"And I think the presence of Boston citizens at our jury trials in other cases is, if you will excuse me, simply a matter of indolence on the part of our local constables. Remember, most of them are either agents of the Crown or certainly Tories in their political affections."

"Seems logical..."

"So, we must *motivate* them to ride farther out into the countryside," Adams mused, "and to get out of the city of Boston...to enlist our potential jurors for this trial."

Nathan nodded. The strategy seemed reasonable to him. And then Adams stopped pacing, and turned to face Nathan.

"So...what are you waiting for?" Adams asked.

"Well," Nathan said grasping for an answer, "I am...well...waiting for instructions..."

"Go to the sheriff's office," Adams shot back. "Get them to enlist men from the countryside for our jury...what have I just been talking about?"

"Yes," Nathan said. "I understand that. It's just that, well, sir, exactly *how do I motivate them* to do that?"

"I'm sure you will figure it out," Adams said. "Get on your way.

I suggest you begin on this matter immediately. Now, if you will excuse me, I have work to do."

Nathan floated into his own office, a little bewildered about how he was going to order the sheriffs, all of whom were loyal to England, to do his bidding. But he knew better than to dawdle. So he put on his coat, and decided to don his wig, which he usually reserved for more formal occasions, and headed over to the constable's office.

After a two-block walk, he strode into the office. There was a desk officer on duty who had removed his coat, and he was working in his white frock shirtsleeves.

"Could I speak to the sheriff's deputies who are assigned to summon the jury panels in Boston?" Nathan asked.

The officer glared at him, then asked, "And who might you be?"

"A lawyer."

"Well, Boston is very full of them, I am afraid," the officer barked back. "You're going to have to do better than that."

"All right then, my name is Nathan Mackenzie. I am one of the attorneys in the Massacre case."

The officer stopped his writing, and put the quill down and studied Nathan. Then he began to chuckle.

"You with that John Adams fellow?"

Nathan nodded.

Then the officer called out the names of several deputies who, in a few moments, trudged into the lobby and asked why they were called.

"This here," the desk officer announced, "is Mr. Mackenzie. He and Mr. Adams are representing Captain Preston and his men. He wants to talk to you about summoning the jury panel..."

The deputies all began laughing. Then one of them spoke up.

"You and Adams must be real popular with the locals here in Boston..."

Nathan didn't appreciate being the butt of their insensitive jesting, and he did not respond.

"So," the deputy finally said, "exactly what business is it of yours, sir, how we conduct our jury summons?"

For a moment, Nathan froze. He hadn't the faintest idea what he was going to say next. Then a thought came to him, and as it became clearer, Nathan stood up taller and walked over to the deputy.

"No deputy, you misapprehend. It is not *my business* as much as it is *yours*...that is, unless you wish to be the next target of a grand jury here in Boston..."

"What is that you said?" the deputy roared. "Do you threaten us, then?"

"No, sir, not in the least. I only impart a warning. If justice is not done in this trial, because you have *only* summoned local Boston citizens as jurors—citizens who seem all too quick to convict any friend of the Crown of England—then you have set the trapdoor for your own hanging. Once Captain Preston is found guilty, then it will be the constable's office next that the mobs will target. And when you defend yourself against such attacks, and find yourself also in court—will it be merely residents of Boston who will decide your fate at trial?"

There was silence in the constable's office. Finally, the desk officer spoke up.

"Deputies, perhaps you need to go into the countryside hereabouts...outside of the city of Boston...when it is time to round up jurors. Besides, the weather is mild...and the ride in the country will do you good."

"An excellent idea," Nathan said, beaming. "Officers, I commend you for your sound decision."

Chapter 30

When Nathan returned to his office, he found that John Adams had gone. He was disappointed at that, as he was bursting with good news about his handling of the sheriff's deputies and the jury issue and hoped to share it with Adams.

But when he entered into his own interior office he found someone there, waiting for him.

"Edward!" Nathan exclaimed, happy to see his older brother sitting in a chair opposite his desk.

Edward rose with a smile and extended his hand to his brother.

"I hope you will excuse me," he said shaking Nathan's hand warmly, "for barging in like this, unannounced. Mr. Adams showed me into your office…he was on his way out. He said to tell you that he had a dinner engagement with his wife and some others tonight."

"It is no inconvenience to have you here, brother," Nathan said. "In truth, I was surprised, of course…but very pleased to see you sitting in my office. I had regretted our last words, in this very place, many weeks ago. I'm glad to see you."

"I was talking with Edith," Edward said seating himself back in the chair, "and something arose in our conversation…actually a matter that has been stirring me in my prayer closet…and the Lord has impressed on me that I should do something about it. Something in line with Scripture…"

"What is that?"

"Coming to you as a brother in the Lord, and my own flesh and blood kin, in the spirit of the gospel Matthew chapter eighteen, and asking you to reconsider your decision to engage yourself in this hopeless cause…"

Suddenly, Nathan's enthusiasm at his tactical victory with the sheriff's office, and his optimism at seeing Edward seemingly holding out an olive branch, all of that was now dashed. His brother had not changed his position; rather, he had only changed his manner of approach.

He tried anger before to intimidate me, Nathan thought to himself, *and now he's quoting the Bible and coming to me in peace. But the message is still the same.*

"Do you consider my legal defense of these men to be sin?" Nathan asked forthrightly.

"I consider it foolishness…and akin to partnering with unrighteousness."

"I do not, Edward," Nathan said. "Furthermore, without making too much of a point of it," he continued, "if I look to my Savior as an example, He is called our heavenly Advocate before the bar of God…and by the way, all of His clients are hopeless sinners. So, *even if every one of my clients were guilty,* which I do not believe to be the case…even if that were true, then defending them and insuring that they receive a fair trial would be merely following the tradition of Jesus Christ, Who is, after all, our example."

Edward saw that his discussion was yielding no fruit, and he quickly rose to his feet.

But as Nathan studied his face, and looked into his eyes, he saw something he had not expected to see—indecision. Edward was one of the most decisive, self-assured men Nathan had ever known. But now, just for an instant, Nathan saw something in Edward's expression that led him to believe that his older brother was searching his own heart, like a man might search his trunk, pulling out clothes, books, and papers, hunting for some lost possession, or for some misplaced remembrance. Perhaps a family Bible or some record of the life of generations of family members from ages past.

"There is, in your coming here, I believe," Nathan said, reaching out, and taking hold of Edward's sleeve, "more to this than just the massacre case…"

"What do you mean?" Edward said, not looking Nathan in the eye, but staring at the floor.

"I mean only this…perhaps you hope that the conviction of these men, and their severe punishment, will somehow appease the radicals of Boston, and quiet the citizens. And if that happens, then all will be well. Peace will return. No further violent conflict…no talk of confronting mother England…and no decision to make…"

"Decision?" Edward said. "What decision?"

"*Your* decision, brother," Nathan said quietly. "Your decision, on where you stand if the great cataclysm comes upon us…if we find ourselves having to choose between our brothers and sisters, the fellow settlers of these American colonies, and the arrogant and tyrannical Crown of England…and I think that you fear that choice, brother. For you truly do not know, if that day comes, how you will choose."

There was a look that Edward gave his brother before he left the room. It was not despair, or resignation. But it was something close to both of those emotions. Edward did not speak, and he showed no anger. But he gathered his three cornered hat, carefully placed it on his head, and then quietly left Nathan's office.

Hundreds of miles to the south of Boston, in the foothills of western North Carolina, Robby Mackenzie was approaching a wayside tavern. It was located on a stretch of lonely dirt road that was lined on both sides with pine tree forests. Robby was tired and hungry. He carried only the dusty clothes on his back, and the leather satchel that contained his only few possessions. He had been traveling for days.

There were several farm wagons and packhorses tied off around the outside of the tavern; and, quite conspicuously, there was one very fine looking coach as well.

Robby beat some of the dust off his clothes, wiped the sweat from his face, and walked in.

Inside there were a dozen men; most of them looked to be frontiersmen and dirt-poor farmers. One man, however, stood out: he was well dressed in a fine coat and shiny black boots. He was standing by the barkeep with a tankard in his hand. He was engaged in a lively discussion with one of the farmers who were seated at the tables eating and drinking.

"What good does it do," one of the farmers said loudly and angrily, "if we continue running our own kind of government here, if we still feel King George's pitchfork in our hind sides, prodding us to pay taxes…but gettin' nothing in return…"

"Look here," the well-dressed gentleman said in reply, "we have accomplished much. When the Crown of England stopped providing us with judges and courts to settle disputes like civilized people, well…then we created our own local courts, did we not?"

A few of the farmers nodded in agreement.

"And when crimes occurred, and the Crown refused to provide protection," the gentleman continued, "we employed our own private constables and established our own local laws, and our own jails to enforce civility. And when the English-backed sheriffs collected excessive taxes and then corruptly paid them to themselves, we ceased paying taxes...Now I don't know about you, but I believe we have made progress..."

"Yes, but Roger here made a point that you're not answering!" another one of the farmers said. "All of that is well and good. But England doesn't care. We are taxed as if King George was doing something to provide government for us...yet he has failed to do that! Now what we members of the Regulators are proposin'...is that we take things to the next step..."

"Next step?" the gentlemen said. "I fear you speak treason, sir. You must be careful..."

"We can't let things lay as they are, I tell ye! Something has to be done to wake up old King George..." said one of the rough-looking frontiersmen in a fringed, animal hide coat.

"I have supported you men, and put up with the protestations of you so-called Regulators," the gentlemen said, shaking his head, "but I will not join you in any vigilante acts. Make no mistake about that. Now I am one of the few East Carolina men from the tidewater who's been willing to support you wild-eyed Westerners. But my patience is wearing thin..."

Then the gentleman put his tankard down on the bar, stepped toward the door, and turned to address the farmers.

"I counsel patience," he said with urgency in his voice. "*Patience,* men. For pity's sake, what further steps could you possibly take that would not spell disaster for us all?"

Then he exited the tavern and climbed in the back of his coach, while his coachmen scrambled to the front and lashed the horses into action.

"We don't need him," one of the farmers said.

"Oh, we don't?" another asked. "Mr. Gallway is one of the richest merchants in his part of the tidewater, and the only tidewater patriot who isn't a Tory sympathizer…I always thought we were lucky to have him backing us."

"Then we will do it without him," another said.

That is when the group of frontiersmen and farmers were aware that Robby was standing in the corner.

"You there," the frontiersmen in the fringed jacket shouted to him. "Show yourself!"

Robby stepped forward out of the shadows, still holding his satchel.

"So, you're travelin' through here," the man said. "You got kin hereabouts?"

"No, sir. My kin are all from Boston."

There was a momentary hush.

"Be they patriots? Or Crown kissers?" the frontiersman growled.

"Well, one of my brothers is a lawyer. I do know he is a patriot, sir. As for my other brother…he is a preacher in a well-established church in Boston…but I cannot tell you where he stands."

"Where do you stand?" another one of the men shouted out.

"I do not know all your grievances, men. But I have traveled up and down the Eastern Seaboard. And one thing I've heard from my brother, the lawyer…that God created men to be free, and governments to keep them that way. But it's a pitiful sight when a king across the ocean says he wants to pick our pockets, just so he can use *our* money to buy chains for *our* wrists."

The crowd burst into laughter. The frontiersman walked up to Robby with a smile and slapped him on the back.

An old farmer in a dirty slouch hat, and leaning on a cane, hobbled up to Robby and spoke up.

"He sounds honest and goodhearted, men, and stouthearted as well. Barkeep…I think he deserves a meal. He looks hungry."

Robby thanked him and sat down at a plank table with the old farmer. "Hadfield Fergusson is the name," the farmer said, stretching out his leathery hand to shake Robby's. "But everybody knows me as Fergusson. So, son, are you movin' on then…or are you settlin' here…?"

"Not sure," Robby said.

A tavern keeper placed a small block of cheese and a slice of bread on the table in front of Robby.

Robby thanked him and took his knife out of his coat pocket and began slicing the cheese. He offered the first bite to the old farmer, but he only smiled and declined.

"Not sure," Robby said with his mouth full. "Depends on whether there is a reason to stay a while…"

"Well," the old farmer said. "I may have such a reason. I manage a small farm. My hired help left to go east where the money is. I live alone. Need help. You look like a strapping lad. Want to work my farm a spell, for food, bed, and a few coin pieces?"

Robby kept chewing. After a while he swallowed and smiled at the farmer.

Divine Providence may have brought me here, Robby thought to himself. *I will have a bed and food for a while.*

Robby wiped his right hand on his pants, and then extended it to the farmer who grabbed it.

"You have yourself a new hired hand," Robby said, beaming.

Chapter 31

In the weeks leading up to the trial, Nathan and John Adams had spent each day, from the break of dawn until the late hours of the evening, working together in preparation for the murder charges against Captain Thomas Preston. Deborah was consumed with her new infant son, William, while still managing the house. Abigail Adams visited her a few times, with her two toddlers in tow, to give her a hand with the duties of the home, and to commiserate about the temporary loss of their husbands to the demands of the law.

Because Nathan's motion for severance had been granted by Justice Cushing, the trial of Captain Preston was "severed" from the cases against the other English soldiers. That meant that the Preston trial would proceed first. The soldiers' trial was set for a month later. John Adams had impressed upon their defense co-counsel, Robert Auchmuty and Samson Salter Blowers, the necessity of splitting up the legal defense team. Auchmuty, who was a Tory, and had experience as a vice-admiralty judge, was clearly the keener trial advocate of the two. He was to handle the defense of Hugh Montgomery, one of the foot soldiers, in the second trial. The dour, lackluster Mr. Blowers, assisted by Auchmuty, would defend another defendant soldier, Matthew Killroy. Adams and Nathan would represent the remaining soldiers.

But in the first trial, that of Captain Preston, it would be John Adams and Nathan Mackenzie for the defense.

By the fall, the trial was ready to commence. The leaves in the maple and elm trees in and around Boston were already starting to turn to colors of scarlet, yellow, and blaze orange, and the all-too-brief warmth of the summer had fully faded into crisp days and cold nights.

On the first morning of the first day of trial, Nathan rose early, just before sunrise. He had not slept well that night. His tossing and turning in bed had been so violent that he worried that he would wake up little William, who was slumbering in their bedroom in a small rocking cradle, next to their four-poster bed. So he quietly arose, when it was still pitch black, and crept down the stairs to the front room, and then stretched out on the gold and black embroidered love seat. But though he tried to close his eyes, his brain would not cease its grindings.

So he got up and threw on his heavy wrap over his nightshirt, thrust his feet into his boots, and slipped out through the kitchen to the rear yard where the woodpile was. Then he made several trips into the house with armfuls of logs, and kindling. He stacked it all into the brick-lined firewood storage cavity underneath the kitchen hearth. Nathan wanted to make sure that Deborah would have plenty of firewood to keep the house warm during the day. He did not want her to have to leave the house and have to trudge in and out with heavy logs in her arms.

After that, he stoked up the fire until it was roaring in the kitchen fireplace. He hung a teapot filled with water from the iron hook over the fire.

As Nathan leaned against the brick surround of the hearth, and felt the warmth of the bricks, he felt overwhelmed at the importance of the case which was to begin in just a few hours.

Oh God, he prayed out loud, *bless the efforts of Thy servants at law, and give us Thy justice…*

But then suddenly a woman's voice joined his.

And give a special blessing to my dear husband, Deborah said, standing behind him, *and reward him for his courage and his sacrifice…*

Then Deborah hugged him from behind, wrapping her arms around him tightly.

Together they stood in front of the blazing fireplace, saying nothing for several minutes.

Then Nathan turned around, and kissed her and hugged her again.

"I thought you were asleep," he said. "I hope I didn't wake you."

"Mothers always sleep with one eye half open, haven't you heard that?" she said with a smile. "Besides, I didn't want my husband trotting off to his trial without an affectionate hug from his wife!"

"Thank you," he said. "I am afraid I didn't sleep a wink last night."

"The Lord will wake you up," she said, "and will make you attentive today…together with the Tory lawyers for the Crown who oppose you!"

Nathan dressed himself, wearing his finest dark waistcoat and dark pants with the fine stripes, and his powdered wig, and his formal cape.

He ate no breakfast, for he simply could not stomach any food. Then Nathan kissed Deborah, gathered his leather satchel full of papers and notes, and walked hurriedly for the four blocks to the courthouse.

John Adams was already there in the courtroom, as was the entire prosecution team at their table, huddled together talking. One half of the courtroom was filled up with prospective jurors who had been hailed by the sheriffs to report for jury duty. The other side of the courtroom was already filling up with curious audience members.

Nathan sat down next to Adams. Nathan had been trying to conjure up an optimistic attitude about the case as he walked to the courthouse that morning. After all, he thought to himself, his motion for severance had been granted. Adams' masterful ploy to get the Governor to demand a delay of the trial date had worked. And most recently, Nathan had been successful in convincing the sheriff's deputies to draw potential jurors from outside of the city. After reviewing those several procedural victories, Nathan was already starting to feel fairly sure of their ability to gain an acquittal for Captain Preston by the time he had reached the courthouse steps.

"I am feeling very sure about this whole case," Nathan whispered to Adams with a smile, as the two lawyers sat at the defense table awaiting the arrival of Justice Edmund Trowbridge, the presiding judge. "I feel that we shall surely be victorious…"

Adams stopped what he was reading, put his papers down, and turned to face Nathan in his chair.

"Don't be a fool, man," he replied back in a strained whisper. "Do you realize what we are up against here?"

Nathan was taken aback. He was going to reply, but Adams beat him to the punch.

"I realize that we have won a few minor skirmishes in this fight," Adams continued. "But the war, Nathan, the legal war is about to begin. And frankly, our opponents have the better facts, as well as a judge who will likely side with them, and jurors who, though they be not from the city, may well have the same hatred of an English officer as do the city folks…in short, man, we face a Herculean task…make no mistake about that…"

Then, almost as an afterthought, Adams reminded Nathan of his duty during the first day of trial when the jury would be picked.

"Remember, also," Adams said, "that you will lead the defense questioning of the jurors…"

Nathan was still pondering Adams' somber assessment when Captain Thomas Preston was escorted into the courtroom and over to their table. Adams and Nathan shook hands with him, but had no time to sit.

For then the bailiff and clerk scurried into the courtroom, followed by a short, squat man named John Hodson, who was to be the court's reporter of the proceedings. All three stood at attention.

Then the clerk called out for the attention of the court, and uttered the preamble and the *oyez*, commanding all present to rise for the Honorable Edmund Trowbridge.

The justice, a middle-aged man of moderate height, strode in the courtroom with his scarlet and ermine robes. He wiped an errant hair from his powdered wig back into place, nodded to the crowded courtroom, and then sat down at the bench.

Trowbridge was something of an enigma. Adams had previously tried cases before him, but they were perfunctory types of proceedings. Not the type from which he could possibly glean some indication how he might rule in a highly charged, politically incendiary case like this.

A man of good looks that made him look younger than his age, Trowbridge was a man who always chose his words carefully and artfully. He never said more than he needed to in his rulings. While his political leanings could have been presumed to be Tory, he conspicuously avoided ever mentioning them, and did not join any of the clubs and fraternities that favored the Crown of England. On the other hand, it was a known fact that he detested civil unrest and had never uttered a single word in favor of the patriot cause.

In short, Justice Trowbridge held the potential, from the defense standpoint, of either being the best of all possible judges to try the Boston Massacre case, or else, the absolute worst.

There was nothing further Adams or Nathan could speculate on that matter. They would simply have to wait and see how this secretive Justice would approach their case.

"Defense counsel," Justice Trowbridge began, "I have decided to depart with normal protocol...which would usually have the prosecution begin the jury voir dire...and will call upon the defense to begin."

Nathan was stunned. He had counted on the prosecution to open up the questions, giving him a chance to mentally survey the legal landscape before he had to dive in.

But that would not be the case.

The first juror, a merchant by the name of Howard Palling, was called to the stand. He answered the judge's preliminary questions about his name, occupation, and date of birth.

But then, with a startling revelation, he answered the judge's question about his place of residence.

"I live on King Street, Your Honor," the juror said, "about a block from where this terrible massacre took place. In the city of Boston."

Boston! Nathan shouted silently to himself. *I thought they were going to call jurors from outside the city!*

Then Nathan turned over to Captain Preston, who was staring directly at him.

Nathan stared back. And then, quite unexpectedly, a thought flashed into Nathan's mind…an image…of Captain Preston, with a thick rope around his neck, staring at Nathan from the top of the gallows…and then the trapdoor of the gallows opened and the face disappeared from his sight, and then Nathan heard a thud, as the body reached the very end of the rope with a terrifying jolt, and all that could be heard was the creaking of the rope as the body swung to and fro at the bottom of the gallows.

"Counsel!" Justice Trowbridge called out to Nathan, breaking into the imagery of his mind, "Did you hear my command? I said that the defense will proceed with the voir dire of the jury…will you now proceed, sir, or not?"

Adams flashed an angry look to Nathan.

"Get to it!" he whispered harshly to Nathan.

Nathan slowly rose to his feet.

Now it begins, he heard himself saying silently.

Chapter 32

The juror in the witness stand had a complacent, almost bored look. It was as if he did not understand, or at least did not care about, the stakes in the murder case.

"Mr. Palling," Nathan began a little nervously. "You...you said that you live in Boston...the city of Boston...is that correct?"

"Nothing wrong with your hearin', counselor," Palling said with a smirk. "That's what I said."

"And you are a merchant..."

"That's what I said..." Palling remarked, shaking his head a little.

"And you do a good business, do you?"

"Not since the boycott, no..."

"So, you participate in the boycott, do you?"

Palling began to shift a little in his chair. Samuel Quincy, the lead prosecutor, was immediately on his feet objecting.

"Your Honor," he complained, "Mr. Mackenzie is trying to do exactly what we warned this honorable court he would try to do during the pre-trial motion hearings...we argued that the defense would try to convert this trial into a blatant political statement, rather than a proceeding founded on a decent, civil view of the law. This is intolerable!"

"Your Honor," Nathan said, "I am merely trying to determine whether this particular merchant has any biases or prejudices that could affect his impartiality as a juror..."

"Then why don't you simply ask him that question?" Justice Trowbridge said, a little irritated.

But Nathan knew better than that. No juror openly admits being unfairly biased in his judgments. No, that is not how to reveal a deep-seated matter. Rather, the way to disclose a prejudiced juror was to set a trap, with a hidden trapdoor, and then let the creature sniff the bait and lead himself right into it, unawares.

"Mr. Palling," Nathan continued, "I will spare you any embarrassment, and will withdraw my question. I would not want to make you the least uncomfortable by asking whether you align with the patriot cause and oppose the English government. I will not do that, sir."

With that, the juror, Howard Palling, relaxed a little in his chair and a half smile appeared on his face.

"Let me only ask you whether you have lost income in your business as a result of the boycott against English goods..."

"Of course I have," Palling said.

"Lost a grievous amount of revenue?"

"A goodly amount..."

"Was that loss of revenue your own fault?"

"Of course not..."

"So you blame the English Crown...you blame King George for that loss of revenue?"

"No, certainly not!" the merchant thundered, nervously looking over at the English justice sitting on the bench.

Of course, that left only one last party to blame—the patriots of Boston. But Nathan was smart enough to not ask that question.

"Your Honor," Nathan said with some confidence, "I find myself befuddled. I was at first struck by the fact that this juror might be biased against the Crown of England, and by logical deduction, biased against Captain Preston, an officer of the English military. But it would appear that I was quite wrong. The defense is very pleased with this juror. We have absolutely no objections to him…"

John Adams looked up from the defense counsel's table at Nathan, who could see his senior partner out of the corner of his eye. Adams knew that Nathan was taking a risky gamble with that ploy; he knew he would have little sympathy with the judge if the defense tried to block the man from serving on the panel, so he was attempting to cause the prosecution to be the ones to insist on removing the merchant from the jury. But if he lost his gamble, they would have a Boston merchant on the jury; something both Adams and Nathan did not want.

There was a pause for a moment. Justice Trowbridge lifted an eyebrow and glanced over at prosecutors Quincy and Paine, who were whispering to each other.

Then Samuel Quincy rose slowly and managed a meager smile.

"Your Honor, we would be most pleased also with this Boston merchant as a juror…"

Nathan's heart sunk at that last comment.

"Except for…"

"Yes?"

"Well," Quincy continued. "Except for his…his proximity of residence to the scene of the crime. He may have, however unintentionally, formed some opinions about the crime based on his heightened knowledge of that area of the city of Boston..."

Quincy knew he could not afford to offend the patriots in the courtroom, for they were going to be his best witnesses against Captain Preston, so he was trying to disqualify this man who harbored a hidden resentment of the patriot-imposed boycott, but in the gentlest way possible.

Justice Trowbridge looked a little perplexed.

"Mr. Quincy, I am not sure that is a basis for rejecting this juror. Mr. Mackenzie, do you want to still retain this juror?"

Nathan rose again and smiled confidently.

"Your Honor, with Mr. Quincy's advanced trial experience and sharp reasoning powers, I must defer to his judgment on this matter...if he thinks that this juror should not serve, then who am I to disagree?"

"All right then," Justice Trowbridge announced, "this juror is disqualified. Next juror..."

Nathan breathed a sigh of relief. But it would not last long.

Chapter 33

Following the dismissal of juror Howard Palling, another potential juror was called by name; he rose slowly, a little hesitantly, and then situated himself in the box for questioning. As Nathan interrogated him, it soon became apparent that he had a personal acquaintance with one of the victims, namely, Samuel Gray.

"So, you knew Mr. Gray, is that it?" Nathan asked.

"Knew him like my own kin," the juror responded. "I worked for him in his shop for the last five years. He gave me work when I was destitute. Treated me like his own son, he did..."

"Now, when did you become aware that he had died of gunshot wounds, suffered in the shooting by certain English soldiers?"

"The very day he died. I knew he was lingering, and we were all hoping and praying that he would pull out. But it was not to be..."

"What was your reaction?"

"Cried like a baby, I did."

"Did you feel angry at anyone?"

"Sure enough, I did."

"At whom?"

"At the captain there, that Preston fellow, and his soldiers."

"Did you wish that you could revenge your employer's death?"

"The thought did pass my mind on occasion..."

"But you knew that would be wrong..."

"Well, in a manner of speakin', I guess you could say that..."

"But what did you feel, and think, when the sheriff's deputies summoned you to this case and told you that you might be a juror who would decide the fate of Captain Preston?"

"Very pleased," the man in the box said, holding himself up very straight.

"And why was that?" Nathan asked.

"'Cause then I could vote to put the neck of that Captain Preston in a rope noose, and then would hope to see him drop with my own eyes..."

Nathan thanked the man for his honest and forthright responses, and then moved Justice Trowbridge to excuse the man from jury duty on this case on the grounds of prejudice against the defense.

But Samuel Quincy rose up and strode forward toward the man, advising the judge that he wanted to ask him a few questions.

"Now, sir," Quincy said to the prospective juror, "you consider yourself a good man? An honest man?"

"I suppose."

"Not prone to do evil?"

"Not rightly on purpose, no..."

"So that having been said, you would agree with me, sir, that you will not do evil against this court...but you will weigh the evidence, and arrive at a just verdict, will you not? And you will not convict Captain Preston except upon good and well-founded reasons?"

"What was that?" the man said. "Did you say *not convict* Captain Preston?"

"I said not convict except upon—"

But the man would not allow him to finish his question again, and interrupted him so as to make his intentions extraordinarily clear.

"No sir," the man said, "I came to *convict* that English captain… elsewise, why would I have come to this trial in the first place?"

Quincy tried not to look distressed at his blunder and the man's self-disqualification but was not entirely successful.

Justice Trowbridge dismissed the man from serving as a juror in the case.

By midday, a jury was finally picked. To the satisfaction of John Adams and Nathan, none of them resided in Boston, and none seemed to harbor any extreme anti-British animosity. Nathan looked to Adams for some happiness at that development, but his mentor looked no more optimistic than before.

"Mr. Quincy and Mr. Paine," the judge said to the prosecutors. "Shall you commence with opening statements?"

Quincy rose and addressed the court.

"We waive opening statements, Your Honor. But will reserve the right to make closing arguments at the end of the trial."

"This is our golden chance," Nathan whispered to Adams. "If you give an opening statement now, you will be the only counsel giving a theory of the case."

But Adams shook his head.

"It's a trap," he whispered back. "The facts in this case are so jumbled, and confused, that if I say one thing that is not later substantiated by witnesses, he will hang me up like wet laundry. No, Nathan. I'll not do it."

Then Adams stood up and also waived his opening statement.

Robert Treat Paine then stood up and announced to the court that he was about to direct the questioning of the prosecution witnesses.

The first witness was a man named Peter Cunningham. He heard a bell ring that night and rushed down to the area near the King's Customs House, and saw Captain Preston assembling his soldiers to stand fast against a mounting crowd.

"Now Mr. Cunningham," Paine said in a slow, booming voice, "did you hear the captain give orders to his men at that time and place?"

"Sure enough I did."

"And what order did he give?"

"He ordered his men to prime and load their muskets."

"Are you sure you heard him give that order?"

"Positive. Quite sure."

"Was this shortly before the soldiers started shooting into the crowd?"

"It was."

Nathan glanced over at Captain Preston, sitting next to him at the defense counsel table. Preston's eyes were slightly glazed over and unfocused. As if he were hearing testimony that was crushing him internally.

"How far were you from him?"

"Only about four or five feet away. I was in the crowd."

"And then, shortly after he ordered his men to prepare their weapons, then you saw and heard the firing?"

"I did. It was terrible. The soldiers started firing at us. Men screaming and dropping. Blood all around. I ran for my life. It just came out of nowhere. Without warning."

Paine strode over to his seat with a satisfied grin and sat down.

John Adams then began his cross-examination.

"You say the shooting *just came out of nowhere. Without warning.* Those were your words just now, sir?"

"Yes. That is what I said."

"*Without warning,*" Adams repeated again. "So therefore, it would be correct to say that you *did not hear Captain Preston actually order his men to commence firing?*"

The witness paused a moment, and then answered.

"I am not sure...he could have said that...but the crowd was noisy so I may have missed that."

"But you are not very sure that you heard him say that?"

"That's right. Not sure at all that I heard Captain Preston actually tell his men to fire."

Adams rested his cross-examination. Paine jumped up and briskly approached the witness.

"Mr. Cunningham, you testified that Captain Preston ordered his soldiers to prime and load their weapons..."

"Yes, sir."

"Would it do much good to order soldiers to prime and load their weapons...*if the Captain was not also entertaining the idea of having them shoot those weapons?*"

"Well, sir," the witness said. "Everybody knows that you don't prime and load your weapon unless you're pretty sure you're goin' to fire it..."

"Indeed," Paine said with a smile. "One last question. Where was Captain Preston standing when he gave the order to prime and load the muskets?"

"To the rear of his men," the witness said. "Standard military position for a commanding officer who is about to have his men commence shooting."

As the witness was excused and walked through the courtroom, Adams leaned over to Nathan with a grim look.

"Now you see," he said quietly, "why I was not jubilant about our several small tactical victories. The battle has been joined. And I am afraid that we have just suffered casualties."

But the casualties were about to mount higher.

The next witness Paine called was William Wyatt.

Like the other witness, Wyatt was at the scene at the time of the shooting. But he had some testimony that would be several times more devastating than the prosecution's first witness.

"Mr. Wyatt," Paine said. "Did you observe the English soldiers?"

"I did."

"And did you see Captain Preston with them?"

"Plain as day."

"What was he saying to them?"

"He was angry and swearing...about the crowd gathering...he told his men to prime and load their weapons."

"So, he was angry and swearing when he told them to prepare their weapons for firing?"

"Indeed he was."

"Then what was the next thing that you heard Captain Preston say?"

Wyatt leaned forward in the witness box, with his arms folded in front of him, and a look of bitter determination on his face.

"I heard that Captain Preston there," he said, pointing to the defense table, "I heard him say—*Fire, men!* But they did nothing at first. So he shouts, and starts swearing and says, again, even louder—*Fire your guns!* And then, that's when the muskets start firing, and belching smoke, and men start dropping in the snow where they stood..."

Robert Treat Paine knew how to end a direct examination on a high note. So with that, he ended his questioning. He did not need to carry a look of smugness on his face, as he often did. So catastrophically effective was the testimony of his witness that Paine concluded that it was at that very point that the criminal case against the English officer was probably won.

As John Adams slowly stood to his feet to begin his cross-examination of the witness, Nathan sunk back in his chair.

He felt as if he had just been punched in the gut.

Chapter 34

John Adams was on his feet strolling slowly toward William Wyatt, the prosecution's potent eyewitness.

There was a relaxed, almost nonchalant demeanor to Adams, which Nathan found bewildering. At first he thought that it was a tactical ploy; that Adams was trying to bluff the jury into believing that the testimony of Mr. Wyatt had not damaged the defense case. Of course, from Nathan's perspective, to believe that would be utter foolishness.

Or, there was another explanation contemplated by Nathan. Maybe John Adams, though he was a principled and impassioned advocate for justice, had nevertheless concluded that this case simply could not be won; that the rest of the trial would be a mere ceremony, a legal bit of play-acting.

Yet everyone knew that there would be a deadly outcome at the end of this piece of legal theater if the defense did not begin rewriting the script.

"Mr. Wyatt," Adams began softly, "I listened intently to your testimony. You said that you saw Captain Preston."

"That is correct."

"And you heard him say several things."

"That also is correct, Mr. Adams. Things I heard with my own ears."

There was a pause. Adams took a moment to adjust his wig which had slipped slightly forward. After he pushed it back gently, he continued his questioning.

"So the point is, Mr. Wyatt," Adams said. "The point is…well, whether your eyes were cooperating with your ears."

The witness gave an almost comical grimace at the question. Then he muttered, "I ain't got the faintest idea what you mean."

Justice Trowbridge, who was characteristically expressionless, now lifted an eyebrow and wrinkled his forehead.

"Do you want to rephrase that rather…quizzical question, Mr. Adams?" the judge asked.

"No, Your Honor," he replied. "Thank you for your suggestion, but I would prefer not."

"Do you understand the question?" the judge asked Wyatt.

"Not by a far sight, judge," he replied.

"Then I must strike the question, for I do not understand it either," the judge ruled.

Strangely, Adams did not seem fazed by the ruling.

"Mr. Wyatt, where was Captain Preston facing when he ordered the soldiers to prime and load their muskets?"

"Half toward me and half toward the soldiers."

"Well, how could that be?" Adams asked with a loud voice. His face showed an overblown expression of disbelief. "How could the captain be half-facing you and half-facing the soldiers, if you were in front of the soldiers, and the good captain was standing *to the rear of the soldiers?*"

"'Cause you are mistaken," Wyatt said proudly. "Preston wasn't to the rear of the soldiers. He wasn't in back of them. No sir, he was *standing in front of them.*"

"No, sir!" Adams said, exploding with his loudest voice. "I am not the one mistaken. The one mistaken in this case is Mr. Cunningham, the prior prosecution witness…who testified that Captain Preston was *standing at the rear of his men.* He would be mistaken, right? Because you are not mistaken, correct?"

Wyatt took a while answering, trying to determine what trap was being prepared for him.

"No…I am not mistaken…"

"Good," Adams proclaimed. "Then let's proceed. Now Captain Preston was half-facing you when he told his men to load their weapons?"

"That's what I already said."

"Standing *in front of his men?*"

"Yes."

"Now, Mr. Wyatt, do you think it would be prudent for a commanding officer to order his men to load their weapons if they were facing an angry mob, and that mob had weapons and clubs, and that mob was moving in against the soldiers?"

"I didn't see no clubs…"

"No, I didn't say that you did. But *if the mob* had clubs and were using them against the soldiers, shouldn't a prudent officer tell his men to load their weapons, just to be ready?"

"Maybe…"

"Now were you in the middle of the mob…this crowd of Boston men?"

"Pretty much so…"

"And there was shouting and yelling going on?"

"Yes, but with good reason…"

"But a lot of commotion?"

"Suppose so."

"Then the next thing you hear is the order to *Fire, men!* Those words, *Fire, men! Correct?"

"Absolutely."

"And is it a fact that when those words were shouted out, that Captain Preston's back was to you, as he was facing his men?"

Wyatt took a little time answering that, but when he had settled on a reply, a grin broke over his face.

"Yes, his back was to me because he was facing the soldiers... and that was because he was shouting out his order to them...his order to fire..."

"His order to fire?" Adams exclaimed with incredulity. "While he was standing directly *in front of them?* Do you contend that the good captain wanted to die that day? That he wished his own men to fire directly upon him while he stood in front of them?"

There was another pause.

"Maybe it was Preston's plan to jump out of the way at the last moment..."

"But he didn't jump away at the last minute, did he? In fact, would you agree that the muskets started firing while Captain Preston stood in front of them, and that he only narrowly escaped being hit himself?"

"Don't know...maybe..."

"Oh, come now, Mr. Wyatt. Didn't you give a written statement to the Sons of Liberty—in fact I have a copy right here," and with that Adams flourished a piece of parchment. "And in that statement you said that Preston was standing in front of the soldiers and almost got hit himself?"

"If that's what that paper says there..."

"And you said something else too. In this statement you say that immediately after the muskets were fired, 'Captain Preston swore at his men, and took his sword and batted the rifle barrels of his men upward so they would stop shooting?'"

"Maybe that's what I wrote. Maybe..."

"Do you wish me to have Justice Trowbridge read your written document and then confront you as to whether you wrote those words?"

That is when William Wyatt sat up straight and answered promptly.

"No, sir. Not necessary."

"One last thing," Adams said. "You say that when the first order to fire was shouted out, that the men did not commence firing. It was only after the *second time that the order was shouted out* when the men began firing their muskets into the crowd. Right?"

"Yes. So what?"

"It is a question of rank and authority, Mr. Wyatt," Adams replied casually. Then he turned and walked back to the defense table.

"I still don't understand," the witness muttered. "So what if they didn't fire the first time?"

Justice Trowbridge folded his hands, and then leaned toward the witness.

"I believe the point that counsel is making," the judge said, "is that the order of an officer, such as a captain, would be followed immediately. Whereas the command of another...for instance, a command from an ordinary foot soldier...might cause the other soldiers to hesitate..."

Wyatt's face seemed confused. But then the light broke in on him, and when it did, he spoke up, while still in the witness box.

"You mean to say that one of his soldiers might have given that order to—"

"Mr. Wyatt!" Robert Treat Paine shouted out, to stop his witness from saying anything further damaging to the prosecution's case. Then Paine strode quickly up in front of Wyatt.

"Did I hear correctly that you saw no clubs or weapons among the crowd of victims who were fired upon?"

"That's right, sir."

"No weapons," Paine said, then turning to the jury and opening his arms wide in bewilderment. "You mean to say that they were totally unarmed?"

"Yes, sir."

"And yet Captain Preston ordered his men to load and ready their weapons against these unarmed civilians?"

"He did indeed."

"And the soldiers were ordered to fire upon unarmed civilians?"

"*Someone* ordered them to shoot, that's for certain..."

"Have you ever seen or heard of such a thing ever occurring before, sir? A squad of trained soldiers firing their muskets directly at unarmed civilians?"

"Not in no civilized nation, I certainly haven't. No, sir."

Paine nodded in dramatic agreement and then dismissed the witness.

Wyatt climbed down from the witness box and quickly walked through the courtroom. But now, something was different from when he first entered the courtroom before his testimony.

Now, Wyatt's face had an uncertainty about it. Like the look of a boy sitting in front of a wooden puzzle, trying to figure out where a small piece was supposed to fit.

Nathan's gaze followed Wyatt's exit through the courtroom until he noticed someone seated in the very last row.

It was Samuel Adams. His arms were crossed across his chest, and he had a lip-pursing scowl on his face. Seated next to him were several members of the Sons of Liberty, who were equally outraged.

"I think we have made some enemies today," Nathan whispered to Adams, and then motioned for him to notice his cousin Samuel in the back of the courtroom.

"Not surprising," Adams replied. "They are wondering, at this very moment, whether, as part of my defense, I will try to show that our patriot brothers, the Sons of Liberty, had actually provoked that mob into attacking the soldiers in the first place."

Nathan thought on the matter for a few seconds, and then his eyes widened, as he considered the devastating impact that such an argument would likely have on the future of the patriot cause in Boston, and even beyond.

"Will you, sir," Nathan asked in a low whisper, "have to make that argument in this trial?"

Adams did not answer. But he only mounted a meager smile and then turned back to his notes, as Robert Treat Paine announced his next witness.

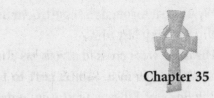

Chapter 35

The prosecution then followed up with several witnesses who, more or less, both corroborated, and yet also opposed, the Crown's theory of the crime. Some testified, as the prosecution was trying to show, that Captain Preston had issued the order to fire; yet those who did also confessed that they either did not recall where the captain was standing at the time, or else they recalled him standing in front of the soldiers. Those who placed the captain squarely behind the soldiers could not swear that they heard the captain actually give the order for the troops to fire.

But the final witness of the prosecution revealed a devilishly effective ploy by the Crown's lawyers. His name was John Wilme. The purpose in calling him was to enter into evidence, for the first time, facts that suggested the clear, premeditated intent by the British military command to eventually put down the Boston patriots with excessive force; in fact, with deadly force should the opportunity arise.

"Mr. Wilme," Robert Treat Paine began, "you are a merchant here in Boston, are you not?"

"Aye, I am, it's a fact," he replied.

"Your shop has been frequented by English soldiers, has it not?"

"Yes, sir."

"And English officers also?"

"It has."

"Do you know Captain Preston?"

"I do. Very well."

"He has frequented your place of business?"

"Yes, along with other officers…"

"Other officers, such as Officer Christopher Rumbly, also an English captain?"

"Yes."

"Have you ever seen Captain Rumbly together with Captain Preston?"

"I have, sir. In fact, sir, both captains have come in my shop together."

"Do they seem to enjoy each other's company?"

"They do. They often jest with one another. Talk about their wives and families back in England. Quite often."

"Have you ever heard Captain Rumbly say something that Captain Preston disputed?"

"No, can't say that I have…"

"Now then, shortly before the massacre of the civilians in this case, did both captains happen to come into your place of business?"

"Yes, but then Captain Preston left. And only Captain Rumbly remained."

"Did he say something about 'blood running in the streets of Boston'?"

"He did, I am afraid."

"What did he say?"

"Captain Rumbly said, and it startled me when he uttered it…he said that at the sign of any disturbance the English would march their troops right up to King Street...and that they had been in battle before...and that when the shooting began, they would make sure their aim was sure, and not miss, and that the blood was soon to run in the streets of Boston. It practically made me shiver down my spine to hear such a thing."

"And then, just hours later, Captain Preston's men were ordered up King Street, just like you were told it would happen, and soon those same English troops were firing on the crowd, killing them dead where they stood—just as he said it would happen?"

"Yes, sir. Exactly as the captain said it would."

"And moments before Captain Rumbly said that to you, he had been discussing something with Captain Preston?"

"That is the truth, yes sir."

"And Captain Preston then left, and then commanded his men... and then the shooting began. Right?"

"Yes. And the blood did run in the streets of Boston..."

Pained nodded in agreement, and then walked back to his seat, slowly passing by the jury box where the jurors were still fixed on the witness and his last, powerful description of the Boston massacre.

John Adams rose to his feet and strolled to the witness. Nathan had now learned not to judge Adams' grasp of the case by his casual demeanor.

"Mr. Wilme," Adams began. "You have spoken a great deal about Captain Rumbly, but very little about Captain Preston. You do realize, do you not, that it is Captain Preston on trial here today...and not Captain Rumbly? You do know that?"

"Yes, I did gather that."

"Good. Now that we have established that as fact, let me ask you another, fairly simple question." Now Adams was starting to build up steam, and his pace was getting quicker. "Would you tell the good jury of men over there, sitting in the jury box, what regiment Captain Rumbly belonged to?"

The witness had to think for a moment. Then he remembered and called it right out.

"Yes. I remember now—"

But before the witness could continue his answer a man's voice rang out, saying, "Stop!"

Adams looked around.

John Hodgson, the short, stout court reporter, was waving his writing hand in the air, moving his fingers.

"Your Honor, I need a moment. My hand's gettin' a cramp most awful while I am struggling to take the record of all of this..."

"Yes, most certainly," Justice Trowbridge said sympathetically. "And Mr. Adams, do try to talk slower so that our court reporter can keep up."

Adams smiled and nodded. But he was clenching his jaw a bit, as he was about to drive home a significant point, and the court reporter's interruption couldn't have come at a worse time.

After a few minutes of flexing his hand and his digits, Hodgson nodded to the judge, and Justice Trowbridge gave the signal to Adams to proceed.

"You were about to say what regiment Captain Rumbly belonged to."

"Oh, Captain Rumbly...I thought you meant Captain Preston..." the witness said.

John Adams could not help but roll his eyes in dismay.

"Captain Rumbly, man. Give us the regiment he belonged to."

"Rumbly belonged to the 14th regiment."

"Very well," Adams said. Then he took a few steps toward the jury, until he stood directly in front of them. And, like a conductor of an orchestra, he reached out his left hand, with his back to the witness, and with the point of his index finger, directed his question to be answered: "and tell the jury what regiment Captain Preston and his soldiers belonged to."

"The 29th regiment."

"Was it Captain Rumbly's regiment out in the streets that day, shooting at the mob?"

"No, sir."

"Was it Captain Rumbly commanding the soldiers that day of the shooting?"

"No, it wasn't."

"No, of course not," Adams said sarcastically. "And you did not overhear what Captain Rumbly said to Captain Preston, or vice-versa, right?"

"No, I didn't. I couldn't rightly hear..."

"For all you knew, they were discussing the rules of lawn bowling, or the migratory patterns of birds!"

"I truly cannot say what they were talking about..."

Now Adams was starting to boil into full, righteous fury, and he was aiming it at his nemesis, Robert Treat Paine.

Adams delivered his final questions, which were more like closing arguments, while standing directly in front of the prosecution table, looking Paine straight in the eye as he spoke.

"But the prosecution lawyer, Mr. Paine, has called you here, to this courtroom, and sworn you to tell the truth, in a capital case, where an innocent man may hang if the truth is disguised or hidden; and he has asked you to testify...not about the innocent man on trial—Captain Preston—no! Instead, he has asked you about another officer in another regiment altogether, and then hoped that the jury would believe that there was some shadowy conspiracy afoot between the two…a conspiracy, I might add, that has neither been proven, nor even referred to by Mr. Paine. And it has not been referred to by Mr. Paine because he is totally incapable of proving such a ridiculous conspiracy because *none ever existed!*"

Paine finally had enough. He leaped to his feet bellowing several objections, all in a row and quite jumbled together. The last objection included the words "unethical," "scandalous," and "character assassination."

Justice Trowbridge calmly considered the matter and pronounced his ruling.

"There is only one good objection amidst your entire sea of complaints," the judge said. "The question is a compound one, with many compound elements…"

"Mr. Wilme," Adams said briskly. "My question was rather long. But considering each part of my long question, is there any individual part that you would disagree with?"

Paine was leaning forward, ready to pounce on Adams with another objection. But he couldn't quite figure out why Adams' question was objectionable; only that he knew he wanted it to be so, and desperately wished he could mount an intelligent argument to bring about that result.

While Paine was wrestling with that legal conundrum, the witness finally decided to answer.

"Well, Mr. Adams," he concluded. "I would say that, everything considered, you summed it all up pretty good."

As Adams walked briskly back to the defense table, having concluded his cross-examination, Nathan wanted to look at the faces of the jurors. But he was afraid to do it, even as he was afraid to take a breath. So he stared at the table in front of him instead.

The courtroom was stone cold silent.

Then a voice was heard. It was Robert Treat Paine. He had struggled with the decision on whether to conduct further rebuttal examination of the witness. To mitigate some of the damage. But he was too good a trial lawyer to give in to that temptation. The trial of murder cases was always an untidy business. He decided, purely as a tactical matter, to leave the untidiness untidy, rather than try to sweep it up, and in the process litter the courtroom with just more dust.

"The prosecution," he announced, "has decided to rest."

While Paine slowly seated himself, trying to look reassured, John Hodgson, the court reporter, lifted his right hand, and quickly took the opportunity to begin wriggling his fingers in an effort to regain the feeling in his writing hand.

John Adams looked down at his long list of defense witnesses. Then he looked over at Nathan.

"It is now time," he whispered, "to place our trust in the God of all justice."

Chapter 36

While Nathan was walking home he was pondering the final words uttered by John Adams in the courtroom. They were cryptic, and Nathan wanted to ask Adams what he meant.

But Justice Trowbridge took the opportunity to close testimony for the day, and ordered that the trial be commenced the next morning at nine o'clock. At that time the defense would present its case. Adams quickly told Nathan that he needed to go directly home, to attend to some family business with Abigail. And then he shuffled his papers, thrust them in his leather bag, and disappeared quickly out of sight.

When Nathan stepped inside the house, he was greeted by Deborah, who was rocking a crying baby in the rocking chair. She looked distraught and tired. Nathan could smell the odor of burned fish in the pot hanging over the fireplace in the kitchen. He quickly hurried into the kitchen and lifted the pot lid with a rag, revealing a pile of simmering trout that was black, and stuck to the bottom of the pot. He lifted the pot off the hook and placed it on the brick hearth to cool. Then he walked into the front room where Deborah was sitting with their baby.

"I was just thinking," he said with a smile, kneeling next to Deborah, "how much I was *not* in the mood for fish tonight."

Deborah had been holding back tears in her eyes. But now she burst into laughter. The baby started crying louder. And so they both laughed all over again.

Nathan offered to fix them a simple meal that he was able to quickly assemble for his wife—some cooked vegetables, salt pork, cheese, and bread.

Finally when baby William was down and slumbering in his cradle, Nathan and Deborah quietly stole into the kitchen for the meal Nathan had prepared. Deborah was feeling bad that she wasn't able to have dinner ready.

"I am so sorry I didn't have a hot meal for you after your day at trial." she said.

"I had the easy part, just pulling some food together from here and there…you had the important job…caring for wee William."

As they ate and spoke in quiet tones so as to not awaken little William, Deborah asked him about the case.

Nathan explained in great detail the voir dire, and the various witnesses called by the prosecution.

"So, tomorrow the defense case is presented?" she asked.

"It is. But Mr. Adams said something at the end of court that puzzled me."

"What was it?"

"He said—that it was now time to 'place our trust in the God of all justice.'"

"I don't think that's odd," Deborah said, munching on a crust of bread with some cheese on it. "You said Mr. Adams is a godly man. His wife, Abigail, certainly is godly. Why wouldn't he seek God's sense of justice in the matter?"

"It wasn't exactly what he said. I do agree with you that he is the type of man who remembers the role of God in the administration of the law. No, it was more the *timing* of what he said. It was just after the prosecution rested its case, knowing that we would have to present our defense witnesses the next day."

"Did you ask him to spell it out for you?"

"I didn't have the chance…he dashed out of the courtroom before I could speak to him further about it."

"So, what do you think he meant?"

"I think he means to change our strategy. That's what I think. And I think he means to take a dangerous risk in doing so…"

"How would he change your defense?"

"I'm not sure," Nathan said, spooning some cooked vegetables into his mouth. "But of this I am certain…we had a very long list of potential witnesses that we were going to call in our defense case. But now, with his comments on trusting God…I don't know. I really don't."

"Well, you will share your mind with him, tomorrow, when you learn of this new strategy?"

"I will. You know I will. But he is my superior. I will have to abide by his decision."

Deborah nodded, and for a while they were quiet while they ate. Then Nathan asked about William, and how Deborah's day was spent.

They talked for a long while, enjoying the quiet and the chance to share with each other. Finally Deborah pulled a letter from her apron pocket.

"Look, this came today!" she said. "It's from your brother Robby."

Nathan broke the seal and opened it immediately and read it out loud.

In the letter, Robby explained that "due to disconcerting circumstances" he was forced to leave the employ of Jared Hollings; but Robby did not elaborate. Nathan shook his head at that.

"I wonder what form of trouble he has gotten himself into now," he muttered.

But then Robby explained in the letter how he had moved south to North Carolina, and was now in the employ of one Hadfield Fergusson, an elderly, dirt-poor farmer.

"He has little by way of crops, just a few livestock, and his small house is ramshackle, and the roof leaks, and some of the boards are pulled away. His fences need mending. There is much work for me here. He has given me a bedroom in the main house, and some meager meals. I am grateful for that. I feel that somehow Providence has brought me here, and so I will stay on here a while. He is a good man, though I do not think that he knows the Lord Jesus Christ. But he has taken me in with great warmth and much kindness."

When Nathan finished the letter he laid it on the wood board table, and gave a big sigh.

"At least Robby loves the Lord and seeks His divine will in his journeys..."

After considering what his wife had said, Nathan smiled, and nodded. But he said nothing further regarding Robby.

Later that night, after little William arose for another nursing, while Deborah tended to the baby, Nathan carried the cradle up the stairs to their bedroom and placed it on the other side of the room, though close enough for them to hear him if he cried.

William was put to bed, and Nathan and Deborah, after donning their nightshirts, quietly slipped under the goose feather quilt on their four-poster. As Deborah cuddled with him, Nathan whispered evening prayers. He prayed for William, and Deborah, and his trial the next day, and Edward and Edith. And then he ended by praying for Robby.

"As he wanders the world," Nathan prayed in a hushed voice, "may he never wander from You, Lord..."

Then, in a matter of minutes, both husband and wife were both fast asleep.

Chapter 37

Nathan reported to the courtroom early the next day, just so he could engage John Adams in an effort to have him explain his comment from the day before.

"You said we must now trust in God," he said to Adams at the counsel table. "What did you mean?"

"Did you listen carefully to the prosecution's witnesses thus far?" Adams asked.

"Most certainly."

"And what have you heard?"

"You mean, all of their testimony?"

"No, I don't mean that," Adams said in a slightly scolding voice. "I mean the sum total of their evidence, man. What conclusions did you reach?"

"Only this, I think," Nathan said, trying to discern Adams' point. "That they have failed to agree on very many points of fact, it seems to me..."

"Precisely!" Adams responded. "There is confusion. Contradiction. That's where the case lies as of now."

"So how does that relate to trusting God?"

"Because this long list of witnesses," and with that he pointed to the names of the parchment in front of him, "is about to get much shorter."

"Why?"

"Because we don't want the prosecution to use our witnesses to shore up the leaks in its own dike. Let the leaks continue. May the water seep through the holes in its case like a sieve. We can only afford to call those witnesses who are clearly in our favor, and who pose no possibility of being used to the advantage of the Crown's prosecutors...to plug the holes in their dike."

"How short is our list of witnesses going to be?" Nathan asked.

Adams took his pen, dipped it in the inkwell in the table, and then drew a line through every single name on the defense witness list except two.

The first was Captain Thomas Preston himself. Adams would question him.

And the second was a surprise witness. That would be the last witness they would call. And Nathan had been assigned to handle his questioning.

"You realize the risk we take in limiting our case to only two witnesses?" Adams said. "If we are wrong, and we fail to convince the jury of Captain Preston's innocence through these two, meager witnesses...then all will be lost for our client."

And then he added something else.

"And in a way, Nathan, your witness," Adams said nodding to Nathan and tapping his finger on the last name on the witness list, one of the two names that had not been crossed out, "the witness you will be examining, he may prove, in the end, to be the most important witness in this entire trial."

Nathan had little time to meditate on Adams' extraordinary

statement. Suddenly, the bailiffs and the court clerk scurried into the courtroom. Then John Hodgson, the court stenographer, closely followed behind, with his large diary of the proceedings tucked under his arm.

Hogdson sat down, opened his diary, flipped open the brass cover on the inkwell of his desk, dipped his quill in, and held his hand poised, ready to write.

The clerk called all to rise for the Honorable Edmund Trowbridge.

Justice Trowbridge strode in, paused to brush a piece of dust off his scarlet robes, and sat down, tugging very discreetly at the back of his long white wig of ornate curls, so that his wig was perfectly placed on his head. Then he called the case.

"Mr. Adams, is the defense ready to proceed with its case?"

"We are, Your Honor," Adams said. Then he turned to his right side. Sitting next to Nathan was Captain Preston. He was dressed in his red and gold officer's parade coat. His hat, including its white plume, was placed on the table in front of him. He was sitting rigidly in his chair, his back mortar-and-brick straight.

Looking directly at his client, then casting his eye over to the jury box, Adams made his announcement.

"The defense calls Captain Thomas Preston."

A murmur rippled through the courtroom.

Preston stood up, and strode to the witness box where he was sworn in.

"Before the eyes of God," the clerk intoned, "and before this Honorable Superior Court, and in the sight of His Majesty's Crown, George the Third, King of England, and Defender of the Faith, do you hereby swear to tell the truth in all matters of which inquiry is made of you today?"

"I do," Preston said loudly. Then he sat down, adjusting the tails of his coat as he did.

Adams began his direct examination with painstaking detail. He started with the English officer's personal background, and his family history in England. Then he moved to his military training.

"Were you, in your prior military experience, engaged in several significant battles in the French and Indian hostilities?" Adams asked.

"I was," Preston answered.

"And were you decorated for valor in your conduct during those hostilities?"

"I was."

"And as we all know, the Crown of England sent its troops into battle for the protection of these colonies, Massachusetts included, from the violent overreaching and tyrannies of France?"

"That is true, sir."

Then Adams turned his questioning on Captain Preston's assignment to Boston.

"As a military officer, did you have authorization to dispute your assignment, as captain, over your soldiers here in the city of Boston?"

"As a military officer, I had no discretion in the matter. My job was to obey the orders that I received from my commanding officer."

"And so you were ordered to report to Boston, with your men, and you did so?"

"Exactly, sir."

"Even if you may have harbored some personal misgivings about the mission? The mission, being, the quartering and stationing of a standing army among fellow Englishmen, in English colonies, during peacetime?"

"My job, sir, was not to evaluate the mission, unless asked, but rather to carry it out."

"And if asked, you would have voiced your opinions?"

"If asked by my commanding officer, that is correct, sir."

"Were you ever asked?"

"I was not, sir."

Then Adams moved to the events of March 5, 1770. He carefully inquired about the prior acts of mob violence that had occurred in Boston.

As he did, Samuel Adams, patriot leader, and dubbed the chief "agitator" among the Sons of Liberty by the English, was seated in his usual spot, in the very last row of benches in the courtroom.

But as his cousin went in the line of questioning that described prior riots by the patriots, Samuel Adams leaned forward, resting his arms on the bench in front of him; his eyes fixed on John Adams.

"Some in this courtroom," John Adams said, prefacing his next question, "would exhort me to now shepherd my questions, like obedient sheep, into a certain direction…into the legal sheepfold, as it were, where we may dwell on such things as the cause of this mob violence that we speak of today…"

There was a stunned hush in the courtroom.

"Or even more specifically," Adams continued, in a high, crisp voice, "the names of the men, and the identities of those patriot colonial groups that may have actually had a part in stimulating— whether wittingly or unwittingly we do not know—but had a part nevertheless, in causing the outbreak in violence, and even the mob violence that occurred on this March the last, the fifth day."

Samuel Adams and his patriot partners were fixed like stone statues, in suspended animation, waiting for John Adams' next words.

There had long been murmurings amid the Tories and the English overseers in Massachusetts that Samuel Adams himself, along with his Sons of Liberty, may have actually instigated some of the men to confront Captain Preston and his soldiers, and which led to the tragic massacre that ensued.

It was clear to Samuel Adams, indeed to John Adams as well, that if evidence were introduced that in the least even *suggested* such patriot instigation, the entire fabric of patriot resistance in New England could quickly unravel.

The moment was now there. The one that Samuel Adams and his men had been waiting for. The courtroom was packed not only with the curious, but all with the stouthearted. Paul Revere had left his engraving shop and was in the row of patriots along with Sam Adams. In the far corner, prosperous merchant John Hancock was standing, with his arms tightly crossed, waiting without a breath, for the next words of John Adams; this same man who had delivered some of the most rousing speeches Hancock had ever heard on the matter of English tyranny and the need for the recognition of colonial rights, but now seemed perched on the precipice of betrayal of every patriot in every colony of the Americas.

Justice Trowbridge stopped his note-taking and looked up; then he placed his quill pen on the bench and folded his hands, awaiting Adams' next question.

Would Adams reveal some patriot conspiracy of violence as a defense for his client's military judgments?

That was the question that seemed apparent to every soul in that Boston courtroom.

But Adams' next words were not designed to address the minds of the citizens who were attending the trial; or even his cousin

Samuel who he knew to be listening, steely-eyed, in the last row of the courtroom.

Or even the king's prosecutors, Quincy and Paine, who were staring with grim faces at their table, squinting at Adams, wondering where he was heading.

No, John Adams' next statement was intended for the ears of Justice Trowbridge, the implacable, careful, scholarly judge who was trying this case.

"However," John Adams continued, "I shall refrain from asking any questions whatsoever on such a speculative and inherently political issue."

Then, as the entire human assembly seemed to relax back in their seats, Adams announced the direction of his next questions.

"Instead," he said, "I will ask you, Captain Preston, to describe the events of March the fifth."

Preston dutifully nodded, and proceeded to recall how he and his men had been summoned to the Crown's Customs House in the square, near King Street, to protect a military sentry who was being harassed by a crowd of Boston citizens.

How he arranged them in a semicircle and ordered their bayonets fixed in the event of a rush by the crowd.

"The crowd grew larger and uglier," Preston said with restraint in his voice. "We were sizably outnumbered."

"Were there weapons?" he asked.

"There were clubs in the hands of some; I do know that Mr. Attucks, one of the unfortunate men who was killed that day, had a club, as did several seamen standing with him."

"Did they use the clubs?"

"Just before shots were fired, the clubs were swung at us…I was struck, as were several of my men."

"Were there other weapons?"

"Rocks were thrown, and large chunks of ice, and other missiles, some were bottles, I believe."

"Did you, Captain Preston, ever give an order for your men to fire?"

Preston took a breath, then directed his gaze over to the jurymen in the box.

"I did not, sir."

"Where were you, relative to your men, when the shots began to be fired?"

"Directly in front of my men."

"Were you hit by any of the shot from those muskets?"

"Miraculously no, sir. I heard shot whistling past my head from the muskets of my men, but by the grace of God, I was not hit."

"But some men from Boston were hit, were they not?"

"Yes sir, regrettably that is true. And several died."

"What did you do after the first shots were fired?"

"I took my sword and batted the rifle barrels of my men downward, toward the ground, and shouted for them to cease firing."

"When the mob dispersed, did you call for medical attention for the wounded?"

"I did, sir."

Adams took a long breath, nodded, smiled at Preston, and then announced that he had no further questions.

Robert Treat Paine strode up to the witness quickly. He had something in his hand, behind his back.

"Captain Preston," he began in his cross-examination, "you say it was not your place to question the wisdom of the order from the Crown to place troops in Boston, correct? You have no opinion on that matter?"

"No sir, not officially."

"You have never voiced an opinion on that?"

"No, sir."

"And never voiced any opinion about the good people of Boston, whether you like them...or whether you...hate them?"

"I do not gather your meaning, sir..."

"My meaning is clear," Paine said loudly, "but your answer is not. Have you ever said or written anything about your opinion regarding the citizens of Boston?"

"I do not believe I have."

"Never?"

"I think not, sir."

"Well," Paine announced brazenly, and then with a flourish produced a piece of paper he was holding behind his back. "Then we shall now see whether you are telling this court and this jury the truth...or whether you are lying, sir...lying with black heart and corrupt soul—lying, sir, simply to save yourself from the hangman's noose!"

Chapter 38

Robert Treat Paine marched over to the witness box and laid a two-page letter on the rail in front of Captain Preston, who was now being cross-examined.

"Do you admit that the signature that appears at the end of this letter is, in fact, your signature?"

Preston glanced at it, then gave the letter back to the prosecution lawyer.

"Yes, sir, it is my signature."

"And the contents of this letter are yours, also?"

"I presume so," Preston said. "I doubt that I would have signed a letter that I did not author."

"This letter is dated several months ago, when you were in the Boston jail, awaiting trial…dated June of this year, to be exact…"

"Yes, I wrote many letters at that time, as I was concerned about my plight as a defendant in this case."

"This letter was intended for friends of yours in England?"

"It was."

"You did not suspect that it would fall into the hands of others?"

"Most certainly not."

"And for that reason, what you wrote in this letter, I would imagine, was exceptionally candid?"

"I always try to be candid..."

"But this letter, in particular, this one, contained your candid observations?"

"Yes, sir, that is correct."

Robert Treat Paine now held up the letter, and paused to slowly turn until he faced the jury box, waving the letter over his head.

"Captain Preston, do you not express your disgust for the people of Boston in this letter?"

"I would not characterize it that way..."

"You did write, did you not, in this letter, the following—*The citizens of Boston have ever used all means in their power to weaken my military regiment, and to bring them into contempt. They have promoted and aided desertions among my soldiers, by grossly and falsely promulgating lies about them. This city is full of malcontents who are maliciously trying to fish out evidence proving that the March 5 shooting was a concerted scheme to murder the inhabitants*—you wrote this, sir?"

"I did, but if I may explain—"

"Your letter. Your words?"

"Yes, sir, but if I may—"

"No, sir, you may not. You must answer my questions, not your questions."

Now Paine was feeling that he was getting close to the underbelly of this murder case. He would jab his interrogations into Preston's defense like a bayonet into the soft, fleshy part of a man's gut.

"You wrote a letter, though, about the same time, to the *Boston Gazette*, praising the citizens of Boston for *throwing aside all party and prejudice, having the utmost humanity toward me, and stepping*

forth to be advocates for truth in defense of my injured innocence…
those also were your words, were they not?"

"They were, but on a different subject…"

"So, to the citizens of Boston, you praise them for their 'humanity' toward you, but secretly, at the same time, you write to your friends in England, saying that these men of Boston are 'malicious,' and are 'malcontents,' and liars, do you not?"

"In a different context, on a different subject…"

"But those were your words about the citizens of Boston, were they not?"

"Yes, I fear they were…"

"Having despised the people of Boston, and having lied about your true feelings about them in your letter to their local newspaper, you no doubt did not care whether your soldiers fired their muskets at them that night or not, correct?"

"No sir, that is not true—"

"And I notice that you accuse the Boston citizens of *maliciously trying to fish out evidence proving that the March 5th shooting was a concerted scheme to murder the inhabitants*—your words, correct?"

"Yes, I have admitted that…"

"But the phrase 'trying to fish out evidence' is very interesting. You could have used any turn of a phrase, but you picked that one. Are you a fisherman, Captain?"

Preston paused, and for just a moment, there was a flicker of a smile, and a faraway look on his face when he answered.

"When I was younger, I fished the rivers and lakes of the lowlands of Scotland, and some of the running rivers of England…looking for trout…yes, I used to fish…"

"And did you," Paine said in a voice of brutal audacity and piercing volume, "ever fish a lake *knowing there were no fish there?*"

"No."

"So likewise," Paine said, going in for the kill, "you do not accuse the citizens of Boston of trying to manufacture *false evidence* that really was not there—but rather, as you say, you accuse them of trying to 'fish out evidence' of your conspiracy to permit soldiers to start shooting civilians…"

"I am not sure I know what you are saying…"

"Of course you do!" Paine shouted, the veins in his neck bulging, and his face reddening. "You were concerned, as you write here in this letter, that their fishing around for 'evidence' might uncover the truth that there was, as you put it, a 'concerted scheme to murder inhabitants' of Boston!"

"That is preposterous!" Preston shouted back, having reached his limit.

"Is it?" Paine asked. "I do not believe our fine jury of men will find that idea preposterous…especially since you yourself use those very same words in your secret letter to England."

Paine then grabbed the letter, plucked it from the witness rail, and tossed it over to John Adams' table.

"You may redirect your witness, and attempt to rehabilitate his testimony on this letter, Mr. Adams," Paine said with a sneer, "if you are able…and I have no doubts that you will not be able."

The letter had been a shock to both Adams and Nathan. They both had urged their client to hold nothing back, to be forthright with them about every statement, every letter, note, and diary entry he may have ever made about the March fifth massacre, so they could prepare for trial. But Preston had never told them about this letter.

Adams fingered the letter for a few seconds, his face pursed and twisted with anxiety. Then his face relaxed, and he slowly stood up and approached his client.

"Captain Preston," Adams began. "Your letter to the *Boston Ga-zette* praising the people of Boston for coming forward to help you to repair your *injured innocence* as you call it, do you mean to say that witnesses came forward to tell the truth about what happened that night?"

"I do, but there was something else..."

Adams was trying to control his witness. He knew that the case was now at a critical juncture. Any slight error could tip the case one way or another. So he tried to cut his client off.

"Yes," Adams said loudly, "but if I may, Captain, redirect your attention..."

"No, sir, with all due respect, you may not. There is something I intend to say, sir, and I will say it."

Paine was starting to smile. So was Mr. Quincy at his side. They thought they were seeing the unraveling of the defense case before their very eyes.

"What I meant," Preston said, with emotion in his voice, though his face was as passionless as stone, "about those *stepping forth to be advocates for truth,* as I wrote in my letter...I was primarily referring to *you,* Mr. Adams, to you, and to your associate, Mr. Mackenzie, for showing such extraordinary bravery in coming to my defense, when I know it must have been a substantial sacrifice to you both, and to your families, to associate with a British officer accused of such horrible crimes against the people of Boston."

For a moment, Adams did not know what to say.

Nathan, sitting at the defense table, was taken aback by complete surprise with Captain Preston's words. And in an instant, Nathan had to struggle to fight back tears, though he did not know where they had come from, or why they were there.

Adams cleared his throat with embarrassment, glanced down

at the letter, and then, a little awkwardly, said quietly to the witness, "Thank you."

Then Adams regained his composure and continued.

"And now, as for this other letter, the one penned in June, during your imprisonment, to your friends in England, when you referred to those 'malcontents' trying to 'fish out' evidence against you...let's talk about that."

Adams was proceeding on pure hunch, now, as to what his client might say. But he also knew that a request for adjournment to discuss the letter with his client would be a disastrous tactical move—as the jury would then believe that anything that Preston said thereafter would simply be the result of being coached by his lawyer.

"Your reference, Captain, to those 'malcontents'—you no doubt refer to some colonial patriots who have rounded up sworn statements of witnesses and produced them to the prosecution?"

"Yes, that is part of it."

"What is the other part?"

"I was referring to...well, to be very blunt...I was referring to the Crown's two prosecutors, who seem overzealous to see me hang as a sacrificial lamb and with little care for the truth of what happened that night."

Ordinarily, Robert Treat Paine would have leaped to his feet and screamed out an objection. But this time he didn't.

And that frightened John Adams.

Paine must really have a dagger waiting for us if he is not objecting, Adams thought to himself.

With that, Adams sat down and rested his redirect questioning.

But now Paine rose.

"I have re-cross now," he announced loudly to the bench.

Justice Trowbridge nodded for him to proceed.

"Captain," Paine commenced, "you mentioned the local colonial patriots as the 'malcontents.' And during Mr. Adams' original direct examination, he said he would refrain from mentioning those local radicals who instigated the riot that gave you and your men the excuse to murder innocent civilians. Yet Mr. Adams has now opened the door to such an inquiry. So here we go…"

And with that Paine raised his voice to an even higher octave.

"Will you name the names, sir, of the men, these Sons of Liberty, who you understand instigated the mob riot that night?"

As Paine asked that question, he pointed directly to Samuel Adams, who was seated in the rear of the courtroom.

John Adams was on his feet objecting.

"This is beyond the scope of direct examination," Adams barked out. "I specifically advised the court, indeed this entire courtroom, my decision *not to pursue that line of questioning.* The prosecution therefore is barred from going into that on cross-examination or re-cross."

"Mr. Adams waived that limitation, as he opened the door to it," Paine countered loudly, "when he mentioned that business about 'malcontents' being local Boston 'patriots' as he called them. Having opened the door," Pained concluded, "Mr. Adams cannot object if I choose to walk through it."

Justice Trowbridge was clearly troubled by John Adams' reference to "malcontents," as being one and the same with the "patriots" of Boston, which was just another name for the controversial Sons of Liberty. The judge was clearly struggling with whether to open the trial wide to testimony about whether Samuel Adams and others had whipped the mob into a frenzy that night.

As the judge was considering how to rule, Robert Treat Paine quickly slipped over to the defense counsel's table and leaned down so that John Adams could hear him.

"Just one more mistake," Paine said, "by attorney John Adams. But this time it's far worse than a defective writ. This time your client will hang for it."

"You're blocking my view," Adams responded calmly. "Please remove yourself from defense counsel's table."

After a few minutes, Justice Trowbridge announced he had reached a ruling.

"My ruling," he said, "is based on established precedents. A party, such as Mr. Adams, may waive the limitations he has placed on his direct examination, by opening up an area of new ground in his re-direct questioning."

The ruling looked to be a catastrophe for Adams, and Nathan, and Captain Preston.

"However," he added, "the waiver must be clear, and unambiguous, and unequivocal. Mr. Adams, your reference to local Boston 'malcontents' may have been ill-advised, but it did not constitute waiver. Mr. Paine, you shall not be allowed to venture into that line of questioning."

Paine's expression reflected a valiant attempt to save face.

But his voice did quiver a bit when he finally announced how he would proceed.

"My examination of this witness...is...finished," he said and sat down.

Adams finally exhaled with relief.

Then he turned to Nathan.

"All right, then," Adams said, "I think I have repaired *some* of the damage done to my client by Robert Treat Paine. Though I regret to say, not *all* the damage."

Then he put his hand on Nathan's shoulder and offered his last comment on the subject.

"It's all up to you," Adams said. "Up to you with this last witness. I am sorry to place this on your shoulders…but it has come to this…you must win this case now, Nathan. You must…"

Chapter 39

Nathan tried not to consider the weight of responsibility he bore. As Captain Preston dismounted from the witness box, and then walked back to his seat, Nathan tried to shake the feeling that he might be responsible for an innocent man being executed.

"We call," Nathan began, "Dr. John Jefferies, for the defense."

Prosecutors Quincy and Paine bolted upright in their chairs. And then began whispering intensely to each other.

A middle-aged, well dressed man in a long, well-tailored black coat and powdered wig and starched white frock made his way to the witness box and was sworn in.

"Your name?" Nathan asked.

"John Jefferies."

"You reside in Boston?"

"Yes. And work here as well."

"What is your profession?"

"I am a medical surgeon."

"Do you know Mr. Patrick Carr?"

"I do."

"Did you have occasion to be with Mr. Carr on the day he died?"

"I regret to say that I did."

"When was that?"

"On the ninth day after the March shooting in the square."

"From what cause, sir, did he die?"

"From musket shot piercing his body. He died of gunshot wounds from the English soldiers' muskets. He was on the outside perimeter of the crowd when the shooting began. I was his attending physician during those last days of his life."

"Now Dr. Jefferies," Nathan said, "did you and Patrick Carr converse in the last days and hours of his life, about the events that led up to the March fifth shooting?"

Samuel Quincy was now poised to object, if the questioning continued in the same line. He had told his co-counsel Robert Treat Paine to stand down; that his performance with the last witness was lackluster, and that "he was going to take over the prosecution case so we have at least someone in an officers' coat to hang when this is all over."

Dr. Jefferies, a little oblivious to the import of that juncture of the case, answered matter-of-factly.

"Oh yes," he said. "He and I conversed a great deal about the shooting, right up to the point at which he died."

"Very well," Nathan said. "Let us now discuss what he told you…"

Now Quincy was on his feet.

"Objection!" he shouted. "Your Honor, this young advocate's zealousness has obviously exceeded his recollection of the law. It is fundamental that this court cannot admit testimony from one witness quoting another who is not present in court. That is clearly hearsay. Further, testimony about transactions with a man now deceased violates the dead man's rule."

"Counsel?" Justice Trowbridge asked, motioning with his index finger for Nathan and Quincy to approach the bench, outside the earshot of the jurors, who were all leaning forward, staring at Nathan.

When both lawyers were at the side of the judge's bench, he engaged them in a low, hushed voice.

"Mr. Mackenzie," he began, "what road are you taking with this line of questioning? While I do not believe that the dead man's rule applies, as that concerns legal transactions, not conversations as such, the quite primary point is this: Dr. Jefferies' patient, Mr. Carr, is dead. Thus, isn't this all clearly hearsay?"

"No, Your Honor," Nathan replied. "I believe that Patrick Carr knew he was approaching death. Thus, whatever he said would have constituted a dying declaration, and as such, is an exception to the hearsay rule."

"But Your Honor," Quincy shot back, "we don't know what kind of declaration Patrick Carr made to his physician. Perhaps he was confessing guilt over a gambling debt…or perhaps mourning that he would never see his children again…we cannot qualify this as a dying declaration relevant to this case based on the scant record before us now."

"Mr. Mackenzie," the judge inquired. "What do you propose that Dr. Jefferies will say?"

"He will recite Patrick Carr's deathbed description of the incident that took his life…and his opinion about the guilt or innocence of Captain Preston and his men—"

"Patrick Carr is not entitled to any opinion as to guilt or innocence," Quincy barked out.

"He has the *greatest right!*" Nathan heard himself roar back. "He gave his life for the right to make such a judgment. God will surely judge every one of us today if Patrick Carr's dying words—uttered before being ushered into the throne room of the Almighty—are silenced, and hidden, and locked up forever. God will judge us all for that!"

Quincy was so shocked at Nathan's outburst he was speechless.

Judge Trowbridge was stupefied.

John Hogdson, the court stenographer, shifted nervously in his chair, and it creaked a bit as he did.

The judge did not take his eyes off Nathan. There was complete silence, but Justice Trowbridge continued to stare Nathan in the eye.

Then, after an almost interminable period of quiet, Justice Trowbridge made his ruling.

"Mr. Mackenzie, you may put the question to the witness. Mr. Quincy, your objection is overruled. And Mr. Mackenzie—do not try the court's patience, *ever again.*"

"I won't, Your Honor," Nathan said, bowed a little, and then resumed his position standing in front of the witness.

"Doctor," he began again, "please tell us what Patrick Carr said about the incident that cost him his life."

"He said," Dr. Jefferies explained, "that he was a native of Ireland; he grew up there. He had many occasions to see mob violence against British rule in that country…he had even seen soldiers fire upon mobs during such incidents. But Mr. Carr also said that he had never seen soldiers—or any officer for that matter, meaning Captain Preston—endure so much violence, and so much physical assault before they finally fired, as Mr. Carr witnessed in the case of the Boston massacre wherein he was mortally wounded."

"Did he say anything else?"

"He did indeed."

"What did he say?"

"That he forgave the man whose musket fired the shot into him—and forgave the commanding officer, that would be Captain Preston—as Mr. Carr said he believed that there was *no malice in such acts, but that the captain and his men must have been trying to defend themselves...*"

"Did he die in peace?"

"I cannot read a man's soul. But as much as I can read peace on a man's face, yes...Patrick Carr, having spoken the truth about the events of that night, left this world in peace."

Nathan thanked him, then took his seat at the defense table.

Quincy was faced with an intractable dilemma. If he cross-examined the physician of the now dead Boston victim, it would be as if he were attacking the victim himself—a clearly unacceptable position to be in before the jury. On the other hand, if he let this witness go, it would appear as a sign of weakness in his case.

Prosecutor Quincy drummed his fingers nervously on the table, trying to decide.

Justice Trowbridge asked him if he had any questions for the witness.

More finger-drumming.

"Counsel," Justice Trowbridge asked again, "will you cross-examine this witness or not?"

The finger drumming stopped.

"No, Your Honor. The hour is late," Quincy said with a carefully managed smile, "and I am sure the jury is tired. We shall forgo any questions."

"The defense rests," John Adams announced as he stood up.

Justice Trowbridge dismissed the court for the day, and then informed counsel that closing arguments would commence at nine o'clock sharp the next morning.

As Nathan passed by the chair of John Hodgson, the reporter lifted a finger to get Nathan's attention.

Nathan halted in his tracks, and bent down toward the court reporter.

Hodgson had only two words to whisper to the young lawyer. *Well done.*

Chapter 40

As Adams and Nathan left the courtroom together for the day, Adams confided something in his young protégé.

"I had, during this entire trial, been wondering what approach I should use in closing arguments for Captain Preston's defense."

As they walked on, Nathan was waiting for the answer.

"But after your examination of Dr. Jefferies, it came to me. The pieces fell into place...or at least some of the pieces...this is an imprecise art we practice...but in any event I now know what I must argue tomorrow."

But, as usual, Adams would not expand on the vague strategy he mentioned to Nathan.

Nathan was exhausted and when he arrived home, he gave his apologies to Deborah for his lack of appetite, climbed the stairs, then quietly disrobed and climbed into bed. Little William was snoring and breathing loudly in his cradle.

After some time, Deborah, in her nightcap and gown, climbed into bed next to her husband.

Then she moved in closer, sliding over to his side under the covers.

After a while, just as Nathan was drifting off to sleep, Deborah started whispering to him.

"Edith came by today," she said.

There was no response from Nathan.

"You know, your sister-in-law…"

"Yes, of course."

"She said she had an announcement…"

Nathan did not respond, half lingering between sleep and wakefulness.

"Do you want to know the announcement?" she asked.

There was only silence. So she gave a little nudge to her husband.

"Do you want to know the announcement?" she asked again.

"Yes. Whatever you think," Nathan answered groggily.

"She says she is *with child*…"

"What?"

"*With child*," she said in loud whisper.

"That's good," Nathan murmured.

"It just doesn't seem right…"

"What doesn't?"

"Edith. Being in the state…she hasn't had a bit of morning sickness…none of the signs…"

"Wife," Nathan said with exasperation. "You mourn for her because she is without a child. Now she says she is with child, and you doubt her…"

"A woman has wisdom about these things," Deborah said.

Then after a moment, Deborah said, "Kiss me goodnight, husband."

Nathan groaned a little, but then he rolled over and kissed her on the lips.

And then he kissed her again. It was on the third kiss that she intervened.

"Good night, Mr. Mackenzie," she said with a little laugh, and then rolled over on her side.

In a few minutes they were both asleep.

The following morning, in court, Samuel Quincy had a confident air about him. He had stayed up all night, analyzing the testimony, organizing it, and putting together his summation. Today, he felt invincible.

John Adams, on the other hand, went home, had a good dinner with his wife, played with his children, and then after a few hours of preparation in his study, he retired to bed with Abigail.

Nathan thought he would feel relieved that his active duties were done. Adams would give the closing arguments. All Nathan had to do was sit at counsel table next to Captain Preston.

But it was different than Nathan had expected. Now that he could no longer engage the opponents—no longer argue the points, and ask the questions—the tension, in a strange way, seemed even worse; indeed, almost intolerable.

The jury was assembled. The courtroom quickly filled to overflowing.

The clerk, the bailiff, and Hodgson, the stenographer, all filed into the room.

Then Justice Trowbridge entered as he had every day of the trial, with the same announcement from the clerk, with all in the courtroom standing for his appearance.

Samuel Quincy strode up to the jury box to commence his summation.

He warmly thanked the jury for their patience, and their attention to the trial.

And then he lit into the conduct of Captain Preston.

Quincy had honed the case down to a frighteningly simple and elegant picture of abject hatred by an English officer for the local civilian population.

He mentioned the Captain's letter, "wherein this British officer expressed his disgust for the citizens of Boston."

He then matched that with the testimony of John Wilme, the local merchant who had heard a fellow British officer and friend of Captain Preston predict that there would be *blood running in the streets of Boston soon,* and then that very night the massacre took place.

"Now I understand," Quincy argued, "that you could still reject this picture of Captain Preston's total guilt, the evidence of his premeditated murder, were it not for one absolutely undeniable fact that rises above all others: even if we accept the implausible testimony of the defense, that the civilians in that crowd that night were carrying sticks, and maybe threw some snowballs at the soldiers... nevertheless, this much is incontrovertible and undeniable...the civilians *had no guns of any kind*...and the only guns belonged to the soldiers."

Then Quincy concluded brilliantly.

"Captain Preston ordered the soldiers to fix bayonets, and indeed they did just that. Why, I ask you, did he also order them to prime and load their muskets as well? If Preston had stopped at the order for bayonets, they could easily have controlled the mob without firing on them. And today, several men would be returning to their homes for meals with their wives, and could pat their sons on their heads. Instead, today they lie, cold and dead, in the graveyards of Boston. But Preston did more than just order the soldiers to load their weapons, thus giving rise to the catastrophe that ensued…indeed I believe he was *to the rear of the troops when the shots were fired.* What is the proof, as some witnesses say he was there, and some thought he was in the front? The evidence is this…and mark it well, men…*not a hair on his head was touched by the musket shot*…yet several men who stood in front of the soldiers were killed where they stood…do you believe that Captain Preston would have escaped any injury if he had been standing at the fore of his men as he claims?"

Now Quincy's voice was low, and intense.

"And why was he at the rear of the soldiers? Because that is the standard position of a commanding officer who is about to order his men to commence firing. Preston's own letter to his English friends is the capstone…he fears that local Bostonians will 'fish out' the true evidence of his plan to murder innocent inhabitants of this fair city. Gentlemen of the jury, the English army is a paragon of might and discipline. But amidst this stellar institution there is a dastardly and evil officer…a coward. And a liar. And a murderer. The English army needs to be relieved of him. The city of Boston needs to be rid of him. And the world needs to be cleansed of the likes of him. He is guilty of murder. Find him so, men. And put this matter to rest forever, and restore quietude and order to the city of Boston."

It was at that point, after hearing the summation of Quincy, that Nathan feared that this case could not be won. And even worse than that, he wondered whether their client was really innocent after all. Quincy's arguments seemed flawless.

John Adams got up slowly and approached the jury box.

That morning, before the court convened, Nathan asked Adams what his summation would include.

Adams didn't answer the question, exactly. Instead he gave Nathan a word picture.

"When you argue to a jury," he said, "you have to wrap up the case like a package in brown paper with string. The important thing, though, is it has to be small enough to tuck under their arm. If they have to carry it with both hands, you've lost."

When Adams started his summation, he began simply. He listed with monotonous precision each of the Crown's witnesses and then described the factual contradictions between them all.

"If you are going to hang a man," he said, "at least have the decency to base it on at least one witness who got it right. But men of the jury, none of the prosecution witnesses got it right."

Then he quickly stitched his tack, as if he were dancing a reel.

"So, if the prosecution witnesses have it wrong, who has it right?" he asked.

"Gentlemen, facts are stubborn things. And facts produce truth. And truth is the most stubborn thing of all. Hide it if you will. Try to paint it over with varnish. But in the end, if you look for it, it shows itself. Recall Captain Preston's testimony? He was in the front of the men. He did not give the command to fire. One of the prosecution witnesses said the firing did not start with the first command. Who gave the command? It was one of the soldiers—not an officer—for the men hesitated at first. Proof that the Captain had not given that order. Even the prosecution witnesses admit that after the first volley, Captain Preston struck at the musket barrels of his soldiers with his sword as he commanded them to cease firing...how could he do that if he were behind them? And *why* would he have done that if, as the Crown suggests, he hated the citizens of Boston and wanted an excuse to fire upon them?"

Then Adams knotted the string around the entire defense case.

"Recall Patrick Carr, a victim of the shooting, the most honest

man in this trial, whose words come to us from beyond the grave…
his words show that he saw no malice in the actions of Captain
Preston, and found no fault against him at all. He said so on his
deathbed, men. With his last dying breath."

Now Adams was about to tuck the package under the arms of
the jurors.

"But note the closing words of the Crown's prosecutor, men.
Mark them well. He tells you…*put this matter to rest forever, and
restore quietude and order to the city of Boston.* But why would he
say such a thing? Think, men, think. *Why?* Because Mr. Quincy
and Mr. Paine want to make Captain Preston hang as a sacrificial
lamb…in order to convince you that England has paid her pen-
ance for abusing our rights and depriving us of the privileges of
Englishmen. Then all shall be restored. And England shall continue
as she has in the past, to control us, to crush us…why did those
men die in the streets of Boston?

"I will tell you why…because the Crown of England saw fit
to place standing armies in the midst of Boston's citizens during
peace-time, just to intimidate them. But I tell you, men, peace with
England shall not be bought by the price of an innocent man's
hanging…not by a far cry. God in heaven will not permit us to
commit such a travesty as that. If we be patriots, then we must be
loyal to the truth above all else. And the truth, men, is that Captain
Thomas Preston is but a pawn on the chessboard of King George.
Let justice ring out today, men! Let it ring out loudly. And if it does,
then perhaps freedom will be the next to ring out tomorrow!"

Chapter 41

Just as he had promised, Hadfield Fergusson, the old North Carolina farmer, had been providing room, board, and a small coin stipend to Robby Mackenzie in return for his work around the farm. However, Fergusson's "severe lumbago" had made it hard for him to manage his horse drawn cart, particularly when it came time to attend his weekly meetings of the west country Regulators; those rough North Carolina patriots who were planning their next anti-English strategy. They meant to protest, in the strongest way possible, the Crown's abject failure to provide the most rudimentary government for them, while, at the same time, driving them into bankruptcy through exorbitant taxation and the unchecked corruption of their local English overseers.

One balmy moonlit evening, while the twelve jurors in the Boston massacre case were deliberating the fate of Captain Thomas Preston far to the chilly north, on a bumpy, backwoods dirt road down in North Carolina Robby Mackenzie was holding the reigns and driving Fergusson's one-horse cart. The two men were returning to Fergusson's split-log house following a meeting of the Regulators.

Fergusson had gone quiet for the longest time. Then, when

Robby recognized the split-rail fence that marked the boundary of Fergusson's farm, he decided to break the silence.

"Almost home, now," Robby said.

"Yep," Fergusson muttered.

After a few more minutes, Robby chimed in again.

"That sure was a lively meeting tonight…those boys seemed ready to wrestle some wildcats…"

"Uh huh," Fergusson replied.

Finally Robby decided to stir things up.

"Hey Fergusson, did I burn your mouth real bad at dinner tonight with that hot ham and grits I cooked up?"

"Nope," Fergusson said. "Why'd you ask?"

"Just wondering," Robby answered with a big grin, "I thought maybe that's why you quit using your tongue…"

Fergusson gave a chuckle and then coughed a little after he did.

"You think I've gone dumb on you?" the old farmer asked.

"Sort of…you've been real quiet…"

"Just had some things on my mind."

"Like what?"

"Like things pertaining to you, for instance…"

"How so?"

"Well," Fergusson said, "you ain't never told me what brought you to the Carolinas…all the way down from Virginia. After all, I've got you under my roof…I'm feeding you and giving you work on my spread. So, I figure a man's got the right to find out something about the man he has living under his roof…don't get me wrong: You have done fine work for me, and are right friendly company too. But a man's got a right to know…"

"You're right there, Fergusson," Robby replied. "Can't dispute that."

Robby took a moment to collect his thoughts. Then he spoke.

"Here's my story…I worked for a prosperous man, up in Virginia. He was good to me. I had no complaints, and counted myself blessed beyond measure. But he had a daughter. She had dark eyes, and a smile that looked like music would look if it had a face. Real pretty. She led me on…but truth is, I was like a pony with a bridle…I guess that I was too quick to be led."

"What happened?" Fergusson asked.

"I got myself accused of some conduct…things that no gentleman, and most certainly no Christian man would ever do with a lady…I swear, Fergusson, I was innocent of any such thing…but she turned on me, and for the life of me I can't figure out why. Then, to make things worse still, I came to learn that even with all her flirtations and feminine approaches toward me, she had been promised in betrothal to another man…now, can you imagine such a thing?"

"What happened?" Fergusson asked.

"Well, the father was all set to come against me with the full force of the law…so, with the help of one of his chief plantation overseers, and on the advice of one of his slaves, I got myself free, and hightailed it down here…"

"You took the advice of one of *his slaves*, you say?"

"Fellow named Solomon. Couldn't read nor write, but had some handy advice for me, nevertheless. I am much indebted to him."

"Now I've heard everything," Fergusson muttered.

"So, there's my story," Robby said as they headed down the tree-lined lane that led to the log house at the end. "The terrible truth is, Fergusson, even with all that she has done against me…if that woman came to me tonight and asked me back, I'd be fool enough to take her up on it…now, doesn't that make me just about the most mule-stupid man you've ever met?"

Fergusson considered what he had just heard, and then gave his assessment.

"Naw," he replied. "It don't. My second wife, she died trying to give birth to our child, more than thirty years ago. But before her, I had Katrina, my first wife. She left me for a frontiersman who was traveling west. No sir, I don't think you're a fool by any stretch…"

Then, as Robby was pulling the cart up to the barn, Fergusson added something else.

"I appreciate you tellin' me your story. Took some gumption. It would have been easy to spin a tale…I'd never have known the difference."

"I was brought up to tell the truth. My older brother, the Reverend, raised me after both my parents died in a fire. Some folks might call him a mite stern. But he had good reason. He was the one who brought me to the Lord. And my other brother, Nathan, the lawyer, he was sort of like a second father also. They both made sure I knew how to conduct myself as a Christian."

"I notice that you only had a small satchel when you met up with me," Fergusson said. "But I saw that you were carrying that big old Bible…"

"I sure do. It says in that Bible that *thy word is a lamp unto my feet and a light unto my path*:…I figure I need all the light I can get!"

"Well, I don't read but a little, myself," Fergusson said. "Seein' that nobody ever taught me."

"My brothers taught me," Robby said. "And I could teach you. We could start tomorrow. And if you have no objection, I would like to use the Bible, seein' as it is so handy. I would like to start you in the gospel of St. John."

Fergusson nodded in agreement as he climbed cautiously off the cart.

"We'll have you reading in no time," Robby said. "Shucks, my brothers would be proud of me...here I am becoming a regular schoolteacher!"

After Fergusson stretched his back, after climbing down, he looked up at Robby.

"You're real proud of your two brothers aren't you?"

"Sure. Of course. A lawyer and a Reverend. Both of them, men of means, and influence in Boston."

As Robby unhitched the mare from the cart, and was trotting her into the barn, Fergusson called out to Robby.

He stopped and turned around.

Fergusson had a smile on his face.

"Them brothers of yours ought to be right proud of you, son."

Robby laughed, and shook his head. He then led the horse by the bridle into the barn, and slid the door closed.

Chapter 42

It was after midnight when deputies from the court came banging on the doors of the law offices of John Adams and Nathan Mackenzie.

Nathan had curled up and fallen asleep on the loveseat in the small lobby.

Adams continued to work in his office, but as the hours waned, and the candle had burned low, his eyes were getting heavy, and then started closing.

The two lawyers had retired to the office to await the verdict from the jury.

Now the banging at the door woke both of them.

At first, Nathan had forgotten where he was, and it took a few seconds to remember why he had fallen asleep at the office rather than in his own soft bed at home.

I am here, he said to himself trying to clear his head, *because the jury was still out. Still deliberating. The Captain Preston case…that's it. Now, I have to answer the door.*

When Nathan swung the door open, two red-coated deputies from the court were standing on the top step.

"Justice Trowbridge is commanding you, and Mr. Adams, to present yourselves to the courtroom, posthaste."

"Have they reached a verdict?" Nathan asked nervously, his mouth now suddenly as dry as sand.

One of the deputies looked at the other, and then looked back to Nathan.

"I can't say one way or the other."

Then the two deputies turned and quickly walked away.

By then Adams appeared in the lobby, rubbing his face with one hand, and trying to put his coat on with his other.

"Tell me everything," he said.

"We've been called to the court. That's all I know…"

"Is the verdict in?"

"They wouldn't tell me."

"We must go, Nathan. Right away. No delay," Adams barked.

The two lawyers exited the office, locked the front door, and then scurried down the street to the courthouse.

In the moonlight, they could already see a large group entering the courthouse through the front doors.

When Adams and Nathan reached the courthouse there were still a number of men in a line, waiting to file in.

There were a few mumbled profanities, uttered among some of the men, as they glanced back at Adams and Nathan, and as the crowd slowly entered the courtroom.

Prosecutors Quincy and Paine were already at their seats at the Crown's counsel table.

Adams studied their faces. He was aware that occasionally the court personnel would inform the government's lawyers first, unofficially, of the verdict, before the jury would formally announce it in open court.

But as he searched the tense expressions of Quincy and Paine, he realized that they did not know either. That nobody knew, except the jury, how they had weighed in on the guilt or innocence—on the continued life or imminent death—of Captain Thomas Preston.

Hodgson, the court reporter, was sitting in his chair, with quill pen poised. The bailiffs and the court clerk were standing at attention.

The judge's high-backed black leather chair at the bench was empty.

But not for long.

The clerk looked over to the side door which was now opening from the judge's chambers and cried out, commanding that all should rise and give heed the entrance of Justice Edmund Trowbridge.

The judge entered with the exact same innocuous expression that he had worn through most of the trial, and then quickly sat down.

Every seat in the courtroom was taken. In the back, Samuel Adams and his associates were sitting, with arms crossed.

The clerk called out the title of the case—the Crown versus Captain Thomas Preston. Then, two deputies entered, accompanying Captain Preston, one on each side. They hurriedly brought him to the defense table, and then walked, quickstep, to the corner of the courtroom.

"In this matter, I am informed that the jury has reached a verdict…is that true?"

One of the jurors stood up.

"It is, Your Honor."

Justice Trowbridge nodded, and then cleared his throat.

"And is this verdict unanimous among you all?"

All twelve men on the jury nodded in agreement.

There was a look of anxiety on the faces of the jurymen. Not of uncertainty of their verdict; but a hesitation as to the full force, and possible fury, that might be unleashed as a result of their final deliberations, and their ultimate decision, regarding the tragic events of the evening of March 5, 1770, in Boston.

"Pronounce you now, jury foreman, the verdict of you all," Justice Trowbridge said.

The jury foreman, who was still standing, swallowed hard. Then he spoke.

"On the matter of the charges of murder against Captain Preston for...for the deaths of the five men of Boston..."

Then he swallowed again.

"We find Captain Preston..."

Nathan was numb with anticipation.

The entire room was transfixed.

"We find him...*not guilty*, Your Honor..."

Somehow, the words had not landed on the ears. It was as if the pronouncement that Captain Preston was not guilty was still floating, lingering in the air, above the heads in that crowded courtroom.

Then someone gasped.

And another man shouted out a profanity.

And then pandemonium began to break out and shouting from one group of men, several of them sailors, was met by the shouts, against them, from several local merchants.

The deputies rushed up to the crowd to try to restore order.

"Order!" Justice Trowbridge yelled, now standing to command the attention of the courtroom.

It was only after his third command for silence that the crowd started to compose itself.

Justice Trowbridge ordered that Captain Preston be released from custody and escorted out of the building through the side door.

As he was being led out, Preston turned to Nathan and Adams, and said, "God bless you, men…may your courage never be…" but his last words were not heard, as he had then reached the side door, and the deputies, surrounding him, hurried him through it.

Quincy and Paine, clearly perturbed, threw side glances to Nathan and Adams, and then pushed their way through the crowd that was exiting the courtroom.

Adams and Nathan sat next to each other, at the defense table, saying nothing, but waiting for the courtroom to empty.

Adams reached over to Nathan, and grabbing him by both of his shoulders, broke into an enormous smile, nodding as he did.

Thinking they were the last to leave, Nathan and John Adams collected their papers and rose to their feet.

But when they turned around, they saw someone waiting in the last row.

It was Samuel Adams. Sitting alone.

There was a curious expression on his face; unusually placid, considering the fact that the jury verdict that had just been announced had violated every tenet that Samuel Adams and his Sons of Liberty had been passionately espousing.

"Cousin," Sam Adams said sternly to John, who was standing next to Nathan. "We have matters that must be discussed…privately."

"Such as?" John Adams asked, leery of the invitation.

"I can't go into it here. Meet me at the Rising Sun Tavern in ten minutes. You may bring your associate, Mr. Mackenzie, with you."

Then, as Sam Adams stood to leave the courtroom, he added one further caveat.

"But *do not,* under any conditions, bring anyone else."

Chapter 43

When John Adams and Nathan arrived at the Rising Sun Tavern it was darkened, they could see no one inside, and there were no lamps burning.

John and Nathan mounted the steps to the covered porch, and then knocked several times, but no one answered.

"Do you think this was all a ruse?" Nathan asked.

But before his question could be answered, they both heard a voice behind them.

"Come along then," a man said, down on the ground level below the porch. He was standing in the shadows and they could not make him out well.

"Follow me," the man instructed them.

Nathan and Adams walked down the steps from the front porch, and then followed behind the stranger who was leading them around the side of the tavern.

It was then almost two o'clock in the morning, and there were no citizens milling about; no pedestrians on the street, no travelers on horseback on the road that ran past the Rising Sun Tavern. Nevertheless, the stranger looked around, every which way, as he took them to the back of the establishment. He had the air of a man who greatly feared the possibility of detection.

When they finally arrived at the rear of the tavern, the stranger knocked once loudly. Then waited. Then he knocked three times. Then the man waited a few seconds, and followed that with two more knocks. The little square window at eye level, at the top of the door, slid open.

"Mr. Gill," the man announced.

The little square window closed.

In an instant the door opened to them.

Mr. Gill stepped into the rear storage room of the tavern, which was filled with barrels and crates along the walls. There were no windows in the room. A few oil lamps were lighted.

In the center was a small round table. There were several chairs set around the table, and some chairs also set in a larger perimeter around those.

A group of men were sitting in the chairs. John Adams immediately recognized his cousin Samuel. And as he looked at the faces around the room, he recognized most of the others.

"Cousin," Samuel began, addressing John Adams, "would you and your associate please have a seat?"

Adams and Nathan both took seats at the table.

"Gentlemen," Samuel continued, "please introduce yourselves."

"Mr. Benjamin Edes," one man started out. Adams knew him; he was the publisher of the *Boston Gazette*. "And this is my partner, Mr. Gill," the publisher said, pointing to the stranger who had met them in the shadows in the front of the tavern.

"John Hancock," another man announced. He was well dressed, and appeared prosperous. Adams smiled and nodded; he knew him as a successful local merchant with extensive shipping interests.

"Mr. Paul Revere," another man proclaimed.

"Now that we have made our formal introductions," John Adams said, "perhaps you could tell me, and my associate Mr. Mackenzie, why we are having this meeting...particularly considering the lateness of the hour."

"Some meetings," Samuel began, "are better conducted in the lateness of the night...where there are no prying eyes, or listening ears."

"Again," Adams said, "I would ask that your purposes be made clear..."

"Cousin," Samuel replied. "In case you were wondering what my reaction was to the verdict in your case, let there be no question that I was appalled and outraged."

"I was not wondering in the least," John Adams responded. "I already had a good idea of how you would assess the outcome of our case. I knew that you would forever think that my representation of Captain Preston was the worst mistake of my life, and a betrayal of the ideals that I had previously espoused..."

With that, Samuel nodded to Mr. Edes, who was holding an old edition of his own newspaper. Then Edes commenced to read an anonymous letter from the paper.

"*Be it remembered, that liberty must at all hazards be supported. We have a right to it, derived from our Maker.*"

"Do you mean to say," Samuel continued, "*those kinds of ideals?*"

"Do you think, cousin," John Adams responded, "that I would have forgotten my own words?"

Edes passed the newspaper over to Samuel, who glanced down at the page, and then recited its title: *A Dissertation on the Canon and the Feudal Law.* After a moment of glancing down at the piece in the newspaper, Samuel looked up at John and asked a simple question.

"Do you still believe what you wrote there?"

"Of course I do!" John blurted out, in a highly insulted tone.

Samuel Adams looked down at John Adams' essay, and then picked up another quote to recite.

"*But besides this they have a right, an indisputable, unalienable, indefeasible divine right, to the most dreaded and envied kind of knowledge, I mean of the character and conduct of their rulers.*"

Then Samuel looked around the room and said to John Adams, "I believe your writings dare to bring into question the inviolability of the monarchy...you dispute the divine right of kings, counselor...and not only that, but you make an indirect attack on King George himself. So, it appears that contrary to popular opinion, I am not the radical, the agitator, here," Samuel said looking around the room, "rather, *it is you, John Adams...*"

A few of the men in the room chuckled at that.

Then John Hancock spoke up with a sly smile.

"I am feeling rather uneasy, meeting secretly, under cover of night, with the likes of John Adams, here," Hancock said. "After all, who knows where such treasonous and revolutionary ideas of his might lead?"

After a few more chuckles around the room, John Adams leaned back in his chair, realizing that they were all having some good-natured fun at his expense.

"In truth, cousin," Samuel said, "when I first heard the verdict in your case, I was prepared to change my last name, so that I would never risk the possibility of being mistaken for a traitor like you..."

Then Samuel cocked his head to the side, and thought on what he was about to say next.

"But my compatriots here," and with that he nodded to the members of the group, "after the verdict, whisked me into a corner, and immediately convinced me how this blasphemy against justice might actually work a great advantage for us…" Then, Samuel grew pensive, and added, "besides, it seemed, after a few moments reflection, that you had an opportunity to have argued in your defense that your client, Captain Preston, was simply the victim of a violent mob…and that there was a credible argument that the mob had been instigated by myself, and my fellow Sons of Liberty here. Yet, you resisted that temptation, and never advanced that argument. So, here we are, John. Great events now depend on certain…contingencies…"

"In other words, it all depends on *you*, Mr. Adams," Benjamin Edes, the publisher, added.

"And depending on whether you would be a patriot, Mr. Adams," Hancock added, "rather than a Tory lawyer for Tory causes."

"If you are asking me to abandon the defense of the remaining English soldiers," John Adams shot back, "soldiers, many of whom are my clients, and who are set to be put on trial in less than two months hence…then the answer is no!"

But strangely, Samuel Adams was not the least fazed by that last comment.

"No, we are not asking that," Samuel Adams replied, with uncharacteristic calm.

Then he came to the point.

"What we are asking, sir," Samuel said, "is whether you will go deeper into politics, *first*…"

"Deeper?" John asked.

"We know you were elected a selectman for the local population in Braintree, before you came to Boston," Samuel said.

"Now," Hancock added, "we want you to go deeper...soon the Boston town meeting will elect a representative to the Massachusetts legislature."

Adams was trying to sort out this surprising invitation to become a politician. But then a thought came to mind.

"You asked *first* whether I would enter politics...is there a *second* question?"

"Yes," Revere said, breaking his silence. "We want to know if you can be trusted..."

"Why me?" Adams asked.

"What better man to serve as the spearhead for the rights and liberties of the people of Boston," Samuel Adams remarked, "than a man who defended the liberty of an English officer? The English, who of course still control the levers of government in this colony, will likely mistake you for a *neutral*..."

"As opposed to a patriot and a partisan," Hancock added.

"Which is what we trust you will be," Revere added, "if you go to the legislature on our behalf."

"Well?" Samuel Adams said. "What is your answer, sir? This is not personal, cousin. For if it were, we would never speak together again. No...this is something quite...fortuitous...something, dare we say...*providential*..."

"Yes," Hancock said, ruminating a bit on the thought. "A lawyer who barks like a Tory sympathizer, but who bites like a patriot!"

After the laughter died down, Samuel Adams asked John the question again; "So, are you with us on this endeavor, wherever it may lead?"

Adams folded his hands in his lap. He looked over at Nathan, who was basking in the amazement of the moment. Then he gave his answer.

"Though I perceive that the path that we propose shall be paved, at least for the moment, with discouragement, hardship, and trial...I believe there is no other path that can be taken. I am your man...if you...each of you...are able to lend me your most profound trust."

"And by that I mean to say, *each* of you," John Adams said with passion in his voice, and looking straight into Samuel Adams' eyes.

"Then it is done," Samuel responded coolly.

"What else do I need to know?" John asked.

A few of the members of the group glanced at each other. Then Hancock spoke up.

"Mr. Benjamin Franklin, who is the negotiating delegate to the British Crown on behalf of several colonies, including Massachusetts, in attempting to secure more advantageous trading terms, among other things, with Parliament and the King...has also sought to obtain valuable intelligence on the intentions of England toward the future of the colonies."

Then Hancock paused, and considered the gravity of the information he was about to share.

"Mr. Franklin has heard rumors...whether they are true we do not know...but he has heard credible reports that there is, in existence, certain correspondence between the English Governor of Massachusetts and high ranking English leaders in London...correspondence which verifies that the very worst and most malicious strategies are being plotted against us in London."

"It is quite apparent to us all," Samuel Adams said, "that we are fast approaching the river Rubicon. Let us remember that from this point on, cousin, we are all riding in the same boat."

The men rose and all solemnly shook hands.

John Hancock walked John Adams to the door separately, and the two men exited outside, with Nathan following.

"We assumed, I hope accurately," Hancock said, "that your young associate, Mr. Mackenzie, can be equally trusted…and that you may find some use for him in your work with us as well?"

John Adams turned to Nathan.

"Well, Nathan," John said, "will you join me as my political secretary, if I am elected?"

It was all rushing at Nathan too quickly, and he paused for a moment.

Finally, when John Adams, and Nathan, and John Hancock, were standing together, in the chill of the night, under the black sky, illuminated by the haloed white moon, and countless stars, Nathan replied.

"If we are at a great river crossing, and I am already in your boat," he said, "it would be foolish, I would think, to jump overboard."

A little later, when John Adams bid him good night, Nathan noticed how his mentor's face was, by then, showing great weariness from the tumultuous events of the day.

Nathan walked the few blocks to his small brownstone house, alone.

Deborah and little William would be sleeping peacefully, he thought.

He looked up into the silent night sky.

Then Nathan spoke a prayer of protection and blessing over his family; and asked that God might prepare him for the uncertainties of the future, and for the obligations and privileges of the work to which he might soon be called; work that threatened to overwhelm him before he had even begun.

That done, he placed his hand on the iron door handle of his front door, and entered his home.

Chapter 44

In late November, the second jury trial relating to the Boston Massacre, that of the soldiers of the 29th English Regiment, commenced in Superior Court.

As agreed, attorneys Josiah Quincy, Samson Salter Blowers, Quincy's law partner, and Robert Auchmuty represented the two most culpable defendants: foot soldier Matthew Killroy, who had harbored personal animosity against Samuel Gray, a victim who was killed standing directly in front of Killroy, and soldier Hugh Montgomery, who stood next to Killroy in the muster line.

The remaining six English soldiers were represented by John Adams and Nathan Mackenzie.

The jury returned its verdict on December fifth.

Before the jury retired to deliberate, they had heard evidence suggesting two significant excuses for the actions of the squad of English soldiers: first, that some members of the mob had wielded clubs and had struck several of the soldiers; and second, that total confusion had reigned in the seconds just prior to the musket fire from the soldiers.

In fact, it appeared that foot soldier Hugh Montgomery had been struck down by a club, and when he was able to get back on his feet he began to scream "fire, men," adding profanities and further calls for them to "fire." Finally, defendant Matthew Killroy, who had no love for Samuel Gray and the other Boston protesters, was only too happy to finally oblige the command, and fired, followed by Montgomery's weapon being discharged. By that time, the remaining soldiers had tragically believed that a lawful command had come from Captain Preston, and also fired their muskets.

When the jury filed back into the courtroom, they had undoubtedly recalled John Adams' closing argument on behalf of the six soldiers he and Nathan represented:

Whatever may be our own personal wishes, our inclinations, the dictates of our own passions, those things cannot alter the facts and the evidence that you have heard in this trial. What was that evidence, gentlemen? That a motley crew of saucy boys and outlandish jack-tars—what we must call, in truth, a simple mob—cruelly attacked those soldiers. Whether they acted in self-defense of their own safety or life is for you, the jury, to finally decide. But one thing must, indeed, be remembered...and it cannot be gainsaid. That it is inherent in the very nature of things, that when soldiers are quartered in an otherwise peaceful town, in time of peace, and without good reason, that it will always occasion two mobs for every one that they are meant to prevent. Such a military plan is always a wretched conservator of the peace!

The foreman of that jury read out the verdict again to the very crowded courtroom. But unlike the first trial, that of Captain Thomas Preston, when the verdict in the eight soldiers' trial was read out loud, it was not received with any shock by the citizens of Boston. The residents of that city had, it seemed, a chance to reflect on the evidence presented by John Adams and Nathan weeks before in the captain's case, and had resolved that whatever the responsibility of individual soldiers—and there would be a reckoning for two of them at least—the greater fault lay not in Boston nor in the 29th Regiment, but across the sea, and in the palaces of power in London, and Windsor Castle.

All six of the soldiers defended by John Adams and Nathan were acquitted of any wrongdoing.

Hugh Montgomery and Matthew Killroy, however, were convicted of murder in the course of official military duties. But by an arcane procedure of "claiming benefit of clergy," those two evildoers were spared life and limb in return for a "lesser" punishment: they were each branded on the thumb with a kind of "mark of Cain." Such a brand would remain for their natural lives, and would make them veritable outcasts in any villages or towns which they might occasion. They would become, in essence, hunted and haunted men, never finding peace, or safety, or solace.

Almost immediately, the financial and professional fortunes of Adams and Nathan began improving. And the two lawyers would have easily become the most prosperous attorneys in Boston, if they had possessed the time and inclination to develop their law practices.

But they had neither. Good to their word, Samuel Adams, John Hancock, and the other patriots vigorously campaigned for John Adams to represent Boston in the colonial legislature. He won the election handily.

John insisted that Nathan be his political secretary and chief of staff. Deborah was a little bewildered at that turn of events. When Nathan first explained to her, the morning after his late night meeting with the Sons of Liberty, that he might be assisting John Adams in his run for public office, it made little sense to her.

Then, when the law business for John Adams and Nathan began bouncing back, it made even less sense.

"Please tell me, husband," she pleaded, "when your law practice, which had seemed to have been so stricken ill because of the massacre case, finally is showing itself to be in complete recovery, *why you would abandon it altogether, now, of all times?*"

Nathan's only answer seemed to be somewhat enigmatic, even to him: "I wish, dear wife, that I could give you a clearer answer. But this is all I can say—that Providence has given us a very amazing turn of events. Once greatly admired for his patriotism and legal brilliance, then later despised for his defense of Captain Preston, Mr. Adams has now exceeded all his prior accolades, and now intends to enter politics. Deborah, I cannot say it any other way—I believe that his fortunes and mine have been interwoven by the hand of God. It is not for me to try to unwind them."

As usual, no matter how Deborah feared for the future, or disagreed with her husband's decision to place them at risk, Nathan had, once again, in his winsome combination of words, reason, and the reasons of the heart, convinced her that all would be well.

But, all was not well with Edith Mackenzie, Reverend Edward Mackenzie's wife. Her "pregnancy" had created a worsening condition. Her belly had not grown as expected. Her "morning sickness" was absent when it should have been present, and was acute and did not abate when it should have been absent. She had followed none of the usual signs and symptoms of childbearing.

After Christmas, two midwives examined Edith, and then met privately with Edward in the front room of their large house.

"Reverend Mackenzie," the older woman said soberly, "we have assessed your wife's condition, as best we can. We have delivered, between us, nearly seventy babies. And we bring troubling news…"

"Tell me quickly," he said. "What is happening with my wife? What is happening with our baby?"

"We cannot tell you much about your wife," the midwife said. "You may have to consult a physician on that matter. But regarding the baby…"

"Yes?" Edward asked impatiently.

"There is simply no baby, at least that we can determine."

"Absurd!" Edward said, shouting so loud that both of the midwives were taken aback at his reaction. "Of course there is a baby."

"Please, Reverend Mackenzie," the midwife said, trying to soothe him. "Speak to a physician. We would suggest that you do so, as very soon as possible."

Edward, in his haste to believe that they were unskilled, or ill-advised in their opinions, disregarded their warnings. But after they left the house, Edith called her husband into the bedroom where she was resting on the bed.

"Edward, what did they say?" she asked.

"Nothing," he replied curtly, trying to diminish his growing anxiety about her condition. "I have dismissed them. They seemed to have nothing worthwhile to say."

"But husband," Edith said, reaching out a hand toward Edward. "I am in pain." And with that she rubbed her belly with her other hand.

Edward took her hand, and sat on the bed next to her.

"We will consult a proper doctor, my precious wife," he said.

"But who?"

"Never fear. Boston is full of physicians."

"There is that kind doctor who attends our church," Edith said, with a bit of pleading in her voice. "Dr. Jefferies…oh, what is his first name? Oh, yes, John. That is it…Dr. John Jefferies. A kind man, and well-spoken of by some of your parishioners, I think. Can we consult him, Edward? Please?"

Edward knew Dr. Jefferies. Edith was right about him. He was an accomplished surgeon, a man of tender compassions, and was a regular attending member of Edward's church. At another time or place, Edward might have struggled against agreeing to call him. Edward had been reading the accounts of the trial of Captain Preston in the *Gazette*. And he was aware that Dr. Jefferies had been an influential witness for the defense, supporting the theory of John Adams and Nathan that even the victim, Patrick Carr, who died shortly after being tended to by Dr. Jefferies, believed that no improper order had been given by Captain Preston, and that the actions of the mob had precipitated the soldiers' firing, a response of pure military self-defense.

Edward's personal turmoil over the massacre might have otherwise obscured his objectivity: He was still finding reasons to disagree with Nathan's defense of the English captain and his soldiers, believing, as he did, that it was simply a random event of violence, perpetrated by overzealous soldiers—and that with the swift punishment of them all, that Boston would settle back into peace and tranquility; and then the calls of the radicals for protests against mother England would slowly die out.

But now, as he studied Edith's shallow cheeks, her pale, washed-out complexion, and her grimaces of pain, none of those condescensions seemed to matter. Edward did not want to admit what now seemed so very clear: Edith was frighteningly ill; perhaps the midwives were right after all.

In any case, Edward knew what had to be done.

"Yes, my dear," he answered his wife. "I will call on Dr. Jefferies...not to worry..."

That afternoon he stopped by Dr. Jefferies' office. The doctor had a patient in his examining room. Edward waited for nearly an hour. Finally Dr. Jefferies came out and greeted Edward warmly, inviting him into his inner office.

They exchanged pleasantries for a few moments. Dr. Jefferies complimented Edward on his last sermon, part of his ongoing exposition on Paul's letter to the Romans. Then he offhandedly remarked about the massacre case.

"I know," Dr. Jefferies said, "how proud you must be of your brother Nathan's work in the trial of Captain Preston, and the case also involving the other soldiers. In the end, I think, true justice was done. I know, Edward, that you may disagree with me on this, but the clearest thing that came from that trial was the outlandish conduct of the English government in posting a standing army in our midst. Of course, I am sure you have heard that King George has actually ordered the troops out of Boston...though not back to England, I fear. But, enough about politics...what brings you here?"

Edward gave Dr. Jefferies a concise, and hurried, overview of Edith's health, and her difficult and strange pregnancy, and the disconcerting report of the two midwives who had examined her. Dr. Jefferies vouched for both of them as careful and skilled midwives; but there was a sober look on the doctor's face that concerned Edward, especially when the surgeon spoke up.

"I would suggest that I examine Edith as soon as possible...perhaps even today. Can I come over to your house? Is she available?"

Edward agreed.

After his examination, Dr. Jefferies took Edward outside the house, donned his long coat, and prepared to leave for his medical office.

"I fear," the doctor said, "that Edith is possessed of a rather sizeable tumor in the upper cavity of the womb. It gave, at first, some of the same signs as a pregnancy. But I assure you, Edward, that she is not with child. Sometimes the tumor growth will abate on its own...though only rarely. Usually it proceeds to grow, and will complicate itself into the other internal organs. At the end, it can be very painful. I have medications and elixirs, of course, which can help with the pain."

"Can you not cut it out?" Edward asked, his voice pleading for some other hope.

"Not in this case," the doctor replied solemnly. "I would have to resection such a large part of the womb. It would almost certainly result in her death. I am so sorry."

Edward's head reeled, and he felt as if his legs would buckle under him. He thanked the doctor for his candid appraisal.

Then Edward went into the front room, dropping to his knees, and wept and prayed before God. After a long time of prayer, and pitiful supplication, Edward wiped his eyes, rose to his feet and mounted the stairs to the second floor, where Edith was waiting for him in bed.

As soul-shatteringly difficult as it would be, Edward knew he would have to share the whole brutal truth with his wife. Yet, he did not know, as he slowly climbed the stairs, how he would gain the strength to tell Edith the news. He would have to believe, he thought, as he approached the door to the bedroom, that God's grace would be supplied in this time of desperate need.

For he knew of no other means to carry such a burden.

The window in the bedroom was open, as Edward took Edith's hands, kissed them, and then tearfully shared what Dr. Jefferies had said.

A block away, the sound of Edith's mournful shriek could be clearly heard.

Chapter 45

By the spring of that year, 1771, Robby Mackenzie and Fergusson had become fast friends. Robby had never known his own grandfather very well—and so the old farmer, who was a combination of hardheaded toughness, and tender, plain-spoken wittiness, became a kind of replacement grandfather for him.

Fergusson appreciated Robby's strong work ethic. The young man more than justified his board and keep. He repaired the fence lines, fed and cared for all of the livestock, fixed several leaks in the roof of the house, and oversaw a handful of laborers who helped clear away several acres of land that Fergusson wanted to use for the planting of tobacco.

And as he had promised, Robby spent time every night teaching Fergusson how to read, starting with the gospel of John in the New Testament. By the time they had made their way to the end of that gospel, Fergusson asked Robby to call a preacher so that he could talk at length with a clergyman about the state of his soul.

Robby had learned that there was a small country church less than fifteen miles away, so he asked Fergusson for permission to leave for a day; then he swung himself up onto one of the younger bay horses, and rode east to meet Reverend Calvin Beecham.

The pastor was a short, fast-talking man of about fifty, with a wide grin and a hearty laugh. Robby figured that Beecham would be a perfect fit for Fergusson.

And he was right.

The backwoods preacher agreed to return all the way to Fergusson's farm. The three of them ate dinner together. Afterwards, Robby wandered into his small back room bedroom; he wanted to leave plenty of time for Fergusson and preacher Beecham to talk.

It was after midnight when Robby drifted off the sleep. Just before he did, he could still hear the voices of the preacher and Fergusson talking. But by then, the laughter had died out, and there was a quiet seriousness to their voices.

In the morning, the preacher was up very early, sitting on the front step, reading his Bible just after sunrise.

"Say, Robby, my boy," he asked, "do you got yourself a stretch of water hereabouts? A pond, or a river or such?"

"We've got a small stream down the hill a ways," Robby answered.

"Would it be deep enough, somewhere, to take a man sittin' down in it?"

Robby thought about that. Then he remembered.

"Sure enough," Robby replied. "Down toward the willow trees, there is a turn of the stream, and there is a collection of rocks with a small waterfall. Below the waterfall—that's where the stream sort of ponds. It's about four feet deep there."

"Excellent!" the preacher yelled out.

"Preacher Beecham," Robby asked, "what do you have in mind?"

"Ask him," Beecham said, and motioned for Robby to turn around. When he did, he saw Fergusson standing behind him with a big smile.

"I done got saved last night, Robby boy!" he exclaimed. "My sins have been washed by the blood of the Savior, Jesus."

"Now we're goin' to baptize him good and proper," Beecham said. "Down in that stream of yours."

The three men walked down to the deepest part of the stream, just below the shallow waterfall, and there Fergusson confessed that he believed in everything done by Christ on the cross, and that he proclaimed that Jesus was God's own Son, and invited Him to reside in his heart and soul thereafter.

With that, Beecham recited some Scripture, and then carefully walked Fergusson into the stream and dunked him down into the water.

When Fergusson got up out of the water, the preacher was holding onto him. Both of the men laughed together, and Beecham cautiously walked the old farmer to dry land.

By the time Fergusson reached where Robby was standing on the banks of the stream, his laughing had ceased, and he looked at Robby and began to cry great weeping tears. And Robby held onto the old man, and Fergusson held onto Robby and cried in his arms.

Preacher Beecham was treated to a large breakfast. And after eating, he mounted his horse, invited both Fergusson and Robby to attend Sunday services at his church, and then rode off toward the pine tree forest at the end of the farm.

Beecham could still be heard to be singing *When I Survey the Wondrous Cross* with a loud enthusiasm as he trotted his horse into the woods and disappeared.

It was a few weeks later, in mid-May, when the wildflowers were starting to show themselves and the trees throughout the hill country were popping open with green buds, that Fergusson made an announcement to Robby.

"There's going to be a mighty meeting of all the Regulators down near the Alamance Creek," the old farmer said. "All the Regulators will be there. Maybe upward of several thousand."

"What for?" Robby asked.

"Show of strength," Fergusson replied. "The English Governor for the Crown, Mr. Tryon, he's outlawed all such assemblies and meetings, calling them illegal. We say it ain't so. We say that it's about time that Tryon face up to our grievances once and for all."

"When is it?"

"We meet tomorrow," Fergusson said. "I best start riding before sunup."

"I can't let you go alone," Robby said. "No offense, but with your age and infirmities you may not make it to Alamance Creek. I should take you there…"

"This ain't your fight," Fergusson said. "I've felt kind of poorly that I've kept you here in the West Country takin' care of me…instead of finding your way in the world…"

"Here is my part of the world, at least for right now," Robby replied. "The Lord Almighty has confirmed that much for me. So rest assured, Fergusson, I'll be right there with you. We leave together tomorrow, before daybreak."

The two men had a meal of cooked rabbit and a few turnip greens. They talked for a while, and then Robby was ready to turn in for the night.

But as he did, he noticed Fergusson was in the large room, by the fireplace.

He had taken down his musket and his pistol.

And Fergusson was slowly and carefully cleaning them both, preparing them for the Regulators' assembly planned for the next day.

Chapter 46

The following day, Fergusson and Robby arose an hour before sunrise. Robby prepared the one-horse cart, and put some salted meat, bread, and green apples in a burlap bag which he tossed into the back of the cart, along with his Bible, and a large tin bottle of water. Robby tied off another horse at the back. He saw that Fergusson had already packed his musket and pistol, carefully wrapped in a blanket, onto the buckboard.

As they rolled down the rutted dirt road they didn't talk much. Robby noticed that Fergusson was nodding off in his seat. As he drove the horse-drawn cart along the path in the pre-dawn dusk, Robby's mind was wandering. He thought back to Rachael, who, by then, would have been married by Robby's calculations.

In a way, Robby was surprised how he could now think back on Rachael, without the same kind of inner pain that he had experienced before. His short infatuation with the flirtatious beauty had been a heartbreak, for sure, but time seemed to now have softened the edges of the deep hurt, and feelings of betrayal.

Then, as the sun broke through over the mountains, and the clouds began to scatter, Fergusson woke up and reached into the bag and pulled out an apple for each of them.

Fergusson reached into his pocket and pulled out a small knife, then he proceeded to slice down the apple into pieces. The two men crunched down on the apples in big bites. Robby chewed hard, wiped his mouth, and then asked Fergusson a question.

"You plan on shooting someone today?"

"Not if I can help it," Fergusson replied, talking though a mouth of juice and appleful. "Why?"

"Just wondering," Robby said. "I noticed you were carrying your own arsenal in the back there," and with that he nodded to the buckboard of the cart.

"Regulators always believe in being prepared," Fergusson said. "For *whatever* might transpire."

"I thought you said this grand Regulators meeting," Robby continued, "was to hear some hoot-n-holler speeches, and to circulate a petition of grievances against the Royal Governor for ignoring your plight, and to protest the corruption of his local officials."

"You said that real well," Fergusson said. "See, I think you ought to get yourself a job in politics."

Robby smiled, but would not be put off that easily.

"Come on, Fergusson, you didn't answer my question."

"You want to know what's goin' to happen down there?"

"Yes sir, I would."

"Well, the truth is," Fergusson said, "I rightly don't know. But the English Governor, William Tryon, has said some things that make me think there may be trouble."

"Like what?"

"Oh, that he's practically itching to use his paid militia to blast us to kingdom come if we have a big meeting of the Regulators again...things like that."

After a few moments of silence, Fergusson added a thought.

"We got an extra horse at the back of the cart. If you don't got the stomach for this…I wouldn't blame you in the least if you were to take that horse and ride straight back to the farm…wait for me there, till I come back…"

"Listen," Robby said emphatically, "I promised I would stand by you today, and I meant it. Just that I wanted to know what to expect…so…now I know."

After they rode for a while longer, Robby suggested that Fergusson fish out the Bible and do some practicing on his reading. They were now on the Gospel of Mark.

Fergusson said he thought that made sense, and so he started reading out loud where they had left off last—with the story about Jesus healing a man's son who had been occupied by an "unclean spirit."

That was followed by Jesus' prediction that he would be arrested, and then put to death, but would rise three days later.

When Fergusson read that part out, he stopped, and re-read it again. Then he looked at the page with a puzzled look.

"What's the matter?" Robby asked.

"Just wondering at that…knowing that ye're going to die, and knowin' it all beforehand, and knowin' ye're going to rise up from the grave, is all…"

"Not too different from you, Fergusson," Robby said with a smile. "Now that you are a Christian man. You know you are going to die someday…and when it is all over, sometime, in God's patient plan, you, and I, and the other followers of the Savior…we're all going to rise up, and walk with him in paradise…"

After thinking about that for a while, Fergusson's face broke into a big grin, and then he shook his head.

"I was sure wrong about you," he said.

"How so?"

"Just that I said you ought to go into politics…I was wrong about that. I'm thinking you ought to be a preacher like that Reverend Beecham who baptized me!"

Robby laughed out loud at that. But Fergusson just smiled back.

Long hours of tiring riding went by, and then finally Robby and Fergusson arrived near the Alamance Creek. At that point, Fergusson said the meeting place was only a mile or two away. But as they led the cart along a small path that ran on the high ground up from the creek, they heard the sound of shouting, and voices, and cheering off in the distance.

"There they are!" Fergusson exclaimed, cocking his head to listen.

In a half an hour, they were pulling up to a meadow, and a large clearing where the creek took a sharp bend.

In the clearing there were two thousand men who had gathered there—Regulators all—to convene for the purpose of moving their followers to air their complaints against the Royal Governor.

Robby helped Fergusson down, and with the help of a hickory cane, Fergusson started ambling toward the front of the crowd, where, on the back of a wagon, a man was making a speech.

Then, suddenly, Fergusson halted, and turned to look back at his cart. Robby understood what he was thinking.

Fergusson had left his pistol and musket, wrapped in a blanket, on the buckboard.

After staring back at the cart, Fergusson looked at Robby, looked back at the cart one more time, and then decided to keep walking, without the benefit of his weapons.

Robby and Fergusson approached the makeshift platform that

had been constructed on the farm wagon. A sea of men were lounging on the grass, listening to a speech being delivered on the platform by a fellow named Herman Husband.

"You all recall," Husband shouted out, "how the Royal Governor expelled me bodily from the Assembly for this colony, and forbade me from representing your interests there."

There were scattered catcalls and boos from the crowd.

"Then, not satisfied with that outrage, our English overseers illegally arrested me on trumped-up charges of criminal libel and threw me in jail, and then kept me there even though a grand jury found that I had commited no criminal acts whatsoever. Now, men, eventually they had to let me go."

Then one frontiersman, in a dirty deerskin jacket, jumped up and screamed out, "And it's a good thing too, Herman, 'cause I was rounding up the Regulators to march down there and break you from jail and then burn down the town!"

With that, the crowd went wild, and jumped to its feet, with calls of "Freedom for the West Country!"

Husband quieted them down and continued.

"You also know how our royal taskmaster has illegally changed the laws, making new provisions just for us—allowing any Regulator to be tried for any offense, no matter where it is alleged to occur, within the city of New Bern, where the governor's palace is..."

"That's so the governor can try us with one of his own bribed juries, and his own handpicked, corrupt judges!" another man, who was on his feet, called out.

"You see," Husband continued, "you all know the outrages against us. But the point is this: What do we do now? With such a great crowd of witnesses here assembled, we hope to show the

Governor that we cannot be ignored! We intend to make a show of force. To demand the rights to which we are entitled!"

As the large crowd of Regulators cheered, off in the distance, on a bluff, an English militia scout, lying on his belly, was peering through his spyglass at the crowd down below. Then he snaked backward until he was away from the crest and out of sight, and then jumped to his feet and ran to the governor's troops, who were amassing a hundred yards away. There he saluted Major General John Ashe, who was mounted on his horse. Ashe bent forward, received the verbal report, and nodded. Then he rode over to an elaborate tent where Governor Tryon was seated in his shirtsleeves, and enjoying high tea.

The Major General saluted and then delivered the scout's report.

"Your Royal Highness," he said. "There is an assembly of some two thousand Regulators meeting not a quarter of a mile from here. The scout identified Herman Husband and several others of their radical leaders."

"Are they armed?" the governor asked, with his mouth still full of a large bite of sweet cake.

"Poorly armed," the officer said. "With few military quality weapons. They also seem to be disorganized and lacking in any real rank and file."

"Good," the Governor replied. "That will make it all the easier to shoot them down like a gaggle of wild turkeys."

"Beggin' your pardon, Your Highness," the Major General added. "But shouldn't we issue a warning to them first? A chance to disband?"

"Oh, I suppose," the governor responded, wiping some crumbs off his ruffled shirt. "But we both know that they won't bite on that bait."

The Major General then dispatched a Major and a Lieutenant to ride down to the conclave under a flag of truce. The Governor was dressed by then, and watched through his spyglass as the order to disperse was delivered. He watched as Herman Husband and several other leaders huddled, and then walked back to the two Royal militia officers as a group. They were waving their arms athletically. The Governor smiled, and then muttered to the Major General at his side, *just as I thought…these men are savages.*

In a few moments, the two officers came riding back to camp and quickly dismounted and ran up to the Governor's position.

"If you please, Governor," they began. "They have refused the order to disperse. Instead, they are asking that a delegation of their Regulators be permitted to meet, here and now, with yourself, or a delegation of your choosing, to discuss their various grievances."

"Grievances!" Governor Tryon screamed. "Grievances? Meet with me? They shall have a meeting, make no mistake, gentlemen. But not a meeting of the kind that they are expecting. They shall meet the hot lead from our weapons!"

Then Governor Tryon asked for the finest long rifle in the army, which was quickly presented to him by a sharpshooter.

The Governor accepted the rifle, looking at it with satisfaction. Then he commanded that the Major General and a squad of body-guards accompany him to the crest of the hill, overlooking the crowd of Regulators.

"I shall commence this turkey hunt myself!" he exclaimed.

There was the excitement of a small, wicked boy in his voice. The kind of boy who delights in plucking the wings off butterflies, or crushing beetles.

Chapter 47

Down in the crowd, the word had already spread that Herman Husband and several of the other leaders had refused the order to disperse; but instead, they had countered with their own proposal.

There was a nervous anticipation in the air. Many of the men were unarmed. And those who were had brought small arms, old rifles that hadn't been fired in a while, short-aim pistols, hand knives, or swords. A few had brought hatchets and axes. There were no stores of ammunition.

The Regulators had not come for a battle, but merely for a show of force and numbers.

"Surely they'll negotiate," one of the farmers said, who was standing next to Robby and Fergusson. Then he looked at Robby and exclaimed, "They got to. Look at our numbers. They got to pay attention to our grievances…won't they?"

Robby tried to manage a confident smile. But he knew better. He thought back to his work with Jared Hollings in the House of Burgesses in Williamsburg, and how, with the slightest whim, the Royal Governor had dissolved the people's assembly and threatened the delegates with arrest, causing them to scatter for a safe, secret place to meet.

"Personally," Robby remarked to the farmer with resignation in his voice, "I wouldn't expect anything honorable from a Royal Governor. But that's just me."

Up on the crest, Governor Tryon, his Major General, and a few aides were looking down on the crowd.

"Bring the troops up directly behind me," Tryon commanded. "Mine will be the first shot."

The Major General gave the order for the small army of about fifteen hundred well-paid militiamen and mercenaries to advance directly behind the Governor.

"This is the easy way of shooting a wild bird," the Governor said laughingly to the troops that had gathered around him. "You best put some shot into him *before* he takes flight!"

The troops gave out a good-natured chuckle at that.

"Now," the Governor muttered as he lifted the long rifle and aimed it at the crowd of Regulators below, and began to sight his victim, "let's find ourselves a young, healthy buck…a strapping lad who will be missed by these ragamuffins…and who will have a dear old mum waiting for him at home…"

Tryon asked for the spyglass, and the Major General placed his before the Governor's squinting eye while he was aiming.

"Oh yes," Tryon said with a smile, "I have the perfect shot…"

Down in the crowd of Regulators, only fifty feet from Robby and Fergusson, there was a break in the crowd, exposing a tall, seventeen-year-old boy, dressed in an old puffy-sleeved shirt, and buckskin pants. He was standing with his hands on his hips.

Suddenly, off in the distance, there was the crack of a gunshot. And a small white puff of smoke that appeared on the crest of the hill.

The seventeen-year-old staggered back, and then fell to the

ground, clutching his chest with a bewildered look on his face. Several of the men rushed over to him. The boy was struggling to get up, but couldn't. His face was growing pale, and his light colored shirt was now covered over with a spreading stain of bright red blood.

The boy weakly cried out, and then put his head down on the ground.

"I downed him with one shot!" the Governor exclaimed up on the hill, with a kind of youthful pride. "Take note, men," he continued, "to make your shots count like mine."

The Major General ordered the men into lines, and then he ordered the first two lines of riflemen to progress down the hill.

"Down the hill at the quickstep!" he called out. "Then fire at will."

The rows of sharpshooters quick-stepped down the hill toward the crowd of Regulators until they could get a clear shot. The front row of English militiamen dropped to their knees in shooting position, as the row in back kept standing, aiming their muskets over their heads.

When the first volley was fired, the Regulators were already in full panic, grabbing for weapons, many of them running pell-mell for cover, but there was no cover to be had.

A dozen Regulators quickly dropped to the ground, wounded or dead with one shot.

The remaining militia troops of the Royal Governor then quick-stepped in lines down the hill, row after row, taking shooting positions, firing, priming and reloading, shooting again and again, continually advancing down on the crowd.

The Regulators were crying out for someone to take command

of their defense, but the only response was the call, "We are all free men, every man for himself!"

Hundreds of unarmed Regulators began fleeing the meadow, leaving the few with weapons to start shooting back. Here and there, a few of the Royal militiamen were dropping from the return fire from the Regulators, but from Robby's position in the middle of it, it was clear that the battle was already lost.

"Let me carry you!" Robby yelled to Fergusson, and he bent down to throw the old farmer onto his shoulder. He figured that would be the quickest way to get his friend safely to their horse and cart. Fergusson turned around to let Robby pick him up.

But as he did he was hit, and Robby heard Fergusson give out a loud groan.

Fergusson was clutching his midsection—he had just suffered a hit from a musket ball into the middle of his back. He was bleeding profusely.

"Run, Robby," he moaned out as he collapsed to the ground, "leave me be, boy."

"I won't!" Robby yelled back.

But out of the corner of his eye Robby noticed a militiaman with a bayonet fixed to his musket charging right at him.

Robby rolled out of the way as the Royal soldier lunged, and he plunged his bayonet into the ground, narrowly missing Robby.

Robby jumped over onto the militiaman, wrestling him to the ground, and pounding his fist into his face, knocking him out.

But racing toward Robby was another militiaman. His musket had no bayonet and he was out of ammunition, so he took the butt end of his musket and bashed Robby's head from behind, just as Robby was getting to his feet, knocking him back down to the ground, unconscious.

The Regulators were now in full retreat, except for their brothers who were left behind, wounded or dying on the grass.

Governor Tryon was beaming from his position in the rear, on his horse. He was already crowing, rehearsing the report he would later give to London. "A glorious victory, men!" he exclaimed. "A signal and glorious victory over these obstinate rebels!"

On his side in the meadow, Fergusson, mortally wounded, was feeling the life drain from him. He thought his friend Robby was near him, but he could not see that Robby was lying but a few yards from him, unconscious on the ground.

See ya at the resurrection, boy, Fergusson muttered into the air. He mouthed a few more words, and then the talking stopped. Finally, the old farmer was motionless, with his eyes half-open, looking up blankly into the sky.

The officers ordered that the dozen Regulators captured alive be lashed up tight with rope. They would be taken down to New Bern for trial on the grounds of treason. Governor Tryon planned on making a spectacle of them.

A few of the militiamen passed though the field, looking for dying rebels, helping them on their way to the next life by stabbing them through with their bayonets.

One of them came up to Fergusson. He was pale, and dead, so the militiaman didn't bother with him.

But then he saw Robby on the ground. He didn't appear to have any gunshot wounds. He looked closer, and then Robby moaned a little and began to stir.

"What have we here?" the militiaman said out loud looking down at Robby.

Then he took his musket and lifted it up. He adjusted the bayonet so that it was tight on the end of the barrel.

"Dead rebels are the kind our good Governor likes!" the militiaman called out, and lifted his musket over his head, with the barrel end pointing straight for Robby, readying himself to plunge his bayonet into Robby's helpless body.

Chapter 48

The Major General was riding through the battlefield, when he spotted the militiaman raising up his musket over his head, and ready to thrust the bayonet end into the body of Robby Mackenzie.

"Halt there!" he cried out, and then rode over to where Robby was lying.

The militiaman saluted and put his musket to his side.

"Look here," the Major General said. "This man is unarmed," he said, pointing to Robby. "There's been enough slaughter for one day. Stand down and join the rest of the troop over at the end of the clearing."

The militiaman gave a reluctant smile and then scurried off.

The Major General called for one of his captains, and ordered him to have Robby hand-tied and laid in a cart till he regained consciousness.

"We'll try him with the other captives," the Major General said, "when we get to New Bern. He'll probably swing from the rope, but that won't be on my head at least."

The Royal militia army camped for the night at that spot, then rose with the sun the next day to make the slow return to the

Governor's palace in New Bern with a dozen captured Regulators roped together in one wagon, and with a semi-conscious Robby in another, smaller cart.

That day Robby could not tell whether he was dreaming or asleep. In his groggy half-consciousness, as he lay in the cart, he was vaguely aware of movement all around him. His eyes couldn't focus, and his head was reeling with a crazy-quilt patchwork of pain, dizziness, and nausea.

By the time the Royal army, with Governor Tryon in the lead, made their entry into New Bern, Robby was starting to gain full consciousness. And the pain had become unbearable.

It was aggravated by the yelling, hooting, and hollering by some of the merchants and English sympathizers who had lined the street; they had been instructed to show themselves along the street for Governor Tryon's victory march into town.

Robby's cart stopped in front of the jailhouse. Several militiamen dragged him roughly off the cart, with his hands still tied behind him, and shoved him into a jail cell. He found a corner to sit down in. The remaining rebels were placed in a separate locked cell.

"We are keeping this one away from the others," the captain of the guardhouse told another guard, pointing to Robby.

"Why's that?"

"'Cause they think he might not be one of the Regulators. Or that he might be willing to spill his guts about who was leading the rebels in any event."

After a few hours the guard came up to the cell and called for Robby to step closer to the iron bars.

Robby arose with some dizziness, and after steadying himself from falling, slowly shuffled over to the bars.

"What's your name?" the guard growled.

"Robby…"

"What's your given name, you scum?"

"Mackenzie."

"And where's you from?"

"No place in particular…"

The guard grabbed Robby by the shirt through the bars, and slammed his face up against the iron bars.

"Then you'd better tell me where your people is from…*or else.*"

"Boston…I have family in Boston," Robby muttered in pain.

"That's better," the guard said, and released him from his grip. Robby trudged over to the corner of the cell and laid down, hoping to find a position that would lessen his head pain.

Meanwhile, in the officer's quarters, Major General Ashe was hosting a reception for some of the officers of the 14th Regiment who had recently arrived from Boston.

Captain Rumbly who was one of them, saluted, and then shook hands with Major General Ashe.

"So sorry, Major General, about your problems with these…what do you call them? These Regulator rebels…" Captain Rumbly said, while sipping from a glass of wine and helping himself to the banquet table of chipped beef, sausage, and cheese. "Perhaps we can help you now that we will be stationed here for a while."

"No need now," the Major General replied. "I think they are well in hand. We just defeated them soundly up by Alamance Creek. Killed quite a few. We captured a dozen of them. They're in custody down here, awaiting trial for treason. I'm sure those poor devils will hang."

Just then, the head jailer approached the Major General, who bowed and excused himself.

"Beggin' your pardon, General," he said. "Sorry to interrupt.

But you wanted the names of all prisoners captured up at the Alamance...here they are, sir." And with that he handed a piece of paper to the Major General.

Ashe glanced down at the list.

"Too bad," he muttered. "We were hoping to have captured some of their leaders, particularly Herman Husband. But none of them are on this list..."

Then he took a closer look at something written on the paper.

"Didn't I hear, Captain," the Major General said, "that your Regiment, the 14th, had been up in Boston, before shipping down here to North Carolina?"

"That is correct, General. A rowdy bunch of rebels up there, for sure. One of our sister regiments had to shoot several of them down in the main streets of the city..."

Major General Ashe tapped the piece of paper with his finger.

"It looks as if one of your Boston rebels may be down here among the Regulators."

"Oh?"

"Look here," the Major General said, showing a name on the paper to the Captain.

"Mackenzie," Captain Rumbly said out loud as he read Robby's name from the list. "The name's familiar...give me a minute..."

Rumbly squinted as he thought hard, plopping a piece of beef in his mouth as he tried to remember.

"General, I've got it!" Rumbly announced proudly. "There was a rebel sympathizer up in Boston, a lawyer that went by the name of Mackenzie. He teamed up with another rebel lawyer by the name of John Adams."

"Good show!" the Major General exclaimed. "We may be onto something here. A rebel family, tried and true, then?"

"Well, General," Rumbly said a bit apologetically. "It is not quite that simple, I am sad to say. This Mackenzie fellow, and this other lawyer, John Adams, teamed up to defend a British captain named Preston, when he was charged with cold-blooded murder during an insurrection in Boston."

"Defended the English officer, you say?"

"Yes, sir."

"Then the Mackenzies are Tories?"

"Not exactly, sir."

"Well, make this clear, Captain. What are they?"

"We had always thought," Rumbly replied, "that Mackenzie and Adams were rebel lawyers, and I believe in their hearts they are, sir. Yes, indeed. But very cleverly, they defended Captain Preston, and actually got him off those murder charges, they did. So, in a manner of speaking, I believed they had done that to throw the English off their scent, if you know what I mean."

"Yes, I do," the Major General said.

Then after a few moments of reflection, the Major General excused himself from the reception and made his way over to the jail. There he met the head jailer again.

"Is that Mackenzie?" he whispered to the jailer, pointing to the slumbering Robby.

"It is," he replied.

"Wake him up...and ask him something..."

"Certainly, sir, and what would that be?"

"Ask him," the Major General said, "if he has a relative in Boston. A family member, by the same last name...a lawyer."

Chapter 49

The Regulators had suffered heavy losses as a result of the battle at Alamance Creek. Some twenty rebels were killed, and one hundred were seriously injured. The momentum that had been started as a protest to the gross corruption and mismanagement of the local government that had been permitted by the Royal Governor was now in disarray. The back of the resistance movement in North Carolina, for all appearances, had been broken.

Following the battle, and the arrest of a dozen of the Regulators, half of them received quick trials in the shadow of the Governor's palace, quicker convictions, and a predictable sentence: death by hanging, as traitors against the Crown of England.

But Robby Mackenzie, recovering in his jail cell from a skull fracture, was in a unique situation. Based on the report from Captain Rumbly, Major General Ashe believed that he needed to speak personally with the Governor.

Arranging for a private meeting in the Governor's luxurious palace reception room, Major General Ashe laid out the predicament.

Seated on the silk embroidered settee, Governor Tryon sipped tea as he listened to his General's assessment.

"It appears that Robby Mackenzie's family in Boston has ties to the rebels in that area. However, his brother's successful defense of an English officer makes this a very delicate situation."

"Speaking of delicacies," the governor said, "General, please help yourself to the candies and ladyfingers on the table there. They are most delicious!"

"Thank you, Governor. Very gracious of you, but I think I will pass on that. Now, as I was saying, we have a dilemma…"

"I really don't see the dilemma," the Governor retorted. "Put him on trial, and let him hang with the rest of those agitators against the Crown."

"Well, it may not be as simple as that," the Major General explained. "Some of our Tory friends may wonder why we have executed a relative of a Boston lawyer who came to the aid of an English regiment in Boston in their time of need. On the other hand, simply releasing Mackenzie won't do either. If he later joins up with the rebel cause, it would prove most embarrassing to you."

Governor Tryon munched on a ladyfinger cookie and thought on the matter. Then his face brightened.

"I believe I have an excellent solution," Tryon said. "I know that King George has been contemplating what to do if the hostilities here in the colonies continue to escalate. I have privy myself to conversations with the Crown on that very matter. They are planning, I believe, a crushing imposition of force…revocation of privileges and liberties here in the Americas…institution of a new form of colonial servitude…but also, a plan for evacuation of rebels was discussed. Those who could not be immediately executed should be shipped far away from colonial soil. And I know just the place: Far away from the colonies, yet a location of confinement under the direct control of the Crown of England."

Major General Ashe nodded.

"Do you want me to start making the necessary arrangements?" he asked.

"Yes. Outstanding idea," the Governor replied. "If this Mackenzie fellow becomes important to us for any reason, we will know where to find him. On the other hand, if he is not missed…then, we can have him executed at some time in the future. No one will miss him. No one will wonder about him. And my administration will be spared any political embarrassment. You see, General? This is why my administration over this colony is going to survive and flourish. Because I know how to make principled decisions!"

The Major General smiled courteously, bowed, and then exited the room.

Robby had no way of knowing about the conversation between the Major General and the Governor. Yet he did sense that something was afoot; while the other rebels were being tried and hung, he was still languishing in jail after several months.

Then one day several jailers arrived outside Robby's jail cell, and opened the iron barred door with a loud clang.

"Up you swine!" they yelled.

Robby stood up, his head still mildly hurting, and shuffled over to the open door.

The jailers slapped iron wrist manacles on him, then leg irons, and then shoved him down the hall and over to the side door that led to the outside.

The bright sunlight blinded Robby's eyes, and he covered his face with his arms. Then they pushed him onto the back of a wagon, with two armed guards to accompany him.

"Where am I going?" Robby asked.

"You'll speak *only* when I tell you to speak," one of the guards growled, and he slapped Robby on the side of the head.

Robby moaned from the blow as the world inside his head started spinning, and he grew dizzy with the excruciating explosion of pain in his skull. The guards giggled as he bent over, and nearly passed out.

The uncomfortable ride in the wagon lasted for several hours, until the road they were traveling on led down to a landing at the side of a brackish water inlet, not far from the ocean. The guards dragged Robby off the wagon, and pushed him forward, as he shuffled in the sandy soil over to a rowboat. They told Robby to climb in, and the two guards hopped into the boat.

One of them started rowing, while the other guard sat facing Robby, with his pistol trained on Robby's face.

Robby was facing back toward the landing, so he was unable to guess where the boat was being rowed, or what his ultimate destination might be.

But then, after an hour of rowing up the inlet, Robby was able to see land disappearing away from him on either side. Large waves were washing up against the small craft, and the boat was bobbing wildly up and down with the surf as the guard struggled to keep rowing them ahead.

Then, for an instant, Robby had a frightening thought.

If this rowboat becomes swamped with water, and we have to jump overboard, my heavy irons will make me sink like a stone. I will be drowned in an instant.

But that idea was followed quickly by another—just as disconcerting.

Perhaps that is what they want. Maybe they plan to throw me overboard themselves…rather than a public hanging like the others, is it a private drowning at sea they have planned for me?

Robby was tempted to ask his questions aloud. But the pain

he had experienced from the hand of the guard when he asked his last question convinced him to remain silent—at least for the time being.

Finally, out of his peripheral vision, Robby was able to see a large, looming object behind him. He heard a sound, and he looked up in the cloud-filled sky. There were flocks of seagulls circling above, cawing loudly. Then there was another sound. The creaking and moaning of a large ship just behind him. Then shouts from the crew for the guards to toss up the rope from the bow of the rowboat.

The guard rowed furiously, bringing the skiff closer to the side of the ship. Then he set his oars down, and tossed the bow rope up. He missed the ship, and reeled the rope back in and then tried it again. A sailor caught it and pulled the rowboat up closer until it was lying next to the ship, the sides of the rowboat banging into the vessel with each wave.

A larger rope with a loop tied off at the end was lowered down to the rowboat. The guard pulled it over Robby's torso, and then yanked it up under his arms, and pulled the slipknot tight.

"When they pull you up, don't move your arms," the guard said with a crooked smile. "Unless you want to end up visiting Davy Jones' locker, that is!"

Both of the guards laughed, and then signaled the sailors on the ship to "heave away."

Robby suddenly felt his body yanked off the rowboat, as he swung into the side of the ship, bouncing off it, and then was pulled higher and higher by the sailors on the deck.

When he was almost at the top deck, Robby looked down, and realized the dizzying height of his journey up the rope pull.

For a second, he felt as if he might be sick, so he closed his eyes and tried to breathe easy.

With a last big tug, the group of sailors yanked him over the railing and onto the top deck with a thud. Robby landed on the deck like a large beached fish.

The rope was cast down to the rowboat. Two sailors pulled Robby to his feet. The first mate, a fellow named Jackson, who wore a blue short jacket, and a black, broad brimmed skimmer hat, stood in front of Robby with his hands on his hips.

"So you're the lucky fellow," the first mate said in a raucous voice, "who'll be taking a sea voyage with us! I fear, though, that the accommodations will not exactly be to your liking!"

Several of the sailors belly laughed.

Jackson ordered two of the sailors to lock him away in the hold below.

"Can you tell me, sir," Robby asked, as he was being led away. "Do you know where I am being taken?"

When Robby asked that, Jackson told the sailors to halt. Then he strode up to Robby, and put his face right into Robby's.

"Aye, my boy-o," he shouted back. "I do know. That I do. From what I know of it, ye're bein' taken to the darkest pit in the bottom of hell. Where the key is thrown away, and the sunlight never shines. That is where ye're bound. So enjoy the *comfort* of our damp, stinking hold down below. It will be luxury compared to where you are headin'."

Chapter 50

Through the summer of that year, 1771, and into the fall and winter of the following year, John Adams, and Nathan, and Samuel Adams' political aides worked hard to convince the citizens that John was worthy of their votes. Every village that had a square, every farmer's field that had a farmer walking behind an oxen plow, was visited by Samuel Adams and John; when they would meet the voters, Samuel proudly introduced his "famous cousin John, a man so honest that even the English soldiers trust him…and a man so brave that he will kick those same British soldiers right out of Boston!"

At election time, John Adams won handily. Immediately, he and Nathan began to turn down legal work so they could focus on their work in the colonial assembly.

While Nathan and John were wrangling with other legislators, debating bills, and plotting strategy to advance the cause of the colonies while lessening England's grip, Deborah took little William, upon the invitation of Abigail Adams, and retreated for days on end to the Adams' farm in Braintree.

Deborah missed Nathan desperately, but, in her pragmatic view, if they had to be separated, then there was no one she would rather spend time with than John's wife Abigail.

Together, the women rose at five in the morning, sewed and wove clothing, jarred fruit and vegetables, made entries in the farm ledger, balanced the business books, managed the farm's livestock, watched over their children, and still had time to entertain themselves by playing musical instruments or simply talking.

Conversation—that was Deborah's favorite part of that time with Abigail. She found her friend to be a brilliant and learned woman. Abigail could quote Shakespeare and Milton at length. And she was a woman of particularly well-defined opinions.

"Men and women each have their sphere of contribution," Abigail would say. "Each important in their own right. Now, to act well your part, that is where the true honor lies."

It was in that time that the two women forged their closest bond.

Deborah's time with Abigail was so invigorating that she sometimes felt guilty that she had neglected returning to Boston sooner. Not only to check in on Nathan, but to visit Edith, whose health had continued to deteriorate.

When Deborah did visit her, she was shocked at what she saw: an emaciated face, and lusterless eyes, with a look of helplessness brought about by the unceasing presence of pain in her body. The medicines and elixirs had only partially reduced her discomfort.

In the final days, though, Deborah was there almost constantly. She couldn't help but notice that Edward, who hovered by Edith's bed all day and all night, was adding more to his own burden by somehow contriving, in his own mind, a vague responsibility for her impending death.

"If only I had prayed more fervently," he would whisper to

Deborah, confiding in her whenever Edith would fall into lapses of fitful sleep. "If I had been more possessed of faith…more righteous and less sinful in my arrogant, prideful ways…"

Deborah found it both odd and troubling that she was entertaining the most confidential confessions of a minister of the gospel.

But she found that ultimately, her best duty was to make herself available, and to simply listen—not only to Edward's tearful pleas, but also to Edith's almost unbearable cries for help to lessen the pain that could no longer be lessened.

Deborah had never understood how death could be sometimes described. She had heard it from her own relatives as a child as a "blessing" or as a "reprieve."

But now, being with poor Edith, she understood. Nathan took off from his duties with John Adams at the Assembly to join his wife at Edith's bed in those last days.

While Edith slipped closer to death, Nathan and Edward, who would sit together in the bedroom, did not talk much. Yet Deborah could sense that even in their silence there was a bond. Nathan would occasionally convince Edward to take short walks with him, to stroll on the sidewalks of Boston, just to clear his head. But the walks would not last long. And after a few minutes, they would quickly walk back to the house, to make sure, when Edith drifted back to consciousness, that Edward would be there with her.

Edith died at three-thirty in the morning. When she was buried, it was not in the city. She had always wanted to live in the country, she said. But she knew that her life as a big city pastor's wife would not lead to that. "If I can't live in the country, then let me be buried in the country," she occasionally said.

Though in life she was denied her fervent desire for a child of her own, when she was finally laid to rest, Edith's wishes for her burial were honored in her death. She was buried with a fine view of the countryside in a small cemetery, beneath a spreading chestnut tree.

Chapter 51

At last, Robby Mackenzie's long sea voyage was coming to an end. He had spent most of it in the damp, disgusting hold of the ship; his wrist and leg irons chained to a post. He was fed twice a day on rations that barely kept him alive. And, for the first days of sailing, he was not allowed any liberty on the ship at all.

Finally, Robby decided to engage Jackson, the first mate, in an attempt to convince him that he might be of some use.

"You should know," Robby remarked one day, trying to convey a chipper, upbeat attitude despite his dismal plight, "that I have sailed as a deckhand on several ships up and down the coast of the colonies."

"You don't say," Jackson said sarcastically. "Why, that practically makes you a candidate for admiral now, don't it!"

"No," Robby replied, "I don't claim to be an expert seaman like yourself. Just a helpful hand. And I do notice that for a four-masted rigger such as this, you are short on sailors to trim her."

Jackson strolled up closer to Mackenzie, and looked down at him. Robby's face was beginning to become darkened with soot and whiskers. His clothes were filthy.

"You just want to move about, lad, with some salt sea air on your face. That's all you want."

"Surely it is," Robby answered. "But I think my hard work is a fair trade-off for some fresh air."

Jackson thought on it for a few more seconds. Then his brow furrowed.

"You prisoners is always a problem, you is. One bit of problem with you and it's my back at the captain's lash. And don't think it won't be!"

"I'll be no problem. None at all," Robby said. "You can trust me on that."

"Why should I? You're a dangerous criminal, by my account. Though you certainly don't look the part. Still…the Governor himself has banished you to the bottom cave of God's green earth. He must have had a reason."

"Sure he had a reason," Robby replied with urgency in his voice. "I was an innocent man caught in the middle of an ugly battle. They couldn't hang me, but they didn't want to release me. So here I am. Haven't you ever got yourself caught in the middle of something that wasn't of your doing?"

Jackson screwed up his face a little while he pondered Robby's request. Then he bent down close to his face.

"You make one wrong move—you make one mistake—and we'll lower you down on a rope for shark bait. And I will let the sharks eat you slowly, starting at your feet!"

"Then I have just one regret," Robby said with a smile.

"What's that?"

"Those poor sharks are going to go hungry."

The next day, Jackson had his sailors come down and unlock Robby's chains. He climbed the ladder to the top deck, and when he opened the hatch, he felt the cool, moist air of the ocean. He climbed up on deck, and for the first few moments he let the winds wash over his sore, dirty body, and listened to the rolling ocean waves washing up against the bow of the ship.

But that would be the last time he would be standing still. They had him swab the deck, and then swab it again. He coiled and uncoiled the ropes; he trimmed the sails and repaired a few tears in the sheets up near the crow's nest. He polished the rails, cleaned the tin dishes after meals, and boiled the soiled clothes of the sailors, stirring them with a long stick in the washing pot.

When finally one of the men cried out landfall from the crow's nest, there was a part of Robby that felt sorry that the journey had ended.

He had never forgotten Jackson's warnings about the "hell hole" which was his destination. Whatever it was, he was sure he was better off as a servant deckhand on this ship—or any ship for that matter—than the place where he was heading. Yet, Robby had been careful not to probe Jackson about his ultimate destination. The sailors had been forbidden to discuss it with him.

Part of Robby felt that perhaps, if he worked hard and proved himself to be trusted, that something would change for him. But then he recalled the sermons he had heard from his older brother Edward who preached from the book of Acts; about the apostle Paul, who was a prisoner on the ship bound for Rome. And how even though Paul had saved the entire ship's crew, he was still their prisoner, and was still delivered to his jailers in Rome at the end, to finally die at the executioner's sword.

If that happened to the great apostle Paul, Robby would think to himself, *then what hope is there for me, a lowly sinner, and a Christian of no special account…and a man who holds no particular importance in God's kingdom?*

Robby was on deck, standing next to the other sailors when the port city came into view.

In many ways it looked like the harbors of Boston, or New York. The men at the wharfs looked like the American colonials he knew. Yet Robby knew it could not be. He wondered what journey could have possibly taken so long, just to end up at a place that looked so much like home.

Then it struck him.

I must be somewhere in the British Isles, he thought to himself. He looked at the faces of the sailors. Those were the faces of men who were finally returning home.

As the ship dropped anchor in the waters of the sound, Jackson walked up to Robby. Next to him was the bosun's mate who was carrying Robby's wrist and leg irons.

"Put him back in irons," Jackson said to the sailor. "Then put him ashore with the first boat. Make sure that a fellow from Castle Rock, a big fella by the name of Cameron, is there to take custody of the prisoner."

The first boat was lowered, and, along with several other sailors, Robby scurried down the rope climb that was draped over the side of the ship, and into the long boat.

Robby turned to look back at the ship, and to take his last glace at First Mate Jackson who was standing on the top deck, leaning on the railing.

There were no goodbyes or farewells.

It would be the last time that Robby Mackenzie would ever see Jackson, or that English ship, again.

When they arrived at the dock, there were several uniformed British guards. In the midst of them was a large, red-coated man with a red beard, who was carrying a piece of paper.

"How many prisoners, then?" the large man called out, with a powerful Scottish brogue.

"Just one," a sailor called out.

They lifted Robby out of the boat and onto the dock.

Cameron, the tall Scot, strode up to Robby.

"Ye're Mackenzie, then?" he said, glancing down at the paper in his hand.

"I am."

"It's a pity," Cameron shot back, "that ye're a Scotsman. You give us all a bad name, you sorry son of a mongrel dog."

"I would never want to give my people a less than honorable name," Robby said as he was being led behind Cameron with guards on each side, and away from the docks.

"Oh you wouldn't now, would you?" Cameron roared. "Then the best thing you can do is to die quickly—and to do it quietly."

Suddenly, everything that Jackson predicted seemed to be coming true.

And when Robby asked his next question, he was about to find out how accurate Jackson had been.

"Can you tell me where I am going?" he asked.

"Castle Rock," one of the guards said, as they hoisted him onto a horse-driven cart.

"What kind of place is that?" Robby asked.

The guards burst into laughter.

Cameron, who was sitting next to the driver, shook his head, and then he turned around to answer the naïve lad who was his prisoner.

"Well, now that depends," Cameron said. "It depends on exactly where in Castle Rock you happen to be sleeping and living."

The men kept laughing.

"Now up in the barracks, where we poor sons of the devil have our quarters, that is to say, we soldiers of the Crown of King George, up there in the barracks, it is not too bad by a wee sight. Decent meals and clean beds..."

Now the men were laughing louder.

"But that is not where you will be spending your time," Cameron said. And now the men were in gales of laughter. "No, Mr. Mackenzie, you'll be down in the...shall we say...*lower* apartments. Down in the considerably less luxurious accommodations."

The men riding in the cart were doubled over in laughter.

When the laughter finally died down, Cameron turned to Robby.

Off in the distance, Robby could see a high, dark mountain of stone rising up over a large city. And atop the mount was the structure of a forbidding castle.

"That is the city of Edinburgh," Cameron shouted out. Then he pointed to the dark castle, which was the highest point on the horizon.

"And that is Edinburgh Castle. Where you will be confined," Cameron said. "Down below, in the bowels of that castle—in the deepest dungeon that man has yet devised. And may God help you, for the Crown of England surely won't."

Chapter 52

At any other time, and under almost any other circumstances, Robby Mackenzie would have been ecstatic to experience Edinburgh firsthand. After all, in addition to being one of the great cities of the world, the streets of this famous Scottish capital had been walked by Robby's ancestors, as they witnessed some of the most turbulent and historic events of the last two hundred years. Robby, and his brothers Nathan and Edward, had frequently heard the same stories which had been passed down over the course of six generations of Mackenzies.

Ransom Mackenzie, the aide-de-camp of Minister John Knox, had passed through the fires of the Scottish Reformation. Here in Edinburgh he rescued his bride-to-be, fought the French soldiers of Marie de Guise, the queen mother, stood fast for the gospel despite designs against his life, and, along with Knox, had resisted Mary Queen of Scots to her face.

Ransom's son Andrew was counsel to the Scottish assembly in Edinburgh as they fought the religious tyranny of King Charles of England, with his ruthless attempts to eradicate Protestant worship throughout England and Scotland.

And then there was Peter Mackenzie, Ransom's grandson, who

preached at Greyfriars Church in Edinburgh, and rallied an army of Gospel "Covenanters" who stood fast for the truth of the Bible as Scotland and England, once again, were plunged into a bloody confrontation over religious freedom.

As Robby sat in chains in the back of the prison cart, as it slowly winded its way up the Royal Mile, through the narrow, steep main avenue that ran from the tollbooth at the bottom ultimately up to the very top, where the dark stone walls of Edinburgh Castle loomed large on the skyline, he couldn't help but feel that his slow journey of humiliation through the streets of that city was not unobserved.

Of course there were the onlookers and gawkers, carrying baskets of wares on the street who stared at him as he passed; sometimes they would simply shake their heads. Others would hurl insults. Groups of children, dirty street waifs who lived off stealing and who populated the countless alleyways and cramped closes that ran between the dizzying buildings and tenements, would jeer and throw rocks and refuse. The well-dressed merchants in coaches, or on horseback, would look the other way as they passed him.

Yet Robby felt, in a strange way, that there were other witnesses to his slow ascent to the dungeons of Castle Rock, where he was heading. Those who had gone before. His ancestors, who had risked life, limb, and fortune to preach the Gospel, and to fight against cruelty and tyranny.

Robby knew they were in God's eternal pavilions, and yet they were studying him nevertheless—somehow waiting, and watching—to see if his courage would measure up.

Their eyes are upon me, Robby heard himself saying out loud.

"What are you talkin' about?" one of the guards remarked; he had been dozing off but Robby's comment had awakened him.

Robby did not reply, but simply shrugged.

He looked up at the buildings upon buildings of this city, many stacked five stories high and even higher, crammed so close together that they blocked out the sky.

The streets were choked with a human tide, noisy, mostly soiled and tired looking, dodging wagons and horses, and carts; beggars in rags, rough looking sailors, and tavern brawlers, and lounging soldiers, women in shawls rushing to their destination but looking down at the ground, fearful of making eye contact.

As Robby took in the city of Edinburgh, and thought back to the examples of bravery by those Mackenzies who had come before, he remembered something. He was told about the house of John Knox, the great Scottish Reformer, and how it had been situated on this very street.

"Excuse me, sirs," Robby said to his captors. "Can you tell me where the house of John Knox is located?"

The two guards just shook their heads.

Cameron, who was sitting next to the driver, slowly turned around until he was facing Robby.

"There," he said, pointing to an overhanging apartment on a second floor, which now had someone's laundry draped from its windows.

"Sorry to disappoint *your majesty*," Cameron said sarcastically. "But things have changed a wee bit here in Edinburgh, in case you haven't been told."

Robby was still overwhelmed by the immensity of this busy, dirty, forsaken city when Cameron spoke up again; and when he did, Robby was astounded. At that point they were almost up to the Edinburgh Castle.

"*You however*," the big Scot proclaimed loudly, "*I will scatter among the nations and will draw out a sword after you, as your land becomes desolate and your cities become waste."*

Robby was certain that Cameron's quote originated in the Bible, though he could not remember where it was from.

But it was at that moment, as they neared the top of the road that led to the main gate of the castle, that Robby first began to think that perhaps there was more to Mr. Cameron than met the eye.

As Robby looked up to survey the castle, and the guardhouse which was located against the outer wall of the castle, he noticed a wide courtyard just outside of the castle grounds. There was a crowd of hawkers and merchants milling about, just before the gate. They were selling a variety of flowers, trinkets, knives, and cheap bracelets and rings, arrayed on flat carts, along with men's gloves and ladies' silk handkerchiefs. They were calling out the value of their wares, in a cacophony of songs and chants, to the soldiers and officials filing in and out of the gatehouse.

By then, after the long, rambling cart drive that day, Robby's head was beginning to ache. He closed his eyes and tried to think away the pain—but it wasn't working.

He opened up his eyes, and looked over the sea of faces of the merchants lining the street and the courtyard. A heavyset, round-faced woman selling gloves looked right through Robby and yelled over to the soldiers guarding him, "Why don't ye buy yourself a new pair of gloves for yer strong hands, my love? Come now and be the dapper one, won't ye? New gloves to hold the hand of yer pretty one..."

But the guards grunted and never looked her way.

As Robby passed by the round-faced woman, a girl selling flowers behind her suddenly appeared, her deep blue eyes met Robby's, and he found himself staring at her pretty face, which was framed by red hair tucked underneath a worn bonnet.

But then as the cart continued to travel up the road, Robby craned his neck to get a second look; but the crowd, which was milling about, blocked his view, and an instant later he could see the flower girl no further.

When Robby arrived at the top of the hill, at the gate to the castle, the cart came to a halt, and he was pulled off roughly by the guards.

Cameron paused to talk to the two guards a moment. Robby could not hear what they were discussing. But when they were finished, Cameron stepped away, glanced over at Robby as if he wanted to say something—but for whatever reason could not—and then disappeared into the quartermaster's office.

The two guards pushed Robby into an arched entrance of the castle, and then through a heavy wooden doorway, and then down a steep pair of stone steps that seemed to wind endlessly downward, farther and farther, into the darkness below. Occasionally there was a burning torch set up on a sconce in the stone wall, which lit the way so they could see where they were going. But after they had traversed several succeeding levels, lower and lower, each becoming cooler, and damper, they came to the last torch, and one of the guards plucked the flaming torch out of the wall sconce, and held it in front of them as they continued downward.

Several more levels later, the guard came to an iron gate. He reached down on his belt, fetched a huge key and unlocked the gate. They shoved Robby forward until they came to a cell with a six-inch thick wooden door. The guard unlocked the door, and swung it open. The darkness was so enveloping, that even with the flaming torch to light their way, Robby could not see clearly into the dungeon cell.

But another of Robby's senses came alive.

Robby could smell the overpowering odor of death, and disease, and human waste, and animal droppings, and damp fungi, all mingled together, and it was emanating from the dungeon cell that was now to become Robby's place of confinement for some indefinite period of time—perhaps for the remaining days of his life, however long or short that might be.

Pushed from behind, and still in chains, Robby was sent into the dark dungeon.

And then he heard the monstrous sound of the heavy wooden door slamming behind him. And then the clanking of the iron lock being turned and secured. The last shadows from the guard's torch, which was the only medium of illumination, quickly faded away as the guards scurried up the stairs, not wanting to remain for even a minute in the belly of the dark, stinking dungeon.

And then Robby was plunged into an abysmal pitch blackness. He walked clumsily around in the dark, measuring the size of his small cell. There was no bed. The only other object in the cold stone enclosure was a wooden bucket; it was, he presumed, to be used to relieve himself.

He listened in the dark void, for some sounds of any other life around him.

But he found none. All he could hear was the beating of his own heart, and the dripping of water somewhere in the dungeon.

A few hours later there would be one more sound.

The scrapping, skittering feet of rats, as they scampered through the dungeon.

Dear Lord, Robby said breathlessly. *I do not think I can do this...*

Upward, a hundred feet above the dungeon, in the courtyard, the flower girl was packing her cart to roll it back to the flower shop that was halfway down the Royal Mile. She said good night to the woman with the round face, and then began rolling her cart down the steep, brick-paved avenue.

When she finally arrived at the flower shop, her employer, a tall, rough looking man, was waiting in the adjacent alley, which was barely wide enough for two people, side by side, to travel.

"Took ye long enough," he muttered. "Ye know I gots several other establishments that I own in the city. This ain't the only one. When ye're late, it costs me time. Do ye understand that?"

"I do, Mister Campbell," the flower girl said. Then she pulled a bag of coins from her pocket and handed it over to Campbell.

"Now, that's a good girl," he said, grabbing the bag, and beginning to count the day's revenues.

After he finished, he handed three coins to the girl.

"Flora," he said, "here's yer pay. An extra pence—as you will notice."

"Thank you," she said. Then she turned to leave.

But he laid his arm across the alley, to block her way.

"Is that the way you thank yer employer and yer benefactor?" he growled.

"'Tis," she said, with a little anger in her voice.

"Come now, girl," he said. "Ye've got no one. Ye live in the most despicable room in the underground of the city. Ye could do worse than to be matched with me."

"I do not want to be *matched* with you. Now please let me pass," she said sternly.

"Well, now," Campbell replied. "If ye will not choose wisely, then perhaps I will have to take for myself what I crave..."

And with that he grabbed her by the shoulders, and began sliding his hands downward, tugging at the top of her dress.

Flora reached into her dress pocket and pulled out a knife, and in an instant, had it pressed hard against his neck.

"If ye think ye can take me by force," she said with an iron determination in her voice, "then ye will end up losing much more than yer pride in the bargain."

Campbell paused, then he released her. As she hurried off down the street he burst into laughter and yelled several profanities after her.

A few minutes later, Flora was at a narrow alley. She walked down in, and then entered a side entrance in a five-story-high tenement building. She entered it, and made her way down the winding stairs, to the windowless, airless "underground" below. Once there, she pushed her way through drunks and prostitutes and beggars, and the sick, the poor, and the lame.

Until she came to a small room without windows. She plopped down on a straw bed.

And she stared at the ceiling.

Only one good thing today, God, she whispered.

And then she thought on the young man that she saw being carted up to the Castle Rock in chains.

Chapter 53

The first few months of Robby's confinement in the Edinburgh Castle dungeon were wretched. He was fed once a day. A wooden bowl was slid through a small opening in the bottom of his cell door. The bowl contained a mixture of gruel, moldy meat, and a crust of bread. Following the bowl, a small metal canister of water would follow.

Twice a week he would be allowed, though still kept in his chains, to walk up the spiral staircase, and outside to the blinding light of day. He was allowed thirty minutes of exercise. And then he would be led back to his cell.

He found that even though he licked his bowl clean, the cockroaches would soon be swarming over him in the darkness in an effort to get to the bowl. So he learned, as soon as he was done eating his meager meal, to shove the bowl back outside through the little trapdoor.

The rats were a constant menace. Once night he woke up with a start, and realized he had been bitten in the ankle. He was feverish and sick for days after that; unable to eat, too sick to move, he was not strong enough to mount the stairs for exercise. Miraculously, Robby slowly recovered.

But it was the silence, and the abject, unlighted blackness that tormented Robby the most. He felt himself slipping into delirium at times. He saw images that were not real. Frightful visions that haunted him, but were merely the product of his being deprived of sunlight and human contact.

In order to survive, Robby found that prayer was his only life-line. But it was the kind of prayer that he had never experienced before. Sometimes he was relegated to moaning or weeping. Inarticulate sounds from the bowels of his soul, as he cried out to God to rescue him. For a while, Robby comforted himself by remembering the story of Joseph in the Old Testament: the young man betrayed by his brothers, thrown into a pit, sold into slavery, wrongfully accused, and left for dead in a prison.

I was betrayed only by men I do not know, Robby would tell himself over and over again as he laid in the darkness, on the cold stone floor of the dungeon; *but not by my brothers...never by my brothers.* And he thanked God for that. But when he tried to conjure up the faces of his brothers Nathan and Edward in his mind, he found that he was too sick, and too mentally deprived to do so. His family had become only a vague reality to him, one that he could not fully grasp.

And in his heart, Robby was believing, more and more, that he would never see his brothers again.

Then one day something happened. He did not understand, at first, why it had occurred.

Robby heard a guard coming down the stairs. He saw the familiar torch being carried by the jailer.

Then he saw a second light still burning outside his cell, even after the guard had left. For the first time since his incarceration, the guard had lit a torch in a wall sconce on the wall opposite the door to Robby's cell.

Light was now pouring into Robby's wretched room.

Robby began to weep.

Thank you for the light, Lord, he was crying.

The following day, his food rations were doubled. He was now eating twice a day. Though the food was still putrid, he forced himself to consume it to build up his strength. Robby began a regimen of walking around the circumference of his cell so that the humors of his blood would be stirred.

Then, his outside time in the yard was expanded. He was taken out every other day. And not just for thirty minutes, but for more than an hour. And he was not kept close to the door that led down to the dungeon, but was allowed, under the watchful eye of a guard, to stroll around the courtyard, and eventually, even over to the main gate.

Robby discovered that the same time every day, usually in the late afternoon, the local merchants, and the sellers of trinkets, and the flower girls would show up to peddle their wares to the soldiers leaving the castle, or those entering the grounds during the change of the castle guard. Occasionally he would see civilians being led into, or out of the castle grounds, though he did not understand their business.

Nor did Robby understand what had accounted for the change in his fate, or the special favors that he was now being shown.

It was not long after these changes, and Robby's newfound freedoms in the courtyard of the castle, that on one day he noticed a familiar face. In the crowd of peddlers on the other side of the gate he recognized, for just an instant, the pretty face that he had seen on the day that he was first being carted up to Edinburgh Castle.

But when he saw the girl again, and she looked at him through the iron grates of the front gate, he turned away in shame. He knew his beard was unruly, and his clothes were disgustingly dirty.

I do not want her to see me this way, he thought to himself.

But when he was led back down to his dungeon cell, and for the rest of that day and throughout that night, he could think of nothing else except the pretty girl on the other side of the gate, selling her flowers. He knew it was foolish to be so possessed with a woman whom he had never met; and with whom he had no contact, and would probably never meet. But somehow her face was something he could hold on to, and it helped him forget his plight.

But two days later, when Robby was next allowed out in the courtyard, he quickly scanned the crowd of peddlers outside the castle gate.

The pretty flower girl was not there.

He didn't know what to think about that. But he had made a decision of sorts in the intervening days, and he would now put it to the guard.

"Can I ask you a question, sir?" Robby asked the guard as he was leaning against the outer wall of the castle.

The guard straightened up a bit, and eyed Robby suspiciously.

"What do ye want?" he asked.

"I was wondering," Robby said, "whether it would be possible…if it wouldn't be too much trouble…if I could have a bowl of water to wash my face…and a straight-edge to shave my beard…"

The guard thought on it for a moment before he answered. Then he called out to another guard from the quartermaster's office to come out. He whispered something to the other man, who then returned to the office.

"We're not promisin' anything," he said.

But the next day, a bucket of water was brought down to his cell. It felt so good to splash water on his face and torso that Robby laughed out loud. Then the guard cautiously gave him a straight-edge and a piece of mirrored glass, and watched him as he shaved the long whiskers off his face.

When Robby was done shaving he passed his hand over his face, and feeling the clean, smooth skin, he couldn't help but smile.

The next day Robby was not expecting to be exercised; but to his surprise, another one of the guards arrived and told him he would be given time to stretch his legs outside. Unlike his prior walks, today the ankle manacles were removed, and he was left only with his wrists in chains.

But then, when he passed out into the courtyard, he was surprised to see no guard waiting there to observe him.

Instead, Captain Angus Cameron, the big red-bearded Scot, was standing nearby with one hand behind his back. There was a blanket tucked under his underarm.

It was late fall by then, yet the weather had been uncharacteristically mild for Scotland. But on that day, a chill wind had come blowing in.

Cameron strode over to Robby, and without looking directly at him, Cameron tossed the blanket at him.

"A wee nip in the air today," Cameron said. "Let's take a walk, Mr. Mackenzie from Boston."

They walked along the fortifications of the castle. It was far beyond the normal area to which Robby had been allowed to walk.

Upon coming to one of the large cannons at the palisade, Robby paused to study it. He had never seen such a formidable piece of artillery.

"What's the matter, boy?" Cameron said. "Have ye never seen a cannon before?"

"Not this big," Robby said with amazement. "I've been a mate on some ships, and I've seen guns all right. But nothing like this."

"This little thing?" the big Captain remarked with a laugh. "This is nothing. You should have seen the big *Mons*—a real giant of a cannon. She used to toss a four-hundred-pound ball a mile if it was an inch. But then, oh, about fifteen years ago, the English moved her from here to the Tower of London. She's been there ever since."

Robby swept both of his hands, chained together, along the smooth iron surface of the cannon. Cameron was a few feet away from him, looking out from the perch of the castle battlements, which loomed high over the city.

"The thing about a cannon," Cameron remarked, looking out over the rooftops of Edinburgh while he spoke, "is that it *levels* the battlefield. The great *Mons* cannon was built back in the late 1600s. It was intended for the Scots to use it against the English—all of that was long before the Union of the Crowns of course, and the 'marriage' between London and Edinburgh. But it leveled the field between Scotland, which was always poor and understaffed military-wise, and England, which was prosperous and had powerful armies."

Robby was listening carefully. Though he could not then figure out why Cameron had decided to accompany him on his exercise that day; nor why the imposing Scotsman had bothered to share a bit of military history with him.

Then Cameron turned to Robby and said, "Walk about the courtyard by yourself, Mackenzie. Just don't get any ideas of trying to scale the walls or get through the gate. My men have orders to shoot, and they are all excellent marksmen."

With that, Cameron turned and walked away. Robby followed him with his eyes until he saw him disappear into the quartermaster's office.

I would like to see if the flower girl is out there today, Robby thought to himself, and then hurried over toward the gatehouse.

Chapter 54

As he walked quickly toward the guardhouse and the main gate to the castle grounds, Robby had a strange thought. *What if Captain Cameron was giving me a signal of some sort...allowing me to walk freely by myself...permitting me to do so without ankle manacles...what if he is allowing me to escape?*

The thought would have been a wild and fanciful one, except for two incontrovertible facts: that Robby had been given extraordinary privileges of late, which Robby could not help but feel were from the hand of Cameron himself; and also that Cameron was a proud Scotsman, himself. Perhaps, Robby thought, there was some motivation on his part to help a fellow Scot.

But those imaginations soon came to a halt, when Robby approached the guardhouse and saw that there was a full contingent of armed soldiers at their usual places on either side of the wide, iron-barred gate.

He looked through the bars out into the crowd of peddlers that were plying their wares on the other side. There seemed to be a smaller group than usual.

Robby scanned the faces.

Then he saw her.

Now he could get a better look. She had the same worn bonnet. Her red hair was not combed up as the well-to-do ladies would often wear it; but instead, her locks were cascading down her back, from underneath the bonnet.

She was even prettier than he had remembered. Large, delicate blue eyes.

But there was a firmness, even a hardness, about her. She carried herself as if she had been forced to fend off the ugly aspects of Edinburgh all by herself.

The flower girl was calling out to passersby, most of them local merchants or soldiers.

"Bonny flowers!" she yelled out. "Buy a flower and win the heart of yer bonnie lass!"

As she called out she turned toward the gate. And then she caught sight of Robby.

That is when their eyes met, and for a moment, she stopped walking, and stopped her calling.

As the two of them gazed at each other though the gate, Robby grew bolder, and began walking to the gate. He could hear bits and pieces of the guards' conversations. One of them, the shortest one, was speaking about his wife's birthday coming up.

The four armed guards, two on each side of the gate, stopped their conversations and riveted their attention on the young man in wrist manacles who was walking toward the iron bars.

"See here now," the short guard called out to Robby, "what do ye think ye're doin'? Get back now, before we put a bayonet into ye."

"Sorry," Robby said with a smile. "Didn't want to cause you alarm. Just wanted to spy out the flowers that the pretty girl here is selling."

"And why would that be?" the guard shot back.

"Dunno," Robby said with a smile. "Maybe I wanted to give you some advice on which ones you should buy for your wife…"

One of the other guards laughed and said, "Hamish…now you've got the prisoners tellin' ye how to give flowers to yer beloved!"

"You there!" the first guard said to Robby, with anger in his voice, "I don't need the sorry likes of ye to tell me how to buy flowers for my wife!"

"Of course not," Robby said, noticing that the flower girl had made her way up to the gate and was listening intently to the conversation. "But you have an impressive position as a castle guard…just would have thought that you would want the best for your lady."

And then, Robby added, "And I think the ladies all prefer the heather and bluebells…"

"But then," he continued, "what do I know? You would know best…"

"That's the truth, you scum, and dinna forget it!" the guard barked out.

One of the guards from the quartermaster's office was walking toward Robby to fetch him back to the dungeon cell, so Robby started toward him.

After Robby was a distance away, and the other three guards were gathered together to discuss their schedule of rotation, the short guard stepped up to the gate and motioned for the flower girl to come closer.

When she did, he lowered his voice and called through the gate to her.

"How much for the heather and bluebells?"

The flower girl broke into a brilliant smile.

"Only fivepence, sir. And thank ye!"

"Come back in an hour," the guard said with a lowered voice, "when I'm off watch…and have the flowers with ye…and I'll pay ye as I leave for the day."

"Oh thank you!" the flower girl said, beaming. And as she turned to walk back to her cart, she quickly threw a frantic look to where Robby had been standing to see if she could find him.

But by then, he had been led by the guard through the castle door, and was already walking down the spiral stone steps that led to his cell far below.

The next day, Robby was led outside again for an hour of fresh air and exercise. He swept his hair back with his hand as he stepped out into the daylight, suddenly embarrassed by his manacles, and his soiled, shabby clothing. The guard who escorted him disappeared as soon as Robby walked outside.

At least I have had a shave and a wash, Robby thought to himself, and immediately looked down toward the gatehouse and the peddlers on the other side, searching for the flower girl.

Captain Cameron was not with him on that day, and he realized that he was free to roam around the courtyard by himself.

As he glanced down toward the group of peddlers, he spotted the flower girl toward the front of the crowd.

Then, an instant later, she saw him. She looked down at her cart and pretended to be rearranging the flowers that were contained in funnels made of newspapers.

She glanced up out of the corner of her eye, studying Robby as she fiddled with the flowers.

Robby took a few slow steps toward the gatehouse and the main gate.

Then the flower girl took several bunches of flowers into her arms, and strolled up to the gate. There she spoke for a few moments with the guard.

When he stopped talking with the red-haired girl with the armful of flowers, the guard swung the iron gate open for her and let her pass though.

Now she was about twenty feet away from Robby.

Robby tried to be nonchalant, but was careful to walk in the same direction as she was, and was perfectly parallel to her. Then he quickly angled himself closer to her as he walked until he was then about five feet away.

"I would be a perfect gentlemen, and offer to carry that for you," Robby said with his best, polished smile, "but my hands and wrists are already busy holding up these chains."

Then he raised his wrists to show his manacles.

"Of course it is an important matter, this business of holding onto these chains," Robby continued. "Not anybody can do it. Certainly not. Takes a great deal of skill and strength, not to mention perseverance. That's why they picked me to do it!"

The flower girl struggled to look disinterested, but her smile and her deep dimples betrayed her.

"So," she said as she walked. "You consider yourself as possessing those qualities then?" She had a definite tone of skepticism in her voice as she spoke.

"Oh, I do, yes indeed," Robby replied.

Then the flower girl halted and swung around to face him.

"Ye know," she said with an air of exasperation, "I must be mad, talking like this with a prisoner. Simply mad! Ye are not to be trusted. Ye must know that…"

Robby lowered his head a little.

"I am sorry, Miss, I truly am," he responded. "I sure do not want to make you feel ill at ease. I surely don't. Please forgive me…and I won't be bothering you again."

Robby turned to leave.

But as soon as he did, the flower girl called after him.

"Thank ye, anyway," she said, "for helping me sell my flowers to the guard yesterday. And now, as a result, I'm selling flowers by the bunch for an officers' banquet being held here at the castle tonight. So…thank ye…sir…"

Robby stopped walking and turned to face her.

"You are most welcome," he said with a wide smile.

Then the girl turned and walked away from him, entering through the large arched entrance of the castle, toward the inner courtyard and the officers' quarters within.

Robby strolled aimlessly around the same spot waiting for her to return.

Finally, after delivering her flowers, the girl returned and crossed into the outer courtyard, heading toward the gatehouse and the main gate.

Robby scurried up to her until he was about four feet away and kept pace with her as she rapidly walked toward the guards.

"I see you managed to drop off all your flowers!" he called out to her.

"So," she said with a smile, but never turning her gaze toward him. "In addition to yer other sterling qualities, it appears that ye have the use of both of yer eyes too!"

He chuckled and nodded his head.

As they neared the gatehouse, still walking side by side, Robby asked her a question.

"Would it be improper for a gentleman to ask you for your name?"

"No," she replied, "it wouldn't. But there seems to be some doubt about yer qualifying as a *gentleman,* now wouldn't ye agree?"

"I suppose it would *appear* that way," Robby admitted reluctantly. "But," he added, "appearances can be deceiving."

She kept walking.

"So," he persisted. "What is your name, if I may ask? Just so… just so I may know how to lead more customers to you in the future!"

She stopped in her tracks and looked back to him with a smile.

"*Flowers!*" she called out to the guards who were milling about at the gatehouse. "*Pretty flowers!*"

And as she called that out, she glanced back at Robby with a bright, dimpled smile.

Suddenly, as Robby stood there staring back at her, and finding himself lost in her smile, he forgot for a few, fleeting moments that he had manacles on his wrists, and that he was still an inmate of the dungeon of Castle Rock.

"Prisoner!" a guard in back of him called out gruffly. "Back to your cell!"

Robby turned reluctantly, and was led to the doorway from which the steep, spiraling stone staircase led down to his cell.

But then a thought broke through, into his mind, and when it did, his brain exploded with a sudden revelation about the pretty girl.

Of course! Robby thought to himself, and he turned back to cast one last look down to the flower girl on the other side of the iron gate.

Flowers… "pretty flowers" she said…that's it…her name must be Flora…her name is Flora!

Chapter 55

Over the weeks and months that ensued, as Edinburgh slowly eased into winter, and then Christmas, and into the dreary months of January and February, Robby found himself the recipient of a wonderful and growing friendship with Flora.

By then, another unexplained aspect of unexpected grace had been bestowed on Robby: He was finally allowed to stroll around the castle grounds during his exercise period without wrist manacles of any kind.

By the time that the city was blanketed in a light snow, and the temperatures dipped, there were few peddlers that gathered outside the castle courtyard gate.

And, of course, it was far past the flower-selling season, so Flora was unable to visit the castle as much as before; though there was a benefit in the flower season coming to an end; she was able to finally quit her position with the cruel, barbarous Mr. Campbell, the owner of the shop. Flora had, over the course of many weeks, discussed more and more about her life in her talks with Robby, each time she had contrived reasons to pass through the gate and walk with him in the courtyard; during those walks she explained how both her parents had died in the plague. How her only brother, Sean, had left for Ireland, and his whereabouts were unknown. Yet still, she did not tell him the reasons why she had quit working with Campbell.

In one of her many jobs, she worked as a seamstress and a weaver, and she had talked her employer into allowing her to sell woolen scarves and jackets up at the castle gate. She had managed to sell enough so that her continued trips to the castle were justified—and so she could time it perfectly, enabling her to visit with Robby during his daily exercise periods.

In turn, Robby had explained much to her about himself. About his family in Boston, and his brothers; about his vagabond life, his work with Jared Hollings—though he did not share the unfortunate events that precipitated his sudden departure, and the reasons for his fleeing to North Carolina.

And he shared with Flora the details of his friendship with Fergusson, and the old farmer's sad death in the Battle at Alamance Creek, and how Robby's wrongful arrest and the unwarranted suspicion that he was a member of the Regulators had led to his being shipped over to Edinburgh to be held captive there.

But one day, as winter began edging its way into the beginnings of spring, in the year 1772, Robby heard an offhanded comment from one of the guards; but it substantiated a speculation that Robby had long been harboring.

And after Robby heard it, he couldn't wait to share it with Flora.

"One of the guards," Robby said, barely able to control his enthusiasm, "told me that Captain Cameron had asked for the papers for my incarceration here. He wanted to read himself the background of my being transported for imprisonment to Edinburgh dungeon."

"So, what do you think that means?" Flora asked, as they strolled together along the high stone castle abutments.

"If my hunch is correct," he replied, "it means that Cameron is searching for some reason to get me released. That for some reason, he is trying to help me."

"Do you really believe that?" Flora asked excitedly.

"I believe it in my heart. Yes, I do."

"Why would he do such a thing?" Flora asked.

Robby knew why she questioned it. Flora had lived a hard life, and, for many years since her parents' deaths, was forced to defend herself against the wiles of unscrupulous men.

"I don't know—not for sure. But I do know that God can work miracles through the hearts of men."

Robby had learned that Flora was a Christian woman herself, but she had developed a slightly suspicious view of miracles.

She had learned that life was, by and large, a tough pilgrimage, and that spectacular "acts of God" could not always be counted on to rescue the downtrodden, or the oppressed.

But two more months went by and Robby heard no further news about Captain Cameron's inquiry into his state of imprisonment. Occasionally Robby would see Cameron, but as much as he was tempted to confront him directly, he chose not to.

Robby had prayed for wisdom, and his sense was that if the Scots Captain had some news to share, then he would have shared it.

Then worry began to set in. Flora had been up to the castle less than usual. She had never fully bared her heart to Robby, and he, in turn, had never fully disclosed his love for Flora. For Robby, it would have been irresponsible to pledge his love to a young woman who lived on the outside of the prison, while he was still a resident of the dungeon within; particularly because he did not know whether he would ever see freedom outside the castle grounds again.

It had been more than a week since Robby had seen Flora, and his mind was running wild with awful possibilities. She was beautiful and clever, and the way Robby saw it, she must be receiving offers of betrothal on a regular basis.

When he coupled that with the fact that Flora, despite her hard work in multiple jobs, lived a life of destitution, and was forced to rent a public room in the horrid "underground" of Edinburgh, the eventual outcome seemed obvious to Robby: some wealthy merchant would most certainly sweep her off her feet, and place her in the safety, luxury, and comfort that she deserved.

Besides, Robby thought to himself, *why would she want to risk her future on a man who was incarcerated in the Castle dungeon, and whose future was so dim, and hopeless?*

Those were the thoughts that were racing through Robby's mind, and which had plunged him into a deep melancholy.

But he was about to receive news that would plunge him even deeper still.

Captain Cameron strode out, that day, as the weather was mild, and the birds were flitting to and fro, all around the buttresses of the Castle.

His look was a stern one, so much so that it startled Robby and caused him to begin thinking the worst before the large Scottish captain of the castle guard had said a word.

Robby was outside in the courtyard when Cameron approached him.

He had a piece of parchment in his hand. There was a gold seal and a ribbon dangling from the end of it.

"Do ye know," Cameron began, "that I have made certain inquiries into yer confinement? Do ye know that?"

"I did know that," Robby said.

"It was not out of sympathy for ye, for a man in my position cannot afford to suffer sympathies. The world is a world o' woe, and only the hardy and the steadfast survive."

Robby said nothing, but his eyes kept darting down toward the sealed document that Cameron was holding in his big fist.

"So, after my inquiries," Cameron continued, "I find out that back in the American colonies things are not peaceful. That England is bracing to give yer homeland a thrashing that she'll not long forget. His Majesty does not abide rebels, and yer brother and others with whom he is joined have been tarnished as rebels. And so, as a result…"

Then Cameron lifted up the sealed document.

"As a result," he went on, "this warrant has been delivered to me."

Then his booming voice lowered, and there was a kind of tenderness to it.

"A warrant," Cameron said softly. "Oh, son…I am afraid that it is a warrant for yer execution. And I am the one to make sure it is carried out."

For a moment, Robby felt the earth underneath him grind, and shake, and begin to open up under his feet. He looked down, but it was not the ground that had opened up. It was Robby's life, and everything in it, being shaken to the foundations.

Cameron was looking him straight in the eye.

"Did ye hear what I said?"

"I did," Robby answered quietly.

Now Cameron's voice was gaining momentum, and there was a rising of anger in it.

"Let me tell you something about *me*," the big Scot said, almost shouting. "Because ye're just young and foolish and ye've got much to learn…you see…the thing about me, about bein' a Cameron such as I am, is that we are loyal. Do ye understand? Loyal to the death we are. And ye're probably thinkin' 'loyal I am to the King of England,' and ye can bet that I surely am."

Robby was trying to listen and understand, but Cameron's ramblings seemed so very irrelevant compared to the earthshaking news he had just revealed to Robby.

But in a moment, Robby would begin to understand.

"Now there was an ancestor of mine, by the name of Geordie—Geordie Cameron. He lived in the wilds of the Great Glen, the Highlands to the north of here. Have ye ever been there?"

Robby shook his head.

"Of course ye haven't," Cameron said with a strange exuberance. "But I have. And I have learned the history of my clansfolk, as you should have too. Now my ancestor Geordie was best friend, and a fellow cattle drover, to a man named Hamish Chisholm. Well, one day, these two friends were out in the fields together, and some French mercenaries hired by another clan came upon Geordie and Hamish, and ran them through with their swords and their arrows. Murdered them in cold blood—and then murdered their families as well. Only one girl survived. Her name was Margaret Chisholm, and she fell in love with a young man named Ransom Mackenzie. Does any of this ring a bell in that thick skull of yours? Margaret became the wife of Ransom Mackenzie—yer line—yer kinsman."

Now it did sound familiar, as Robby had heard the stories about his ancestor, Ransom Mackenzie.

"Now which clan do ye suppose ordered the French mercenaries to slay my ancestor, Geordie, and Hamish, the father of your ancestor Margaret?"

"I don't know…" Robby stuttered.

"The Campbells! Of course it was the Campbells!" Cameron shouted. "Those dirty rotten Campbells!"

Then Cameron came right up to Robby's face, and lowered his voice to a whisper.

"And as for this warrant for yer execution…did ye know—no, of course ye didn't, but I will tell ye that I know it to be so—that a local merchant here in Edinburgh, a lowlife snake of a man, learned that a young flower girl had fancied you and refused to fancy him, and so he made certain inquiries through certain acquaintances of his—his contacts with a Crown's counselor in the Court of King George—and urged them, purely out of spite, to make sure that they put you to death as a rebel?"

Then Cameron grabbed Robby's shirt in his fist, and lowered his voice down to a whisper so low that Robby had to strain to hear it.

"And what do you think the *clan name is* of this snake of a man who wants you dead? He is a *Campbell!* So a Campbell wants me, a Cameron, to have ye, a Mackenzie, executed, when in fact the Campbells were responsible for killing kin of both of us in ages past!"

Cameron straightened up and looked around quickly to make sure that no one was around.

"Now," he concluded. "I have to leave ye, for I am greatly distressed by the fact that this time tomorrow there will be *only one guard at the guardhouse*, and a man with very poor eyesight I might add. And so, I leave you—*Robby Mackenzie*—to ponder that fact…and to let it roll around in that thick skull o' yers."

After Cameron had disappeared into the quartermaster's office, Robby was left alone to his thoughts.

But when he turned toward the guardhouse, he now realized that Flora had been cleared through the gate, and was walking, her arms across her chest, toward him.

And the look on her face was grim.

Chapter 56

Flora was clearly troubled as she approached Robby.

"I have not seen you," Robby said quietly, "for over a week..."

"Aye, and with good reason," she retorted.

"Flora, I've something to tell you," Robby began. "Something terrible I have just heard."

"Well I've something to tell ye first," she blurted out. "And I am not sure how to say it."

Robby was paralyzed now, with apprehension.

"So I will just say it," she began.

Then Flora took a deep breath, closed her eyes, and then proceeded to tell Robby the news.

"It so happens that Kenneth Halloway, a very successful shipping merchant, and a customer of our knitting and tailoring shop, has sought out my company on several occasions when visiting the shop."

Somehow, Robby should have been expecting it; but it still came as an excruciatingly painful disclosure.

"And more than that," she explained, with her eyes still closed, "he has sought my hand in marriage."

By now, tears were streaming down Flora's face and she could not hide the misery of her predicament any longer.

"I need you to say something," Flora said with a pleading urgency in her voice.

But Robby was dumbstruck and did not know how to respond, except to feel crushed within, and he wondered whether the execution that Cameron had mentioned to him might be an enviable end to all of it.

"Won't ye say *anything* to me?" she pleaded.

"What would you want me to say?" Robby said, lashing out. "I have no future, Flora. None! Even though *I love you more than my life itself*...and my soul only sings when I am with you, now it does not matter. None of it. Because I am destined for the hangman's noose, as I learned today. Unless I escape immediately, and then what would I have to give you? A life on the run from His Majesty's soldiers? What kind of life would that be?"

Now Robby, whose voice was trembling as he struggled against the tears, noticed something in Flora.

Her face had softened, and a smile started in the corners of her mouth, as she wiped the tears from her cheeks and grabbed his face in her hands.

"What kind of life?" she asked, her voice cracking with emotion. "I will tell you something, Robby Mackenzie. Any life would be a good life if I can spend it with you. Do ye hear me, laddie?"

"How...why..." he stuttered.

"Because I now know that ye love me. It certainly took you long enough to tell me that."

"I couldn't share that with you," Robby said, stammering, "because my life has been in jeopardy."

But then Flora's smile evaporated and she suddenly thought back to something he had said.

"Yet, ye said *hangman's noose*...that's what ye said..."

"I did," Robby said, but then he put his arms around her shoulders and drew her close to him. "But I believe there may be a way of escape. I fear to involve you dear Flora, my precious Flora..."

"If ye *don't* involve me," she said angrily, "then I will curse yer grave forever if this plan of yours fails. Now tell me all, and tell me how I can help ye, my precious love of a man."

"You need to be here at a certain time tomorrow," Robby said.

"Anything," she whispered, looking about to make sure they were not being overheard.

And then he added something else.

"And we will need the help of a trusted friend..."

Chapter 57

It was a rainy day, the kind typical of Scotland. It was a slow, misty, soaking rain that had started late in the night and continued into the next day. The skies were iron-gray and there was a gloom everywhere.

Down at the guardhouse, there was a solitary soldier named Haversham who was posted there. He was in the small guardhouse, hiding out from the rain. A tall man, in his forties, Haversham had been in numerous military campaigns, and he bore a slashing scar across his face, and a left eye sewn shut, to prove it.

Then he heard a female voice.

"Excuse me, good sir," the young woman on the other side of the gate called out.

Haversham poked his head out of the guardhouse to look. He saw two women standing in the rain—a small one, and a larger one—both of them dressed in hooded coats. Each of them was holding a large, covered cooking dish. The larger one had a pleasant, round face. She was the friend of Flora's whom Robby has seen on his first day in Edinburgh, as he was rolled up the Royal Mile on his way to the dungeon.

Flora, the smaller woman, addressed him again.

"Beggin' yer pardon," she said. "But we have some cooked goods for the officers' mess hall."

"Nobody told me to be on the lookout for such as that," the guard grumbled.

"I am sorry," Flora continued. "But Captain Cameron requested these."

"I doubt by a far sight that he *needs* anything more to eat," Haversham muttered. Then thinking better of his comment against an officer, he turned to both of the women and added, "And ye didn't hear me utter any such words as ye just heard. Ye understand that?"

Both of the women nodded their heads. Then Flora spoke up again. "Sir, we have an abundance of sweet cinnamon bread. Perhaps you could relieve us of one of the small loaves?"

"I might," he grunted in response. "I just might at that…"

Flora reached in her cape and pulled out a small loaf of bread and passed it through the ironwork of the gate. Haversham snatched the loaf, then tore off a bite with his teeth and started chewing. He grunted, and then tore off another bite.

As the guard was chewing noisily, Flora and her companion shifted their feet nervously. The only audible sounds were that of the guard's discourteous lip-smacking and swallowing as he gorged himself on the cinnamon bread, the clopping of a carriage a few blocks down the Royal Mile, and the dribbling of the rain as it ran off the roof of the small guardhouse.

When he was finished, the guard licked every one of his fingers and then wiped his hands on his pants.

Why doesn't he just let us in? Flora was saying to herself.

Flora's hands were gripped tightly on the inside of her cape as she waited for the guard's response.

Finally she had waited long enough.

"Will we be allowed, sir, to bring these dishes of food inside?"

"I really ought to clear this with an officer," the guard said. "I could go inside and find out what's what with this story of yours..."

"Yes, I understand," Flora shot back. "But, uh...what should we say if someone goes by and asks us why you have left your post unguarded?"

Haversham stared at Flora. Then he looked back toward the castle, trying to judge exactly how long he would have to leave his post unattended while he tried to locate an officer to authorize their entry.

Then he turned back to the two women and eyed them closer.

"Let me see the food ye got there," he growled. And then he took out a huge key and unlocked the gate and swung it open.

When the two women walked through the gate, the guard ordered them to lift off the lids to their food dishes.

Flora looked nervously over at her companion, but said nothing.

"Are ye sure?" Flora said.

"Aye, of course I'm sure, ye daft woman!" Haversham shouted and grabbed her food dish.

He took his hand and lifted off the lid, and handed the lid over to Flora.

Haversham looked closer at the contents. Then, with one hand holding the bottom of the dish, he reached into the dish with his other hand.

After a moment, he withdrew it.

He had snatched a loose piece of roast beef, dripping with gravy, and popped it in his mouth.

"Ye see," Flora said trying to be cheery. "I wanted to spare ye the temptation."

Haversham waved both of them through.

At that exact moment, several stories down in the castle dungeon, Robby was pacing impatiently in his cell. The guard was supposed to have come to unlock his cell door at the usual time, so he could go out to the courtyard for exercise.

But no guard had come. Robby knew that his plan of escape could only have any chance of success if *everything* worked perfectly, and already there seemed to a problem.

Help me, Lord, Robby prayed quietly as he walked back and forth in his cell.

Finally, after a few more minutes, he heard the steps of the guard, slowly descending the stairs.

When the guard did arrive, a few minutes late, he didn't unlock the cell.

"It's raining out there," he said in a tired monotone. "We'll exercise ye tomorrow instead."

"I don't mind the rain," Robby shot back.

"Well, I do," the guard replied.

"Captain Cameron has ordered fresh air for me *every day*," Robby said firmly.

The guard sighed, then slowly unlocked the cell door.

Robby started to walk quickly up the stairs ahead of the guard.

"Wait up," the soldier said behind him several steps. "What's yer hurry?"

Robby slowed down a bit as he climbed the spiraling stone steps.

Wait for me, wait for me, Robby was thinking as he considered the two women whom he was hoping would be waiting for him; *don't let them panic and leave, dear Lord...*

When Robby got to the top of the stairs, and opened the door from the Castle turret which led out to the courtyard, he looked around frantically.

But neither Flora nor her friend were there.

The rain was now coming down in sheets. The guard was standing right next to Robby.

Then Robby caught sight of Flora and her female companion walking in the rain, heads down, having left the officers' mess hall in the castle and heading toward them across the courtyard. Their hands were empty.

As they approached Robby and the guard, who were both standing in the doorway of the castle turret, both women veered over toward the men.

As they did, Robby announced to the guard, "I think I'll stretch my legs a bit—rain or no rain..."

The guard nodded his approval as Robby stepped quickly into the rain, and disappeared around a corner of the castle.

As Flora and her friend approached the guard, Flora flashed a bright smile, and engaged him in conversation.

"We have just dropped off some food in the officers' mess, roast beef, sweetbread, boiled potatoes. I hope you and the others enjoy it," she said. "You must be having a banquet for the officers' families?"

While Flora was talking, her taller friend stepped past the guard and pretended to shelter herself from the downpour, by leaning against a stone wall, under the tile eaves.

"Don't know anything about any banquet," the guard muttered.

The other woman froze her posture while slowly edging her way sideways, inch by inch along the wall, in the direction that Robby had headed, trying not to catch the attention of the guard.

"Of course I suppose ye're married," Flora said brightly to the guard. "Ye bein' a handsome one and all…"

The guard tried to act casual, but he smiled a little at that, and he and Flora carried on small talk for a few minutes.

Then suddenly, the guard looked around and said, "Where is yer friend?"

With that he stepped out of the enclosure of the doorway and into the pouring rain and began looking around.

Suddenly, around the corner, the caped figure appeared, scurrying through the rain toward them, head bent down low.

"All right, Rosalie," Flora said loudly, "we've got to get back to the kitchen at Lord Williston's house."

Both of them turned and began walking, with their backs to the guard, strolling quickly now toward the guardhouse gate, where Haversham was still standing at his post.

Their heads were hunched down as they approached the last guard who was posted; the last line of detection between the inside of the secured castle courtyard, and the City of Edinburgh outside the Castle Rock.

"Keep yerself dry now!" Flora cried out to Haversham as they approached the iron barred gate, and then stood there, waiting for him to open it, and to let them pass.

Haversham looked at both of them. He had the heavy ring of large keys dangling from his hand. He swung the ring back and forth a little, and the keys jingled and jangled together.

Then Haversham stepped toward the big square lock on the gate to open it. But something caused him to stop, just as he was fishing out the key for the gate.

It was nothing about Flora that gave him concern. Rather, there was something different about her companion, and he couldn't exactly figure out what it was. He let the key ring dangle from his hand, as he moved his head a little to study the other person in the hooded cape a little closer, and this time with his one good eye.

The companion's head was down, and the face was covered by the hood of the cape.

"Let me see yer face," he growled. "Pull down that hood and let me see ye better..."

As he said that, Haversham used his other hand to swiftly pull his sword from the scabbard. The rain was pouring along the smooth, gleaming steel of the soldier's blade.

He was a soldier who had killed his share of men in battle. He knew well how to use his sword, and wouldn't hesitate to use it again.

"I said show yerself!" Haversham barked, and poked the tip of his sword against the middle of the caped figure.

By then, the other guard up at the castle side door had caught sight of the interchange, and saw Haversham draw his sword. That guard started running quickly toward the guardhouse, and was drawing his sword as well.

"Show yerself now!" Haversham yelled.

Flora's face showed a controlled panic, as the sheets of rain continued to cascade down.

The figure slowly reached up to the edges of the hood, paused a minute, and then pulled the hood of the cape fully down.

The face that was revealed was the round face of a middle-aged woman, who was beaming a big smile.

"Nice weather we're havin', ain't it?" she said.

Haversham grunted. Then he unlocked the gate and let the two women pass through. He then waved to the other guard, to signal to him that everything was alright.

The other guard stopped in his tracks, sheathed his sword, and then sauntered back to the doorway that led to the dungeons. He looked around as he walked, trying to catch sight of Robby.

But Robby was nowhere to be seen.

The guard picked up his pace and started jogging around the castle battlements. He kept running, now at a full sprint until he came to the cannon that was fixed in its position at the outer wall. It was the cannon where Robby and Captain Cameron had passed the time, and had talked together.

But what the guard saw there sent him into a frenzy.

There was a length of rope attached to the heavy cannon, and swung over the wall, and then down the sheer rock cliff that surrounded Edinburgh Castle.

"Escape!" the guard screamed and started running to the quartermaster's office. "Prisoner escape!"

Chapter 58

At the bottom of Castle Rock, under the foreboding shadow of Edinburgh Castle, behind a grove of tall bushes, Flora was embracing Robby, and kissing him on the lips and face with wild exuberance. Though the sky was still overcast, the rains were subsiding. Behind the clouds, the sun was ebbing down over the sky, and in an hour or two it would be edging to the horizon. Here and there, shafts of yellow sunlight were starting to break through the cloud banks.

"I canna believe it!" she said. "Ye're here in my arms, a prisoner no more."

"My love," Robby said, "we can't dally, or else I'll be back in that dungeon and awaiting a hanging."

"Leith is where ye have to go. You can ship out there."

"You're right," Robby said. "If I try to hide here in Edinburgh that will only work for a short period of time. From what you've told me, with all the beggars in the streets, surely someone will be willing to give me up for the Crown's heavy coin. But I worry about you…"

"Don't," she said, almost short of breath with excitement. "I know where to hide for a day. That won't be a problem. Rosalie says she can get a ride in a coach that is bound for Leith, and I can join you there. But the coach won't leave until tomorrow."

"So, I need to leave you now," Robby said. "Even though it pains me to do that."

"Ye must!" she cried out, and then kissed him hard on the mouth again, and then urged him again. "Ye must leave now. The quickest way is the westerly road. But for five miles or so it is open field. But that is the shortest. If you start running, ye can make it through the fields and out to the countryside where there is a thick forest that runs for miles and miles on the way to Leith. Once ye make it to the forest, the sun will be going down, and between the thickness of the woods and the dark, ye'll be hidden as cozy as a beetle in a bog."

"Five miles you say?" Robby asked.

He had calculated that by that point his absence had been noticed, the castle grounds searched, and a hunt on horseback was already started down the Royal Mile and the adjacent roads. It would be a race to the forest, as he now saw it.

"Five miles of open road and field," Flora said. "Oh how I wish I could have found a horse for ye!" she cried out.

"No, Flora dear. You mustn't worry about that. I can handle the five miles."

"But ye'll have to run like the wind, dear Robby. Like the wind…"

"Don't worry," Robby said, and then, taking her in his arms one more time, he broke into a broad smile and added, "Besides, Flora darling, I'm quite a good runner!"

And then he kissed her goodbye.

And then turned, when he realized they had forgotten one last detail.

"But Flora, where in Leith will we meet?"

"Outside a tavern called The Wolf and Rose," she called out, as she turned to run toward the east end of Edinburgh; she planned to enter the underground from that lesser traveled end of the city. "May God protect ye until then!" she cried out, and began running in the opposite direction.

"He will!" Robby yelled after her. "I know He will!"

Then Robby started trotting along the shrubs, bushes, and trees that ran, like an apron, around the circumference of the rocky base, and sheer cliffs that vaulted up to the castle. He wasn't familiar with Edinburgh except that he did vaguely remember coming into the city on the road from Leith, when he had first arrived in Scotland as a prisoner. And from what he could recall, Flora was dead-on: There were open fields and a winding road for five miles before the road cut through dense forest.

The forest and the coming darkness would be able to hide him all the way to Leith; if only he could make it there undetected.

For a moment he toyed at the idea of hiding in the city until nightfall. Then he realized the folly of that. He could never find Flora. And by then, she would be on a coach to the port city, and he would be trapped in Edinburgh, as an army of soldiers continued to swarm through the area.

It's now or never, Robby decided.

He continued at a trot, to wind his way around the circumference of Castle Rock, and then he headed in a westerly direction, as the sun was peeking through the clouds, traversing its arc in the same direction as Robby.

By the time he had made his way to the fields that lay outside of Edinburgh, and to the crossroads that intersected the dirt road to Leith, he had only seen two men on horseback, and a farmer driving a two-horse hay wagon, all of them trying to make it into Edinburgh before sundown.

As Robby stood on the dirt road, looking at its winding path ahead of him, he surveyed the scene. There was low meadow on all sides. After the rains, in particular, it would be soggy and poor going. His best bet would simply be to run on the road until he reached the forest. He turned all the way around and looked back at Edinburgh. There were no signs of soldiers or horse riders coming out of the city.

Don't waste time here, Robby told himself. *Start running, man.*

Robby limbered up, but he was amazed how stiff and painful his joints had become from his months in the damp dungeon.

He said a quick prayer, and then started off at a fast trot.

Robby knew that he could not afford to become winded too quickly. And he couldn't risk stopping to catch his breath or to walk any part of the road. It would be just a matter of time before the castle guard came thundering down the road.

And when they did, if Robby had not reached the protection of the woods by then, it would be disaster.

Robby kept up his pace for the first ten or fifteen minutes.

But then he started having problems keeping his breathing steady. He was almost out of breath before he had even covered a half mile.

Four and a half miles left, he told himself. *Surely I've covered at least a half mile by now...Lord, give me victory...I've come too far to fail now...fill my lungs with the breath of your Spirit and my legs with Your power...I am weak...but You shall be my strength...*

Robby finally worked himself into a pace that he could manage. It was slower than he wanted, but he felt that he was making good progress.

He still couldn't spot the forest yet, but he wasn't worried about that. He was running at that point on the lowest part of the road as it ran against marshy bogs on both sides.

All Robby could hear was the sound of his own feet hitting the dirty road in a monotonous cadence. His lungs were burning, and his legs were starting to get wobbly. But he yelled at them to give him more.

This body will not give out! he said in gasping breaths as he ran.

After a while the road started to rise up a bit, and it was clear that he was running up to a higher plateau.

Good, he thought to himself, *when the road comes to higher ground, I can look forward to see how far the forest is, and look back to the city to see if I am being followed.*

It was then that Robby was deciding to do what he swore he would not do. With his lungs exploding with pain, and his legs like loose ropes that were coming uncoiled, he had decided that if the forest was close enough, and if there were no riders behind him, then he would stop running.

He would walk for a while. Surely he would be out of danger by then. After all, he told himself, the sun was now dipping down toward the horizon. In the next thirty minutes it would go down, and then darkness would set in.

And then he would be safe.

Robby was panting and moaning as he started up the rise in the road that led to the plateau.

When the road finally reached the level plateau, Robby was already slowing his pace down, finding it difficult to continue. He was barely running now, and he looked up ahead for the forest. He could now see it.

But his heart sank, because it was at least another mile or two up the road.

Then he turned around, almost stumbling as he did.

What he was about to see would send a shiver down his spine, and all the way to the ends of his toes.

A few miles down the road behind him there were riders approaching. They were riding fast, because even with the damp dirt, they were kicking up a dusty trail behind them.

He squinted, and thought he saw four riders.

Yes, they were soldiers. One was carrying a spear with the Crown's standard on it. And they were coming from Edinburgh. From the castle.

For Robby, there was no doubt about it. They were searching for him.

Robby looked around him for a place to hide.

There were no trees, no bushes, only scrub plants, and wet, soggy bogs, and no rocks large enough to hide behind.

And there was now, only the road, which curved this way and that; and there was the forest, which, if he reached it, would be his safety.

Robby started running. His slowdown in pace had caused his legs to seize up with stiffness.

But his breath and his lungs were better.

He pushed his pace, going faster and faster. It would not be a matter of pacing now, he would have to run himself to near-death, if need be, in order to reach the forest. The only thing he had going for him was the fact that the plateau was now undulating with lower and then higher spots, so he would be less visible to the riders until they got closer. But his legs were rubbery and mounting the rises in the road was becoming nearly impossible.

Behind him the riders were still two miles behind, and coming around a curve in the road.

Robby knew that when he came within the vision of the riders, of course, they would see him, and whip their horses and catch up to him.

Robby was now running up the last rise in the road.

When he mounted the rise, he saw that the forest was about one mile ahead. The road was flat.

There were no dips in the road to hide him, but only a long winding curve.

Now there could only be a full run with total speed, fueled by total determination to survive.

Robby pushed himself to the fastest he could run, pumping his arms to try to urge his legs on.

A mile and a half behind him, the sergeant of the squad told the other three riders to hold up. He called for a spyglass.

"The prisoner may be alone, which is what I am guessing," he muttered.

Then he looked through the spyglass at the winding road up ahead.

When he did, Robby had just hit the beginning of the curve and disappeared from the soldier's line of sight.

"What's that?" the soldier blurted out. "I think I saw something...then it was gone."

"Was it a man?"

"I think so...maybe not...I'm not sure," he said, handing back the spyglass to the other soldier.

He paused for only a moment, and then he gave the order.

"We're going to ride fast. We're not going to take any chances," he barked. Then he ordered the two riders with the fastest horses to run down the man; and the sergeant and the other soldier would follow behind.

Up ahead, Robby thought he could actually hear the horses on the road in back of him. He glanced back at the last curve in the road, but the riders were not there yet.

Robby's heart and chest were bursting with pain. His head, at the place where he had suffered his skull fracture months before, was now pounding with flashes, like lightning bolts.

His legs were so exhausted they felt like dead meat that had been attached to his waist.

Don't give up...don't give up, Robby was saying in breaths and gasps.

The forest line was now only a hundred feet from him, dead ahead. But he could hear the horses' pounding hooves approaching the curve.

When the riders made the curve they would see him.

It would be over.

Faster, faster, Robby was screaming in his own head. His eyes were bugging out and his head was back, as if the string had been cut, and his mouth was wide open in the amazement of enduring a kind of suffering he had not experienced before.

Now Robby was twenty feet from the thick underbrush and the tall trees. He could see there was a deep trough just beyond the first line of trees, with some large boulders.

His body was giving out. He had no idea where his feet were or what his legs were doing.

The two fastest soldiers were now rounding the curve at a full gallop.

Robby wobbled forward, and fell through the underbrush of the forest, rolling and tumbling down the ditch and landing behind a large boulder.

The two riders came thundering up to the forest which lined the road on both sides and when they did they then slowed their horses down to a trot.

As Robby lay in the ditch in the forest, he tried to keep from panting out loud for fear of being heard. But as he did, he could barely breathe, and felt as if he were suffocating.

His head and chest and heart and lungs and legs all felt as if they were being set on fire.

The two riders stayed absolutely still and listened. They looked around into the forest from their position, scanning the trees and everything between them.

The sun was now low on the horizon, streaking through the woods. A dark gloom was now over the countryside.

Finally, one of the soldiers spoke up, as he saw the sergeant and his aide approaching them on horseback from behind.

"I say that it was no man that the sergeant saw. I say that we head back to the castle. We'll probably get word when we get back that they found him along the Royal Mile."

Robby tried to keep the sound of his breathing low, so he could listen.

When the sergeant and his aide rode up to join the other two soldiers, Robby could hear the sound of the men talking.

Then the talking stopped.

Then he heard the whinnying of horses, and the sounds of hooves, as the four soldiers turned around and headed back to Edinburgh Castle.

Chapter 59

It was the end of the next day by the time Robby had made his way to the outskirts of the port city of Leith. He had walked most of the night, then lay down for a two-hour nap in a wooded thicket about a hundred feet off the road. He was awakened when the sun breached the horizon and the gray shadows gave way to the first light of day.

He was dirty and exhausted, but greatly exhilarated by the fact that he had, it seemed, escaped the castle guards, and would be able to make it safely to the rendezvous with Flora at Leith.

The port was a large expanse of warehouses and storage buildings with a few churches and smaller businesses sandwiched in. There were huge piles of coal stacked everywhere, due to the vibrant coal-shipping business done there. And because of that, there was a black dust that settled everywhere—the narrow cobblestone streets and cramped closes were covered with it; the stone buildings were blackened, giving the entire city a dirty, depressed aura.

As Robby entered the outskirts of the city, he could see the harbor off in the distance against the setting sun, and the spiny tangle of masts from nearly two dozen sailing vessels.

When he reached the first mercantile establishment he could

find, a cotton goods shop where the owner was closing up for the day, he asked him for directions.

"Pardon me," Robby asked, "but could you direct me to the Wolf and Rose Tavern?"

The owner thought for a minute. Then he nodded and started talking.

"Aye, I can tell ye," he said. "And it isn't too hard to find."

Robby's face lit up.

"Ye direct yerself toward the harbor and the yardheads, see," he began. "And take the Tollbooth Wynd—a main avenue, larger than most, and follow that good and proper. As ye're headin' to the coal hill shore, in that direction, look for Riddell's Close. It's a narrow alley, ye can easily miss it…and then head down that, about halfway…and there ye'll find the Wolf and Rose."

Robby thanked the gentleman. The merchant looked Robby over—his dirty clothes and unwashed face.

Then he added a thought.

"Now, sir, if ye don't mind my tellin' ye, ye look a bit rough like…don't look like ye have a pence to yer name. They charge a goodly price for food, drink, and lodging down there. We don't take kindly to more of the riffraff and cudgel boys robbin' our folks and all. We've had enough of that."

"No fear there," Robby said with a smile. "I've had to walk a far distance, sir, is all, and haven't had a proper change of clothes. And at the tavern I hope to be refreshed with a meal and a bath when I meet my…my…enterprise partner."

The merchant nodded, though his expression belied some skepticism at Robby's story.

But as Robby walked down the Wynd, looking for Riddell's Close, he had a disconcerting thought.

The merchant talked as if this city were crawling with criminals, he thought to himself. *Will poor Flora be able to make her way safely through this place without being robbed or accosted?*

With that thought in mind, despite the weariness in his body, Robby picked up his pace, first at a quick walk and then at a jog.

He turned down Riddell's Close just as dusk was settling over the city. It was a winding, narrow alley, with warehouse buildings and stores rising up on either side. A misty fog was starting to seep into the lanes and alleys from the harbor. Halfway down the Close there was a solitary street lamp flickering. Then beyond that, he could see a tavern sign hanging out over the street, though he couldn't read it yet.

As he got closer, he saw several drunken sailors spilling out of the tavern and onto the alley yelling and fighting and laughing. Just beyond them, farther down the Close he saw a newsboy with a floppy hat and worn clothing, leaning against the wall of a building, holding up a newspaper in each hand.

He stopped and turned around. No one else was around. There were no signs of Flora.

Robby was tempted to panic, but he had to remind himself that there was no guarantee that Flora was going to arrive before him. And even if she had, perhaps she had already entered the tavern by herself.

However, as Robby judged the rough neighborhood, that last thought increased Robby's fears, and now he was picking up his pace once again.

In a few moments, he could make out the tavern sign.

It read *Wolf & Rose.*

At last, he muttered to himself.

A few of the sailors had meandered off down the alley. But one of them, together with a friend, was arguing loudly with the newsboy, trying to grab his papers without paying. Judging the boy's size, Robby guessed him to only be around ten or eleven years old.

The bigger of the sailors was shoving the boy against the wall, and then was attempting to go into his coat pockets.

The other sailor was standing back laughing.

"Hey!" Robby yelled out. "Leave the boy alone..."

But as Robby tried to intervene, the other sailor grabbed him and pulled him back.

"Stand back!" he yelled. "Unless ye want to learn a hard lesson."

But Robby took the sailor by the coat and swung him into the bigger sailor, knocking them both to the ground. The newspaper boy hurriedly scooted back a few feet along the alley to safety.

"I was never a very good student in school," Robby muttered.

The bigger sailor leaped to his feet, and charged at Robby with his head down, like an enraged bull.

Robby stood his ground until the sailor was almost on top of him; then he gripped his hands together, and batted the sailor, head-first, into the brick wall next to him.

The sailor's head glanced off the wall and he tried to keep standing, but his knees were buckling. With one powerful blow, Robby sent him to the cobblestones.

The smaller sailor was on his feet, trying to decide whether to charge in against Robby or not. But as he looked down at the big bruiser of a sailor who was out cold, he decided to turn, mutter a few profanities, and then disappear down the alley.

That is when the proprietor of the tavern came out with a club in one hand and a set of chains in the other. He took a quick look at the downed sailor and then smiled at Robby.

"Ye done me a service, sir," he said. "This here's Dirk Connelly. He just roughed up my barmaid, and left without payin'. I had enough of this character."

The man then bent down, wrapped the unconscious sailor's wrists together with the chain, connected him to the iron gate outside his tavern, and then secured it with a lock. He would remain there until the sheriff arrived.

The newsboy ran up and wrapped two arms tightly around Robby.

When that happened, the floppy hat fell off, and long, red hair flowed down.

Robby pulled back, and looked down: He was looking into Flora's blue eyes which were now tear-filled as she started laughing and crying at the same time.

"Now I seen everything!" the proprietor cried out with a chuckle.

"Flora, you're safe!" Robby cried out. "But...dressed as a newsboy...?"

"I fooled you and the sailors, didn't I?" she said brightly. "I couldn't take any chances. I know how the streets down here are full of undesirables." Then she turned to the proprietor and added, "No disrespect meant, sir, for yer establishment."

"None taken, young lady," he said. "Sir," he said to Robby, "let me thank ye by giving ye, and yer lady friend, each a room for the night free of charge, and the best beefsteak stew we've got."

"We'll take the meal," Robby shot back, "with much gratitude. But we'll only need one room for the two of us."

"Well, now, I am sorry," the man said with regret, "but I do try to run a respectable establishment here."

"I'm sure you do," Robby replied with a smile. "But we plan, sir, on being both legal and respectable by the night's end."

Then he turned to Flora.

"Flora, darling, I saw a church just a block from here—the South Leith Church—and it looked to have the lights burning in the parsonage…"

Then Robby kneeled down on the cobblestones.

"If you will have me in marriage, Flora, I will cherish and love and protect you all the days of my life. And if you will, then let's get to the church before the Reverend goes to bed for the night!"

Flora was laughing a belly laugh, and then it turned into a torrent of tears. When she finally wiped her face and took his hands and pulled him up to his feet, she said, "Oh, Robby my love, because I know well that ye will, I say aye…and aye…and aye!"

By the time they were embracing, a barmaid and several customers were standing in the doorway, and they were all applauding wildly.

"Coo-ee!" the proprietor shouted. "This has been a night to remember!"

Robby and Flora scampered up the street to the parsonage. And as they hoped, the Reverend was still awake; and his wife and his caretaker were up also to witness the marriage.

Flora, who had gathered all of her wages and savings for her trip, gave a few coins to the pastor. And as Robby was carrying her down the street to the tavern, she told him that she had enough money to book them a passage the following day—but no farther than Ireland.

"But, perhaps that is for the best," Robby said with a smile, and then kissed her. "Didn't you say," he added, "that your brother was last seen there? Who knows, perhaps we can locate him. We'll have family there at least. I will look for work, and save up until I can afford to ship us, together, to the colonies. We shall not be separated again, my love..."

When Robby carried her into the tavern, the cheering from the customers started all over again.

Chapter 60

As the summer months of 1772 made way for the fall, in England there was an increasing tension rising in Parliament about the fate of the American colonies. Some members favored leniency and negotiation, feeling that the rights of Englishmen had been denied their kinsmen across the Atlantic.

But most members of Parliament deferred to the royal prerogative. King George was cemented into the idea of full-scale retribution.

In his hotel room in London, Benjamin Franklin was pacing. He was expecting a package to be delivered by courier.

But the package was overdue by several days. He was now concerned that his covert intelligence-gathering and spying had been found out.

He walked over to the French doors leading to the outside porch, and opened them up, taking in the cold air.

Without clear evidence of the true intentions of our cruel custodians, he thought to himself, *we Americans are simply blind men, groping and stumbling in the dark.*

Then there was a single knock on the door.

Franklin hurried across his stateroom and opened the door.

A tall fellow from the east end of London, in a wide-brimmed hat and long black coat, was standing in front of him, holding a package under his arm.

"Is ye Mr. Franklin?" he asked.

Franklin nodded.

"Got a delivery for ye," he said, and held the package out in his open hand.

Franklin reached for it, but the man pulled the package back, and then stretched out his other hand toward the diplomat.

"It's a matter of righty and lefty," the man said. "I gives you what's in my right hand, and ye gots to fill what's *not* in my left hand."

"Oh, a game," Franklin said with a sigh of irritation. "How fun. Why not make it easier still? Perhaps by my guessing what is *not between your ears.* That one's easy."

"Oh, a regular humorist, are ye?" the man said angrily. "Then see if ye can laugh at this: one *gold sovereign* please and thank ye."

"That's practically highway robbery," Franklin muttered as he walked over to his desk and pulled out his coin bag. But then a thought came to his mind, and he chuckled a little to himself.

On the other hand, Franklin thought to himself with a chagrined smile, *this fellow probably is a highway robber.*

He delivered the gold coin to the man in black, who took the time to bite it firmly and feel its heft before turning the package over to Franklin.

After the courier had left, Franklin bolted and locked the door and took the package over to the ornate desk, tearing its brown paper away quickly to reveal a small cache of letters.

He arranged his quill pen and inkwell, and a few sheets of parchment on one side, and the letters on the other; then he started poring through the correspondence, making notes as he read.

At first he found little revealing in the letters from the Royal Governor of Massachusetts to the King of England, to his various members of the Privy Council, and to various key members of Parliament.

If I am going to risk being tried as a spy for treason, he said to himself out loud, *I hope at least to find something worth the price of the rope they'll use to hang me.*

But then, after almost an hour of painstaking review, he came across some alarming information.

There, in front of him, was what appeared to be an original of a letter from the Royal Governor of Massachusetts, to Thomas Whately, the personal secretary to Lord Grenville, the Prime Minister of England. And also in the packet were original letters from the Royal Secretary of Massachusetts, also an appointee of the king, written to Whately as well.

The tone of the letters regarding the handling of the colonies was ugly to the extreme: but the ideas contained in the letters, as an expression of English intentions, was downright explosive.

Franklin adjusted his spectacles, brought his oil lamp closer, and read with astonishment.

On the issue of whether American colonists actually enjoy "English liberties," they said, nothing could be further from the truth. "There must be an abridgment," the Governor's letter said, of anything close to such liberties. More English troops, not less, must be posted in the streets of Boston and elsewhere. The colonists, they concluded, must be suppressed; and oppressed if necessary.

Franklin was stunned that such a gold mine had found its way into his hands. He had been using a small network of spies to ferret out letters; there was a small, underground industry dealing in stolen official correspondence at that time, in the alleys and backrooms of London. But who could have guessed that these letters, from Royal officials in Massachusetts, would have so clearly outlined the requests from the king's own men to tyrannize the very people who had previously presumed they were entitled to inalienable rights?

Franklin knew what he had to do. Before anything else, he began to copy the letters verbatim. Here, before him, was the best evidence of the English plan of official government oppression of the American colonists. The diplomat would have to insure that there were plenty of copies to circulate among his allies across the Atlantic.

When he finished copying the letters, he then authored a cover letter to his contacts in Boston explaining the find, emphasizing the authenticity of the correspondence, and sharing his own thoughts. These letters, Franklin wrote, explained the rude mistreatment he had been receiving from the English government as of late.

The chasm that had developed between America and Britain was now becoming a yawning, gaping abyss.

When Franklin's letter and copies of the accompanying English government correspondence reached Boston, a hasty meeting between Samuel Adams, John Hancock, John Adams, and several of the other patriot leaders was arranged.

Sam Adams took the opportunity to formalize a plan that had been in the works for months.

"It now appears," he said, "that the time for our Committees of Correspondence has come."

"The same plan as we discussed?" Hancock asked. "A committee of twenty-one, to maintain regular contact by confidential letters, with all of the towns and villages of this colony. To unify our collective effort."

"That, yes," Sam Adams replied. "But, John, what about your idea?"

And with that he turned to his cousin.

John Adams had been unusually silent during the meeting. Behind him, on a chair in the corner, taking notes as usual for Adams, was Nathan Mackenzie. Then John Adams spoke up.

"It had occurred to me," he said with a tone of studied resolve in his voice, "that the time has come—long overdue I now conclude—for a concise statement to be voted on at the next town meeting. A proclamation, setting forth, in logical and clear fashion, the assertion of the rights of all colonies to the right of self-rule. Assuming we can get the votes on that, we can then bullet that proclamation through the colony by means of this Committee of Correspondence."

Sam Adams smiled at that. There was a moment of quiet, and then John Hancock added, "Sounds like a grand idea, John. Let's see to it."

For the rest of the morning they hammered out the technical details of the Committee and the wording of the first draft of the proclamation for self-rule.

They took a break for lunch, and Nathan dashed home to spend a few minutes with Deborah and little William.

But when he arrived, Deborah was waiting in the front room, holding William. She had a message for Nathan.

"Your brother stopped by," she said. "Edward was here, at the house, with another gentleman, another pastor, though I didn't catch his name. They said they needed to meet with you immediately. He said it absolutely could not wait, whatever it was."

"Deborah darling," Nathan replied, "we are right in the middle of some extraordinary business, John and I are..."

"I'm sure you are," she said with a firm smile. "But your brother Edward looked to have some *extraordinary* need for you to meet with him. And he is your brother, after all. I am sure that Mr. Adams will understand. Abigail is coming by shortly. Do you want me to have her soften her husband up for you?"

Deborah chuckled when she said that.

Nathan smirked, and then shook his head.

"I am sure that I lack the brilliant wit of both you and Mrs. Adams," Nathan remarked with a smile. "As well as your *powers of persuasion*. But I think I can handle Mr. Adams myself."

"Edward said that he and his friend will wait for you at Edward's church," Deborah added. "In the sanctuary."

Nathan kissed Deborah and then ran back to the meeting house, where he confided in John Adams. His mentor smiled and patted him on the shoulder, and bid him to take care of his family business.

Then Nathan headed down the street toward Edward Mackenzie's church.

He had no idea what it was that had overtaken his brother with such a sense of urgency. Or why it was that he, a lawyer, would be meeting with two ministers of the gospel in the sanctuary of Edward's church.

Chapter 61

In the sanctuary of the First Church of Boston, Edward Mackenzie was seated on the steps leading to the pulpit that jutted out, from a high, prominent perch, overlooking the pews. It was a beautiful dark walnut pulpit, intricately carved. From that pulpit Edward had preached his Sunday morning and evening sermons for nearly fifteen years.

But now he was not in the pulpit. As he sat on the bottom step, in the shadow of the looming pulpit, he was directly across from the first row of pews.

As Nathan entered the sanctuary he spotted Edward sitting, with his hands folded on his knees. There was a large pulpit Bible next to him.

As Nathan walked down the center aisle he could then see that another man was in the front pew, facing Edward. But Nathan could only see the back of his head, and he could not recognize him.

Then as he rounded the pews, Nathan saw a man in his early forties, dressed in a traditional clergyman's frock and black coat. To Nathan, the man could well have been any minister from any church in Massachusetts.

The man gave a friendly smile to Nathan, rose to greet him,

and extended his hand and shook Nathan's with an uncommonly strong, confident handshake.

Nathan could feel that the man's hands were rough, with layers of calluses.

"Brother Nathan," Edward announced, "this is Reverend Jonas Clarke. He is a minister of the Gospel from Lexington. He has come at my request."

Nathan sat down on the pew next to Rev. Clarke, but Edward remained standing as he spoke.

"In fact, Rev. Clarke has been with me these last two days, staying in my parsonage, going with me on my home visits, but mostly discussing matters that have borne down on me, and occupied my heart, my mind, my soul, for longer than I can remember."

Nathan waited for an explanation, why his brother had called him to this meeting. But the reason was about to become clear.

"So, brother," Edward continued, "here is the issue, and the reason for your presence. Rev. Clarke has taken a very bold stand in his church, and in his community, regarding the patriots' cause against English rule. But I have taken a very different course, as you know, Nathan."

It was then that Nathan realized who Rev. Clarke was. In his dealings with John and Samuel Adams, and John Hancock, he had learned a little of Mr. Hancock's family background.

"I believe," Nathan said, "that I have heard of you, Rev. Clarke. In fact, was not John Hancock's father the previous pastor of the church you are now shepherding in Lexington?"

"Indeed, yes," Clarke replied with a smile. "Rev. John Hancock, Sr., was my predecessor. Our church is only a short distance down from Buckman Tavern, if you have ever traveled to Lexington."

"I have, only once, on a legal matter," Nathan said. "But I believe that I recall seeing your church there as I passed by."

"Rev. Clarke has been kind enough," Edward continued, "to let me air my various concerns and speculations about the colonial cause, and our resistance to England, and the role, if any, of the clergy in this matter of great public debate."

"I am afraid," Nathan explained, "that things have gone far beyond just being *a matter of public debate*. The letters we have received from Mr. Franklin in London give us indisputable proof that the Crown, through our colonial masters, intends to subjugate us. Militias are being formed, and drilled here in the colonies, as we speak. The time to painstakingly consider your own course, Edward, may soon disappear. Events will soon force you to choose which side you shall serve."

"Yet Romans chapter thirteen requires," Edward said, his hands clasped together, and his eyes closed in intense emotion, "that the Church of Jesus Christ be subject to the governing authorities. That resistance to such authorities is in opposition to God."

"Was it not William Tyndale," Rev. Clarke countered, "who said that *resistance to tyranny is obedience to God*? If we were to require absolute submission at all times in all places, without objection, and without exception, then how do we explain Naboth's dispute against evil King Ahab in the book of Kings, chapter twenty-one? Is not England, through its king, like King Ahab? Lusting after our vineyards which belong to us, the American colonists and our heirs, and now, like Ahab, threatening to kill us to secure those vineyards? And how do we explain Daniel's refusal to have his religious liberties, and his sacred conscience, violated by the edicts of a pagan king?"

Edward was pacing, gesturing energetically at the foot of the pulpit.

"Yet does not the apostle Peter," Edward said, his voice rising, "in his first letter, also agree with the apostle Paul's inspired pronouncement in Romans, that we be subject to the government in all things?"

"And *exactly what government* would that be?" Nathan said loudly, his voice filling the church sanctuary. Nathan stood now, and took a few steps toward his brother.

Nathan's voice was filled with a passion that Edward had not heard before. This had ceased to become a mere political debate, and Edward could see that now.

"*Which government* is it, brother," Nathan continued, "to which we are to be subject? We have duly elected assemblies and town councils here in the colonies. Shall we be subject to them? Then, let us be subject. They are calling for us to resist the oppression of England. Does not Scripture command, then, that we obey them? We were given a promise of a new form of governing here, beginning with the Royal Charter at Jamestown, Virginia, and we Americans have freely and joyfully built our government here just to have *another government* in London tell us that we shall no longer enjoy the rights of Englishmen. All right then, so be it. But we *shall* have the rights as *Americans* then, for I believe that God has ordained that."

"But has the King of England violated the Church of Christ here in the colonies?" Edward said, his voice pleading.

"Most certainly," Rev. Clarke added. "Edward, remember my telling you the other day the sad history of this. More than a decade ago, the king arbitrarily vetoed the application for a colonial charter for the establishment of a Christian Missionary Society. London tried to block the printing of Bibles here. And in Virginia," Clarke continued, "Baptist preachers are jailed because of their failure to be licensed under the rules of the Church of England. And then there is the matter of slavery, that pernicious scourge. Every time our colonies have passed laws outlawing slavery, the King has vetoed them; His Majesty has forbidden us to outlaw it!"

Edward was rubbing his forehead with his hand, his eyes closed so tightly that his brow was furrowed and his face slightly contorted.

For several minutes, as Edward held his head in his hands, there were no voices, and no sound.

Finally, Rev. Clarke broke the silence.

"I admire your diligence, brother Edward," Rev. Clarke said, "in searching the Scripture and seeking the will of God in this matter. But the Bible tells us that for a man to know to do what is right, but fail to do it, for that man it is sin. Search your heart, Edward. Does it not tell you that there are, as your brother says, two governments at play here? Not one. You will have to choose which one you shall obey. But for me, I have made my choice. In my church basement there is a collection of weapons that I permit to be stored for our militia. It is for the self-defense of our community against England's cruel tyranny."

Edward stepped down toward Rev. Clarke, until he was standing in front of him. His eyes were moist with emotion, but there was the beginning of a resolve that was dawning in his heart, and it was being reflected in his face.

"So," Edward said to Rev. Clarke, "you say that your church will fight, if need be?"

"I pray fervently against that day," Clarke said. "But if that day does come, then yes, they will fight. For I have trained them for that very hour. They will fight, and, if needs be, will die, too, under the shadow of the House of God."

Chapter 62

Two and One-half Years Later
Early April, 1775

When Robby and Flora fled to Ireland, they had hoped to locate Flora's brother. But they were never able to do so. Work was hard to find, and they only had what was left of Flora's savings after they had booked passage out of Leith, Scotland. They subsisted on a near-starvation diet, and lived in a squalid single-room tenement in Dublin.

Yet Flora kept up a cheery disposition. She talked often of how happy she was to be married to Robby, and how, in her words, "Leavin' Edinburgh was the best thing for me, as it likely saved my life."

But Robby knew that Flora was trying hard to buoy his flagging spirits. He remembered how his wife had received an offer of marriage from a successful merchant and had turned him down for Robby, a former prisoner and now an escapee on the run.

Robby tried hard to vindicate Flora's decision to marry him; he worked whatever odd jobs were available, sometimes days in a row without sleep. But most often, days would pass with no work at all.

Then one day, Robby was able to secure a job in a fishing business owned by a man named Harry Donegal. He had a fleet of four fishing boats, as well as other enterprises. Robby spoke of his experience aboard ships, and soon was going out every day on one of the boats, before the break of dawn, and returning after sundown.

At the same time, Flora found some occasional work in a tailoring shop and a dry goods store and kept herself busy, waiting for her husband's return from his fishing trips.

After several months of Robby diligently working on the boats, Donegal started bringing him into his office and asking him to assume some clerical work; a few times he accompanied him to meetings with grocers where he learned how Donegal negotiated the price of the catch that his boats would bring in. A little bit at a time, Robby was not only able to make enough money to move Flora and himself into proper housing, but he was able to set aside a small amount each month for their eventual journey back to his homeland.

Robby and his boss began spending more and more time together, and their conversations become more and more revealing.

One day, before closing up his harbor office for the day, Donegal leaned back in his chair and asked Robby a question.

"So, ye want to return back to the colonies?" Donegal asked.

"I do, sir," Robby replied. "It's home for me. I have two brothers there, with their families in Boston. My heart yearns to return. No offense to you, though," he was quick to add. "You have been very kind and generous to me here in Dublin."

"Ye've earned it, lad," Donegal said. "Every bit of it."

Then he paused a moment before venturing into his next comment. Donegal leaned forward and lowered his voice slightly.

"Ye know," he said to Robby. "We Irish and you American colonists have a certain amount in common..."

Robby leaned forward to listen.

"Namely, English boots on the back of our necks," Donegal said.

Robby had not told Donegal about his imprisonment in Edinburgh. Though he appreciated his employer's goodwill, Robby felt that there were still certain things that he could not risk divulging.

"I too, have felt that boot," Robby said guardedly.

"I'm sure ye have," Donegal said with a knowing smile. "Yes, I just had that feeling…"

Then Donegal, after eyeing Robby for a few moments, decided to venture further.

"I hate to lose ye, lad," he said with a sigh. "But I know what it is like to be apart from yer land, and yer kin. So, here it is—take it or no—I don't exactly know of any ships headin' for Boston—even here in Ireland we've heard of the troubles over in Boston—and there is scarcely anyone willin' to risk being plundered or sunk by the English navy while trying to enter Boston Harbor."

After another pause, Donegal got to his point.

"But I do know that there is a ship bound for Portsmouth, in New Hampshire, weighing anchor in a month. That'll get you to the colonies. From there ye can travel down to Boston if ye like to join yer kinsfolk."

Robby was beaming.

"I should have enough for passage," he remarked. "That is wonderful news!"

"Well, and if ye're short a few quid, then let me know, and I may be able to fill in the gaps for yer tickets, for ye and yer bride."

"You've been a true friend to me," Robby said. "I don't know how to thank you."

"One other thing," Donegal added. "I have a brother, who settled in New Hampshire some time ago. He writes me regular…he could put ye up for a fortnight until ye make yer plans for Boston or no."

"That's very generous of you."

"Righty-o," Donegal said with an air of finality. "Then it's to New Hampshire for ye. My brother Sean tells me all about the goin's-on in the colonies in his letters. He says that trouble is brewing and bubblin'. He's gone and joined a militia group of some kind."

"Militia?"

"Aye," Donegal replied. "Sean writes that they call themselves the Green Mountain Boys."

After that conversation, Robby was quick to author a letter to his brother Edward, in Boston, and asked that he share its contents with Nathan as quickly as possible. He explained his plan to travel to Boston by way of Portsmouth, New Hampshire, and he shared his good fortune in marrying Flora.

Robby had refrained from writing ever since his escape from Edinburgh Castle, for fear that English sympathizers might read his mail, and learn of his whereabouts. But now that he was determined to leave Ireland soon, he reasoned that he needed to send off one letter to his brothers.

In Boston, when Edward finally received Robby's correspondence, he was elated to have heard from him; and to learn that their younger brother was alive, and prospering, was married no less, and most importantly, was bound for the colonies with his bride, and ultimately, for a Boston reunion with his family.

Edward strode quickly over to Nathan's office to share the good news. As was the case by then, the law office of John Adams and Nathan Mackenzie had been transformed into a clearinghouse of political activity, correspondence out to the patriots throughout Massachusetts, and strategy against the eventual English military advance.

There were two dozen men scattered through the offices, all engaged in loud discussion, and buried in a flurry of papers.

Edward called Nathan outside to share Robby's letter with him. Edward's eyes were filled with tears, and together the two of them praised God for his protection of their young brother, and rejoiced at his eventual arrival in Boston.

As the two men sat on the bench outside the office, studying Robby's letter again, poring over every word, both of them were thinking the same thing: how far a road it now seemed that they had traveled over the years.

A road that had included Edward's loss of his wife, Edith; the birth of little William for Nathan and Deborah; Robby's disappearance, but now his reappearance.

And, of course, there was the powerful divergence, at first, between Edward and Nathan regarding the conflict with England.

But in the months and years since their meeting together with Rev. Clarke in Edward's church, Edward had finally come to a resolution on the matter. He began preaching a series of sermons on the biblical balance necessary between obedience to government and the resistance to tyranny. He held prayer vigils for peace to reign in the land; yet he also openly discussed with his congregation and his board of elders the preparations necessary in the event of military conflict with England.

And as Edward thought back, sitting on that bench, to his new path, he felt a strangely comforting kinship—an invisible bond—to his ancestors in Scotland and England; to Ransom Mackenzie and his sons Andrew and Philip, and their sons and daughters. A bond with all those who had come before, linked by the mystery of a bloodline that worshiped the one and true God, and had believed fiercely in His Word, and then had taken it into the halls of power, into the battlefields of sacrifice, and not only before both kings and tyrants, but also before the common folk as well, reluctant to compromise, and quick to stand fast when standing fast was the hardest thing to do.

Edward was deep in thought as he folded the letter and handed it to his brother Nathan.

"Why do you want me to keep this?" Nathan asked.

"I am going on a trip...to Lexington," Edward said quietly.

"Lexington?" Nathan said, a little aghast. "There is intelligence we have—reliable information—Edward, we have heard that the English may be planning a military advance there. You may be walking into the middle of a vipers' nest."

"Yes, I know that," Edward replied with a look of resolve on his face. "That's why I am going. To help Rev. Clarke. I am not sure how long I will be gone. I've spoken to the elders. We have made preparations for my associate pastor to take over my duties until my return."

It was a strange irony that Nathan, as he looked into his brother's face, wanted now to dampen his brother's commitment to the patriots' cause. That he wanted to protect him from danger. To have him choose a safer course.

But Nathan knew better than to try.

"Do me this one favor," Edward said. "As you gather with your men and set forth your ideas for the future, and however this conflict is resolved, please always remember..."

Then Edward's voice trailed off.

"Remember what?" Nathan asked.

"Remember," Edward continued, with emotion choking off his words, "where true liberty comes from. That the source of our liberty can only, and always, come from our Lord, the Almighty, our blessed Redeemer and Creator."

"I will," Nathan replied, carefully studying his brother's face.

Nathan knew then that his pledge had a preeminent importance, for he saw that in Edward's eyes; yet Nathan also had the sense that there was a greater importance even beyond his promise to his older brother, though the shape and image of what was to come was still shadowy, and indistinct.

Nathan shook Edward's hand firmly and then nodded to him.

"I pledge that I will remember that, brother," Nathan said again.

Chapter 63

April 19, 1775

It was well past midnight. In the darkness, with little moonlight to illuminate the way, the rider was whipping his steed frantically. The pounding of hoofbeats from the sweating horse could be heard echoing on the dirt road to Lexington. Paul Revere had been given the fastest horse that could be found—a sturdy mare named Brown Beauty. With Revere, who was an excellent horseman, clinging to her back, Beauty was now making the twelve-mile ride to Lexington in record time.

In Boston, a large contingent of British troops had been dispatched from the English ships, and the *HMS Somerset* was now blocking off the estuary river leading from Boston Harbor to Charlestown; the heavily armed English soldiers were soon boarding longboats; from there they would make landfall, on their march to their eventual destination of Concord. On the way the British regulars would pass by Lexington, and any hostile colonials would be killed, and their arms seized. When they reached Concord, their mission was to obliterate all of the ammunition and arms being stored by the colonists, and to use deadly force against anyone slowing them in their path.

There would be no talk; no negotiation. No discussion.

Now was the time for the exercise of the full, brutal might of the English army.

Just before sunrise Revere came galloping up to Rev. Clarke's parsonage. In addition to Edward Mackenzie, and a house full of family and relatives, the parsonage was temporarily housing Sam Adams and John Hancock. Outside the house, Hancock's elegant coach was parked. Inside the guest bedroom, Hancock had his large wooden trunk, which contained all of the papers relating to the soon-to-be convened Second Continental Congress.

In that one trunk alone there was enough evidence, if it fell into British hands, to hang all of the patriot leadership from Massachusetts as traitors to England, and the leaders of several other colonies as well.

At Rev. Clarke's farm, Revere leaped off Brown Beauty and raced to the front porch.

"The regulars!" Revere yelled at the front door, his voice strained from having delivered the same message to several other minutemen posts on his journey that night.

The front door swung open.

"The regulars are coming! Turn out!" he yelled again.

Hancock and Sam Adams scampered to collect their belongings. Hancock ordered Revere and another man to fetch his trunk immediately and arrange for it to leave with Hancock.

"Women and children upstairs, now!" Rev. Clarke yelled to his household, all of whom were in their nightclothes. "Do not show yourself until I give the all clear."

"What's going on?" Edward Mackenzie asked hurriedly, as he scampered down the stairs.

"British regulars are on the march, coming this way," Clarke snapped back. "The minutemen will be assembling the militia on the Lexington Green to stop them if necessary."

Edward thought on the matter for only an instant, then he bolted up the stairs and into his bedroom.

A few minutes later, Edward appeared in the front room with his leather britches, and shooting coat. He had a powder horn slung over one shoulder and a musket over the other.

"Edward you can't," Clarke began, "you'll be safe here."

"And that is why I do not belong here," he said with a smile. "You need to make sure that John and Samuel get safely away and that your household is in order. I have no household, my friend. There is just me. And God. And so brother Clarke, I am on my way to the village green."

Rev. Clarke grabbed Edward firmly by the shoulders.

"Look for Captain Parker on the green. He is a good man. A trained ranger. He is commanding our militia."

Edward nodded, and then bolted through the front door and out to his horse.

As he mounted his bay, he could hear Rev. Clarke shouting after him.

"Godspeed, Rev. Edward Mackenzie..."

A few miles away, the patriot drummer was beating out the call to arms, as the colonial militia was assembling on the Lexington Green. They formed two ranks.

There were only seventy of them, to face seven hundred highly trained, professional English soldiers.

The Lexington colonial militia was made up mostly of farmers, and some merchants. A few of them were former soldiers, with experience in the French and Indian wars.

For almost an hour they listened for the advance of the British regulars.

Then, at the last moment, the seventy militiamen were joined by a pastor from Boston.

Edward Mackenzie dismounted his horse, and ran over to the front line, introducing himself to Captain Parker.

Parker told him to take a position on the other side of a nearby stone wall.

"There may be a need, very shortly, I fear," Parker said solemnly, "for a man of God to give final comfort to such men as may enter the gates of glory."

Edward took his position on the other side of the stone fence. Women and children peered out of the windows of nearby houses, watching their fathers, husbands, and sons, prepare to meet the enemy.

All was still. The sun was breaking over the horizon, and a mild breeze was blowing.

Off in the distance the only sounds were the chirping of birds, and the whinny of a horse.

And then it began.

Hundreds of English shoulders, running ahead on the quick-step, were flooding the road and heading directly for Lexington Green.

"Hold yer fire," Captain Parker said.

Major John Pitcairn and several other English officers were riding astride their horses, behind the advancing troops. One of them was holding a pistol.

Column upon column of British regulars, armed with muskets fixed with bayonets, were charging toward the meager American colonists.

Atop his horse, Pitcairn shouted to the colonials, "Throw down yer arms! Villains! Rebels!"

Commander Parker saw that a stand at such a time would be suicide.

"Disperse, men!" Parker shouted out. Dutifully, the patriot militiamen turned and began to run in the opposite direction, away from the advancing troops.

Then, while the American militiamen had their backs to the British, a shot rang out.

"What was that?" one of the militiamen shouted to his companion as they ran.

"Sounded like a pistol..."

That was all the English soldiers needed.

Fueled by a long, pent-up hatred for the colonists, though no order had been given, the English soldiers began firing at will. The sky was filled with white smoke, and the crackling of muskets.

Musket balls were whizzing everywhere.

As they shot, the English soldiers then began to disperse in all directions, firing as they went, and bayoneting the men running from them, and then reloading and firing again. Some of the British troops started firing at private homes and headed there with the intention to sack them.

Militiamen were dropping in their tracks. Some stopped long enough to get off shots. Others leaped over the stone fence where Edward Mackenzie was now standing and aiming his musket. The men started firing across the stone fence at the advancing ranks of hundreds upon hundreds of British regulars who were charging them.

Some twenty feet from the stone hedge, a sixteen-year-old boy who had lost his weapon was running like a wild animal toward the safety of the stone wall.

"Faster lad!" Edward was yelling to him. "Run faster!"

But a musket ball whizzed toward the boy and struck him in the rear of his calf. He screamed and went down, writhing in pain, and grabbing his leg.

Suddenly, from the flank, a red-coated British soldier came charging toward the boy, raising his bayonet to thrust it into the unarmed lad.

Edward fired one shot, hitting the soldier in his right arm. The soldier staggered and dropped his musket, and then fell to the ground, holding his bleeding arm.

Dropping his musket and then leaping over the stone wall, Edward raced over to the fallen lad and began bending down; he planned to heft him over his shoulder, and carry him to safety.

But there was a crack of a musket fire, and then a musket ball exploded into Edward's left chest.

Edward dropped the boy, turned halfway around, and then fell down into the grass.

Major Pitcairn ordered the drummers to begin beating out *down arms*. After much effort, he finally brought the marauding English troops under command and managed to halt their assault.

On the village green, eight colonials were dead. Nine others were seriously wounded.

In the tall, green grass, lying on his back, Edward Mackenzie was groaning and panting, blood pouring from his chest wound.

He was watching the sunlight breaking over the blue Lexington sky. But then the sky became dimmer for him.

Edward was seeing the face of his departed wife, Edith, smiling at him. It was the smile she had on their wedding day, when she was in her white, lacy wedding dress. And then Edward, feeling the life drain from him, thought that somewhere there was the sound of his brother Nathan's voice.

Edward mumbled and tried to force the words which he wanted to say.

But all was jumbled in the growing darkness that was overcoming him.

He struggled to speak.

Only one word would be uttered, before he breathed his last.

Remember…

Chapter 64

May 10, 1775

It was dawn over Lake Champlain where it conjoined Lake George, in upper New York state, along the northern border with Canada. Within the hour, the horizon of tall treetops of pine and fir which lined the wide lakes would be rimmed with a thin line of fiery red from the rising sun.

But for now, the world was still enveloped in a grey dusk, and there was an early damp in the air.

The two hugelong boats that were nearing the shore were full of rough frontiersman, Ethan Allen's Green Mountain Boys, some eighty-three of them.

Word of the British attacks at Lexington, and later at Concord, had already reached Allen's patriot raiders in New Hampshire.

And now, as the men in the boats sat rock-solid, muskets across their laps, faces like carved granite, they were thinking about the daring mission they were about to undertake. But they were also thinking about the patriots who had already been killed at Lexington and Concord.

The boats slipped up to shore, and the men at the bow quietly slipped out and then pulled on the bow rope, tugging the boats forward until they hit the gravel beach. Then the men began to pour out.

In the boat where Ethan Allen had been sitting at the bow and was decked out in his blue cutaway coat, fur hat, and a long saber at his side, there was a young man who had been sitting directly behind him.

As Allen hopped out of the boat, the young man was right behind him. Allen turned around slightly toward the young man as his squad of rebels all walked towards the woods ahead of them.

"What's your name?" Allen whispered to the young man, trying to make conversation and cast an aura of calm before the battle.

"Mackenzie," the young man replied. "Robby Mackenzie."

"Where you from, Robby?" Allen whispered back.

"All over, sir, but I have family in Boston."

"Any of yours in that engagement at Lexington and Concord?"

"Yes, sir," Robby said, his voice growing somber, "I just heard that I lost my oldest brother, Edward, at Lexington."

Allen halted and waited for Robby to catch up next to him.

Then the frontier commander patted him on the back, and said, "Robby, I would like you to stick close to me on this expedition. Will you do that?"

Robby nodded.

"Good," Allen replied quietly with a big grin. "Now, let's capture ourselves an English fort."

The frontiersmen made their way through the woods, and then snaked in a narrow line across a short clearing toward Fort Ticonderoga, the wilderness outpost of the English army that was stocked with cannons, muskets, munitions, wagons, and uniforms.

There were only two sentries strolling along the outer wall of the fort.

The Green Mountain Boys, with innate precision, dispatched two men for each sentry. Simultaneously, they scaled the sides of the fort, and then jumped the two sentries, quickly overpowering them. The front gate of the fort was swung open, and the remaining patriot rebels poured in noiselessly.

"Take this lantern," Allen whispered to Robby, "and follow me. We've got to locate the commandant's quarters."

By the time Allen and Robby came to the structure in the middle of the fort where the commanding English officer resided, the rest of the patriots had already engaged the sleeping British troops. Shots were being fired, but resistance was futile. The Green Mountain Boys had secured every strategic location within the fort.

Soon, ranks of surrendering English soldiers were appearing here and there, with their hands up, in the exercise yard.

At the front door of the English commander's quarters, Allen pounded on the door as Robby stood next to him with his lantern.

"Come out you old rat!" Allen shouted. "Come out now! Your fort's been taken and your men captured!"

The door swung open, to reveal a bleary-eyed English officer in his nightclothes.

The officer was handed over to two of Allen's men.

Then Allen turned to Robby.

"Now we have the pleasure," Allen said to Robby, "of deciding where we start our plunder."

"The cannons," Robby shot back without thinking.

Allen smiled as they trotted across the fort, side-by-side.

"Oh?" the military leader asked with a smile.

"Yes sir," Robby replied without hesitation. "The thing about cannons is that even with unequal armies, they can level the battlefield..."

"That's a smart word," Allen said. "Where'd you learn that?"

"In Edinburgh," Robby replied. "From an English soldier."

And then Robby added, "Who was also a good Scotsman."

Chapter 65

A Year Later
June 11, 1776

A terrifying armada of the world's mightiest navy was filling New York Harbor—thirty battleships manning over one thousand cannons, thirty thousand soldiers, ten thousand sailors, and a full three hundred supply ships to support the English war effort to crush the American colonists forever.

Or so they planned.

In the city of Philadelphia, in the humid heat of an already sweltering summer, colonial delegates from the Continental Congress had just adjourned for the day, and were filing out of the hall. Shirts were sweated-through, and ruffled collars were wilted and stained with sweat.

Roger Sherman, the Connecticut merchant, lawyer, and student of Scripture, came striding out first, as the doors were flung open. He wiped his wide forehead, smoothing his tied-back hair which was, like him, kept in simplicity; and then he donned his brown coat which he had stripped off during the meeting in order to survive the heat.

In the outside vestibule, Nathan Mackenzie was waiting.

Sherman walked straight over to Nathan. During the months

of congressional wrangling, Sherman had struck up a friendship with Nathan, who had been assisting as unofficial secretary for the Massachusetts delegation.

"Nathan," Sherman remarked, "we are making progress. Sorry that you had to wait outside during that last debate, but there are still a few grumblings against the Massachusetts delegation. Mistrust. Particularly from Rutledge and the South Carolina group. They seem to think that by having you assist John Adams and the Massachusetts men in the hall and during debate, that this somehow gives Massachusetts an unfair advantage."

Sherman smiled and shook his head at that.

"I've just been happy to serve," Nathan said warmly. "So, do we have our Declaration Committee?"

"We do," Sherman replied. "Myself, John Adams, of course, Livingston from New York, Mr. Franklin, and Jefferson. John has already suggested to me that we delegate the initial drafting to Tom. Which I think is a capital idea. I am confident the rest of the Committee will go along with that handily."

"And the timing of this Declaration?"

"Within the month or shortly after, we must have it presented and voted on. We can't afford to dally much longer."

"Any further news of the British invasion of New York?" Nathan asked.

"Nothing yet. But the General may need to launch a counter-offensive against the British troops in the Long Island area. May God be with our brave men if that happens. They will, I fear, be greatly outnumbered."

Then Sherman turned to Nathan and recalled his wife's name.

"How is your dear Deborah and your little son?"

"Doing well, sir," Nathan replied. "I have long since removed them from Boston. They are renting a house not far from the Adams' farm in Braintree. She and Abigail have been fast friends for years. I know that their friendship has been a great comfort to Deborah."

Just then Nathan spotted John Adams exiting the hall, chatting vigorously with another Massachusetts delegate, Robert Treat Paine.

Nathan watched the men dialogue together, sharing strategy. When their discussion was over, Paine smiled, and shook Adams' hand and congratulated him "on the progress made thus far toward enlisting the last few reluctant colonies in the move for independence."

"Strange, isn't it?" Nathan said, watching Paine and John Adams. "Those two men were locked in bitter enmity in Boston when we tried the *Boston massacre* case. Now look at them. Comrades in arms. Brothers for a common cause."

"Not so strange," Sherman replied. "God weaves His ways through our lives in a perfect exercise of sovereignty—often when we are least aware of it. If only we could learn to drink even deeper at His Son's well of Living Waters. What great things might we then accomplish for His glory?"

Adams broke free from Paine and scurried over to Nathan and Roger Sherman. Jefferson was exiting from the hall behind Adams, but was waylaid by Lyman Hall from Georgia, who had a few comments for him.

"All right, Nathan," Adams began energetically. "Jefferson is going to do the first draft. Then the Committee will give it a look-over. I will need you desperately at that point."

"I am leaving today," Nathan said. "I am meeting with my brother Robby back at Braintree. I haven't seen him in years. He has been up in New Hampshire, fighting with Captain Allen and the Green Mountain Boys."

"Oh yes," Adams said brightly. "You tell him, for me, how brilliant that engagement at Fort Ticonderoga was. General Washington will make great use of those cannons."

"I will, sir," Nathan replied.

"Jefferson says he can give us a first draft in a day. Can you be back then?"

"I would rather say three days," Nathan said. "I also want to see Deborah. I haven't seen her in so long. And my little son…"

A wistful expression washed over John Adams' face.

"Do drop in on Abigail then," he said. "Tell her…that I miss her so…and that my love still burns so very bright." And then Adams glanced down at the floor for a moment, and squinted as if he had something in his eye. "And that…I will write her again very soon."

"I will, sir," Nathan said.

Jefferson broke free of Mr. Hall and quickly joined Adams. The two men, Jefferson and Adams, turned and were about to leave, when Nathan spoke up and caught their attention.

"Mr. Jefferson?" Nathan called out.

The tall, auburn-haired lawyer turned around.

"Yes Nathan?" Jefferson replied.

"I understand you will author the first draft of our Declaration?"

Jefferson looked over at Adams, and nodded.

"Yes, my colleagues have constrained me to do so."

"Well then, in that event," Nathan added, his voice rising to a kind of firmness that Adams found a bit surprising, "I must insist on something."

"What is it?" Jefferson asked.

Adams had his hands behind his back, and he had a perplexed look on his face as he stared at Nathan.

"I must insist," Nathan continued, "that you remember, in the drafting of it, from Whom our true liberties derive. That we are endowed with them, sir, from the Lord God, our Creator and Redeemer. Please remember that."

Jefferson looked off for a second, pursed his lips, and then spoke up.

"A worthy thought."

"Yes, most worthy," Adams said, his face relaxing into a smile. "Well done, Nathan."

Adams and Jefferson were about to turn and leave the building when Nathan added one final thought that halted them in their tracks.

"My brother Edward wanted me to tell you that."

The two men smiled, with John Adams smiling the broadest, and then they left the building together, talking while they walked. Mr. Adams, his arms gesturing excitedly, was doing most of the talking, and was pointing back to Nathan as he spoke.

Nathan and Roger Sherman chatted for a few more moments as the two of them walked out into the sunlight, and crossed the muddy street. Sherman confided in Nathan how John Adams would often extol the "magnificent" help Nathan had given both he and the effort for Independence. Mr. Sherman commented that he personally believed that Nathan's days of true public service had not yet begun; and that America would benefit from Nathan's intellectual prowess, his strength of character, and his faith in God. Nathan, humbled by such flattery, nevertheless was anxious to see his family, and said his goodbyes, fetched his bag from his rented room, and mounted his horse for the ride back to Massachusetts.

The following day, in the late afternoon, in a small cemetery in the Massachusetts countryside, Robby Mackenzie was standing at the gravesites of Edward Mackenzie, and his wife Edith. It was, in retrospect, an unexpected blessing that they had both always expressed the desire to be buried, not in the city of Boston, but in the country. Boston, by then, had been overrun by British forces. And Robby had to carefully avoid several English sentries on his way to the little country cemetery as it was.

Robby glanced down at Edward's gravestone. On the stone marker there was a simple inscription:

In all these things we are more than conquerors,
through him that loved us.
Romans 8:37

As Robby gazed down at the gravestone, and felt the emotions of his long journey, and his own personal loss, welling up inside, he began to wipe tears from his eyes.

Then he heard a voice from behind him.

"You look so much taller and sturdier than I remember," Nathan said with a smile.

Robby wheeled around, and the two brothers embraced.

They both laughed, and then laughed again at the fact that their reunion was actually upon them.

Finally Nathan spoke up.

"We have so much to catch up on. And you, sir, have much explaining to do!" he said, jesting his younger brother. "Now where is your beautiful bride?"

"At your house in Braintree," he said. "I preferred to meet you here alone. But Flora is so anxious to meet you, Nathan."

"Come, Robby, let's go home together. We'll have a feast. And talk the night straight through. I only have a short time till I'm off to Philadelphia again. Oh, my brother, I don't want to waste a single moment."

"If you don't mind," Robby said, looking down at Edward's grave, "I think I will spend a little time here. You go ahead. Then I will join you and your family and my beauty of a bride back at your country house." Then Robby looked back at his brother.

Nathan looked into his brother's eyes, and he recognized there that thing which remains when one has traversed the lonely valleys, the uncharted seas, and the breathtaking mountaintops of life, and then arrived home safely to tell the tale.

"I will meet you at home, brother," Nathan said. "I long to speak to you about so many things."

When Nathan trotted his horse down the long, familiar dirt lane that snaked through the apple orchards and led to his rented farmhouse, he had felt a feeling of profound resolve. He had lost one brother; and yet, he had found another.

But as he caught a glimpse of the house at the end of the road, he spotted Deborah in the front yard, walking with their toddler. Then, for Nathan, there was only one thought and it propelled him to urge his horse into a full gallop.

"My darlings!" he was shouting out as he thundered down the lane.

And so he galloped down the road, dust billowing behind him, to meet the souls he cherished more than any other in the world.

And as he cast his eyes ahead to his wife and his child, he cried out a prayer of thanksgiving to his God and his Redeemer.

The peace and tranquility that he would experience in those next days with Deborah, and little William, and Robby and Flora would be all too fleeting. He would return to Philadelphia and his work with John Adams and the Continental Congress.

And in the grinding, insufferable months and years to come after that, the drums of battle cadence would beat.

The blood would flow.

The brave would fight—and many would die.

But eventually peace would come, and a new nation would be born, struggling but alive.

After the war, Robby and Flora would settle for a while in New England. But later the two of them would decide to head west, to help forge new lands, and cross new rivers; first in Ohio, and then all the way to Illinois, where they would raise a family in the wilderness. Robby and Flora would never be apart. And Robby would always take his Bible with him, wherever the two of them ventured.

When the last battle had been won, and the drumbeats of the War of Independence had ceased, Nathan's famed co-laborers, and even Nathan, would eventually be showered with honors and recognitions from a grateful people. In that respect, Roger Sherman's prediction would come true. Nathan would live a life of noted public service in the state of Massachusetts, and later in America's new capital.

Yet for Nathan, there had been other, even more profound lessons he had learned along the way. He had come to know, after all, the deepest treasures of family, and the unmistakable touch of God's providential hand.

He would always say that for him, to know such things, was glory enough for any man.

About the Authors

Besides *Captives and Kings* and *Crown of Fire,* the first two books in the Thistle and the Cross series, **Craig and Janet Parshall** have authored three nonfiction books together, including *Traveling a Pilgrim's Path.*

Craig is senior vice president and general counsel of National Religious Broadcasters. He speaks nationally on legal and Christian worldview issues, is a magazine columnist, and has authored six legal-suspense novels: the five installments in the Chambers of Justice legal-suspense series and the stand-alone novel *Trial by Ordeal.*

Janet is the host of *Janet Parshall's America*—a nationally syndicated radio talk show originating in Washington, DC. An author and a cultural commentator in the national media, as well as a frequent television host, she is also a much sought-after speaker on biblical issues that impact the family and the church.

THE THISTLE AND THE CROSS SERIES
Craig and Janet Parshall

CROWN OF FIRE

St. Andrews, Scotland, 1546. The great William Wallace—"Braveheart"—is long dead. But not the Scottish people's desire for freedom. The truths of the Reformation have set Scotland aflame again . . .

When Ransom Mackenzie witnesses one of the Scottish Reformers being burnt at the stake, he becomes an ardent follower of the great Protestant preacher John Knox.

In hiding, Ransom meets the captivating Margaret, who shares his religious convictions. But when he joins Knox in London, the allure of the court...and a young aristocratic lady...enthrall him. Ransom finds himself at a crossroads...where a man can burn for his beliefs, and silence is betrayal.

CAPTIVES AND KINGS

London, England, in the year of our Lord 1606. Andrew Mackenzie, an ambitious aide to King James, has little but contempt for his wayward and adventuring brother, Philip...who in turn resents Andrew's high-handedness and superior attitude. The rift is deep, and it seems it will be permanent after Andrew learns of Philip's unwitting involvement in a plot to kill the king—and insists that he and his son, Peter, flee England.

After sailing to the New World with his son—whose heart is left behind with the lovely Rose Heatherton—Philip struggles for survival amid the dangers of Jamestown, Virginia. Back in London, Andrew is the target of a spiritual battle surrounding the King James Bible translation, and of palace intrigues involving yet another plot against the Crown.

Separated by oceans and bitter resentment, will the two brothers survive their own battles to meet on the common ground of forgiveness?